HOUSE of SALT and SORROWS

ERIN A. CRAIG

A Rock the Boat Book

First published in the United Kingdom, Republic of Ireland and Australia
by Rock the Boat, an imprint of Oneworld Publications Ltd, 2025

Text copyright © Erin A. Craig, 2019
Cover art copyright © Vault49, 2019

The moral right of Erin A. Craig to be identified as the
Author of this work has been asserted by her in accordance with the
Copyright, Designs, and Patents Act 1988

All rights reserved
Copyright under Berne Convention
A CIP record for this title is available from the British Library

ISBN 978-1-83643-164-0
eISBN 978-1-83643-161-9

Printed and bound in Great Britain by Clays Ltd, Elcograf S.p.A

This book is a work of fiction. Names, characters, businesses,
organisations, places and events are either the product of the author's
imagination or are used fictitiously. Any resemblance to actual persons,
living or dead, events or locales is entirely coincidental.

No part of this publication may be reproduced, stored in a retrieval system,
or transmitted, in any form or by any means, electronic, mechanical, photocopying,
recording of otherwise, or used in any manner for the purpose of training artificial
intelligence technologies or systems, without the prior permission of the publishers.

The authorised representative in the EEA is eucomply OÜ,
Pärnu mnt 139b–14, 11317 Tallinn, Estonia
(email: hello@eucompliancepartner.com / phone: +33757690241)

Oneworld Publications Ltd
10 Bloomsbury Street
London WC1B 3SR
England

Stay up to date with the latest books,
special offers, and exclusive content from
Rock the Boat with our newsletter

Sign up on our website
rocktheboatbooks.com

*With so much love to my grandparents
Phoebe and Walter,
who always said I would write a book.
I'm so happy you were right.*

1

CANDLELIGHT REFLECTED OFF THE SILVER ANCHOR etched onto my sister's necklace. It was an ugly piece of jewelry and something Eulalie would never have picked out for herself. She loved simple strands of gold, extravagant collars of diamonds. Not . . . that. Papa must have selected it for her. I fumbled at my own necklace of black pearls, wanting to offer her something more stylish, but the battalion of pallbearers shut the coffin lid before I could undo the clasp.

"We, the People of the Salt, commit this body back to the sea," the High Mariner intoned as the wooden box slid deep into the waiting crypt.

I tried not to notice the smattering of lichens growing inside the gaping mouth, drawn wide to swallow her whole. Tried not to think of my sister—who was alive, and warm, and breathing just days before—being laid to rest. Tried not to imagine the thin bottom of the coffin growing fat with condensation and salt water before splitting asunder and spilling Eulalie's body into the watery depths beneath our family mausoleum.

I tried, instead, to cry.

I knew it would be expected of me, just as I knew the tears were unlikely to come. They would later on, probably this evening when I passed her bedroom and saw the black shrouds covering her wall of mirrors. Eulalie had had so many mirrors.

Eulalie.

She'd been the prettiest of all my sisters. Her rosy lips were forever turned in a smile. She loved a good joke, her bright green eyes always ready for a quick wink. Scores of suitors vied for her attention, even before she became the eldest Thaumas daughter, the one set to inherit all of Papa's fortune.

"We are born of the Salt, we live by the Salt, and to the Salt we return," the High Mariner continued.

"To the Salt," the mourners repeated.

As Papa stepped forward to place two gold pieces at the foot of the crypt—payment to Pontus for easing my sister back into the Brine—I dared to sweep my eyes around the mausoleum. It was overflowing with guests bedecked in their finest black wools and crepes, many of them once would-be beaus of Eulalie. She would have been pleased to see so many brokenhearted young men openly lamenting her.

"Annaleigh," Camille whispered, nudging me.

"To the Salt," I murmured. I pressed a handkerchief to my eyes, feigning tears.

Papa's keen disapproval burned in my heart. His own eyes were soggy and his proud nose was red as the High Mariner stepped forward with a chalice lined with abalone shell and filled with seawater. He thrust it into the crypt and poured the water onto Eulalie's coffin, ceremonially beginning its decomposition. Once he doused the candles flanking the stony opening, the service was over.

Papa turned to the gathered mass, a wide shock of white streaked through his dark hair. Was it there yesterday?

"Thank you for coming to remember my daughter Eulalie." His voice, usually so big and bold, accustomed to addressing lords at court, creaked with uncertainty. "My family and I invite you to join us now at Highmoor for a celebration of her life. There will be food and drink and . . ." He cleared his throat, sounding more like a stammering clerk than the nineteenth Duke of the Salann Islands. "I know how much it would have meant to Eulalie to have you there."

He nodded once, speech over, his face a blank facade. I longed to reach out to ease his grief, but Morella, my stepmother, was already at his side, her hand knotted around his. They'd been married just months before and should have still been in the heady, blissful days of their joined life.

This was Morella's first trip to the Thaumas mausoleum. Did she feel uneasy under the watchful scrutiny of my mother's memorial statue? The sculptor used Mama's bridal portrait as reference, transmitting youthful radiance into the cool gray marble. Though her body returned to the sea many years ago, I still visited her shrine nearly every week, telling her about my days and pretending she listened.

Mama's statue towered over everything else in the mausoleum, including my sisters' shrines. Ava's was bordered in roses, her favorite flower. They grew fat and pink in the summer months, like the plague pustules that claimed her life at only eighteen.

Octavia followed a year later. Her body was discovered at the bottom of a tall library ladder, her limbs tangled in a heap of unnatural angles. An open book adorned her resting place, along with a quote etched in Vaipanian, which I'd never learned to read.

With so much tragedy compressed into our family, it seemed inevitable when Elizabeth died. She was found floating in the bathtub like a piece of driftwood at sea, waterlogged and bleached of all color. Rumors ran from Highmoor to the villages on neighboring islands, whispered by scullery maids to stable boys, passed from fishmongers to their wives, who spread them as warnings to impish children. Some said it was suicide. Even more believed we were cursed.

Elizabeth's statue was a bird. It was meant to be a dove, but its proportions were all wrong and it looked more like a seagull. A fitting tribute for Elizabeth, who always so badly wanted to soar away.

What would Eulalie's be?

Once there were twelve of us: the Thaumas Dozen. Now we stood in a small line, my seven sisters and I, and I couldn't help but wonder if there was a ring of truth to the grim speculations. Had we somehow angered the gods? Had a darkness branded itself on our family, taking us out one by one? Or was it simply a series of terrible and unlucky coincidences?

After the service, the crowd broke up and began milling around us. As they whispered their strained condolences, I noticed the guests were careful not to get too close. Was it in deference to our station, or were they worried something might rub off? I wanted to chalk it up to lowbrow superstition, but as a distant aunt approached me, a thin smile on her thin lips, the same question flickered in her eyes, just below the surface, impossible to miss:

Which one of us would be next?

2

I LINGERED IN THE MAUSOLEUM AS EVERYONE LEFT for the wake, wanting to say goodbye to Eulalie on my own, free from prying eyes. His services rendered, the High Mariner gathered up his chalice and candlesticks, his salt water and my father's two coins. Before setting off down the little path to the shoreline and back to his hermitage on the northernmost point of Selkirk Island, he paused in front of me. I'd been watching the servant boys seal the tomb's entrance, piling bricks slathered with gritty mortar over the crypt and obscuring the rush of swirling eddies below us.

The High Mariner raised his hand in what appeared to be a blessing. But somehow the curve of his fingers was off, more like a gesture of protection.

For himself.

Against me.

Without the press of people in the crypt, the air felt colder, settling over me like a second cloak. Sickly-sweet incense still danced through the room but couldn't quite block out the tang of salt. No matter where you were on the island, you could always taste the sea.

The workers grunted as they hoisted the last brick into place, silencing the water altogether.

Then I was alone.

The crypt was really nothing more than a cave but for one unique feature: a wide river ran underneath, carrying fresh water—and the bodies of departed Thaumases—out to sea. Each generation had added their own bits to it, fashioning stonework around the burial site or gilding the ceiling with an elaborate mural of the night sky. Every Thaumas child learned to read their way across the constellations before ever picking up a book of letters. My great-great-grandfather started adding the shrines.

During Elizabeth's funeral—an even bleaker affair than Eulalie's, with the High Mariner's thinly veiled chastisement of suicide—I counted the plaques and statues dotting the cavern to pass the time. How long before the shrines completely overran this hallowed space, leaving no place for the living? When I died, I wanted no monument to remember me by. Did Great-Aunt Clarette rest better in her eternal slumber knowing her bust would be gazed on by generations of Thaumases?

Thank you, no. Just push me into the sea and return me to the Salt.

"There were so many young men here today," I said, kneeling before the wet masonry.

It was honestly a wonder they bothered bricking it up at all. How long until these stones would be broken open for another of my sisters to be shoved inside?

"Sebastian and Stephan, the Fitzgerald brothers. Henry. The foreman from Vasa. And Edgar too."

It felt unnatural having such a decidedly lopsided conversation with Eulalie. She normally dominated everything she was a part of. Her stories, outlandish and full of hyperbolic wit, held everyone in her audience captivated.

"I think, of all the mourners here today, their tears were the biggest. Were you sneaking out to meet one of them that night?"

I paused, picturing Eulalie out on the cliff walk, in a billowing nightgown of lace and ribbons, her lily-white skin drenched blue in the full moon. She would have made sure to look especially lovely for a secret assignation with a beau.

When the fishermen found her body smashed on the rocks below, they mistook her for a beached dolphin. If there truly was an afterlife, I hoped Eulalie never learned that. Her vanity would never recover.

"Did you trip and fall?" My words echoed in the tomb. "Were you pushed?"

The question burst from me before I could stop to ponder it. I knew without a shadow of a doubt how my other sisters had died: Ava was sick, Octavia was notoriously accident-prone, even Elizabeth . . . Drawing a short breath, I dug my fingers into my skirt's thick, scratchy black wool. She'd been so despondent after Octavia. We'd all felt the losses, but not as keenly as Elizabeth.

But no one was there when Eulalie died. No one saw it happen. Just the brutal aftermath.

A drop of water hit my nose and another fell on my cheek as rivulets ran into the crypt. It must have started to rain. Even the sky wept for Eulalie today.

"I'll miss you." I sucked in my lower lip. The tears came now, pinpricking at my eyes until they fell freely. I traced an elaborately scrawled *E* across the stones, wanting to say so much more, to spit out my grief, and helplessness, and rage. But that wouldn't bring her back.

"I . . . I love you, Eulalie." My voice was no more than a whisper as I fled the dark cavern.

Outside, the storm raged, churning the waves into frothy whitecaps. The cave was on the far side of the Point, a peninsula on Salten, jutting out into the sea. It was at least a mile back to the house, and no one had thought to leave me a carriage. I pushed aside my black veil and began walking.

"Aren't you forgetting something?" our maid, Hanna, asked before I headed down to join the wake.

I paused, feeling the weight of the older woman's motherly eyes on my back. I'd had to immediately change clothes once I returned. The storm had soaked me through, and curse or not, I wasn't planning on dying of a cold.

Hanna held out a long black ribbon with a look of expectation. Sighing, I let her encircle my wrist with the thin strip, as she had many times before. When death visited a household, you wore a black ribbon to keep from following after your loved one. Our luck seemed so bad, the servants even took to tying the maudlin bits around the necks of our cats, horses, and chickens.

She finished off the ribbon with a bow that would have been pretty in any other color. My entire wardrobe was nothing more than mourning garb now, each dress a darker shade than the last. I hadn't worn anything lighter than charcoal in the six years since Mama passed away.

Hanna had chosen a satin bauble, not the itchy bombazine from Elizabeth's funeral. It left welts on our wrists that stung for days.

I adjusted my sleeve's cuff. "I'd rather stay up here with you, truth be told. I never know what I ought to say at these things."

Hanna patted my cheek. "The sooner you get there, the sooner it'll all be over with." She smiled up at me with warm brown eyes. "I'll be sure to have a pot of cinnamon tea waiting for you before bed?"

"Thank you, Hanna," I said, squeezing her shoulder before going out the door.

As I entered the Blue Room, Morella made a beeline for me. "Sit with me? I don't really know anyone here," she admitted, pulling me toward a sofa near the tall, thickly paned windows. Though speckled with a confetti of raindrops, they offered a spectacular view of the cliffs. It seemed wrong to hold the wake in this room, showcasing the very spot where Eulalie fell.

I wanted to be with my sisters, but Morella's eyes were so large and pleading. At moments like this, it was difficult to forget she was much closer to my age than to Papa's.

No one was surprised when he took a new bride. Mama had been gone for so long, and we all knew he hoped to have a son eventually. He met Morella while in Suseally, on the mainland. Papa returned from the voyage with her on his arm, utterly smitten.

Honor, Mercy, and Verity—the Graces, as we called them collectively, all so young when Mama passed—were delighted to have this new maternal figure in their lives. She'd been a governess and took to the little girls immediately. The triplets—Rosalie, Ligeia, and Lenore—and I were happy for Papa, but Camille stiffened whenever someone assumed Morella was one of the Thaumas Dozen.

I stared across the room at the large painting dominating one wall. It depicted a ship being dragged into the blue abyss by a kraken, giant eyes enlarged in fury. The Blue Room held many treasures from the sea: a family of spiny urchins on one shelf, a barnacle-encrusted anchor on a plinth in the corner, and specimens from the Graces' shell collection on any surface tall enough for them to reach.

"Are the services always like that?" Morella asked, spreading her skirts across the navy velvet cushions. "So serious and dour?"

I couldn't help my bemused look. "Well, it was a funeral."

She tucked a wisp of pale blond hair behind her ear, smiling nervously. "Of course, I only meant . . . why the water? I don't understand why you don't just bury her, like they do on the mainland?"

I caught sight of Papa. He'd want me to be nice, to explain our ways. I tried to allow a trickle of pity into my heart for her.

"The High Mariner says Pontus created our islands and the people on them. He scooped salt from the ocean tides for strength. Into that was mixed the cunning of a bull shark and the beauty of the moon jellyfish. He added the seahorse's fidelity and the curiosity of a porpoise. When his creation was molded just so—two arms, two legs, a head, and a heart—Pontus breathed some of his own life into it, making the first People of the Salt. So when we die, we can't be buried in the ground. We slip back into the water and are home."

The explanation seemed to please her. "See, something like that at the funeral would have been lovely. There was just such an emphasis on . . . the death."

I offered her a smile. "Well . . . this was your first one. You get used to them."

Morella reached out, placing her hand on mine, her small face earnest. "I hate that you've gone through so many of these. You're far too young to have felt so much pain and grief."

The rain came down harder, shrouding Highmoor in muddled grays. Great boulders at the bottom of the cliffs were tossed about by the raging sea like marbles in a little boy's pocket, their crashes blasting up the steep rocks and rivaling the thunder.

"What happens now?"

I blinked, drawing my attention back to her. "What do you mean?"

She bit into her lip, stumbling over the unfamiliar words. "Now that she's . . . back in the Salt . . . what are we supposed to do?"

"That was it. We've said our goodbyes. After this wake, it's all over."

Her fingers tinkered with restless frustration. "But it's not. Not truly. Your father said we have to wear black for the next few weeks?"

"Months, actually. We wear black for six, then darker grays for another six after that."

"A year?" she gasped. "Am I really meant to wear these dour clothes for a whole year?" People near the sofa turned their heads toward us, having overheard her outburst. She had the decency to blush with chagrin. "What I mean is . . . Ortun just bought my bridal trousseau. Nothing in it is black." She'd borrowed one of Camille's dresses for today, but it didn't fit her well. She smoothed down the edge of the bodice. "It's not only about the clothes.

What about you and Camille? Both of you should be out in society, meeting young men, falling in love."

I tilted my head, wondering if she was serious. "My sister just died. I don't exactly feel like dancing."

A crack of thunder made us jump. Morella squeezed my hand, bringing my eyes back to hers. "Forgive me, Annaleigh, I'm not saying anything right today. I meant . . . after so much tragedy, this family should be happy again. You've mourned enough for a lifetime already. Why continue to shroud yourself in pain? Mercy, Honor, and dear little Verity should be playing with dolls in the garden, not accepting condolences and making idle small talk. And Rosalie and Ligeia—Lenore too—look at them."

The triplets perched on a love seat truly only big enough for two. Their arms linked around each other, holding themselves like a fat spider as they sobbed into their veils. No one dared approach such concentrated grief.

"It breaks my heart to see everyone like this."

I slipped my hand free of hers. "But this is what you do when someone dies. You can't change traditions just because you don't like them."

"But what if there was a cause for joy? Something that ought to be celebrated, not hidden away? Shouldn't good news triumph?"

A servant approached, offering glasses of wine. I took one, but Morella dismissed him with a skilled shake of her head. She'd quickly settled into her role as mistress of Highmoor.

"I suppose so." I hesitated. Another roll of thunder boomed through the air. "But there doesn't seem to be much to celebrate today."

"I think there is." Leaning in, Morella dropped her voice to a conspiring whisper. "A new life." She discreetly placed a protective hand over her stomach.

I swallowed my mouthful of wine, nearly choking in surprise. "You're pregnant?" She beamed. "Does Papa know?"

"Not yet. I was about to tell him, but we were interrupted by those fishermen, with Eulalie."

"He'll be so pleased. Do you know how far along you are?"

"Three months, I think." She ran her fingers over her hair. "Do you really think Ortun will be happy? I'd do just about anything to see him smile again."

I glanced back at Papa, surrounded by friends but too lost in memories of Eulalie to respond to their conversation. I nodded. "I'm sure of it."

She took a deep breath. "Then such happy news shouldn't keep, should it?"

Morella crossed to the grand piano in the center of the room before I could answer. Picking up a bell from the lid, she rang it, effectively quieting the room.

My mouth went dry as I realized what she was about to do.

"Ortun?" she asked, jarring him from his thoughts. Her voice was high and thin, like the chiming of the bell in her hand.

It was my mother's bell. Camille and I had found it years ago while playing dress-up in the attic. We had loved its silvery tone and brought it to Mama when she grew too weak to be heard throughout the house. Now every time I heard it ring, memories of her last pregnancy came back to me with the force of a cold wave crashing into my chest.

When he was at her side, Morella continued. "Ortun and I

want to thank you all for coming. The last few days have been an unending night of darkness, but your presence here now is like the first warm tendrils of a beautiful sunrise creeping across the sky."

Her words, though obviously chosen with care, flowed easily from her. My eyes narrowed. She'd practiced this beforehand.

"Your memories of dear, beautiful Eulalie paint our hearts with gladness, lifting them from the gloom. And we are happy—joyful, even—for in this bold new morning, a fresh chapter dawns on the House of Thaumas."

Camille, who had been in conversation with an uncle across the room, shot me an uneasy look. Even the triplets broke their tight link; Lenore stood next to the love seat, her fingers digging into the cushy arm.

Morella held Papa's hand and rested her other on her flat stomach, erupting into a wide grin as she relished the attention. "And just as night is chased away by morning's glow, so too will the shadows of grief be pushed aside by the arrival of our son."

3

"THAT WOMAN!" HANNA SPAT OUT AS SHE FINISHED unfastening the tiny jet buttons running down the back of my dress. She helped me step out of it before pushing back her salt-and-pepper curls with a huff. "Using what was supposed to be Eulalie's day to announce such startling news. What gall!"

Camille flung herself backward onto my bed, next to Ligeia, rumpling the embroidered coverlet. "I can't stand her!" She twisted her voice into a high-pitched mockery of Morella's. "And just like the god of light, Vaipany, with his sun, my son will be a shining, sunny ray of sunlight, like the sun, my son." Camille buried her snort in a pillow.

"She could have chosen her timing with better care," Rosalie admitted, leaning against a bedpost, twirling the end of her russet braid. The triplets, identical in every way, had a shade of auburn hair I envied, completely different from the rest of us. Of all my sisters, Eulalie had been the fairest, her hair nearly blond but not quite. Mine was darkest, the same shade as the black Salann sand, unique to the island chain's beaches.

I released the garters around my thighs with a low hum of

agreement. Though I was happy for her and Papa, the news truly ought to have been announced at a later date. Rolling the drab, dark stockings down my legs, I wondered what Morella's trousseau was filled with. Had Papa lined it with white silk hose and ribbons and laces, thinking a new wife would put an end to his bad luck? I threw a black voile nightgown over my head, whisking away thoughts of satin underskirts and jewel-toned dressing robes.

"What does it mean for us if it is a son?" Lenore asked from the window seat. "Will he become heir?"

Camille sat up. Her face was puffy from crying, but her amber eyes were sharp and peevish. "I inherit everything. Then Annaleigh, whenever the curse claims me."

"No one is being claimed," I snapped. "That's a bunch of nonsense."

"Madame Morella doesn't think so," Hanna said, stretching on tiptoes to hang my dress in the armoire. The row of its identically shaded companions depressed me.

"That we're cursed?" Rosalie asked.

"That you girls will inherit first. I heard her talking to your aunt Lysbette, gushing about how in her stomach is the next duke."

Camille rolled her eyes. "Maybe that's how they handle things on the mainland, but not here. I'd love to see the look on her face when Papa corrects her."

Sinking onto the chaise, I pulled a light throw over my shoulders. I'd never fully warmed up after my walk in the rain, and Morella's announcement had cast a further chill in my heart.

Ligeia tossed a bolster back and forth. "So your husband would become the twentieth Duke of Salann?"

"If I wanted," Camille replied. "Or I could be duchess in my own right and let him carry on as a consort. Surely Berta taught you all this ages ago."

Ligeia shrugged. "I try not to remember anything governesses say. They're all so dreary. Besides, I was eighth-born. I hardly expected to inherit anything."

As sixth daughter, I certainly understood how she felt. Born in the middle, I now stood second in line. The night after Eulalie died, I couldn't sleep, feeling the heavy weight of new responsibilities pressing on my chest. The Thaumas crest—a silver octopus with arms flailed, grasping a trident, scepter, and feather—dotted the architecture in every room of Highmoor. The one opposite my bed stared down with an importance I'd never noticed before. What if something happened to Camille and suddenly everything fell to me? I wished I'd spent more time on my history lessons and less at the piano.

Camille taught me how to play. We were stair-stepped, the closest in age of all the sisters, save the triplets. I was born ten months after her, and we grew up as best friends. Whatever she did, I was eager to follow after. When she turned six, Mama gave her lessons on the old upright in her parlor. Camille was an apt pupil and showed me all she learned. Mama gave us four-hand versions of all her favorite songs, soon deeming us proficient enough for the grand piano in the Blue Room.

The house was always full of music and laughter as my sisters twirled around the house, dancing to the songs we played. I spent so many afternoons on that cushioned bench, pressed close to Camille, as our hands traveled up and down the ivory keys. I'd still rather play a duet with her than the most perfect solo all on my own. Without Camille next to me, the music felt too weak by half.

"Miss Annaleigh?"

Drawn from my reverie, I looked up to see Hanna's eyes on me, eyebrows raised.

"Did she say how far along she is?"

"Morella? She thinks three months, maybe a little more."

"More?" Camille smirked. "They've only been married four."

Lenore left the window and joined me on the chaise. "Why does she bother you so much, Camille? I'm glad she's here. The Graces love having a mother again."

"She's not their mother. Or ours. She doesn't even come close."

"She's trying," Lenore allowed. "She asked if she could help plan our ball. We can use it as our debut, since we can't go to court during mourning."

"You can't throw a ball either," Camille reminded her.

"But it's our sixteenth birthday!" Rosalie sat up, a pout marring her face. "Why does everything fun have to be put on hold for a whole year? I'm tired of mourning."

"And I'm sure your sisters are tired of being dead, but that's how it is!" Camille exploded, pushing off the bed. She slammed the door behind her before any of us could stop her.

Rosalie blinked. "What's gotten into her?"

I bit my lip, feeling as though I should go after her but too tired for whatever fight might ensue. "She's missing Eulalie."

"We all miss her," Rosalie pointed out.

A blanket of silence descended over us as our thoughts drifted back to Eulalie. Hanna roamed the room, lighting tapers before lowering the gas sconces until they flickered out. The candelabras cast wavering shadows to the corners of the room.

Lenore stole part of my throw and burrowed under it. "Do you think it would be so very wrong to go along with Morella's plan? To have a ball? We only turn sixteen once. . . . We can't help it that everyone keeps dying."

"I don't think it's wrong to want to celebrate, but think of how Camille feels. Neither of us debuted. Elizabeth and Eulalie didn't either."

"So celebrate with us!" Rosalie offered. "It could be a grand party—to show everyone that the Thaumas girls aren't cursed and everything is fine."

"And we don't turn sixteen for three weeks. We could mourn till then and just . . . stop," Ligeia reasoned.

"I don't know why you're trying to convince me. Papa is the one who will have to approve it."

"He'll say yes if Morella asks him." Rosalie smiled slyly. "In bed."

The triplets fell into fits of laughter. There was a knock at my door, and we all hushed, certain it was Papa coming to chastise us for making so much noise. But it was Verity, standing in the middle of the hallway, drowning in a dark nightgown two sizes too big for her. Her hair was mussed, and glittering tracks of tears ran down her face.

"Verity?"

She said nothing but held out her arms, begging to be picked up. I hoisted her into an embrace, smelling the sweet warmth of childhood. Though she was sweaty with sleep, goose bumps ran down her bare arms, and she snuggled into my neck, seeking comfort.

"What's the matter, little one?" I rubbed soothing circles over her back, her hair as soft as a baby robin against my cheek.

"Can I stay here tonight? Eulalie is being mean to me."

The triplets exchanged looks of concern.

"You can, of course, but do you remember what we talked about before the funeral? You know Eulalie isn't here anymore. She's with Mama and Elizabeth now, in the Brine."

I felt her nod. "She keeps pulling my sheets off, though." Her thin arms encircled my neck, clinging to me tighter than a starfish at high tide.

"Lenore, check on Mercy and Honor, will you?"

She kissed the top of Verity's head before leaving.

"I bet they were only teasing you. Just a game."

"It's not a very nice one."

"No," I agreed, and carried her over to the bed. "You can stay tonight. You're safe here. Go back to sleep."

Verity whimpered once but closed her eyes and settled into the bedclothes.

"We should go too," Rosalie whispered, sliding off the bed. "Papa will be checking on us soon."

"Shall I walk you back to the second floor?" Hanna offered, holding out a pair of candles for Rosalie and Ligeia.

Rosalie shook her head but accepted a hug and the light before stepping out of the room.

"Think about what we said," Ligeia added, kissing my cheek. "Ending the mourning would be good for us all." She hugged Hanna good night and scurried down the hall.

The triplets refused to have their own bedrooms, saying they slept better together.

Hanna's attention shifted to me. "Will you be going to bed too, then, Miss Annaleigh?"

I glanced back at Verity, snuggled deep in my pillows. "Not yet. My mind feels too full for sleep."

She crossed to a side table, and I drifted back to the chaise, folding and unfolding the throw in my lap. Hanna returned with cups of cinnamon tea and sat down beside me. Something about her movements transported me back six years, to the night of Mama's funeral.

Hanna had sat exactly where she was now, but I'd been on the floor, my head buried in her lap as she comforted as many of my sisters as she could. Camille was next to me, her eyes swollen and rimmed red. Elizabeth and Eulalie knelt near us, folding the triplets into a sobbing embrace. Ava and Octavia bookended Hanna, each holding a sleeping Grace. The only one missing was Verity, just days old and with her wet nurse.

None of us had wanted to be alone that night.

"It was a lovely funeral," Hanna said now, twirling her spoon and bringing me back to the present. "So many young men. So many tears. I'm sure Eulalie must be pleased."

I took a shallow sip, letting the spices linger on my tongue before agreeing.

"You've been awfully quiet tonight," she prompted after the silence grew too long.

"I just keep thinking how strange this day felt. How strange everything has been since they . . . found her." My mouth tripped over the words, as if the idea behind them was too unwieldy a shape to break into neat sentences. "Something feels wrong about her death, doesn't it?"

Hanna was watching me. "It always feels wrong when a young person dies, especially someone like Eulalie, so full of beauty and promise."

"But it's more than that. I could understand why the others

died. Each death was horrible and sad, but there was a reason for it. But Eulalie . . . what was she even doing out there? Alone and in the dark?"

"You and I both know she wasn't meant to be alone for long."

I remembered all those tearstained faces. "But why would she meet someone there? She didn't even like going to the cliffs in broad daylight. The heights scared her. It doesn't make any sense to me."

Hanna clicked her tongue, setting aside her cup before pulling me into a hug. I caught just a trace of her soap then—milk and honey. Hanna was far too practical for perfumes or bath oils, but the warm, no-nonsense scent comforted me. I breathed it in as my head rested against her shoulder.

It was softer now, more giving, and the skin that peeked over the neckline of her shirtwaist was lined and crepe-thin. She'd been the nursemaid at Highmoor since Ava was born, always there to help patch skinned knees and soothe bruised egos. Her own son, Fisher, was three years older than me and grew up alongside us. Hanna laced us into our first corsets and helped pin up our hair, drying tears as the untrained curls refused to cooperate. There wasn't any part of our childhood she missed, always nearby for a warm hug or a good-night kiss.

"Did you turn down the bed for her that night?" I asked, sitting up. Hanna would have been one of the last people to see Eulalie. "Did anything seem off?"

She shook her head. "Not that I recall. But I wasn't with her long. Mercy had a stomachache. She came in asking for peppermint tea."

"What about . . . after? You helped with . . . her body, didn't you?"

"Of course. I've taken care of all your sisters. And your mother."

"How did she look?"

Hanna swallowed deeply and made a sign of protection across her chest. "Such things shouldn't be spoken of."

I frowned. "I know she must have . . . it must have been terrible, but was there anything . . . amiss?"

Her eyes narrowed skeptically. "She plummeted more than a hundred feet, landing on the rocks. There was quite a bit amiss."

"I'm sorry," I said, deflating. I longed to ask her if anyone else helped prepare the body for its return to the Salt, but Hanna was done talking about it.

"You're tired, love," she said. "Why don't you settle into bed and see how you feel in the morning?" She kissed the top of my head before leaving. The door clicked quietly shut behind her.

After checking that Verity had truly gone back to sleep, I crossed to the window, drawn by a strange restlessness. My bedroom overlooked the gardens on the south side of the house, three stories below. A wide fountain, showcasing a marble clipper ship, was at the center of the lawn, just off a decorative hedge maze.

Verity rolled over, murmuring sleepy incoherences. I'd drawn half the heavy drapes when a flicker of light caught my attention. Though the rain had ended, the sky was choked with dark clouds, obscuring the stars.

It was a lantern, flickering in and out of sculpted topiaries—sets of breaching humpback whales. As the light broke free from the trees, I spotted two figures. The smaller carried the lantern, setting it to the side before sitting on the fountain's rounded lip. The candlelight caught the white streak in Papa's hair.

What was he doing out in the gardens so late on the night of

Eulalie's funeral? He'd sent us all to bed early, saying we ought to use this time for solemn prayers to Pontus, asking for the sea god to grant our sister eternal rest in the Brine.

The hood of the other figure's cloak fell back, revealing a headful of blond ringlets. Morella. She patted the empty space beside her, and Papa sat. After a moment or two, his shoulders began to shake. He was crying.

Morella leaned against him, wrapping her arm around his back and drawing him closer. I looked away as she reached up to stroke his cheek. I didn't need to hear what she was saying to know her words consoled Papa like a soothing balm. She might not have understood our island ways, but I was suddenly glad of her presence at Highmoor. No one should have to bear such compounded grief alone.

Turning away from the window, I crawled into bed and snuggled up next to Verity, letting her measured breathing lull me to sleep.

4

THE FIRST THING I SPOTTED AT THE BREAKFAST TABLE was Morella's blue satin dress. Pleats of white organdy wound around her elbows, and a choker of pearls dotted her neck. It dazzled like a jeweled hummingbird in a room full of covered portraits and crepe wreaths.

She looked up from the side table as she picked through the trays of food. Highmoor kept a relaxed morning schedule. Everyone drifted in and out of the dining room, serving themselves.

"Good morning, Annaleigh." Morella added a gingered scone to her plate and slathered it with butter. "Did you sleep well?"

In truth, I had not. Verity was a restless sleeper, lashing out like a mule whenever she turned. My mind kept wandering back to Eulalie and the cliff walk, too full to properly doze. It was well after midnight before I drifted off.

"Hello, my love," Papa called out from the doorway.

We turned, both assuming his greeting was for us, but he crossed over to kiss Morella good morning. Though his frock coat was dark, it was a sooty charcoal, not the raven black I'd grown accustomed to.

"How well you look," he said, turning her in a circle to admire the barely discernible bump.

"I think pregnancy agrees with me."

She did radiate a flushed happiness. Mama's pregnancies were full of terrible morning sickness, with bed rest prescribed long before the usual confinement period. When I was old enough, Ava and Octavia let me help with her care, showing me the best oils and lotions to ease her pains.

"Do you think so, Annaleigh?" Morella asked.

I supposed she was trying to be kind, including me in the conversation.

I studied the bright lapis satin. She looked lovely, but it was the wrong thing to wear the day after laying a stepdaughter to rest. "Are Eulalie's dresses already too small for you?"

"Hmm? Oh yes, of course." She used the moment to run a satisfied hand over her stomach.

"Actually," Papa interrupted, reaching over to add a pile of kippers to his plate, "we have something to discuss with everyone on that very subject. Annaleigh, can you get your sisters?"

"Now?" I glanced at the eggs I'd just spooned out. They would not keep warm.

"Please?"

Purposefully leaving my half-assembled plate on the center of the table, I trudged upstairs. I was an early riser, but not all my sisters shared my morning habits. Mercy and Rosalie were absolute bears to wake up.

I chose Camille first.

She'd opened the curtains, letting weak gray light play over her rich plum-colored furnishings. I was surprised to see her in front of her vanity, stabbing a pin through a lock of hair. Though her lips and cheeks were bare, pots of color and cut-glass vials of perfume lay scattered across the tabletop. A black crepe cover, twin to the one shrouding my own mirror, was crumpled at her feet. I wondered when she'd thrown it there.

"Back from breakfast already?" she asked.

"Papa wants everyone downstairs. He has something to tell us."

Her hand paused over a box of jewelry, then reluctantly picked up a jet-black earring. "Did he say what?"

I sat next to her on the bench, running fingers over my own chignon. I hadn't seen my reflection in nearly a week. "Morella's blue dress said plenty. Eulalie would have an absolute fit if she knew what was going on. Do you remember after Octavia died, when Eulalie wanted to go see—what was it, a traveling circus or something?—and Papa wouldn't let us leave the house? He said"—I deepened my voice to a close approximation—"'Grief such as ours shouldn't be seen by the public eye.' And Octavia had been gone for months!"

"Eulalie sulked for weeks."

"And now we honor her by wearing black for what, five days? Papa is already wearing gray. It's not right."

My sister opened a jar and examined the wine-colored lip stain. "I agree."

"Do you really?" I asked, pointedly looking at the mirror. I took the pot away from her, spilling some of the color in the process. Running down my fingers, it looked like blood.

She smoothed out a stray ringlet. "I never was any good at doing my hair without a reflection."

"I would have helped. What if Eulalie—"

Camille rolled her eyes. "Eulalie's spirit won't see a shiny surface and get stuck here. She could hardly stand being in this house during life; what makes you think she'd want to stick around in death?"

I set the lip stain down, unsure of what to wipe my fingers on. "You're in a mood."

She offered me a handkerchief. "I slept poorly. I couldn't get Ligeia's stupid comment out of my head." She picked up a different shade of stain and wiped a small sheen of berry across her mouth. Guilt weighed heavy on her face. "I'll never get a husband if something doesn't change."

"That's not true," I protested. "Any man would be honored to have you at his side. You're clever and every bit as lovely as Eulalie."

She smirked. "No one was like Eulalie. But if I hide myself away in this gloomy house, buried under layers of crepe and bombazine, I'll never find anyone. I don't want to disrespect the memory of Eulalie or any of our sisters, but if we go through every step of mourning each time someone dies, we'll be dead ourselves before we're finished. So . . . I'm ready to move on. And no amount of hangdog looks from you will change my mind."

I picked up the mirror cover, sinking my fingers into the dark fabric. I wasn't upset with Camille. She deserved to be happy. We all did. We all had dreams of greater things. Of course my sisters would rather be out, at court, at concerts, at balls. They wanted to be brides, wives, mothers. I'd be a monster to begrudge them that.

Still, I clung to the cover.

"Papa wants us downstairs," Rosalie called out, interrupting our moment. The triplets crowded in the doorway, peering in. Caught in the strange morning light, their reflection was a grotesque mass of limbs and braids. For a second, they were one conjoined entity, not three separate sisters.

Lenore broke free of the clump, clearing the strange vision from my mind. "Will you tie this for me?" She held out her black ribbon. "Rosalie does it too tight."

She knelt beside Camille, lifting her heavy braid to expose the pale length of her neck. The triplets wore their ribbons as chokers. When we were little, Octavia delighted in telling us lurid, spooky stories at bedtime. She'd conjure up tales of pining damsels wasting after their true loves, ghosts and goblins, Tricksters and Harbingers and the foolish people who bargained with them both. Later, certain we were still cowering in terror under our covers, she and Eulalie would creep into our rooms and snatch the blankets from us.

One of her favorite stories was of a girl who always wore a green ribbon around her neck. She was never seen without it, at school, at church, even on her wedding day. All the guests said she made a lovely bride but wondered why she chose to wear such a plain necklace. On her honeymoon, her husband presented her with a choker of diamonds, sparkling like mad under a starlit sky. He wanted her to wear them, and only them, when she came to bed that night. When she refused, he stalked away, upset. Later he returned to find her asleep in their big bed, naked save for the diamonds and the green ribbon. Snuggling next to her, he stealthily removed the ribbon, only to have her head roll off her body, neatly severed at the neck.

The triplets delighted in that horrid story and asked for it again and again. When Octavia died, they wrapped black crepe around their necks with ghoulish affectation.

Bow securely tied, Lenore twisted it around to a jauntier angle. "The Graces are already downstairs. We woke them first."

Camille rose from the bench. When I offered out the cover, she tossed it aside, leaving the mirror bare and sparkling.

Mercy, Honor, and Verity sat at the far corner of the dining room table. The older girls worked on plates of eggs and kippers. Verity had a bowl of strawberries and cream but pushed the berries about without eating. I noticed she sat as far from Honor and Mercy as she could without actually switching seats. Apparently, she'd not yet forgiven them for their late-night prank.

We didn't bother making up plates of our own. Papa sat at the head of the table, obviously wanting to announce his news.

He started without preamble. "After breakfast, there is a marvelous surprise for all of you in the Gold Parlor."

The Gold Parlor was small and formal, used only for important guests—visitors from court or the High Mariner. Many years ago, the King and his family came to stay with us during their summer progress, and Queen Adelaide used it as her sitting room. She'd complimented the shimmering damask drapes, and Mama vowed to never update them.

"What is it, Papa?" Camille asked.

"After careful consideration, I've decided the time for our family's sadness is over. Highmoor has spent too many years in darkness. I'm ending the mourning."

"We buried Eulalie yesterday," I reminded the table, crossing my arms. "Yesterday."

My leg slammed back as someone kicked me under the table. I couldn't prove it, but I would have placed bets on Rosalie.

Papa raised an eyebrow at me. "I know this may seem premature, but—"

"*Very* premature," I interrupted, and was kicked again. This time I was certain it was Ligeia.

Papa squeezed the bridge of his nose, warding off a migraine. "You seem to have something you'd like to say, Annaleigh?"

"How can you possibly think of doing this? It's not right."

"We've mourned too much of our lives away already. Now is the time for new beginnings, and I can't bear to have our fresh start cloaked in sorrow."

"*Your* fresh start. Yours and Morella's. None of this would be happening if she wasn't pregnant."

The triplets let out a stricken gasp. I saw hurt flash in Morella's eyes but pressed on. Feelings be damned: this was too important.

"She said it's a boy, and you're ready to move earth and moon to please her. You're willing to forget all about your first family. Your cursed family." The word fell out, black and ugly.

Verity let out a noise halfway between a shriek and a sob.

"There's no curse." Lenore rushed to her side, snapping at me. "Tell her there's no curse."

"I don't want to die," Verity wailed, knocking over the bowl of cream.

"You're not going to die," Papa said, gripping the arms of his chair so tightly that it was a wonder the wood didn't splinter. "Annaleigh, you're out of line. Apologize immediately."

I rose and knelt beside Verity, hugging her and stroking her soft hair. "I'm sorry. I didn't mean to upset you. There's not really a curse."

Papa's voice was cold and flat. "I didn't mean Verity."

I pressed my lips together in silent defiance. Though my knees felt weak, I willed myself not to look away from him.

"Annaleigh," he warned.

I counted the seconds ticking by on the little silver clock on the mantel. After two dozen passed, Camille cleared her throat, drawing Papa's attention.

"You said there was something in the parlor?"

He rubbed his beard, suddenly looking far older. "Yes. It was Morella's idea, actually. A treat for you all." He sighed. "To celebrate the end of our mourning, we've brought in dressmakers to design new clothes. Milliners and cobblers too."

My sisters all squealed, and Rosalie rushed to Papa, then Morella, throwing her arms around their necks. "Thank you, thank you, thank you!"

I kissed Verity on the top of her head and stood up, intent on returning to my room. I didn't want new clothes. I was not going to forget the old customs, bribed by shiny baubles and silks.

"Annaleigh," Papa called out, stopping me. "Where are you off to?"

"As I have no need of new clothes, I'll leave you to them."

He shook his head. "We are all coming out of mourning, you included. I'll not have you in drab weeds while the rest of us get on with our lives."

I sucked in my breath, but the fiery barb could not be contained. "I'm sure Eulalie wishes she could get on with her life as well."

He was across the room in three quick strides. My father wasn't a violent man, but in that moment, I truly worried he might strike me. Grabbing my elbow, he pulled me into the hallway. "This obstinacy will end. Now."

Drawing on mettle I didn't know I possessed, I shook my head, openly defying him. "Go, move on, since you're so set on this new life. Leave me alone to mourn my sisters as I see fit."

"No one can move on if you're wandering about the house draped in black, never letting them forget!" He turned toward the window with a curse of frustration. When he looked back, deep creases wrinkled his forehead. "I don't want to fight, Annaleigh. I miss Eulalie as much as you do. Elizabeth and Octavia and Ava too. Your mother most of all. Do you think it brings me joy to have returned half my family to the Salt?"

Papa dropped onto a small conversation bench. It was too low for him, and his knees buckled to his chest. After a moment, he gestured for me to join him.

"I know most men want strapping young sons to follow after them, to take over the estates, to carry on their names, but I was always proud to have so many girls. Some of my best memories were with the eleven of you and your mother, playing dress-up, picking out dolls. I loved those times. And when Cecilia was pregnant with Verity . . . it was such a wonderful surprise. When she passed away, I thought I'd never have happiness like that again."

A tear fell, running down the end of his nose. He pushed it aside, gazing at the tiles beneath our feet. Small chips of sea glass made a mosaic of waves crashing down the hall.

"After so many years of tragedy and sadness, I have the chance to grab that happiness again. It's not as complete—how could it be, with so many gone?—but I need to take it while I can."

The ribbon around my wrist was already frayed, and I toyed

with the fringed ends, overcome by a sense of déjà vu. Wasn't this exactly what Camille and I had just spoken of?

"I suppose these dressmakers might have some light gray silks?" I reasoned, conceding.

"Cecilia always loved you in green," he confided, bumping his arm into mine. "That's why she made up your room in all that jade. She said your eyes reminded her of the sea right before a big storm."

"I'll see what they have," I said, accepting his hand as he pulled me up. "But you will not catch me wearing pink."

"Look at this satin! It's the most delectable shade of pink I ever saw!" Rosalie exclaimed, hoisting the rosette cloth above her head.

The Gold Parlor was a mess of fabrics and trimmings. Crates of bows and laces lay open like treasure chests, their contents spilling out. There wasn't a bare surface to be found. I'd tripped over three boxes of buttons already.

Camille held a swatch of saffron up to her face. "What do you think of this shade, Annaleigh?"

"It suits you beautifully," Morella cut in. She was in the middle of the chaos, sitting on a tufted chaise longue like a pampered queen bee. She hadn't looked at me since the incident in the dining room. I needed to find a way to apologize.

"Something blue would bring out your eyes more," I said, scooping up a bolt of cerulean. "See? And it sets off your coloring—you look so rosy. Don't you think, Morella?"

She nodded faintly but turned to inspect a glimmering bit of ribbon Mercy pulled from a box.

"This chiffon is perfect for my lady," a seamstress said, stepping into the conversation. "Have you seen these sketches yet?" She offered Camille a handful of designs. "We can have that made into any of these dresses."

Camille took the drawings and sat on a pouf covered in glittering pastel damasks. The seamstress knelt beside her, taking notes.

On the rack near me, lengths of cream-colored linens and beautiful green silks rested on padded hangers. I'd selected three patterns for long, flowing dresses and even a ball gown for the triplets' party. Despite my misgivings, the seafoam tulle—dotted with sparkling silver paillettes like twinkling stars—made me giddy with anticipation. It would be a truly magnificent dress.

Lenore opened an ornate box. "Oh! Look at these!"

Nestled inside the velvet lining was a pair of slippers. The silver leather looked as soft as butter and shimmered in the afternoon light. Silk ribbons were sewn on either side to tie around the ankle.

These shoes were meant for dancing.

Verity grabbed one and held it close to her face, inspecting the pattern of beads around the toe with awe. "Fairy shoes!"

"How stunning," Morella said, admiring the other.

Reynold Gerver, the cobbler, spoke up. "Each pair takes two weeks to make. The soles are padded for extra comfort. You could dance all night, and your feet wouldn't mind at all come morning."

Rosalie snatched the shoe away from Verity. "I want a pair of them for our ball."

"No, I saw them first!" Lenore protested. "I want them."

"We should all get a pair," Ligeia said. She joined Morella on the chaise, touching the ribbons. "We only turn sixteen once."

Camille looked up from the sketches. "Can they be made in other colors? I'd love a pair in rose gold, to match my gown."

Gerver nodded. "I have samples of all my leather here." He pulled a book out from under the discarded yellow fabric. He paused, eyeing Morella. "Because these slippers are so unique . . . they can run quite dear."

"Quite dear?" Papa's voice boomed from the doorway. "I leave my girls alone for an hour and you've spent me out of house and home, have you?"

Rosalie held up the shimmering slipper. "Papa! Look at this! These shoes would be perfect for our ball! May we get them? Please?"

He looked at each of my sisters' hopeful faces. "I suppose you all want a pair?"

"Us too?" Honor asked, standing on tiptoe to peer over a stack of hatboxes.

He kept his face as a neutral mask. "I'll need to see them. One of the most important lessons of trade: never shake on an agreement until you've inspected the cargo."

Rosalie gave the slipper back to Verity and nudged her. She stepped forward, holding it out with reverent, chubby fingers.

"They're fairy shoes, Papa."

He turned it over and over again with theatrical interest. "Fairy shoes, you say?" Her round eyes, the same green as mine, beamed. "They seem awfully delicate. Very insubstantial."

The cobbler stepped forward. "Not at all. I assure you, they will last a whole season's worth of balls. I make my soles from the finest leather in the kingdom. Flexible but tough."

Papa looked unconvinced. "How much for eight pairs?" From

the chaise, Morella sniffed. "Nine pairs," Papa corrected. "Nine pairs, delivered before the end of the month. My daughters are having a ball. We'll need them ready by then."

Gerver whistled through his teeth. "That's not much time. I'll have to bring in extra hands. . . ."

"How much?"

Gerver counted on the tips of his fingers, then adjusted the gold spectacles hanging from the end of his nose. "Each pair is one hundred and seventy-five gold florettes. But to have nine pairs made up, in only three weeks . . . I couldn't charge less than three thousand."

The room's playful mood died away. There was no chance Papa would agree to such extravagance. I couldn't begin to calculate what the new dresses and underpinnings were already costing him.

"Surely nine pairs of shoes won't send us to the poorhouse, Ortun," Morella prompted with a winsome smile.

Verity stood on her toes, watching his expression with rapt attention. He knelt beside her. "Do you really think these slippers are worth all that, child?" She looked back to us, then nodded. His face broke into an unexpected grin. "Go on, then, and pick yours out. Fairy shoes for everyone!"

5

WITH A FINAL TUG OF THE OARS, I PULLED MY DINGHY into the marina at Selkirk, slipping alongside the sun-bleached dock as the sun rose over the horizon. At Eulalie's wake, Morella had mentioned she'd been about to tell Papa about the baby but had been interrupted by the fishermen bringing Eulalie's body home. Perhaps they had seen something, some small detail they might have forgotten to tell Papa because they believed the fall was an accident.

I threaded my rope through the eye of an open cleat and tied off the excess line, then pulled myself out.

I needed to find those fishermen.

The five islands of Salann spread across the Kaleic Sea like jeweled clusters of a necklace.

Selkirk was the farthest to the northeast, home to fishmongers, captains, and sailors. A bustling wharf handled the seafood arriving daily on the boats.

Astrea was next in the chain, and the most populated. Shops, markets, and taverns sprang from its rocky shores, a glittering city of commerce and wealth. The triplets had been there nearly every day since their ball was announced, scouring the stores for little treasures. An extra pair of stockings, a new shade of lip stain. Somehow Morella convinced Papa they were all absolute necessities for young ladies about to make their societal debut.

We lived directly in the middle of the chain, on Salten.

Vasa stretched out like a long, skinny eel, with ports on the north and south sides. Papa oversaw the massive shipyard that took up the whole island. Most of the King's naval fleet had been built on Vasa. Someone at court once heard him boast the Salann ships were the swiftest in his navy, and Papa had beamed with pride for months.

The final island was the smallest but most important. Hesperus was one of the most pivotal defense posts in all of Arcannia. Its lighthouse, affectionately named Old Maude, stood taller than any other in the country. Not only did it assist ships coming in and out of port, it was also an excellent perch for spotting enemy boats.

I loved the lighthouse. It felt like a second home. When I was small, I'd volunteer to clean the windows in Highmoor till they sparkled, imagining I was polishing the lighthouse gallery. I'd climb to the highest cliffs and pretend to be atop Old Maude, spying on foreign ships—really, fishermen out for their daily catch—and noting all the pertinent details in a giant ledger, as I'd seen Silas do.

Silas had been Keeper of the Light for as long as anyone could remember. He grew up in the lighthouse, learning the beacon's workings from his father. When it became clear Silas would never have children of his own, Papa realized an apprentice would need to be chosen as an eventual replacement. I prayed to Pontus every night it would be me.

Hanna's son, Fisher, was chosen instead. He worked on the docks, but Papa said he was destined for greater things. As young girls, Camille and I followed him all over Salten, in awe of his every move and hopelessly smitten. When he left to begin his apprenticeship, I cried myself to sleep every night for a week.

Looking across the Selkirk wharf now, I could just make out the beacon's flash and wondered what Fisher was doing. Probably cleaning windows. Silas was fanatical about them.

I made my way down the docks and stopped at the first boat I found, asking the captain if he'd heard of any men who'd discovered a body near Salten. He waved me off, saying it was bad luck for a woman to be near the ships. Two other crewmen followed suit before I found a dockhand willing to talk with me.

"The Duke's girl?" he asked around a wad of chewing tobacco. The juice drizzled down from his lips, staining his beard yellow. "A couple of weeks back?"

I nodded eagerly, hungry for information.

"You'll be wanting to talk with Billups. . . ." He scanned the wharf. "But his boat is already out."

"Do you know when he'll return?" With all the party preparations, I could stay away for most of the afternoon without being missed.

"Not today," he said, crushing my plan. "Nor tomorrow. He's wanting one last big catch before Churning sets in." He held up his hand in the breeze. "Feel that cold snap in the air? It won't be long now."

I tried to hide my disappointment, arranging my face into a smile of thanks.

"Wasn't Ekher with him?" asked the dockhand's companion, who'd overheard the conversation as he rolled an enormous spool of thick rope.

"Was he? Didn't think he left the docks these days."

The second man grunted, and together they flipped the spool over, setting it upright. "He's a couple of piers down, the old netter. You can't miss him."

I navigated the maze of connecting docks, keeping my eyes out for someone with nets. Three piers down, I saw him.

Ekher sat on a bench, surrounded by coils of cobalt and indigo cording. Decades of life on the docks had left his skin dark and leathery, with wrinkles worn in deep. His sinewy fingers were hooked around a wickedly curved needle used to knot the nets together. As they lightly danced over a pile of cords beside him, searching for the right piece, I realized he could not see them.

He was blind.

I paused, wondering what I ought to do next. It was obvious he wouldn't be able to tell me any details about finding Eulalie—Billups must have been the one who spotted her. I was about to leave when he slowly turned from his net and stared directly at me with milky, unseeing eyes.

"If you're going to ogle an old man all morning, girl, at least come and keep him company." He reached out, beckoning with clawed fingers.

Pushing back a nervous laugh, I approached his bench. "I didn't realize you could see me," I apologized, smoothing out my linen skirt.

"Of course I can't see you. I'm blind," he retorted.

I cocked my head. "Then how—"

"Your perfume. Or soap. Or whatever it is young girls wear. I could smell it at a hundred paces."

"Oh." My heart dropped with surprising disappointment, saddened his answer was so pragmatic.

"What do you want with an old blind netter anyhow?"

"I heard you were with the fisherman who found that body. . . ."

"I'll be ninety-eight next Tuesday, my girl. There have been a lot of bodies in my life. You'll need to be more specific."

"Eulalie Thaumas. The Duke's daughter."

He lowered the needle. "Ah. Her. Terrible business."

"Did your friend—Billups—think there was anything unusual about it?"

"It's not very usual to see pretty young ladies falling from cliffs, is it? Is that what you mean?"

I sank down on the bench beside him. "So you believe it was an accident?"

Ekher raised two gnarled fingers toward his chest, as if warding off bad spirits. "What else would it be? She wouldn't have jumped. We saw the locket."

"Locket?" I echoed. I'd never seen Eulalie with a locket.

He nodded. "Chain was smashed to bits, but we could still make out the inscription."

Before I could ask more, he stiffened and grabbed my hand in his. His fingers dug into my palm, and I cried out in surprise and pain. His grasp was too strong to jerk away from.

"Something's coming." His voice rasped, hoarse with panic.

I raised my other hand to my eyes, shielding out the bright sunlight. The wharf bustled along with its usual rhythms and sounds. Gulls screeched overhead, plotting to filch bits of chum from unsuspecting fishermen. Captains shouted at dockhands, issuing orders and sometimes curses as the wayward lads struggled through headaches undoubtedly the result of a wild time at the tavern the night before.

"I don't see anything."

His grip tightened; he was clearly frightened. "Can't you feel it?"

"What?"

"Stars. Falling stars."

I cast a dubious glance overhead at the morning sky, colored deep peach and amber. Not even Versia's Diadem—the brightest of all constellations, named after the Night Queen—was visible.

"What happened to the locket?" I asked, trying to turn his attention to the matter at hand and away from unseen stars. "Did you bring it back with the body?"

He fixed his milky eyes on me, clearly affronted. "I'm no thief."

I thought back to Eulalie's funeral, remembering that horrible necklace she'd had on. It was the only time I'd ever seen her wear it. Had that been the locket?

I let out a sigh of frustration. The funeral was over two weeks ago. Her coffin had undoubtedly split open by now, returning Eulalie to the Salt, necklace and all.

"Do you remember what was written on it?"

Ekher nodded. "Billups read it out loud. Brought a tear to both our eyes." He cleared his throat as if preparing to recite a poem. "'I dwelt alone / In a world of moan, / And my soul was a stagnant tide, / Till the fair and gentle Eulalie became my blushing bride.'"

My mouth dropped open. "Bride? Eulalie wasn't a bride."

He shrugged, stabbing the needle back into the cording. Ekher missed his mark, and the curved metal sank into the pad of his wizened thumb. He didn't seem to feel it. The dark blood stained the indigo net black.

"You're hurt."

His mood shifted abruptly again as the blood welled up and he rubbed his fingers together. "Get away from me before I lose the whole finger, you daft girl!" He wrinkled his nose and spat.

I jumped away from Ekher and raced down the docks, but I kept looking back as he shouted curses at me. I'd never seen someone's moods turn so quickly. Had so many years in the sun addled his mind? As I cast one look back toward him, I bumped into someone and nearly fell over my feet.

"I'm so terribly sorry," I exclaimed, reaching out for balance. The rising sun was directly behind the stranger, casting around him a brilliant corona that blinded me. Spots, dark blue and white-hot, danced before my eyes.

Like the old man's stars.

"I believe this is yours?" he said, stepping closer, arm outstretched. Shaded from the sun's glare, I made out friendly blue eyes staring down with concern.

I felt completely dwarfed by him, barely coming to his shoulders. My eyes lingered on their broad expanse for a moment longer than was entirely proper. He must be a sea captain, I thought, sensing the muscles beneath his fine wool jacket. It wasn't hard to picture him raising a heavy sail, one hoist at a time.

His hair was unfashionably long, the dark curls stopping just shy of his jawline. One curl brushed the corner of his mouth, caught on a passing breeze, and I had a sudden and thoroughly horrifying desire to push it aside, just to feel its softness.

He cleared his throat, and my cheeks burned, so terrified was I that he'd somehow read my mind. He'd been holding out a coin between his fingers while I openly gaped at him, my mind racing with wild thoughts.

"You dropped this." He took my hand and pressed the piece of copper into my palm.

Such a simple gesture, performed every day by merchants and tradesmen, should not have felt so singularly intimate, but his touch thrilled me. His thumb caressed the center of my hand, leaving a tingling sweep when he released the money into my possession. My breath caught as I irrationally wondered what that same movement would feel like against my neck, my cheeks, my lips. . . .

"Thank you," I murmured, finding my voice. "That was very kind. Most people would have kept it."

"I wouldn't dream of keeping something that didn't belong to me." I sensed he was about to smile. "Besides, it's only a copper florette. I'd rather lose the money and seize the chance to talk with the pretty girl who owns it."

I opened my mouth, willing anything to come out, but words failed me.

He stepped in closer as a pair of fishermen barreled down the pier, a heavy crate balanced between them. "Actually, perhaps you could be of some assistance?"

My guard shot up. Papa always cautioned us to be on the

lookout for pickpockets and thieves when outside Highmoor. Perhaps returning my coin was merely a ruse to swindle me out of greater sums.

"I'm new here and was looking for the captain."

I squinted, keeping a wary eye on his hands. Papa said many were so skilled in the art of thievery, they could steal the rings from your fingers without you being the wiser.

"It's a large wharf," I stated, gesturing to the dozens of boats around us. "With many captains."

He smiled guilelessly, his cheeks betraying a trace of his chagrin, and I thought perhaps his intentions were pure. "Yes, of course. I'm looking for Captain Corum. Captain Walter Corum."

I shrugged, wishing the light in his eyes didn't fluster me. After so many years of being locked away at Highmoor, I had almost no experience with men. Even speaking with Papa's valet, Roland, for more than a question or two left me a rosy, stammering mess.

I pointed toward the marketplace farther down the harbor. "Someone there will know."

The stranger's eyes dimmed a touch, his disappointment evident. "But not you?"

"I'm not from Selkirk."

He turned to go.

"Are you to sail for him?" The question burst out too loudly. "For Captain Corum?"

He shook his head. "He's sick. With scarlet fever. I've come to take care of him."

"Is he very ill, then?"

He shrugged. "I suppose I'll find out soon enough."

I remembered how everyone gathered at Ava's sickbed when she fell ill. The room was kept dark, the curtains shut tight against the light. The healers said to heat the plague out of her body, and it grew unbearably stuffy with the fires stoked as high as Papa dared. Even so, Ava's teeth chattered so loudly, I feared they'd crack apart, falling from her bloodied lips like hailstones raining down.

But the stranger didn't look like a healer. He was made to be on a ship, high above the sea in the crow's nest, halfway to the stars. I could picture the wind tugging at his dark curls as he scanned the horizon for adventures.

"I hope he's soon on the mend," I offered, my hands fumbling, unsure of what they were supposed to be doing. "I'll say a prayer to Pontus tonight for a swift recovery."

"That's very kind of you . . ." He trailed off, clearly seeking my name.

"Annaleigh."

His mouth curved into a smile, and my breath caught as a bundle of nerves fluttered deep within me.

"Annaleigh," he repeated, and on his tongue my name sounded full and lush, like a line of poetry or a hymn.

"Thaumas," I added, though he didn't ask. I sounded like a staggering simpleton and wanted to sink into the waves.

His eyes lit up, as if he recognized my surname, and I wondered if he knew Papa. "Annaleigh. Thaumas." His grin deepened. "Beautiful." He swept into a deep bow, holding his arm out like a gallant courtier. "I hope our paths soon cross again."

Before I could voice my surprise, he'd left and was halfway down the busy pier, ducking around another approaching crate.

"Wait!" I cried out, and he paused, turning back.

His face was painted in unexpected pleasure as he waited for me to continue.

Though my cheeks warmed, I stepped closer. "I can show you the way to the marketplace . . . if you like."

He glanced toward the covered stalls several docks down from where we stood. "That marketplace over there?"

His light tone suggested he was teasing, but my stomach writhed in its foolishness. I forced myself to smile. "Yes, well, I'm sure you'll be able to find your way." I nodded once. "Good day . . ." I didn't know his name, and the farewell felt open-ended. "Sir," I added, two seconds too late.

As I retreated toward my dinghy, my face burned scarlet. Suddenly I felt a hand slip loosely around my wrist, twirling me to face the handsome stranger once more. I grabbed his forearm to steady myself. He seemed taller somehow, and I noticed a thin, crescent-shaped scar on his temple. I knew I was staring and quickly took two steps backward, allowing for the proper amount of space between us.

"Cassius," he supplied. "My name is Cassius."

"Oh."

He offered the crook of his elbow. "I'd be very grateful for your assistance in finding the marketplace. It's my first time on Selkirk, and I'd hate to get lost."

"It is an awfully large wharf," I said, peering about the marina as if it had tripled in size.

"Will you help me, then, Miss Thaumas?" His eyes danced, his face about to break into another grin.

"I suppose I ought to."

He led us down another dock, taking a left, then a right, then a left again, drawing out the short walk.

"So you're a healer?" I asked, skirting a coil of rope. The wharves were quickly filling up with fishermen hauling out for the day. "You said you were here to take care of your friend?"

"My father," he clarified. "And no. I've no special training. Just familial devotion . . . familial obligation, really." His smile turned stiff. "This will be our first time meeting, I'm afraid." He ducked toward me to avoid a catch of lobster traps that had been hoisted onto the dock from a nearby boat. Leaning in, he whispered conspiratorially, "You see, Miss Thaumas, I'm a bastard."

He said this with a devil-may-care recklessness, intending to shock me.

"That doesn't matter," I responded honestly. "It shouldn't matter what your parents did, just what you do as a person."

"Very generous of you. I wish more shared your opinion."

We took a final turn, coming directly off the pier and into the marketplace. Tables and booths were set up under makeshift canopies, shielding the fresh catches from the unforgiving rays of the sun. A light breeze kept the worst of the smells at bay, but there was a sharp underlying tang of gutted fish that no amount of wind could clear.

"Well"—I gestured to the stalls—"this is it. I'm sure any of the fishmongers can show you where he lives. It's a small community. Everyone knows everyone."

After the words left my mouth, I saw how true they were. As we wandered into the crowd, eyes fell on us, instantly recognizing me as the Duke's daughter. Though most of the merchants had the decency to murmur behind discreetly raised hands, I could still hear their whispered accusations.

"That's that Thaumas girl."

"Such a shame about . . ."

". . . not even dead a month . . ."

". . . cursed . . ."

The hairs on the back of my neck bristled at the mention of the curse. It was a foolish rumor, but rumors had a way of morphing into something big and ugly. I didn't know if Cassius noticed I was too embarrassed to meet his gaze.

"What's she wearing? It's not even gray. . . ."

". . . make her leave . . ."

". . . she'll bring their bad luck to us . . ."

"Hey! You there!" a voice rang out over the murmured buzz. "You shouldn't be here!"

"I have to go," I said, releasing my hold on his arm. The urge to run from the whispers overpowered any desire I had to stay with him. "I hope you find your father and he gets well soon!"

"But—Annaleigh!"

Before he could stop me, I turned on my heel and sprinted back to the safety of my dinghy. I needed to be out on the water, out among the waves. I needed the sea breezes to push the building panic from me, needed the rhythmic pull of the ocean swells to set my mind right again.

We weren't cursed.

Hopping down into my boat, I tried to cast the crowd's whispers from me. But they lingered in my mind, echoing and growing until the handful of fishmongers became a jeering crowd, then a mob, with torches and knives.

I stood on tiptoes, peering over the planks of the dock to see if anyone had followed me. A small part of me hoped Cassius had, but this end of the marina was quiet. He was back in the marketplace, probably receiving an earful on the Thaumas sisters. My heart sank low as I pictured his golden smile fading away when he learned of the ghoulish passings at Highmoor.

Though the only one to see my foolishness was a little fiddler crab skittering along the planks, my face flushed. I didn't know Cassius, but I couldn't bear the thought he might be thinking ill of me.

"Don't be absurd." I hastily untied my rope from the dock and pushed off. "He was nothing more than a skilled flirt, and you have bigger things to worry about."

Out of the harbor, I paused to splash a handful of water over my heated face. There *were* bigger things to worry about.

What had the inscription in the locket meant? Eulalie, a blushing bride?

It didn't make any sense. Though she'd had many suitors, none of them had ever proposed.

Had they?

Frowning, I set the oars against the waves. There were only two reasons Eulalie wouldn't have told us about a fiancé.

It was either someone Papa would never have approved of . . .

Or someone Eulalie didn't.

My imagination pounced then, conjuring up Eulalie's fateful last night. She must have been meeting this would-be suitor, rebuffing his advances, telling him they could never be together. They quarreled and tempers rose, flaring to a feverish pitch, until he shoved her from the cliffs. Had he thrown the locket after her to erase the evidence of his unrequited desire? I pictured her falling through the air, the look of confusion on her face turning to horror as she realized there was no escaping this, no way to go back and make it right. Had she screamed before smashing into the rocks?

A wave struck the side of my dinghy, slapping me back to the present with a gasp. Though it was all conjecture, I felt I was on the right path.

My sister's death had not been an accident. It had not been part of some dark curse.

She was murdered.

And I was going to prove it.

6

CREAK.
Creak.
Creeeeeeeak.

My fingers were on the handle of Eulalie's desk drawer when I heard the floorboard in the hallway and froze, my heart high in my throat, certain I was about to be caught. While there was no actual rule about not entering our departed sisters' rooms, it didn't feel like the kind of thing I wanted anyone to know about. A flood of possible excuses crashed into my head like a tidal wave to the shore, each sounding weak and unbelievable.

When no one raced into the room and accused me of trespassing, I tiptoed to the door and peered out into the hallway.

It was empty.

With a sigh of relief, I quietly shut the door and studied Eulalie's room, wondering where to look next.

When I returned from Selkirk, I found a nearly empty house. Morella had taken the triplets to Astrea again, and the Graces were still at their lessons with Berta. A series of erroneous notes clunked loudly from the Blue Room's piano as Camille practiced a new solo. With everyone preoccupied, it was the perfect time to slip into Eulalie's room and search for something to prove my theory of a scorned lover.

In her absence, everything had straightened into an orderly neatness she would have hated in life. Books were stacked into tidy towers on her writing desk, not strewn about at the end of her chaise. The floor was remarkably free of clothes, and white drop cloths covered most of the furniture.

I wandered around the room, unsure what to look for until I spotted the tall pedestal near the window. A maidenhair fern, now wilting and in desperate need of attention, languished on it, concealing a hidden drawer I remembered Ava once mentioning. Eulalie kept her most beloved treasures within it.

After several moments of poking and prodding, I discovered a lever and released it to reveal a cache of objects. I pulled out three slim volumes, hoping they were diaries filled with accounts of her days and secrets. Skimming the first few pages, I saw they were novels Papa had forbidden her to read, citing passages too graphic for young ladies' eyes. I set the books aside, oddly pleased she had read them anyway.

At the bottom of the drawer was an assortment of hair ribbons, jewelry, and a pretty little pocket watch. I opened it and found a lock of hair tied together with a bit of copper wire. Twisting it between my fingers, I wondered at its color. When Mama and our sisters died, we all received snips of their hair to keep in memory books or braid into mourning jewelry, but this lock was a pale blond, almost white, far too light to have come from a Thaumas head. I slipped it into my pocket to mull over later.

There was also a vial of perfume and a handkerchief too devoid of embroidery and lace to have come from Eulalie's collection. It singed my nostrils, reeking of a particularly strong pipe smoke.

"What are you doing?" a voice called out, startling me.

I jumped, dropping the handkerchief. It fluttered to the floor like a butterfly at first frost. Heart pounding, I snapped my head toward the doorway, where Verity stood, sketchbook in hand. Her short chestnut curls were swept back with a large bow, and her pinafore was already dusty with pastels. I let out a sigh of relief, grateful I'd not been caught by Papa.

"Nothing. Aren't you supposed to be in the classroom?"

She shrugged. "Honor and Mercy are helping Cook with petits fours for the ball. Berta didn't want to teach just me." She nodded toward the triplets' room across the hall. "I wanted to see if Lenore would sit for a portrait."

"They're out with Morella. Final fittings on their dresses." I shifted, letting my back close the pedestal's door.

Her mouth pursed into a rosebud as she studied me. "I don't think Eulalie will like you being in there."

"Eulalie isn't here anymore, Verity."

She blinked once.

"Why don't you go see if Cook needs more help?" I suggested. "I bet she'll let you taste the icing."

"Are you borrowing something?"

"Not exactly." I stood up, letting my skirts cover the handkerchief.

"Did you come in here to cry?"

"What?"

She shrugged. "Papa does sometimes. In Ava's. He thinks no one knows about it, but I hear him at night."

Ava's room was on the fourth floor, directly above Verity's.

She leaned in, peering about the room with curiosity but unwilling to actually enter it. "I won't tell if you are."

"I'm not crying."

She reached out, beckoning me over to her. I left the handkerchief on the floor, hoping she wouldn't see it. Verity traced one fingertip across my cheek and looked disappointed when it came away dry. "I still miss her."

"Of course you do."

"But no one else does. No one remembers her anymore. All they talk about is the ball."

I squeezed her shoulders. "We haven't forgotten her. We need to move on, but that doesn't mean they don't miss and love her."

"She doesn't think so."

I frowned. "What do you mean?"

"She thinks everyone is too busy with their lives to remember her." She glanced back out into the hall as if worried our conversation was being overheard. "Elizabeth says so too. She says we all look different now. But she doesn't."

"You mean when you remember her?"

She shook her head. "When I see her."

"In your memories," I pressed.

After a moment, she held out the sketchbook, offering it to me.

Before I could take it, Rosalie and Ligeia rushed down the hall, carrying a tower of boxes marked with the names of several Astrean shops.

"Oh good, you're both here!" Rosalie said, struggling to throw open their bedroom door. "We need to go downstairs, all of us, right now!"

"Why?" Verity asked, her shoulders suddenly tense, worry evident on her face. "Did someone else die?"

I winced. What other six-year-old worried an announcement meant someone had died?

"Of course not!" Ligeia said, depositing her treasures at the foot of her bed. "They're here! The fairy shoes! We stopped by the cobbler's shop, and he was sewing on the last set of ribbons!"

Verity's eyes brightened, and the sketchbook was instantly forgotten. "They're here now?"

"Come and see!" Rosalie tore down the corridor, shouting upstairs for Camille to come quick. She must have retreated to her room after her practice session. Ligeia raced after Rosalie, their footsteps heavy on the back stairs.

"We should go," I said.

"Don't forget about Eulalie's handkerchief," Verity said, skipping down the hall before I could stop her.

I blinked once before turning to snatch it up. When I left, the door slammed shut after me, as if pushed by unseen hands.

It was raining again, a cold downpour that chilled the air no matter how many fireplaces were lit. Raindrops raced down the windows, blurring the view of the cliffs and waves below. The Blue Room smelled damp, with a faint trace of mildew.

Morella sat on the sofa nearest the fireplace, rubbing her back, an uncomfortable grimace drawn on her face. My heart went out to her. Planning and hosting such a large affair was trying even under the best circumstances. Doing so while pregnant must be exhausting. And the triplets had clearly run her ragged.

"Lenore, do you think you could find your father? I'm sure he'd enjoy seeing the shoes. My ankles have swollen something fierce with this storm."

I grabbed a small tufted pouf hiding under the piano. "You should put your feet up, Morella. Mama had lots of problems with swelling during her pregnancies. She'd keep her feet elevated as much as she could." I positioned the stool beneath her legs, trying to make her comfortable. "She also had a lotion made of kelp and linseed oil. We rubbed it into her ankles every morning before she got dressed."

"Kelp and linseed oil," she repeated, and offered a small smile of thanks.

I paused, sensing a way to both help her and make up for my outburst the morning after Eulalie's funeral. "I could mix some up for you. It might help."

"That would be very nice. . . . Has your gown arrived yet?"

It was the first time she'd shown any interest in what I was wearing to the ball. She was trying too, in her own way.

"Not yet. Camille and I have our final fittings on Wednesday. If you're feeling up to it, maybe you'd like to come with us?"

Her eyes lit up. "I would enjoy that. We could get lunch in town, make a real afternoon of it. Remind me what color it is?"

"Sea green."

She paused, thinking. "Your father mentioned something about a chest of Cecilia's jewelry somewhere. Perhaps there would be something suitable for you. I remember seeing a portrait of her wearing green tourmalines."

I knew exactly which painting she referred to. It hung in a study on the fourth floor where Mama had wedged a small writing desk into a sunny nook. On clear days, you could see all the way to the lighthouse. Papa hung the portrait there after her death.

"I would love something of hers for the ball. Camille would too, I'm certain."

"And me!" Verity chimed in, eager to be included.

"Of course," Morella said with a smile. "We'll have to look through it."

Mercy and Honor sprinted in, out of breath and sticky from their treats.

"Rosalie said the fairy shoes are here?" Mercy asked, immediately spotting the boxes.

We'd all taken to calling them fairy shoes. Though I knew they were only little leather slippers—beautifully dyed and styled leather slippers—we'd imbued them with a touch of magic. These shoes would be the beginning of our new start. Once we wore them, we couldn't help but be different from who we were before.

Morella swatted at Mercy's hands. "Wait for your father."

"And me," Camille said, bursting into the room with Papa.

We all piled around the sofa, giddy with anticipation.

"How do we know whom each box is for?" he asked.

"We each chose a different color," Honor explained.

"Except us," Rosalie said, speaking for the triplets. "Ours are a matching silver."

"Well, shall we see if these fairy shoes were worth such a fuss?" Papa flipped the latch, and we all gasped as the box opened.

They were Camille's, a sparkling rose gold. Metallic flecks were embossed into the pink leather, creating a shimmering luster. I'd never seen anything so exquisitely sophisticated.

Next were the triplets' shoes. The leather glinted like Mama's precious wedding silver. The ribbons were different shades of purple, matching the girls' dresses. Ligeia's were a soft lilac, Rosalie's violet, and Lenore's such a deep eggplant they looked nearly black.

Honor's slippers were a dark navy twinkling with silver beads like the night sky.

Mercy had picked a frosty pink to match her favorite flower, sterling roses. She'd even asked the dressmakers to trim her gown with silk versions of them.

Morella had chosen a pair of gold slippers, glinting brighter than the sun. She beamed up at Papa as he presented them to her with a look of such tender admiration, I couldn't help but smile.

Verity crept up to Papa as he brought out the smallest box. She leaned on his leg, pressing in to see her shoes the moment the box opened. As the lid came off, she clapped her hands with delight.

"What fine fairy shoes these are," Papa praised, plucking out the purple slippers. Flecks of gold scattered across them like gilt trim.

"Oh, Verity! They're beautiful!" Camille said. "They might be the prettiest of them all."

Verity pulled off her boots and slipped them on, springing into a happy pirouette as we all applauded our tiny prima ballerina.

"These must be Annaleigh's," Lenore said, pulling out the last box.

Nestled on a bed of navy velvet were my shoes. I'd selected a jade leather, and the cobbler had added glittering seafoam and silver bits, concentrated heavily at the toes and fading as they swept across the slipper. They would match my gown perfectly.

Papa smiled as he handed them over to me. "I don't think these are fairy shoes at all. They look fit for a sea princess."

Verity frowned. "Mermaids can't wear shoes, Papa."

"Silly me!" he said, tapping her nose. "Are we all satisfied?"

Everyone chimed in with our happiness, and Morella grasped his hand. "With shoes like these, no one will be able to tear their eyes away from our girls. They'll be dancing out of the house before we know it, Ortun."

Camille stiffened. "Out of the house? What do you mean?"

Morella blinked once. "Only that you'll be off and married, of course. Running your own households, just like me."

Papa frowned.

"*This* is my household." A bite crept into Camille's voice.

"Until you're married," Morella filled in. Met with Camille's stony face, her smile began to wane. "Isn't that right?" Morella looked over to Papa, seeking clarification.

"As the Thaumas heir, Camille will stay at Highmoor, even once she's married. I know it's a nasty bit of business to think over, my love, but when I die, she inherits the estate."

Morella tugged on one of her pearl drop earrings. "Only until . . ." She trailed off, holding her stomach as her face grew flushed. "Surely you girls ought to be somewhere else?"

The Graces all stood to leave, but Camille grabbed Mercy's arm, stopping her. "This concerns them too. We should all stay to hear it."

Papa looked uncomfortable. He turned toward Morella, trying to create a more intimate conversation. "You thought any sons we may have together would inherit Highmoor?"

Morella nodded. "That's common practice."

"It works that way on the mainland," he allowed. "But on

the islands, estates are passed to the eldest child, regardless of sex. Many strong women have ruled over the Salann Islands. My grandmother inherited Highmoor when her father passed away. She doubled the size of the Vasa shipyard and tripled the profits."

Morella's lips pressed together into an unhappy line. Her eyes raced over us, counting. "So our son would be ninth in line, even though he's a boy? You never mentioned anything about this."

His eyebrows furrowed. "I didn't realize I needed to."

His voice held a stern note of warning, and immediately Morella shook her head, backing down. "I'm not upset, Ortun, only surprised. I assumed Salann followed the same traditions as the rest of Arcannia, lands and family titles passed from father to son." Her forced smile wavered. "I should have known you islanders would be different."

Papa stood abruptly. He was proud of our seafaring heritage, and it hurt him when others thought less of us for living so far from the capital.

"You're an islander now too," he reminded her before stalking out of the room and leaving us with our pile of shoes.

7

I WINCED AS THE CORSET'S LACES WERE PULLED IN and dug into the center of my waist.

The shop assistant made an apologetic noise in the back of her throat. "One more deep breath, please, my lady."

The new stays pressed into my hip bones, and my face twisted into a grimace. The assistant motioned for me to hold my arms up so she could slip the pale green silk over my head. As the full skirt settled around my waist, Camille peeked around a fabric screen and clapped her hands.

"Oh, Annaleigh, you look lovely!"

"You as well," I half said, half gasped. The rose gold brought out bronze shimmers in her hair, and her cheeks flushed with radiance.

"I can't wait for the first dance."

"Do you really think you'll meet someone?"

"Papa did invite every naval officer he knows."

I blanched. "And all those dukes."

Her smile widened. "And all those dukes."

Papa had promised to invite a number of possible suitors to

the ball. After seeing a portrait of Robin Briord, the young Duke of Foresia, Camille had taken an uncommon interest in learning all she could about the wooded province. She spun around the shop, no doubt daydreaming of him.

I wondered about the handsome stranger from Selkirk. Cassius had certainly carried himself like a grand lord. Papa had sent out so many invitations, perhaps he'd be among them. I briefly entertained the thought of us twirling through the room, lit with hundreds of candles, his hand clasped around mine. He'd spin me closer, and just before the music ended, he'd lean in to kiss me. . . .

"I don't even know what I'd say to a duke," I muttered, pushing the fantasy aside.

"You'll be fine. You only have to be yourself, and lines of suitors will ask Papa for his blessing."

Lines of suitors. I couldn't imagine a more mortifying scenario.

My greatest hope was finding someone with the same shade of hair as the lock from Eulalie's pocket watch. I'd been carrying it with me everywhere, studying every blond man I came across, searching for a match.

Morella and Mrs. Drexel, the shop owner, entered the room.

The designer brought her hands to her mouth with theatrical charm before spinning me about in a circle. "Oh, darling! Never have I made such a dress for such a girl. You look just like the ocean waves on a warm summer day! I wouldn't be surprised if Pontus came out of the Brine to claim you as his bride."

"That's the water one, right?" Morella asked.

The rest of us in the room nodded uneasily. There was no quicker way to spot a mainlander than to bring up religion. Other parts of Arcannia worshipped various combinations of gods: Vaipany, lord of sky and sun; Seland, ruler of earth; Versia, queen of the night; and Arina, goddess of love. There were dozens of other deities—Harbingers and Tricksters—who ruled over other aspects of life, but for the People of the Salt, Pontus, king of the sea, was the only god we needed.

"What do you think of the dress?" Mrs. Drexel asked, changing the subject with practiced tact.

I studied my reflection. Intricate embroidery flowed like waves across the silk bodice. My shoulders were completely bare, save for little decorative sleeves scalloped across my arms. Dozens of lengths of gossamer silk and tulle made up the skirt. The top layers were different shades of light green—mint and beryl—with flashes of darker emerald and verdigris peeking from the bottom.

"I feel just like a water nymph." I traced my hand over the metallic embroidery and beadwork of the generous neckline. "A very naked nymph."

The other women laughed.

I tugged at the edging, trying to pull it higher. "Could we add something here? A band of silk or some lace perhaps? I just feel so . . . exposed."

Morella pushed my hand aside, revealing my bared skin. "Oh, Annaleigh, you're a grown woman now. You can't cover yourself up like a little girl. How will this Pontus ever see your best assets?"

Mrs. Drexel frowned at Morella's flippant mention of Pontus but nodded nonetheless. With a quick glance about the shop, she lowered her voice to a furtive whisper. "I shouldn't tell you this, but the other day I had a client come in—a very *special* client. She saw your gown hanging on the rack and demanded I make her one just like it."

"Who was it?" Morella leaned in with wide eyes, hungry for gossip.

Mrs. Drexel beamed with pleasure, keenly aware of how much we all wanted to know. "Oh, I couldn't possibly say. But she's a dear customer. A truly *lovely* creature. Her only request was that I make her gown the most *passionate* pink I could find. Something to truly strike the heart of any man, mortal or . . . otherwise."

"Arina!" Camille gasped. "You design dresses for the goddess of beauty?" She looked around the tiny shop as if expecting Arina to pop out from behind an embroidered screen and surprise us all.

"Truly?" Morella said, her mouth falling open.

The twist of Mrs. Drexel's lips gave everything away, but she raised her shoulders in a dramatic shrug. "I'm not allowed to say." She threw in a wink for good measure. "But that's all to say that this gown is perfectly in style. Modest even, compared to some." She tilted her head toward the triplets' gowns, and I hid a smirk.

"I think you look perfect," Camille said. "Just like Mama."

"I remember her," Mrs. Drexel said as she knelt down to pin my skirt to the proper length. "Such a kind soul. She came here once for something to wear to one of your father's ship christenings."

"It was red, wasn't it? With a wide sash over the shoulder?" Camille pantomimed the dress. "I came with her for the final fitting! She loved that gown."

"You were the little girl? Oh, how time passes! I'd wager your next visit here will be for a bridal dress."

Camille flushed. "I certainly hope you're right!"

"Do you have a beau?" Mrs. Drexel asked around a mouthful of pins.

"Not exactly. There is someone I'm hoping to meet at the ball, though."

"She's been practicing her Foresian for weeks!" Morella confided with a chuckle.

Mrs. Drexel smiled. "I'm sure he'll be impressed. Now, I will put the final touches on these two tonight and can bring them to Highmoor tomorrow."

"That would be most kind, thank you," Morella said. "It seems our to-do list keeps growing longer and longer. Only one day left now."

Crossing the street, I spotted him.

Eulalie's Edgar.

He was down the sidewalk from us, chatting with a trio of men, and dressed head to toe in black. Our eyes met, and I nodded. His face turned pale, and he sputtered something to his companions before rushing to leave.

"Mr. Morris!" I called out.

He froze in his tracks, his shoulders dipped with resignation—caught and unable to escape.

"Mr. Morris?" I repeated.

He turned, eyes wild with panic. They swept over me, then fell to the hem of my cloak.

"Miss Thaumas, good day. Forgive me, I hadn't expected you to look so . . . fresh."

His judgment struck me as sharp as a slap. I'd grown

accustomed to the frenzied glee now infusing Highmoor. Sunlight poured in through open windows and fresh-cut flowers were everywhere. New dresses arrived daily and our armoires were riots of colors.

All traces of mourning were gone. The black shrouds from every mirror and glass plate had been gathered into a big pile on the north lawn. Bombazine wreaths and ribbons, crepe hangings, and all of our dark clothes had been set ablaze, fueling a bonfire that burned three nights long.

I glanced down at my blue gabardine uneasily, rubbing my thumb over the pads of my fingers. "There have been several . . . changes at Highmoor."

He took in the colorful clothes, my uncovered face. "I've heard. I'm so sorry, I must be going, I—"

"How . . . how have you been?" I asked, unable to stop the words from tumbling from my mouth. His dark, appraising eyes turned me into a stammering mess. "We've not seen you since . . ." I couldn't bring myself to finish the sentence and grabbed on to the first topic that came to mind. "We've heard it's been a good fall. For fishing! Out on . . . well, the water, of course. A good fall for fishing."

Edgar blinked once, confusion written across his face. "I don't fish, actually. I'm an apprentice at the clockmaker's shop."

My cheeks burned. "Oh, that's right. Eulalie told us that. . . ."

"How is Mr. Averson these days?" Camille swept in, skillfully saving me.

His eyes grew hard with scorn, taking in her pink organza before answering. "He's well, thank you." He jangled one knee back and forth beneath his dark frock coat, clearly ready for the conversation to be over.

Camille seemed oblivious of his discomfort. "We have a grandfather clock he repaired last spring. Perhaps you remember it?"

Edgar adjusted his spectacles, dismay etched across his features. "Yes. With the Thaumas octopus as a pendulum and the tentacles carved on the weights?"

She nodded. "The very one. As the hours pass, the arms lower on its prey."

He twisted his fingers, knuckles sharp and white.

She smiled, apparently done with pleasantries. "I was just tracking down my sister. Our stepmother is waiting for us."

"Of course, of course." He bobbed his head, edging away even before removing his hat to say goodbye. As he did, the sunlight gleamed across his head.

His head of very fine pale blond hair.

"Wait!" I called after him, but he'd slipped through the crowds, all but fleeing from us.

Camille linked her arm through mine, pulling us toward the tea shop. "Such an odd little man."

My heart rose with hope. "You thought so too?"

"It was as though he couldn't get away from us fast enough." Her laughter rang out over the marketplace. "But of course, not everyone is as keen to talk about the fall fishing as you are, Annaleigh."

8

I TRUDGED UP THE STAIRS, EXHAUSTED FROM THE long afternoon on Astrea. After lunch, I'd wanted to race home and ask Papa if Edgar had ever approached him about an interest in Eulalie, but Morella had other plans. She whisked us from shop to shop, appraising the wares like a magpie in search of treasure.

I planned to drop off the purchases in my bedroom before searching for Papa, but as I walked down the hall, I spotted steamy air billowing from the bathroom. It smelled of lavender and honeysuckle, such a distinct scent I paused as memories of Elizabeth flooded my mind. She had a special blend of soap made in Astrea just for her. I hadn't smelled it since the day her body was discovered. One of the Graces must have come across a bottle and decided to try it for themselves.

Sure enough, wet footprints led down the hallway toward their rooms, staining the carpet runner.

With a sigh, I followed them. They led past Honor's and Mercy's rooms and came to a stop outside Verity's. She lay on the floor, sprawled out with her sketchbook and surrounded by colored pastels.

"You're lucky I caught you and not Papa."

Verity sat up, dropping a blue pastel. "What do you mean?"

"You didn't towel off properly and left a watery mess in the hall. You know how much he loves that carpet."

He and Mama had bought it on their honeymoon at a bazaar. Papa said he'd turned his back for a moment and a merchant had pounced, showing off his hand-knotted wares. Mama had wanted to buy a small one for her sitting room, but her Arpegian was so bad that when the rug arrived at Highmoor, it was fifty feet long. She'd loved to describe the look on Papa's face as the runner rolled out longer and longer.

"I take baths at night. I've been in my room all afternoon. See?" Verity raised her hands, dry and smeared with colors.

"Who was it, then? Mercy or Honor? It's still steaming."

She shrugged. "They're in the garden, tying ribbons on the flower bushes."

I glanced back into the hallway. The footprints were still there, just barely. On closer inspection, they were too big to be Verity's. "Were the triplets up here?"

"No."

"Well, someone left wet footprints behind, and they lead straight to your room."

Verity closed her sketchbook. "Not my room." She gestured out toward the hallway, at the door directly across from hers.

Elizabeth's.

"I know you pilfered her soap. The bathroom smelled like honeysuckle."

"It wasn't me."

"Then who?"

Again, she looked meaningfully at Elizabeth's room.

"No one is in there."

"You don't know that."

I sank down onto the floor next to her. "What do you mean? Who would be in Elizabeth's room?"

Verity studied me for a long moment. I could see her thoughts grinding. Finally, she opened the sketchbook back up and flipped the pages till she found the right picture.

It was a portrait of Elizabeth. I noticed the date scrawled in a shadowed corner. Verity had drawn this recently.

"Are you having nightmares again? Have you been dreaming of Elizabeth?"

Verity often suffered from horrible night terrors. She'd scream so loudly, even Papa would rush up from his study in the East Wing. When pressed, she could never remember what they were about.

"This isn't a dream," she whispered.

I brushed aside the chill that had settled over me. "No one is in there. Come and see."

Verity shook her head, her chestnut curls springing like snakes.

I pushed up off the floor with a frustrated swish of skirts. "I'll go, then."

The footprints were almost gone, fading out of the carpet. If I'd come upstairs only a minute later, I never would have seen them. My fingers closed around the door handle—a burnished seahorse poking out from the dark walnut—and there was a rustle behind me. Verity paused on her threshold, eyes wide and pleading.

"Don't go in."

Something about the way her tiny hand dug into the jamb sent a streak of cold racing through my chest. The hairs on the back of my neck prickled, rising in defense against an unseen horror. It was ridiculous, but I couldn't shake the look of fear in Verity's eyes.

I pushed open the door with resolve but did not step inside.

The air felt thin and dusty. After Elizabeth's funeral, maids stripped the bedding and covered the furniture with thin, gauzy cloths. They never returned to clean it.

After a cursory sweep of the room, I turned to Verity. "There's no one in here."

Her dark green eyes drifted up to the ceiling. "Sometimes she visits Octavia."

Octavia's room, another shrouded, untouched shrine, was on the fourth floor between Papa's suite and Morella's sitting room.

An involuntary shiver snapped me from the eerie trance Verity wove. "Who does, Verity? I want you to say it and see how absurd it sounds."

She pressed her eyebrows together, wounded. "Elizabeth."

"Elizabeth is dead. Octavia is dead. They can't visit each other, because they're dead and the dead don't visit."

"You're wrong!" She raced into her room, snatched up the sketchbook, and held it out, unwilling to enter the hallway.

I flipped the pages, searching for whatever proof she thought these drawings would offer.

"What am I meant to be looking at?"

She flipped to a scene in black and gray pastels. In it, Verity cowered into her pillows as a shadowy Eulalie ripped the bedsheets from her. Her head was snapped back unnaturally far. I couldn't tell whether she was supposed to be laughing manically or the odd angle was the result of her fall from the cliffs.

I drew a sharp breath, horrified. "You drew this?"

She nodded.

I studied my little sister. "When the fishermen brought Eulalie back, did you see her?"

"No." She flipped the page. A chalk-white Elizabeth floated in a red slash of ink, surprising a robed Verity, ready for her nightly bath.

She turned another page. Octavia curled up in a library chair, seemingly unaware that half her face was smashed in and her arm was too broken to hold a book straight. Verity was there too, peeking around the door, a small, scared silhouette.

Another page flipped.

I took the book from her, staring at Ava. We had only one portrait of her hanging in Highmoor. She'd been little—nine years old with short curls and freckles. This . . . this looked nothing like that.

"You're not old enough to remember Ava," I murmured, unable to look away from the festering buboes or black patches of infected skin at her neck. Most disturbing was her smile. It was soft and full, exactly as it had been before the plague. Verity had been only two when Ava got sick. She couldn't know what Ava ever looked like.

I turned the page and saw a drawing of all four of them, watching Verity as she slept, hanging from nooses. In disgust, I dropped the book, and sheets of loose paper—dozens of sketches of my sisters—escaped. They exploded across the hall like macabre confetti. In the pictures, they were doing things, ordinary things, things I'd seen them do all my life, but in every drawing they were unmistakably and horribly dead.

"When did you do these?"

Verity shrugged. "Whenever I saw them."

"Why?" I dared a glance back into the seemingly empty room. "Is Elizabeth here now?"

Verity scanned the room before looking back at me. "Do you see her?"

The hairs on my arms rose. "I've never seen any of them."

She took the book and retreated into her bedroom. "Well . . . now you'll know to look."

9

"IT WAS AVA, I'D SWEAR ON PONTUS'S TRIDENT."

Hanna heaved a basket of violet ranunculus up onto a side table. Her full cheeks were as flushed as rosy apples. Even she had been enlisted as an extra set of hands today. "You're telling me Verity sees ghosts? Of your sisters?"

I'd been trailing Hanna around the dining room, telling her the horrors I'd found in Verity's book. The day of the triplets' ball had dawned gray and overcast. A thick, soupy fog blanketed the island. Even though it was well after noon, the gaslights burned brightly, illuminating the army of workers bustling about with final tasks before the guests arrived.

"Yes." I didn't want to believe it was possible, but the detail with which Verity drew Ava shook me to my core.

"These are to be added into the foyer's bower," Hanna instructed two men on a ladder.

They were adding drops of purple cut glass to the chandelier as footmen worked around them, putting the last touches on place settings. Alongside the silver-trimmed plates, dozens of mercury glass candelabras covered the banquet table; as the dinner wore on, their trick tapers would drip purple wax over the glass, delighting the guests. I dropped my basket of the ghoulish candles onto a chair where Roland indicated they should go.

"Ghosts don't exist. Your sisters are in their eternal rest, deep in the Salt. They wouldn't be here. Verity's imagination runs wild. You know that."

My heart sank. Camille had had a similar reaction when I told her about the pictures last night. She'd then kicked me out of her room, saying she needed a good rest before the party. She'd shut the door without even offering me a candle, forcing me to race down the darkened hallway, certain Elizabeth was going to come out of her room and grab me.

Hanna headed to the solarium at the back of the house. "The girls said they want at least a hundred votives in here," she instructed the servants hidden beneath towering palms and exotic orchids. "Be sure to space them out evenly, and for Pontus's sake, don't set them too close to the plants! The last thing we need tonight is a fire." She turned back into the hallway, running into me. "Don't you have somewhere else to be?" she asked, exasperated.

"I know you're busy, but listen, please. Verity didn't know what Ava looked like. She was so little when she died."

Hanna grabbed my shoulders, drawing me in, face to face. "You all look alike, love. A painting of any of your sisters in black and white could be mistaken for you. I think you're seeing what you want to."

My mouth fell open, hurt. "Why would I *want* to see that? They looked so horrible." A shudder of revulsion swept over me as I remembered the awful angles of their bodies. "And she didn't know Eulalie broke her neck."

"The girl fell a hundred feet from the cliff walk. What else would her neck have done?"

A crash sounded in the kitchens, and Hanna used the moment to push me aside. "Annaleigh, child, you're about to drive me batty. I can't remember whether I'm supposed to be polishing the bedclothes or folding the silver. And Fisher is due any moment. You have plenty of preparations for yourself upstairs. We'll talk about Verity later, I promise. Just please get out from underfoot."

My mind, swirling with gruesome sketches and ghosts, stilled at her words. "Fisher is coming?" I broke into my first smile of the day.

She nodded, her face lighting up. "Your father invited him to the ball. Wants to introduce him to the captains and lords. He's so proud." She swatted at me. "Now scoot! I'll be along soon to start on your hair."

I took the back stairs, narrow and as tightly coiled as a nautilus shell, to avoid the foyer's frenzy. Approaching the second floor, I could hear the triplets squabbling over the best mirrors and who stole whose lip color. As Rosalie shouted for a maid to help search for a pair of wayward hair combs, I hurried away.

Once in my room, I opened my bureau, intending to lay out my undergarments. A worn envelope pressed against the back of the drawer caught my eye.

It was a letter from Fisher, written years ago, after he'd begun his apprenticeship on Hesperus. I ran my fingertips over the familiar handwriting.

I really shouldn't even be writing to you, since you made such a stink when Lord Thaumas chose me as the next Keeper of the Light, but Mother says I ought to take the high road. It's pretty stupid, if you ask me. There aren't any roads on Salten and certainly not on Hesperus.

It's quiet here, and Silas wakes me up at all hours of the night to scrub Old Maude's windows. I hate it. That should cheer you, at least. And if it doesn't, no matter. I wrote you, as Mother said I should. So there.

But write me back, Minnow. I miss home more than I thought I would. You especially.

Sincerely,
The Terrible Traitor Formerly Known as Fisher

"Are you taking a bath or not?" Camille barged into my room, surprising me. I shoved the letter under a pair of wool tights. "I've been waiting all afternoon."

Snatching up a pair of stockings, I ran my hand over the silk, as if checking for runs. "Go on, then."

"Have you bathed?"

I tossed the stockings aside. "No. I'm not even sure I'm going to."

She pulled a face. "Is this about Verity's drawings? Elizabeth isn't going to drown you in the tub, but I might if you make me late. Get in there before I dump you in myself."

"Just take the bath, Camille."

"I won't have you looking anything less than your best tonight. We're both finding suitors." She grabbed my robe from a hook and threw it at me.

"I thought you said I just needed to be myself," I muttered peevishly, trudging down the hall. Camille followed after me, presumably to make sure I actually went in.

"Your best, bathed self," she clarified.

I shut the door in her face with a bit of satisfaction and quickly locked it before she could force her way in, issuing more orders. I faced the bathtub with trepidation. This was silly. I'd bathed here many times since Elizabeth died.

As I turned the brass handles, waiting for the water, the pipes creaked and rattled, like echoes of Eulalie's screams when she discovered Elizabeth's body.

After adding a sprinkle of soap, I stepped out of my day dress and studied myself in the full mirror. Dark spots edged along the beveled lines, clouding the reflection. Had drops of Elizabeth's blood seeped into the glass, staining it forever?

I tried to let the hot water relax my tense muscles, but it was no use. My imagination was working overtime. Noises in the house became my departed sisters creeping in, ready for me to join them. When a bar of soap bumped my thigh, I nearly screamed.

"You're being ridiculous," I chided myself before scrubbing my hair. The soap smelled of hyacinths, and as I breathed it in, I felt my body relax, releasing its worries.

Fisher was coming.

I hadn't seen him in years, not since Ava's funeral. We weren't allowed to leave the estate while mourning, and Silas kept him too busy for frequent visits. But he'd been a constant fixture of my childhood, eager to play elaborate rounds of hide-and-seek or go fishing in the little skiff Papa let us use if the weather was good.

He was twenty-one now. Try as I might, I couldn't imagine him as a grown man. Fisher had been such a lanky beanpole, with a mop of sandy brown hair and twinkling eyes, always ready for mischief. I couldn't wait to see him again.

"Are you still in there? Hurry up!"

"I just need to rinse my hair!" I shouted at Camille.

She groaned and stomped away.

Plunging under the water, my head cracked against the back of the tub. It knocked the wind out of me. I came up crying in pain, and as the stars cleared from my vision, I let out a shriek.

The water had turned dark purple, nearly black. Murky brine burned in my nostrils, sharp and bitter. I struggled to push myself out of the tub. The bottom was slick with a silky viscosity. I tried to stand, but my feet slipped from under me, and I fell with a spectacular thud, splashing black water over the floor. I rubbed at my hip, already feeling a bruise.

I tried to scream for Camille but was suddenly yanked under by an unseen force. The dark water raced into my mouth, filling it with a brackish bite as I sputtered out a cry for help. I pushed upward, gagging on the fishy tang.

It was a surprisingly familiar taste. One of Cook's favorite dishes to make in the summer months was a black risotto, full of clams, shallots, and spot prawns. The rice was an exotic obsidian, dyed with squid ink.

Ink! The tub was impossibly full of ink.

Without warning, a tentacle shot from the water, snaking around my torso and constricting tightly. It was mottled red and purple, with lines of orange suckers latching on to me. Another arm attacked my leg, winding up it with a fierce possession. I flailed and kicked, but nothing could pry the beast from me.

The bulbous head of an octopus broke the surface, intelligent amber eyes surveying me through slit pupils. With my free foot, I lashed out at them, praying it would release me.

The creature reared back, and I could see its muscular

underside. Dozens of suckers pointed directly to its wickedly sharp black mouth. It opened once, twice, as if pondering which part of me to attack first.

It launched at me, and just before I felt the beak sink into my thigh, I woke up. My heart pounded, echoing its racing rhythms up through my chest and into my throat as I gasped for air.

I'd fallen asleep.

It was a dream.

An awful, awful dream.

Lowering back into the cooling waters, I let out a sigh of relief but immediately jerked up as pounding sounded against the door.

"Annaleigh, I swear, if you make me late, I'm going to murder you!"

"Coming!"

I pushed myself out of the water, wondering how long I'd dozed. Looking at the white porcelain as I toweled off, I couldn't remember why I'd been so scared in the first place. It was just a bathtub. Elizabeth dying there didn't change that.

Standing in front of the mirror, I twisted my wet hair up and spotted something on my back. A set of red marks raked down my spine, almost as if I'd been scratched.

"Camille?" I unlocked the door.

"Finally!" She burst in, arms full of towels, soaps, and oils.

"Would you look at this?" I turned, showing her my naked back. "What does it look like to you? I can't see it very well in the mirror."

Her fingertips on my skin were cold, pushing at the tender spot. "You scratched yourself."

"But I didn't."

"Hmm?"

"I didn't scratch myself."

She turned back to me, her face deadpan. "It must have been Elizabeth, then."

"Camille!"

"Well, what do you want me to say? It's a scratch. I get them all the time. It probably happened while you were scrubbing." She pulled her shift over her head and paused. "You did scrub, didn't you?"

A scoff escaped me. I wasn't Verity. "Of course!"

Camille noticed the full bath. "You didn't drain the tub!"

As she leaned in to find the stopper, a hand reached out of the water, grabbing her neck and dragging her under. Elizabeth surfaced from churning waters, her eyes filmed a sickly green.

"Camille!" I shrieked, shattering the horrible image. She jerked away from the tub with an exasperated sigh.

"What now?"

I blinked, clearing my vision. This wasn't like the tentacled monster. I hadn't fallen asleep. I'd seen a ghost, just as Verity said I would, now that I knew to look.

"I . . ." Camille had made it abundantly clear last night that she wanted nothing to do with our little sister's visions.

She stamped her foot with impatience. "Well, then? Get out. I need to bathe. And you need to be sure to see Hanna before she starts on the triplets' hair. You know Rosalie will change her mind at least three times."

I'd barely gotten my robe on before Camille pushed me out. Down the hall was a set of large silver mirrors. When we were smaller, Camille and I would stand in the middle, looking into the reflection of our reflections until we were dizzy with giggles.

Using the double reflection now, I lowered the back of my robe. Camille was wrong. The red marks weren't a set of lines. They were bruises, perfectly round. As if someone had pressed their fingertips in, tapping for attention.

I pulled my robe up, hurried to my bedroom, and slammed the door.

10

BENEATH THE WIDE SWISH OF TULLE SKIRTS, I FLEXED my feet, glad the fairy shoes had flat, padded soles. We'd been standing in the receiving line for what felt like hours. If I'd been in heels, I'd be limping to dinner. Camille needled me in the ribs with her sharp elbow.

"Pay attention," she mouthed.

"This is my wife, Morella, and my eldest daughters, Camille and Annaleigh," Papa said, greeting another couple. He shook the gentleman's hand and kissed the tips of the woman's fingers. "And the birthday girls, Rosalie, Ligeia, and Lenore."

We pasted on another round of smiles, murmuring a hello and thanking them for coming.

Rosalie flashed open her fan with an impatient flutter, sneaking a look at the receiving line behind Papa. "We'll never get to the dancing," she hissed.

I glanced around the ballroom, hoping some of the visitors had ventured into other parts of the manor. Hadn't we greeted more people than this? The hall, which could easily hold three hundred people, felt half full. A string orchestra played underneath the murmurs of the crowd, making the room seem livelier than it really was.

Perhaps the fog had detained some of the guests on the mainland?

At least the ballroom did not disappoint. Velvet drapes, navy with silvery tracings, were artfully swagged throughout the room, creating private nooks perfect for romantic assignations. Lush purple flowers dripped from fluted columns. The chandelier gleamed and sparkled, its crystal drops twisting and hanging down to form the arms of the Thaumas octopus. The center of the chandelier made up the body, refracting the light of a thousand burning candles. The massive beast covered half the ceiling.

But the most spectacular sight was the stained-glass wall. It had been covered for years in black curtains, as if its mere presence stirred more joy than was proper in a house of mourning. Squares of blue and green glass gave way to teal and aqua higher up, with a frosting of white at the top, transforming one wall of the ballroom into a veritable tsunami. The light from dozens of tall braziers on the patio illuminated the wall like a brilliant jewel, casting cerulean and beryl highlights across the guests.

I caught sight of the Graces running through the crowds, chasing Aunt Lysbette's tiny toy poodle and giggling with mad glee.

Camille leaned in, whispering under her breath, "Those were the last guests, thank Pontus. I'm starving."

"Do you remember any of these people's names?" I asked as we headed in.

"Besides the relatives? Just that one." She nodded discreetly to Robin Briord. He was standing in a group of young men looking up at the chandelier. Camille's cheeks flushed with a look of hunger that had nothing to do with our impending dinner. "When should I go talk with him?"

Someone tapped on our shoulders. "No big, fancy greetings for me, then?"

Turning, I couldn't help my squeal of delight. "Fisher! Is that really you?"

The years of working on Hesperus had changed him. He'd grown taller and filled out, becoming a man, with laugh lines framing warm and familiar brown eyes. When he folded me into a brotherly embrace, I felt the power behind all his new muscles.

"I didn't know you were coming!" said Camille. "Annaleigh, did you?"

"Hanna mentioned it this morning, but I forgot to tell you."

She raised one playful eyebrow at me. As girls, we'd both been madly in love with Fisher, trailing after him with all the eagerness of the desperately unrequited. It was the only thing we'd ever truly squabbled over.

"Seems an awfully big thing to forget. I'm sure it was unintentional." Her tone was teasing, but an edge darkened her words. "How long are you here for?" she asked, turning her attention to Fisher. "It's been so long since we've seen you. Hanna must be thrilled you're home."

He nodded. "Your father asked me to stay on till Churning. He wanted to make sure I was at the big First Night dinner."

First Night, only weeks away, was the start of the Churning Festival, celebrating the change of the seasons as Pontus stirred the oceans with his trident. The cold water from below mixed with the cold air above. With fish diving deeper to spend the winter in a state of semihibernation, the villagers used this time to repair their boats, mend their nets, and spend time with their families. The festival lasted for ten days and grew progressively wilder as it wore on. Families of Papa's finest captains were invited to welcome in the turning of the sea with a feast at Highmoor. Even in the midst of our deepest mourning, it was the one celebration we always observed.

Camille beamed. "Wonderful. I can't wait to hear about all your adventures at Old Maude. But first I'm on a mission of my own." She strode away, cutting a roundabout sweep toward Briord, her eyes focused on his every movement.

Fisher took my hand, spinning me around. "You look awfully pretty tonight, little Minnow. So very grown up. Save me a spot on your dance card? Or is it already too full? Mother always said I took too long to get in motion."

I opened my pretty paper fan, holding it out to him. It doubled as a dance card, though the spokes were surprisingly empty. Uncle Wilhelm, after much prodding from Aunt Lysbette, had asked to have my first two-step, and a distant cousin had requested to lead me in a fox-trot. I assumed once dinner was over, it would fill up. I was a sister of the guests of honor, after all.

"Lucky me," Fisher said, looking over the blank spaces. "May I be so bold as to request a waltz?" He scrawled in his name with a flourish.

"Take them all," I said, only half joking. My sisters and I were all schooled in the art of dancing—Berta had us waltz about the drawing room, with Camille always making me lead—but I had no aptitude for witty banter or delicate flirtations. The prospect of an evening of forced small talk made me break into a sheen of sweat.

He studied the card before selecting a polka. "I'm afraid that's all I can offer, Minnow. I've already promised dances to Honor and the triplets."

"Well, it is their birthday," I allowed with a smile. "No one has called me that in years."

"I'd warrant you're far too grand a lady these days to strip to your skivvies and go swimming in tide pools." After a beat, his eyes sobered. "I was truly sorry to hear about Eulalie. . . . I wanted to come to the funeral, but there was that storm. Silas didn't want to be caught alone."

I nodded. It would be nice to have someone to remember Eulalie with, but not tonight.

"Where have they put you at dinner?" I asked, diverting the conversation back to something cheerful and meaningless.

"I haven't had a chance to scour the place cards yet."

Setting my hand on his elbow, I guided us deeper into the hall. "Shall we take a look?"

Mercy flopped into the chair next to mine, breathing deeply. Her curls, pinned at the sides with silver roses, wilted. Though she tried to hide it, I caught her yawning behind her hand.

"Why don't you go to bed?" I asked. "It's nearly midnight. I'm surprised you three haven't been sent upstairs already."

"Papa said we don't have to be little girls tonight. Besides, I can't miss this party! Camille or you could die, and we'll never have another one."

"Mercy!"

She scowled. "What? It might be true."

I sighed at her insensitivity. "Who were you dancing with?"

"Lord Asterby's son, Hansel. He's *twelve*," she said, giving the number grave importance.

"You looked like you were having fun."

Her eyebrows pinched. "He only talked about his horses, telling me all of their sires, five generations back. He said he didn't want to dance at all but his parents made him."

"Hansel Asterby sounds like he needs to learn some manners. I'm sorry you didn't get on with him."

"Are all boys so very dull?"

I shrugged. Though not a total shock, Cassius hadn't been among the guests. Consequently, every other man seemed a shade less by comparison.

"You haven't been dancing much," she observed. "And Camille looks peeved."

I followed her gaze to where Camille stood near the crowd surrounding Lord Briord. Her face was pinched, her laughs too loud. "He hasn't made an introduction yet."

Mercy pushed her chin into her hand—had the orchestra been playing a softer tune, she would have been asleep in an instant. "We should ask him why he's stalling. I don't think he's talked to any of us but Papa. It's so rude. Even if he doesn't fancy Camille, it's the triplets' birthday. He should at least wish them many happy returns."

I'd noticed as much. I was also keenly aware my dance card had never filled up. Without Fisher's kindness, I would have looked like a sour old maid.

"Someone should make him." Mercy glared over the rim of her cup.

Lenore joined us, her full skirts piling up over the arms of the chair like a plum-colored waterfall. She downed a glass of champagne in one swallow. "Octavia's wake was livelier than this."

"You've not been dancing either?" I guessed.

"Just with Fisher. It's my birthday. Can't I insist someone ask me?"

Mercy shot me a knowing look.

"I don't understand it," said Lenore. "We all look lovely."

"We do," I agreed.

"We're all well mannered and have many fine and admirable qualities," she continued, taking on the affected accent of an Arcannian mainlander.

"Mmm."

"We're rich," she spat out, and I began to suspect that was not her first or second glass of champagne.

"That we are."

"Then why are we sitting in the corner with no dance partners?" She slammed the glass on the table. It fell over but did not break.

"I intend to ask Lord Briord exactly that!" Mercy was across the dance floor, weaving in and out of couples with righteous indignation, before we could stop her.

"We should go after her." Lenore made no effort to get up. "She's going to embarrass herself."

"She's going to embarrass Camille," I predicted.

"Won't that be fun?"

Lenore flagged down a server carrying a tray of icy champagne coupes. She grabbed two, giving the second to me. I waved it off.

"I'd almost summon a Trickster here and now, just to have someone to dance with!" she groaned, downing her drink.

"You shouldn't say things like that," I warned her. "There are enough whispers about our family as it is. Besides, if Papa catches you, he'll have your head." As if on cue, he and Morella waltzed by, beaming radiant smiles at each other. It was hard to believe they'd sat at Eulalie's funeral only weeks before.

Setting aside the empty glass, Lenore picked up the one meant for me. "What?" she asked, seeing my pointed stare. "It's my birthday. If I'm not dancing, I might as well be lousy with champagne. Look," she said, pointing. "Even Camille agrees with me."

I glanced across the dance floor in time to see Camille throw back a coupe of liquid courage. She took a deep breath and pinched her cheeks, drawing bright spots of color to her face. Her lips moved, clearly practicing her speech for Lord Briord.

As she made her way to him, I'd never seen her look lovelier.

Reaching the outer edge of his circle, she paused, tilting her head toward their conversation. A moment passed, then another, and the rosy hue drained from her cheeks. She held one hand up to her mouth, and I feared she might be sick.

She pushed a path away from the group, staggering back and bumping into a waltzing couple.

"What's the matter with her?" Lenore asked.

"I'm sorry, I'm so sorry," Camille apologized to the dancers before finding her way to us. She pulled me to my feet and dragged me off like a swimmer caught in a passing ship's wake. "We have to get out of here!"

"What just happened?"

"Now, Annaleigh, *please*!"

Camille didn't stop until we were deep in the garden. Thousands of tiny candles dotted ledges hidden throughout the topiaries. It would have seemed magical had the fog ever lifted. Now the little lights played strangely with the mist, creating shadowy phantoms, there one moment and gone the next.

"Camille, calm down." I sat on the edge of the fountain.

She threw a fist toward the house. "This was nothing more than a stupid farce!"

"I don't understand what's going on. Tell me what happened!"

I hugged my arms around my chest, gooseflesh rippling over all that bare skin. It was far too cold to be out, but the chill only seemed to sharpen Camille's senses. At least she'd stopped pacing.

She studied Highmoor in silence. The ballroom, shining so brightly inside, could barely be seen. The orchestra's music echoed eerily in the fog.

"How many men danced with you tonight?"

I sighed. "Would everyone stop harping on that?"

"How many?" She whirled around, seizing my shoulders. There was a strange sheen to her eyes. In the foggy candlelight, Camille looked half crazed. I wrenched free of her grasp, rubbing where her fingers had sunk in.

"Three."

"Three. The whole night?"

"Well, yes, but—"

She nodded as if she'd already known this. "Relatives, right? And not even many of those."

"I suppose not." My teeth began to chatter. "I saw you try to talk to Briord. Just tell me what he said. We'll catch our death out here."

She snorted. "The curse strikes again."

I stood up. "There's no curse. I'm going back."

"Wait!" She grabbed me, her nails biting into the soft flesh of my arm. "I waited all night for him to introduce himself, but he never did. So . . . I decided I would go over and ask him to dance myself."

"Oh, Camille."

She frowned. "I overheard him talking with one of his younger brothers. The brother was egging him on, daring him to ask Ligeia for a dance. He said no. The brother asked why, since she was so lovely."

"What did he say?"

She exhaled with a shaky breath. "He said that, yes, Ligeia was lovely. As lovely as a bouquet of belladonna."

I wasn't familiar with the word and tried breaking it down into things I did know. "Beautiful ladies?"

"Nightshade. Poison. He thinks we're cursed, that we'll curse anyone who gets too close to us. That's why none of us have been dancing!"

"That's not—"

"Oh, Annaleigh, of course it is! Think about it. Whether there is or isn't a curse, people believe in it. We've been tried and found guilty in the public's opinion. Nothing will change their minds, no matter how many pretty parties Papa throws. We're cursed, and no one will ever believe otherwise."

I sank back down, recalling the whispers in the Selkirk marketplace. The speculations that quickly turned to jeers.

"It's so unfair."

She nodded. "And let me tell you, the Briord family tree is far from perfect. When I was studying up on him, I saw several first cousins who were awfully fond of each other. . . . No wonder he has such big ears."

I smiled, knowing full well that an hour before, Camille had pinned such hopes on those admittedly large ears. "This doesn't mean it's over for us. There are other men. Other dukes, in other provinces. Provinces that have never heard of the Thaumas Dozen. Arcannia is vast."

Camille made a noise of disgust, then joined me on the fountain. With her side pressed against mine, we could have almost been at the piano. I missed those days.

"Even if we could find these other dukes from far away, the second they came here, they'd find out. Everyone would tell them, eager to be the one credited with saving His Grace from a doomed match."

"Then maybe we go to them."

"Papa would never sanction such an idea." She wrapped her hand around mine, squeezing my frozen fingers till a little bit of life sparked in them. "At least we'll always have each other. Sisters and friends till the end. Promise me."

"I promise."

A figure approached us, silhouetted larger than possible against the wall of mist, a cape swirling about his frame. Heels clicked across the garden tiles, heading our way. For a moment, I thought Papa might have come looking for us, but the shadowy shape morphed. It was a woman in full skirts. A curtain of fog swirled around us, growing too thick to see, but I heard her laughter, carefree and breezy.

It was Eulalie. I would stake my life on it.

My mouth went dry as I imagined her ghost, fated to walk an endless loop to the very cliffs where she'd met her end. When the bank of fog dispersed, Camille and I were alone in the garden.

My knuckles were white as I gripped her. She'd have to take Verity's drawings seriously now. "You saw that, didn't you?"

"Saw what?"

"The shadow. The laughter . . . it sounded just like Eulalie, didn't it?"

Camille raised a questioning eyebrow at me. "You've had too much champagne." She turned with a swish of skirts, heading back inside and leaving me in the fog.

Heels clicked behind me again, though the garden was empty, and I scurried after her.

11

MY EYES FLUTTERED OPEN, BLINKING BACK SLEEPY grit from the corners. It felt far too early to be awake. The party had ended after three, perfectly timed with the tides to send the guests back to Astrea. Tinted-glass buoys filled with luminescent algae lit the docks, giving the partygoers an enchanting sight as they hurried away from Highmoor as fast as their court heels would carry them.

After the conversation with Camille in the garden, it had been difficult to ignore her words. I watched as sister after sister approached a conversation only to be met with half smiles and glazed eyes. Papa and Morella seemed oblivious to it.

I rolled over with a groan, wanting to hide under the warmth of the covers. Then a glint of light on my vanity caught my attention.

Eulalie's pocket watch.

I'd meant to show it to Papa days ago, but it slipped my mind after seeing Verity's sketchbook. Even now, a shiver of unease rustled down my spine as I remembered the lurid drawings.

Removing the lock of hair from the watch, I twirled it

between my fingers, studying the golden strands. The bit of wire had baffled me at first—I'd always seen hair tied with ribbons or lace—but as I looked at the inner workings of the pocket watch, it suddenly made sense.

Edgar was an apprentice clockmaker.

He worked with coils of wire and springs.

Had he clipped off a bit of hair as a love offering to Eulalie?

I frowned. Eulalie's killer was undoubtedly a rebuffed suitor, someone upset his affections weren't returned. If Eulalie had kept this watch and lock of hair secreted away, it stood to reason she shared his feelings. Why else would she have kept them?

But such a strong, fidgeting anxiety had radiated off him in the marketplace. Edgar couldn't get away from us fast enough.

Edgar knew something. He must.

I tinkered with the pocket watch, mulling over what to do next. I obviously needed to speak to him, but what would I say? This was too big to handle on my own. I snapped the watch shut with a resolute click and went downstairs to find my father.

I burst into the dining room, but it was clear I'd come in at the wrong moment.

Camille, her fingers deathly white around the fork, was smashing her kippers into little bits until they resembled a massacre more than a breakfast. Rosalie was sullenly nursing a cup of tea, and Ligeia, riddled with anxiety, kept gnawing at her silver-polished nails. Lenore was still in bed, presumably sleeping off a well-earned champagne headache.

Papa sat at the head of the table, his jaw clenched and a tense weariness surrounding his eyes. "It was everyone's first social gathering. Perhaps having so many of you out at once made people uneasy."

Camille frowned, her lips thin and pale. "I agree with you, Papa. The cursed Thaumas sisters did make people uneasy." Her fork screeched across the china plate before she shoved it aside.

She must have filled him in on everything she'd heard last night.

He sighed, waving away her accusation with a flip of his hand. "No one believes in curses but those ridiculous peasants in the village."

She struck the table in a fit of rage. "Robin Briord is hardly a fishmonger, and I heard it directly from his mouth! We'll never find a match, none of us! We've all been tainted by our sisters' deaths."

Rosalie had tears in her eyes. "He really said that?"

Camille nodded. "I suppose we ought to consider our good fortune. We'll always have Highmoor. Once Papa di— When I am the Duchess, you'll always have a home here." She snorted, her eyes dark and moody. "The House of Cursed Spinsters."

There was a small noise beside me. Morella had crept in, still in her dressing gown. I didn't know how much she'd overheard, but it was enough for the blood to run from her stricken face. I offered a small smile, but she pulled away, clutching her belly.

"Is my son to be cursed as well?" she asked with a glint of despair, her reedy words drifting above the breakfast table.

Papa jumped from his chair. "My love, you're supposed to be sleeping in. After such an exciting night, you need your rest."

"Papa, I have something I need to speak with you about," I said, finding my voice as he approached us.

"Not now, Annaleigh."

"But it's important. It's about—"

"I said not now! I've had all I can stand of everyone's important news this morning." He threw a warning glance at Camille before escorting Morella from the room.

My breath fell out in a rush as they left. I jammed the watch into my pocket. Purple floral arrangements still dotted the table, and the smell of wilting lilies curdled my stomach. I poured a cup of coffee, leaving it black, and sat down with a sigh.

"So dramatic," Camille muttered.

I ran my finger over the cup's handle. "No one likes the situation we're in, but we don't have to torment her with it."

Camille turned on me. "Since when did you become her champion? You hated her too."

Rosalie and Ligeia eyed the door, judging whether they might leave the room unscathed.

"I never hated her. She's carrying our new brother or sister and having an increasingly difficult time with it. Shouldn't we allow her a little kindness?"

"How much kindness would she show us if her little sun god was inheriting Highmoor? Do you honestly think she'd allow eight spinsters room and board? We'd all be out faster than Zephyr's arrows."

Verity came in, hopping down the last step. "Who's faster than Zephyr? No one can outrace the wind god!"

I shot Camille a warning look. The Graces didn't need to know of any discord between us and Morella.

"You're sure to be, wearing those shoes," I exclaimed, spotting her fairy slippers peeking out from her robe. She'd worn them ever since they'd arrived. I wouldn't have been surprised if she'd slept in them.

Verity smiled, twirling to best show them off, then spun to the buffet, standing on tiptoes to peer up at the pastries. Camille helped her make a plate. She put a generous serving of kippers on first before adding the berry tart Verity pointed to.

"I feel like going back to bed," Rosalie admitted, sprawling her arms out on the table and lowering her head. "Spending all night not dancing was exhausting."

"No fair! I still have lessons!" Verity exclaimed. She climbed into her seat and waited for Camille to bring the plate over.

"Fish first."

Verity glowered up at her. "Yours are still on your plate."

"I'm the oldest," Camille shot back.

Verity stuck her tongue out but eventually dug in. "What are you doing this morning, Annaleigh?"

The watch burned in my pocket, but I couldn't bring it up now. Not with a fight festering just below the surface. "I ought to walk the beach for more kelp. Morella is nearly out of lotion."

"The beach?"

We all turned to see Fisher standing in an archway. "Fancy company? I could row you out to the little islet with all the tide pools. You should be able to find whatever you need."

I sensed Camille's eyes on me but nodded, smiling up at Fisher. "After breakfast?"

He grinned.

Striding in, Papa said, "We need to talk." Scanning the room, he caught sight of Verity. "Darling, why don't you take your breakfast upstairs today? It can be a special treat."

Her eyes lit up. "Are they in trouble? Camille didn't eat her kippers."

"She didn't? Perhaps I'll speak to her about that."

Pleased, Verity scooted out of the room, tart in hand. The fish were left behind.

"Fisher, would you excuse us? I need to speak with my daughters. Privately."

Fisher vanished down the hall.

Papa waited a beat before starting in on us. "Morella is very upset," he said. "Inconsolable."

Camille bristled, clearly not backing down. "Imagine how we feel. We're the ones in danger of dying off, long before that baby is born."

He sighed. "No one is dying off."

"Then she has nothing to worry about, does she?" She slumped back into the chair. "I suppose you want me to apologize for having a conversation that wasn't about her that she chose to eavesdrop on?"

Papa raked his fingers through his hair. "Just don't bring it up again. Not around her, not among yourselves. I'm placing a moratorium on the curse. Which doesn't exist," he added. "Now, I have to travel to the capital this afternoon. I'll be gone at least a week, maybe more. There's an ugly bit of business King Alderon has requested his Privy Council weigh in on." He sighed. "Morella is more tired than she lets on and could use a little looking after while I'm gone. Pampering, even. Understand me?"

Rosalie, Ligeia, and I nodded. After a pointedly long moment, Camille did as well.

"Good," he said, and strode out of the room without a backward glance.

I longed to run after Papa and show him the watch, but he was in too foul a mood to listen. He'd snap at me, and I'd lose any chance at being taken seriously. I stared down into the depths of my coffee, wondering what to do next.

Fisher poked his head in from the hall. "Annaleigh? All ready?"

I pushed the cup aside. "Coming!"

12

THE SKY WAS A VAST BLUE VOID AS WE SET OUT FOR the little islet on the far side of Salten. The sun hadn't been seen in over a week and now drenched down in radiant splendor, as if apologizing for its long absence.

While Fisher manned the small craft, I peered across the expanse of open water, counting sea turtles. The giant beasts were favorites of mine. In the springtime, females hoisted themselves onto our beaches, laying their eggs. I loved to see them hatch. With powerful pectoral flippers and giant, wise eyes, the little turtles were perfect miniatures of their parents. They'd burst free and work their way down the beach, already drawn to the sea, just like the People of the Salt.

"Look!" I pointed to a great leathery hump breaking the surface yards away. "That's twelve!"

Fisher used the moment to pause, lowering the oars. "Biggest one yet too. Look at the size of its shell!"

We watched it take a gulp of air, then dive below the waterline. The wind tousled Fisher's hair, highlighting the sun-bleached streaks, and I was struck again by how much he'd changed since leaving Highmoor. His eyes fell on mine as he smiled lopsidedly.

"It's so beautiful, isn't it?" He raised his chin, gesturing to the island behind me.

I glanced back at Highmoor. Its four stories rose steeply from the top of the rocky cliffs. The stone facade was a soft gray, covered in ivy. A pretty pattern of blue and green shingles dotted the gabled roof, sparkling like the prize jewel in a mermaid's crown.

My eyes drifted to the cliff walk. "It looks like nothing bad could ever happen there, doesn't it?"

His eyebrows furrowed as he nodded. "I think I walked into something I shouldn't have earlier."

"That makes two of us."

His silence felt like a gentle prod for more information.

"I had something I wanted to discuss with Papa, but he and Camille were locked in a battle over that nonsense about the curse, and I never got to tell him. And now he's left for the capital, and who knows when he'll return."

"Is it really so urgent?"

"It felt like it this morning."

"And now?"

I shrugged. "I suppose it will have to wait, whether it is or not."

Fisher slid his fingers over the oars but made no motion to continue rowing. "You can talk to me about it, whatever it is. Maybe I could help?"

I ran my hand over the pocket watch but did not withdraw it. "I . . . I think Eulalie might have been murdered."

His eyes narrowed, the amber darkening. "Mother said she fell from the cliffs."

Tucking flyaway strands of hair behind my ear, I nodded. "She did."

"You don't think it was an accident," he guessed.

I dared to look up, meeting his stare. "It wasn't."

A heavy wave slapped against the side of the boat, startling us both.

"Why haven't you said anything to Ortun? You always used to go running to him with any problem."

"I wanted to but . . . it's different now. He's different. He's pulled in so many directions," I said, speaking to myself more than Fisher. "He's not a widower with a manor full of daughters anymore. He's a husband again. I just wish . . ."

"Go on," he nudged when it became clear I wasn't going to finish.

My mouth raised into a smile the rest of me did not feel. "I just wish I could let him handle it. It feels too big for me alone."

He smiled. "It's too bad we can't ask Eulalie what happened to her, you know? She was never one for a short story, was she?"

"Never," I agreed.

Our eyes met, and a spark of shared intimacy warmed me. It was nice talking about Eulalie again with someone who truly knew her. With all the preparations for the ball, it felt as though she'd been somehow forgotten.

"Do you remember the time she . . ." I trailed off, my throat unexpectedly thick with tears.

"Oh, Annaleigh," Fisher said, wrapping his arms around me without hesitation.

I pressed my face into his chest, letting him hold me and my heartache. He ran his fingers across the back of my neck in soothing circles, and something decidedly not grief unspooled within me. Against my ear, his heart picked up in tempo, matching mine. I lingered there, counting the beats, wondering what would happen if I allowed him to make the next move. But Hanna's sharp *tsk* of disapproval popped into my head, and I pulled away.

He studied me for a long, silent moment before picking up the oars. He worked them against the waves, turning us toward the islet once more.

I bit into the corner of my lip, longing to diffuse the air between us. It was suddenly too heavy, too weighted with unclaimed meaning.

"Fisher? Do you believe in ghosts?"

The words were out before I could even think them over, and though I feared he'd believe me mad, his eyes crinkled, amused.

"Ghosts like . . ." He waggled his fingers at me, trying to look creepy.

"No, real ghosts. Spirits."

"Ah, those."

The waves around us darkened as we passed the drop-off. Gulls roosted in the islet's nooks and crannies. They drifted above us, scanning for food for their young.

"I did when I was a little boy. I thought it great fun to make up stories and scare the younger children in the kitchens. Once I told a tale so horrid to Cook's daughter, she had nightmares for a week and finally tattled on me. Mother was less than pleased."

"And now?"

"I don't know. I think you get to a certain point in life when ghosts are no longer fun. When the people you love die . . . like my father, your mother and sisters . . . the thought that they could be trapped here . . . it's unbearable, isn't it? I can't imagine a worse fate. Unseen, unheard. Surrounded by people who remember you a little less each day. I would go out of my mind, wouldn't you?"

He stopped rowing. "I've been away for a while, but I still recognize that look on your face. Something's bothering you. Not just the thing with Eulalie. Something else." He reached out, squeezing my knee. "You know you can tell me anything."

"Verity has been seeing ghosts." It fell out in a rush, like a river racing off the edge of a cliff. "Ava and Elizabeth, Octavia and even Eulalie now."

Fisher sucked in a deep breath. "Truly?"

I waved my hand, wanting to push the conversation aside. "It sounds absurd, I know."

"No, no, it doesn't. I just . . . What do they look like?"

I told him about the sketchbook, about the plague pustules and snapped necks, the splayed limbs and bloody wrists.

"Oh, Verity." He sighed. "How awful."

I frowned. "And the thing is . . . now that she's told me about them, I'm certain I'm going to walk into the bathroom and see Elizabeth floating facedown in a bloody tub, or see Octavia's broken body in the study. I can't get the pictures out of my mind. I'm seeing my sisters everywhere."

His thumb traced a warm circle across my knee. "It sounds terrible. But, I mean . . ." He paused. "It's not as though you really are."

"You don't believe me." I folded my arms over my chest, suddenly cold despite the brilliant sunlight.

"I believe they unsettled you—and that's perfectly natural; you don't need to be embarrassed about it. But you don't really believe Verity is seeing ghosts—do you?"

"I don't know what to think. If they're not real, why would she draw such awful things?"

He shrugged. "Maybe they're not so awful to her. Think about it. She's been in mourning since the day she was born. When has she ever not been surrounded by grief?" Fisher pushed his tousled hair from his eyes. "That has to affect a person, don't you think?"

"I suppose."

He squeezed my leg once more. "I wouldn't worry too much about it. It's probably just a phase. We all went through odd ones."

"I remember yours," I said, an unexpected smile spreading across my lips.

He groaned, pulling back against the waves. "Don't remind me, don't remind me."

"I'll never forget the way you screamed." He grinned, but for a moment, I had the strangest feeling he didn't know what I was talking about. "The sea snake," I prompted, raising my eyebrows.

Fisher's eyes lit up. "Oh, that. There's nothing wrong with screaming when you spot a snake that large. That's just self-preservation."

"But it was only a bit of rope!" I exclaimed, laughing at the memory. We'd been combing for seashells on the beach when a length of netting washed up. Fisher had grabbed my hand and hightailed it, hollering his head off about poisonous snakes and our impending doom. We girls left out strands of rope for Fisher to find for the rest of that summer.

"Rope, snake, it's all the same," he said, laughing along with me.

The boat struck the black sands of the islet, thudding us from the topic. I hopped from the dinghy and helped Fisher drag it ashore. Farther up the beach, near the rocky outcrops, were a series of tide pools. At high tide, the tiny island was completely underwater, but as the water pulled away, it left behind all sorts of treasures trapped in the basalt. You could always find starfish and rainbow-hued anemones, sometimes even seahorses, stuck until the tide returned. Long clumps of kelp often became entangled in the jagged edges. Tide pools were the perfect place to find more supplies.

"Did you enjoy the ball last night?" I asked as we searched.

"It was certainly the most glamorous evening I've ever had. And you?"

"I'm very grateful you were there. None of us would have danced otherwise."

Realization dawned across his face. "You said your father and Camille were fighting about the curse. People really believe that?"

"Apparently."

"Your family has had a terrible run of luck, but it doesn't mean . . ." He swatted his hand at a fiddler crab, fighting him for a bit of kelp. "I'm sorry."

"It doesn't matter quite so much for me. But Camille is the heir now. She's expected to marry well, and she's worried she'll never find a husband if she's sitting on the outskirts of every ball she attends."

He cocked his head, musing. "If only there was a way to get everyone off the island . . . get you far enough from Salann that no one has heard of the Thaumas curse."

"That's what I said last night! But she thinks it's impossible."

Fisher's eyes drifted off the island, searching the shores of Salten as if trying to recall a buried memory. "I wonder . . ." He shrugged, laughing to himself. "It's probably just more whispers. Forget I said anything."

"What is it?" I asked, joining him to dump my catch.

"Growing up in the kitchens, you hear lots of stories. And that's probably all they are."

"Fisher," I prompted.

He sighed. "It sounds a little crazy, okay? But I remember hearing something about a passageway, a secret door. For the gods."

"The gods?" What would gods be doing at Highmoor?

"A long, long time ago, they were much more active in the affairs of mortals. They liked being consulted on everything from art to politics. Some of them still do. You know Arina is always showing up at the opera and theatres in the capital. Says she's an important muse."

I nodded.

He rubbed the back of his neck. "Well, it's not as if they can take a carriage from the Sanctum, you know? They need a way to get to our world. So there are these doors. I remember one of the footmen saying there's one somewhere on Salten—for Pontus to use when he's traveling. You say some sort of magic words and they take you to places, far-off places like that." He snapped his fingers. "But it's just a story."

Such a door must be marked as special, and I'd certainly never seen anything like that on Salten. It was probably nonsense. But . . .

"Did he ever say where Pontus's door is?" I asked, cringing at the hope I heard in my voice.

Fisher shook his head. "Forget about it, Annaleigh." He picked up the basket and shook its contents. "This enough, you think?"

"It's plenty, thank you. Morella will appreciate it, I'm sure."

We forced the boat down the beach, letting it meet the water. The sun beamed down, warming everything with a golden glow. My eyes fell on Fisher. Studying the way his forearms flexed as he rowed across the bay, I dared to remember how they'd felt wrapped around me.

A splash sounded ahead of us, breaking my daydream. A green flipper caught my eye.

A sea turtle!

Fisher winced, scanning the waters ahead. "Annaleigh, don't look."

A red tentacle thrashed out of the water, flailing aggressively. My smile faded. Red like that meant squid, and it looked enormous.

As the boat sailed past, I wanted to cry. The sea turtle was fighting for his life. The squid's arms wrapped around him, grasping and writhing and trying to pull the shell apart. Squid, even one as sizeable as this, did not eat turtles.

It only went after him for spite.

13

MY FINGERS TRAILED OVER THE PIANO KEYS, WORKING out a series of notes. It was a complex piece, full of rapidly descending glides and swooping rhythms, requiring absolute concentration. Unfortunately, my mind was not wholly on the piece, and the sound made even me wince.

Papa had been gone for over a week. He didn't immediately send word of his arrival, and an uneasy panic descended over Morella, certain the curse had struck. When we finally received a letter, she snatched it from the silver tray and raced upstairs to read his words in private.

She'd begun to show, a small swell in her stomach that quickly expanded into a round curve. The baby was growing too fast. We summoned a midwife from Astrea, and when she emerged from Morella's bedroom, her face was grave with concern.

"Twins," she said. "Active ones too."

The midwife gave me a salve to rub into Morella's belly twice a day and said she needed to rest as much as possible, keeping her feet elevated and her emotions in check.

After another run of wrong notes, I clunked to a finish and swatted at the sheet music, studying what I should have done.

A maid poked her head into the Blue Room.

"Miss Annaleigh?" she asked, and gave a small curtsy. "There's a Mr. Edgar Morris here."

My breath hitched. Edgar at Highmoor? "For me?"

"And Miss Camille."

"I've not seen her since breakfast, but I believe she's in her room." Since the ball, she had ensconced herself behind closed doors, snapping at anyone who dared disturb her.

I pressed trembling fingers into my skirt. After the boat ride with Fisher, I'd written a dozen letters to Papa, trying to explain my suspicions and begging him to come home soon to help. They'd all ended up in the fire, reading like the musings of a madwoman. A letter wasn't the way to go. How could mere words convey the dark feeling growing in my stomach?

"Miss Thaumas, hello," Edgar said, entering the room. Once again, he was dressed in full black, still observing deepest mourning.

I turned on the bench, watching him take in the room postmourning. The sconces made the mirrors sparkle, and even with the overcast morning, the room looked a great deal more cheerful than when he'd last seen it.

"Mr. Morris."

Though it was the height of disrespect, I remained at the piano bench, too surprised to move. It was as though I was truly seeing him for the very first time, spotting details I'd never noticed before. A small scar slashed just above his upper lip, the same lips Eulalie must have kissed. And those were the hands Eulalie had undoubtedly grasped as he secretly proposed to her. Had she run her fingers through that pale blond hair? Taken off the tortoiseshell glasses to gaze into his squinting hazel eyes?

What secrets of hers did this man keep?

"Mr. Morris, what an unexpected surprise." We heard Camille's voice before she entered. Edgar still stood near the threshold, unsure of what he ought to be doing. "Annaleigh, have you sent for tea?"

I shook my head.

"That's quite all right, Miss Thaumas, I don't intend to stay long," he stammered, holding his hand out as if to stop her.

"Martha?" Camille called out, overriding him. "Tell Cook we'll need tea and perhaps a plate of those lemon cookies she made yesterday."

"Yes, ma'am."

"Have a seat, please, Mr. Morris. Annaleigh?"

"What?" I asked, stubbornly remaining on the bench.

"You'll join us, yes?"

After a long pause, I stood. "Of course."

Martha wheeled in a tea service. As eldest, Camille set to work readying everyone's cups. Once we were served, she straightened, eyeing our guest. "What can we help you with today, Mr. Morris?"

He took a sip of the tea, fortifying himself for the conversation to come. "I wanted to apologize for my behavior in the marketplace. I fear I wasn't wholly myself that day. It was such a surprise seeing you both out in public and looking so . . ." His jaw clenched. "Well . . . your faces reminded me of Eulalie. It caught me quite off guard. I also . . . I hoped to speak with you. About . . . that night."

If Camille was surprised, she was far more skilled at hiding it than I.

"What about it?" she asked, stirring her tea so smoothly the spoon never once clinked.

He squirmed uncomfortably. "I suppose I can admit this now, but I was here . . . the night it happened."

"I know," I murmured, my voice so quiet I wasn't wholly certain I'd spoken.

Edgar's eyebrows rose in surprise. "Eulalie told you about me?"

I shook my head. "The inscription, in the locket . . ."

He dabbed at his forehead with his handkerchief. Even it was black. "I was surprised to see it on her at the funeral. She never wore it in life. It was our secret."

"She must have had it on when she fell, but I don't think anyone ever noticed it. . . . The fishermen who found her read the engraving. If they hadn't, I would never have known Eulalie was engaged."

"Engaged!" Camille snorted. "Don't be absurd. Eulalie wasn't engaged."

Edgar shifted to the edge of his seat, focusing his attention on me with an unnerving intensity. "How did you know it was me? We were so careful."

"I found the pocket watch she'd hidden, with the lock of hair. It wasn't until you took your hat off in the marketplace that I realized you were a perfect match."

"You found the watch?"

"What watch? Annaleigh, what is going on?"

For the first time during his visit, Edgar truly smiled. "I thought for certain it was lost to the Salt. I gave it to her in lieu of a ring."

Camille's mouth fell open. "A ring?"

I rubbed my forehead. "The night that Eulalie . . . she was leaving Highmoor to elope with Edgar."

She burst out laughing. "Is this some sort of prank?"

Edgar shook his head.

"I don't believe you. Eulalie was heir to Highmoor. She wouldn't leave that. She had a responsibility here."

"She didn't want it. She never wanted it."

He wasn't lying. Papa had to all but drag her to visit the shipyards in Vasa and coerce her into studying ledgers and accounts. How many times had I sat at the piano and watched her fall asleep during one of Papa's lectures on family history?

"Even if that's true, she would never have married a lowly watchmaker's apprentice. She wanted better things out of life."

"Camille!"

She silenced me with a look as lethal as a dagger.

Edgar ignored her insult. "We were in love."

Camille let out a laugh. "Then she wouldn't have run away with you. She would have married you in a proper ceremony."

"She was scared."

"Of what?" she snapped.

He shrugged. "That's what I hoped you might know. We were supposed to meet at the cliff walk at midnight. I waited for hours, but she never came. I decided to leave and planned to return in the morning. As I pushed my boat from under the cliffs . . ." He winced, swallowing back a sob. "I'll never forget that sound as long as I live. . . . Like the slap of meat landing on the butcher's block." He wiped his forehead again, tears streaming down his face. "I can't stop hearing it. It's ringing in my ears even now. I fear it will drive me mad."

"You saw her fall?" I asked, aghast. My eyes were wide, and the horror raced down my spine.

He nodded miserably. "I was paddling by the rocks when she struck them." He blew his nose with a great honk. "I thought at first she'd slipped. It was dark, a new moon. Perhaps she couldn't see the path. But when I looked up . . . there was a shadow peering over the cliffs. When it saw my boat, it jerked away, hiding in the brush."

"A shadow!" I exclaimed.

Camille took a long sip of tea, seemingly unaffected by his tale of woe. "What then?"

Edgar looked away, his voice growing small. "I left."

"You left our sister's body on the rocks." Her face was a terrifying mask of placidity.

"I didn't know what to do. Nothing could have saved her. She was dead on impact. She had to be."

Camille's calm broke, her eyes flashing with rage. "You didn't check?"

I put my hand out to steady her. "Camille, no one could have survived that fall. You know that." I turned to Edgar. "You think she was pushed? By this shadow figure?"

"I do."

"Was it a man? A woman? Did you see any features?"

"I couldn't say. I was so close to the cliffs, and the waves were pushing my boat about. It was difficult to see. But I can't forget the look in Eulalie's eyes the last day I saw her alive. She was so frightened. She said she'd discovered something she wasn't meant to and needed to escape. At the time, I thought it was simply dramatic fuel to start our getaway—she always had her nose in those tattered romance novels, you know—but now I wonder . . ." He removed his glasses and wiped them clean, once, twice, three times.

Camille's mouth disappeared in a thin line, and I hardly recognized the look in her eyes.

"How dare you enter our home and suggest that our sister, for whom we are still mourning, was murdered!"

"Mourning?" He bristled, casting his arm around the room with disdain. "Yes, I can see all evidence of that. Fresh-cut flowers and lemon cookies. Polished mirrors and balls. How the cheeriness of that dress must lift your spirits from otherwise abject despair!"

"Get out!" She stood so quickly, her cup dropped to the floor. The spilled tea soaked into the plush weave of the rug, leaving a spot as red as a bloodstain.

"Annaleigh?" He turned to me, imploring. "You know something, you must!"

I dared to meet his pained eyes, but Camille stepped in front of me, blocking my view.

"Roland!" she shouted.

Edgar's eyes widened. "Not him—no! Not him!"

Fisher burst into the room, obviously having heard the commotion. "Camille? Are you all right?"

"Oh, Fisher, thank Pontus!" she replied, racing over to him. "Please escort Mr. Morris from Highmoor. I'm afraid he's upset us both terribly."

Edgar grabbed my hands, his fingers slick and nervous. I went rigid at such an unexpected invasion.

Roland appeared, immediately springing to action. "Come with us, sir." He grabbed at Edgar's waist.

"Easy does it," Fisher said, attempting to pull Edgar away.

"Get your hands off of me!" Edgar snapped. "Annaleigh!"

I shook my head and pressed myself deeper into the chair to

keep from being struck by Edgar's flailing limbs. His cries turned to curses as he was manhandled from the room. After a moment of pandemonium in the hall, the front door slammed shut.

Fisher returned, his shirt pulled free, the sleeve torn. "What on earth happened in here? Who was that?"

"Eulalie's fiancé, if you believe him. Which I don't," Camille said, retrieving her fallen cup.

Fisher took the chair Edgar had leapt from and accepted Camille's offer of tea. "Should we alert the authorities? Did he harm either of you?"

"I doubt that's necessary," she replied. "He'll probably do something extremely foolish and go to them himself."

She glanced at me. "Are you all right, Annaleigh? You've gone all peaky."

I felt rooted to the armchair, unable to move. I'd never seen someone in such a fit of grief and rage. "I'll be fine, I just . . . Who do you think the shadow was?"

She snorted. "There was no shadow. Eulalie wasn't pushed off the cliffs." She sighed, toying with the teacup. "I can't believe the nerve of that man. Lying to our faces."

Fisher frowned, still putting threads together. "He lied? About a shadow?"

"About eloping with Eulalie. She would never have run away, especially not with him. She had so many other prospects, much better ones."

Fisher took a loud slurp of the tea while picking up two cookies from the tray. Camille's eyes tracked his movements. Without a word, she picked up a dessert plate and offered it to him.

His eyes crinkled into a smile. "I suppose my Hesperus manners aren't fit for dining in the presence of such refined ladies now, eh?"

"I said nothing."

He jostled her with a brotherly familiarity. "You didn't need to, Camille. You never need to."

My mind felt like an overturned container of honey. I wanted to join in their ribbing, but my thoughts were stuck on Edgar's theory. I couldn't drop it. "Did she ever mention seeing something she wasn't supposed to? Overhearing something?"

Camille frowned, the light going out of her eyes. "No. And you know she confided in us about everything. That watchmaker realized he lost the best match of his life and is trying to worm his way into ours."

"That's a horrible thing to say. It's clear he loved her."

She laughed, a sharp, dry bark. "No one will ever just love us. That ball made it abundantly clear. If someone shows an interest, it's for our money. For our position. For what they can get out of us."

"You can't believe that."

"And I can't believe you don't. Edgar was just greedy enough to look past the curse."

Fisher froze midbite, glancing between us, unsure of what to do. I waved him away, excusing him from the room. He shouldn't have to witness the brewing fight. With a grateful smile, he put down his plate and ducked out.

"What?" she demanded once it was just us. "You think I'm wrong?"

I crossed to the piano and collected my music. "I certainly hope you are."

Behind me, I heard her sniff. When I turned, her face had crumpled, and she was pushing back hot, angry tears.

"At least she had someone, I suppose. Even if he is such a sad little man, he's still a man."

After a beat, I set the music back down and joined her, the fight seeping from me.

"Oh, Camille. You're going to find someone. You will, I know it."

"How? It's completely hopeless. I'm going to die an old maid, unloved, untouched. I've never even been kissed." She dissolved into sobs.

I stroked her hair and listened to her complaints. In my heart, I knew she was right. Would there ever be a man brave enough to risk the whispers? I wished I could say the magic words to set everything right again, but I didn't know where to start.

I stilled.

Magic words.

Magic words for a magic door. The door Fisher mentioned. Even if it was a silly tale, it would take Camille's mind off her troubles. At least for an afternoon.

"Have you ever heard anything about Pontus's door?"

Nose red and face splotchy, she wiped the corners of her eyes. "What are you talking about?"

"Fisher said somewhere on Salten there's supposed to be a door for the gods. They use them to travel quickly about the kingdom. Far, far distances across the kingdom . . ." I trailed off meaningfully.

She frowned. "That sounds absurd."

"Well, of course it does. But wouldn't it be fun if it wasn't? We could go anywhere we wanted. Do anything we wanted and be back before supper."

Camille pushed aside a lock of hair. "Fisher thinks it's real?"

"He told me about it." I didn't need to mention he'd also written it off as nonsense.

"Where's it meant to be?"

I shrugged. "He didn't know."

Camille glanced at the grandfather clock, a soft smile growing across her face. She looked happier than I'd seen her in days. "The Graces will be getting out of lessons soon. I suppose we could see if they want to make it a scavenger hunt."

I beamed. "I'll find the triplets."

As I entered the hall, I heard Camille snort from the couch. "Nineteen years old and on a treasure hunt for a magic door." She glanced up at me. "At least the Graces will be excited."

14

"A MAGIC DOOR?" HONOR REPEATED, DUBIOUS OF MY claim. Her eyes shifted to Camille.

The eight of us were in the solarium, enjoying an impromptu tea party Fisher brought in. We'd found the triplets there, reclining on wicker chaises, reading poems and snorting with laughter. I caught the last two lines, and it appeared they'd found more of Eulalie's contraband volumes. Rosalie, spotting the Graces, slid the book in her skirts.

Mercy munched on a biscuit and mimicked her sister's skepticism. Her dark hair, pulled back with a bow, fell to the side like silk. "Like in fairy tales?"

"Yes, but for the gods to use," Camille said. "And it could be anywhere, so we'll have to look very hard."

"What does it look like?" Verity asked. Even she seemed doubtful.

I'd been certain the triplets would be the hardest to convince and that we'd have to rein in the Graces.

"It will be fun!" Fisher promised. "Or would you rather stay here with Berta? I'm sure she can dig up more lines for you to copy while we're out."

The three quickly changed their tune and downed their tea with gusto.

"Where should we start?" Rosalie asked, helping Lenore and Ligeia up. "Where would a god keep his door?"

"You said Pontus used it for meetings about important matters. Maybe Papa's office?" Mercy reasoned.

Lenore wrinkled her nose. "He always keeps it locked. We won't be able to get in."

"What about the cove on the far side of the island?" Ligeia suggested. "Maybe he comes directly out of the sea."

Honor rolled her eyes. "It's too cold to go into the water. Besides, when the door opens, all the ocean would flood in."

Fisher nodded. "Good thinking, Honor."

Camille skimmed her fingers around the rim of her cup. "It must be concealed somehow . . . otherwise we would have seen it before now."

Rosalie's face brightened. "I think I know where it is!" In an instant, she was racing down the pathway, pushing through fronds and low-hanging vines.

The rest of us trailed behind at a more leisurely pace. The solarium was too humid for sprinting.

"Come on, come on," she urged from the top of the stairs. "And we'll need our cloaks!"

"It's freezing!" Verity squealed, holding the flaps of her cloak tightly across her body.

A brisk wind whipped across Salten, bringing the brine up off the sea. The long grasses were yellow and dry, and a skim of ice crackled across the fountain. It wouldn't be long till Churning.

"Where are we going, Rosalie?" Camille called out, fighting to be heard over the gale.

"Follow me!"

We trudged after her in single file, heading directly into the gusts. It was easier to just keep my head down and follow the trail made by the feet in front of me. The grass died away, and we were on black rocks. Specks of dirt and salt blown about by the wind stung my eyes.

When I dared to look up, I saw we were heading for the Grotto. A narrow path veered off the cliff walk, taking us down, down, down to a small cave hollowed out of the crag. Inside was our family's shrine to Pontus. Four times a year, at the changing of the seasons, we brought offerings of fish and pearls and left them at the silver altar.

I hated those trips.

The trail was precarious. One wrong step and you'd plummet to the surf below.

Our little game suddenly seemed like a terrible mistake.

My eyes fell on a slab of rocks rising out of the sea like an angry fist. That's where Eulalie's body had been found. If Edgar was to be believed, she was pushed off the cliffs not far from where we now stood, and her killer was still on the loose.

Once inside the cave, I breathed a sigh of relief. We just needed to search the shrine and head back. There should still be enough weak sunlight for us to see the path. We could continue the search safely at Highmoor, until everyone tired of the game.

"Where should we start?" Rosalie asked. She'd marched us here so full of triumph. Now that she was here in the crowded space, doubt crept over her features.

There was no door.

"You said it was probably concealed, right?" Fisher said, sensing our flagging spirits. "Let's look around. Maybe there's a strange rock or a symbol or . . . something."

The far wall of the cave behind the altar was covered over with chips of sea glass, forming a wave that crested over a statue of Pontus. Cast of gold and taller than even Fisher, the sea god raised his trident high above his head, as if ready to strike. He looked like a man, mostly. His chest was broad and muscular, but his lower half was a riot of tentacles.

The twisting arms reminded me of the horrible bathtub dream from the day of the triplets' ball. Even now I could feel the rows of suction cups along my legs, gripping and grasping. With a shudder, I turned my back on the golden statue.

"Does anyone see anything?" I asked, shifting my focus back to my sisters.

Verity and Mercy stooped low over the sides of the stone benches. Honor knelt beside them, running her fingers over the seashells decorating the bases.

"Nothing yet."

Rosalie shook her head. She and Camille traced their hands across the stone walls, looking for catches or hidden hinges. Ligeia was at the mouth of the cave, peering at the cliffs surrounding the entrance. Fisher stood nearby, ready to catch her should she lose her balance.

I joined Lenore at the altar, caressing its silver top. "Where else could it be?" I asked. "Maybe in the gallery? There's the painting of the Brine. Or the bathroom on the fourth floor? The tub is a big clamshell—maybe Pontus put the door there?"

"I thought for sure we'd find something here," Rosalie said. Her eyes narrowed as she cocked her head, sweeping her gaze over the small cave. "Did anyone try the statue?" She circled around it, appraising every angle. "Is it me or does it look like the trident can move? See the gap between his fingers?"

Fisher was the only one tall enough to properly inspect it. "I think it actually does. . . ." He reached out on tiptoe and grabbed at the metal rod. With a rusted shriek, the trident spun around so its jeweled front now faced the back of the altar.

And then the wall began to shift.

It looked like a trick at first, the chips of sea glass glinting and sparkling in the dying afternoon light. But they were moving, spinning on unseen pins. They twisted and twisted until freed from the wall, spilling onto the stone floor with a shower of sparks and revealing a gaping tunnel entrance.

We watched the transformation in stunned silence until Verity darted forward and bent down, pressing her hand to the ground.

"It's wet!" she exclaimed. "The sea glass turned to water!"

"That's impossible," Fisher said, stepping in. He patted the area around Verity. When he looked up, his brown eyes were wide with wonder. "How is this happening?"

"There really was a door," Camille whispered before breaking into a grin. "We found the door!"

"We found *a* door," I clarified, staring at the open maw in front of us. "But where does it lead?"

Honor crept closer, peering down its length. "There are torches. . . ."

Her voice was flat, almost as if she was in a trance. As she approached the entrance, Fisher scooped her up in his arms, waylaying her. "Not so fast, little one." He carried her over to the triplets' safe embrace. "I think I should be the one to go in first. Just in case."

He stepped forward, his hands balling into fists. His breath sounded ragged, and for a moment, I thought I could see puffs of it in the air, as if the tunnel was much colder than the shrine. He glanced back at us. "Do I just think about a place as I go through?"

Though Camille nodded, she looked horror-struck, sickened at what her desire had brought about. "I suppose?"

With one last look at us, Fisher entered the tunnel, ducking beneath the low ceiling.

"Oh!" we heard him gasp, his voice thick with astonishment.

Then he was gone.

Verity looked down the passage, as close as she could without actually going in. "He's not there!"

We all stepped forward then to look for ourselves, but she was right. The tunnel appeared to stretch for miles through the cliffs. Torches hung from the sides, their flames flickering and lush, but there was no trace of Fisher.

"What have we done?" Lenore murmured, clutching her hand to her chest. Her face grew white, her eyes too wide. She stumbled back to one of the shrine's benches. "Where is he?"

"He'll be back soon, I'm sure," Camille said.

"You don't know that! What if he never comes back?" Verity sobbed. She pressed herself into my skirts, trembling. "What if we killed him?"

I reached out into the tunnel as far as my shaking fingers would go. A cry of alarm choked my throat as my hand disappeared before me. There was my arm, my elbow, but at my wrist, I ceased to be. I waggled my fingers, certain I was moving them, but saw nothing.

Seeing my missing hand, Honor let out a shriek and ran into Ligeia's arms. I jerked my arm back, suddenly terrified something on the other side might pull me in. For a horrible moment, my flexed fingers looked as if they were a stranger's.

"Are you all right, Annaleigh?" Ligeia twisted Honor around to show her my hand was still attached.

"I think so?" It was in one piece but felt strange, full of pins and needles.

"Where's Fisher? Why isn't he back?" Rosalie asked, pacing in front of the entrance as the minutes ticked by. "Someone should go in after him." She glanced around the room, her eyes landing on each of us. "Shouldn't we?"

An uncomfortable moment of silence passed. I stroked Verity's curls, ashamed I wasn't brave enough to volunteer.

"Fine, I'll do it," Rosalie said with a snarl and was through the opening before any of us could stop her.

Just like Fisher, she was there one moment and gone the next.

"Rosalie!" Ligeia screamed as she threw herself down the tunnel.

She disappeared in the wink of an eye, and Lenore howled. Camille caught her before she too could fling herself into the great unknown. Her cries of despair echoed through the shrine.

"It's cold, it's so cold," Lenore moaned, her teeth chattering.

The triplets often claimed to be able to feel exactly what the others did, no matter how far apart they were. Most of the family scoffed it off as a childish game, but I remembered once, while I was teaching her scales in the Blue Room, Ligeia grabbed her hand, clutching a finger in surprise. Rosalie had gone fishing with Papa and overzealously gutted her first catch, slicing her pinkie.

Camille placed her wrist on Lenore's forehead. "She feels fine."

"Where are they?" Lenore continued to wail. "They need to come back right away. Something is wrong. I can feel it! Something is horribly—"

"What's going on?" Rosalie cut in, skipping suddenly into existence, a wild grin plastered across her face. "You're acting as though you've never seen a magic door before!"

Then Ligeia appeared, with Fisher on her heels. Both looked dazed and happy.

"Where have you been?" Lenore demanded, leaping up to pull her sisters into a panicked embrace. "I couldn't feel you. It was so cold, like ice!"

"It was cold at first," Ligeia acknowledged. "But it was also . . . so wondrous."

"Where did you go?" Camille asked, edging toward the entrance. She looked as though she wanted to see for herself.

"We'll show you. Tonight!" Rosalie said, beaming.

"Tonight?" I repeated.

She reached into her pocket, withdrew a stack of silver envelopes, and passed them out. "Yes! At the ball. We've all been invited."

"Ball?" Camille flipped over her envelope and ran her fingers under the edge. She scanned the thick, creamy paper within. The edges winked with gilding. Her eyebrows jumped. "This is real?"

"As real as me standing here before you," Fisher said, smiling widely. "It really worked! You said you wanted to find a beau, so when I walked through the door, I tried to think of an elegant ball—the music, the gowns, the dancing. When I opened my eyes, I was in the middle of a palace courtyard, the grandest I've ever seen, and they were preparing for a party."

"And *I* got us invited!" Rosalie crowed, laughing at our dumbstruck faces. "Well, come on! We have to get ready! I do not intend to miss the first waltz!"

15

AS THE CLOCK IN THE HALL CHIMED ELEVEN, I SLIPPED on my fairy shoes. The leather still sparkled as if brand-new.

"They don't really match, do they?" Camille asked, tilting her head to study the whole effect of my outfit.

"I don't have anything else to wear. All my other shoes are boots," I said, poking the slipper out from under my navy hem. "No one will see them, do you think?"

Camille pursed her lips. "I'm sure you're right. And that dress is perfect for you. You can't change that."

I turned, looking in her bedroom mirror. We didn't want Hanna to know we were sneaking out, so we were helping each other dress. The triplets were already down the hall, buttoning the Graces' gowns and attaching their painted-cardboard wings.

Once back at Highmoor, we'd raced to the attic, raiding boxes of Mama's old gowns. There were dozens to choose from. The Graces had found dresses from when Ava and Octavia were small and eagerly rifled through them, looking for their favorite colors.

When I'd unearthed the shimmering waterfall of satin from the trunk, I'd squealed at its elegance. Though it boasted a high, modest neckline in front, the back plunged to a deep V, exposing my skin and ensuring I would not be wearing a corset tonight. A forgotten galaxy of gold and silver stars, embroidered with beads and metallic thread, speckled the bodice and puddled down the trailing skirt, making me think of the first words of the invitation.

I snatched the card off the vanity and skimmed the embossed script again:

> *Flushed with starlight and moonlight drowned,*
> *All the dreamers are castle-bound.*
> *At midnight's stroke, we will unwind,*
> *Revealing fantasies soft or unkind.*
> *Show me debauched nightmares or sunniest daydreams.*
> *Come not as you are but as you wish to be seen.*

"It's a themed ball," Camille had announced as we read and reread the invitations, parsing the rhymes for meaning. "Nightmares and Daydreams."

Verity had frowned. "We have to go as something scary?"

My mind flashed to her sketchbook, and I swooped in, quickly allaying her fears. "No! Some people will, but look: 'sunniest daydreams.' We can go as something happy too."

"Like fairies? Like our shoes?"

I nodded, and Mercy and Honor immediately chimed in, saying they wanted to be fairies too.

"What will you be?" Verity asked, looking over the dress in my hands with uncertainty.

I held it up to my shoulders, letting the blue satin dance over my frame. "A midsummer's night, when the sky is full of sparkling stars and fireflies."

It had seemed like a lovely idea back in the attic, but now, wearing the dress, I hesitated. Running my hands over the glossy fabric, I was shocked at how my fingers felt every curve and hollow of my waist. I'd worn afternoon gowns with soft trainer corsets before, but they were made of heavy laces and pleated silks, nothing like this bias-cut satin. It embraced every bit of me like a lover's caress.

"Do you think people will get it?" Camille asked, giving herself a final sweep and opening her fan with a flourish effect. She'd found the dress Mrs. Drexel had mentioned at our last fitting. Though the silhouette was slightly dated, the blood-red satin was so stunning, no one would take notice. A wide sash cascaded down Camille's shoulder, joining a heavy bustle of rosettes and ribbons. She wrapped a ruby choker around her neck and twisted back and forth to admire the way the candlelight played off it.

Camille had been horribly afraid of fires ever since we were girls. Every fall, the Salann Islands were battered with violent storms, and though Highmoor was dotted with lightning rods—each bearing the Thaumas octopus—it wasn't wholly immune. During a particularly nasty squall years ago, a fire broke out in the nursery. We were too young to truly remember, but Camille swore she could recall the scent of ozone and charred wood.

"Maybe if you added a touch of flames with your makeup?"

Her eyes lit up. "That's genius!"

As she crossed to her vanity, the triplets scurried down the hall in scandalously translucent lavender georgette shifts. They claimed to be sea nymphs, and I was suddenly very thankful Papa wasn't here. We'd never be allowed outside Highmoor again if he caught us.

I eyed the back of my dress in the mirror once more. "Maybe I ought to just wear my green gown."

"What? No, you look lovely." She swished a bit of orange glitter up from her eyes. "And I will not have you make us late."

"It's just so . . ." I ran my fingers down the fabric once more.

Camille's teeth winked from beneath a wicked grin. "Carnal."

"Exactly."

There was a soft knock at the door. "Camille? Annaleigh?"

Camille scurried over. "You can't be up here," she hissed at Fisher.

He stepped back, not daring to cross the threshold. "I know, I know, but I wanted to bring you something." He held up his hands, offering a pair of sparkling baubles.

"Masks?" Camille asked, taking one.

"Vendors were selling these outside the palace. Tonight's dance is a masquerade. We'll need them to get in."

"Oh! Thank you, Fisher." She chose the black domino. Silver sequins danced along the edges, with a plume of peacock feathers off to one side.

She looked at herself in the mirror. "It's perfect!"

He was wearing the same suit he'd worn to the triplets' ball, but Rosalie had coiled a bit of metallic green cloth up the sleeve of his jacket. I recognized Verity's hand in the serpent's face painted across his own.

"You went with a nightmare," I said, spotting his childhood fear.

Fisher turned with a smile, then sucked in his breath. "Oh, Annaleigh . . ." I instantly flushed, feeling his eyes on me. "You look . . ." He swallowed and held out a mask. "Will this do?"

It was a sparkling little band of tulle, dusted with glitter—just enough to obscure my eyes and cheekbones. Camille came up and tucked the ends into my hair, pinning the fabric in place. It skirted my skin like a whispered promise made in shadows.

"I think we're all ready," she said.

Fisher glanced down the hallway, on the lookout for approaching servants. "There's one more thing." He darted down the hall and returned with three glasses of wine. "I filched it from the kitchen—thought we might need a little courage." He raised his glass. "To midnight balls."

"And satin dresses," Camille added, hoisting her wine into the air.

They both turned to me expectantly.

"And to dancing. Always to dancing!"

The moon was a giant blue crescent, lighting our way across the lawn and down the cliff. It hung so low in the sky, I could feel its persistent tug pulling at the water, the waves, even us. A hundred thousand stars sparkled above us, as if vibrating with excitement for the party to come.

The sips of wine had emboldened me, making my steps feel more sure and chasing any worries I'd had to the side.

Once we were in the Grotto, Fisher turned Pontus's trident, and we watched the wave wall twist and dissolve into the tunnel entrance.

"Remember, you need to latch on to a thought as you're entering the tunnel," Fisher warned. "Think about the ball, the invitation. It will take you there, but if something else creeps into your mind, who knows where you might end up."

"Maybe we should go in together," I said, eyeing the mouth of the passage as if it were a beast about to devour us all. "Holding hands. Just in case."

The Graces nodded, their eyes as wide as silver florettes under masks of lace and paste jewels.

"You ought to go first, Fisher," Camille reasoned. "Make sure we're heading to the right place."

Fisher held out his hand to Rosalie, and she grabbed Ligeia's. Lenore was next, then Honor and Camille. She grabbed on to Mercy, who took Verity's hand. My little sister looked up at me before squeezing my hand.

"We're ready!" Verity announced.

He ducked into the tunnel and immediately disappeared. I watched as, one by one, my sisters entered the passage and vanished before me. As Verity faded away with a squeal of delight, I froze. After a beat, she tugged on my hand, pulling me into the unseen.

It was as if a thousand sets of fingertips danced over my skin, tickling and poking, prodding and fluttering. I closed my eyes against their invasion, pressing forward. When they stopped, I was in a forest of dazzling trees. They stood like silent sentinels, towering above us, with branches high overhead. The bark, a smattering of gold and silver, pulled away into papery spirals, like birch; beneath the top layers were hearts of rose gold. Metallic leaves rustled, sounding like bells jingling on the breeze.

"Did it not work?" I asked. It was a beautiful forest, to be sure, but not the ball we'd anticipated.

Fisher turned around, searching the moonlit forest. Plush carpets of emerald moss gave way to a pebbled path. "Let's follow that."

The Graces dashed down the trail, skipping, spinning, and laughing with exhilaration under the star-bright sky. Their joy was contagious, and we chased after them, silken skirts rippling behind us. I had no idea how far away from home we were or how we'd ever hope to return, but in this heady moment, I didn't care. The euphoria was tangible: I could taste it in the air, the sweetness coating my mouth and going straight to my head like champagne. Lenore and I linked arms and twirled in circles, our laughter growing louder and wilder the dizzier we became.

The trees eventually tapered away as we came to the banks of a moonlit lake. The waves that lapped against the shore were perfumed with a rich green algae, not the sharp salt of our sea. On the other side of the lake, high on a hill, was a castle so perfectly designed, it looked like something out of a fairy tale. Scarlet pennants slithered in the breeze as brilliant fireworks burst above them. Across the water, we heard murmurs of appreciation and the sounds of an orchestra tuning.

"That's it!" Rosalie exclaimed. "That's where we were this afternoon."

"Are we supposed to walk all the way there?" Camille asked, squinting at the distance. "The ball will be over by the time we arrive."

Lenore let out a gasp. "No, look!"

She pointed to a sparkling glint on the lake approaching us. It was a little train of boats, each big enough to hold just one passenger. They looked like enormous swans, ferried by enchantment, with no crew. The triplets immediately boarded, their laughter verging on shrieks as the great birds tipped precariously from side to side.

Fisher helped Camille and the Graces into the next four boats.

"Hurry up, you two!" Ligeia called out. They were already halfway across the lake.

Fisher spun around, laughing at the sheer improbability of the evening. "I can't believe we're really doing this! Shall we?" he asked, holding out his hand.

His thumb traced around my palm, sending squirming tendrils of unease into my belly. Even though his smile was full of merriment, his eyes felt too fervent. On such a glorious night, I wanted dancing and stars and champagne, not whatever unspoken promise lay in Fisher's gaze.

"I'll race you!" I challenged, nestling between the giant wings.

The swan seemed to hear me and bumped away from the dock at a rapid clip. There were no oars, no rudder, nothing I could use to guide the boat, but it seemed to know exactly what its course was. On Salten, this would have been terrifying, but near a grove of silvery trees, wearing a sparkling mask, I found it exhilarating.

We reached the other side of the lake in no time at all. The castle towered above us on the crest of the bluff. A set of stairs directly across from the docks zigzagged across the hill and up to the palace gates. We paused to consider the climb ahead of us before scurrying up the marble treads.

"Two hundred and nineteen, two hundred and twenty . . . ," Mercy said, counting each step to pass the time. At three hundred, the triplets begged her to stop. "Three hundred and forty-eight, three hundred and forty-ni-i-ine . . ." She dragged the word out, then hopped up the last step with a puff. "Three hundred and fifty!"

Congregating on the plaza outside the main gates, we paused, flicking our fans back and forth to create a breeze as we caught our breath. The palace, built of obsidian blocks, rose seven stories high, with jagged turrets on every corner. Tall braziers illuminated the crimson carpet leading into the main entrance. The facade reflected the dancing flames, winking as though it too was on fire.

Mountains rose up around the lake, snowcapped and covered with dense forests. A mist settled over the water, giving the scene a mysterious softness.

"Where on earth are we?" Fisher asked, breathing in the cool night air as he stood by the stone parapet. He was the only one who didn't seem affected by the climb. I wondered how many times a day he had to race up Old Maude's winding staircase.

"I've never felt so very far from home," Camille admitted, joining him.

"That's because we've never been past Astrea," Ligeia said.

"Never?" He turned and smiled at us. "Then what a fine adventure your first trip to the mainland will be."

A heavy bell rang out, thudding so loudly I felt it deep in my chest.

"It's nearly midnight!" Rosalie cried. "We need to get in now or we'll miss everything!"

Digging the invitations from our cloak pockets, we joined the queue of stragglers seeking admittance. Everyone was dressed in jewel tones and shimmering blacks. The masks ranged from simple dominoes to elaborately plumed and bejeweled masterpieces. Some had painted faces, giving them a mysterious leer or puckered lips. There were horns and scales, flames and glitter. Everyone vied to outdo the splendor of the palace.

Inside, the halls were festooned in scarlet banners, each embroidered with a howling wolf. It wasn't a sigil I was familiar with, and I made a mental note to look it up once we returned to Highmoor. I felt hopelessly out of my depth navigating the forbidding onyx-colored corridors. Even the air smelled darker here, heavily perfumed with blackened resin, musk, and burning incense. This was far grander than anything we Thaumas girls had ever seen.

"You're the daughter of a duke," I whispered to myself. "You belong here."

Lenore overheard me and patted my hand. "I'm scared too," she admitted with a small smile.

We followed the crowds down hallways lined with full suits of armor. Red plumes and wicked swords bedecked the frozen knights, and I wondered how loudly I might shriek if one suddenly came to life. Mercy reached out and touched a pair of boots before pulling her hand away with ghoulish glee.

Music swelled somewhere to our left. The orchestra was readying for the first number. Around the corner, a great hall opened up, with a series of sharply pointed archways along one side, framing the ballroom.

Crowds of people milled about, talking and laughing. Everyone seemed to know everyone else, and no one took any notice of us. We exchanged breathless glances. The moment we'd been dreaming of was now at hand, yet none of us made a motion to enter.

"Miss Camille Thaumas." Fisher stepped forward with a gallant bow. "I would be so honored to have your first dance."

After a moment's pause, she nodded, visibly relaxing. They went inside, and we all followed, skirting the walls to watch as the dancing began.

16

"MAY I HAVE THIS DANCE?"

A man dressed in dark blue stretched his hand out to Rosalie. With an eager smile, she was whisked onto the crowded dance floor. Lenore and Ligeia soon followed. Their dresses fluttered as they twirled beneath the most unsettling fresco I'd ever seen.

It was a painted forest, dark and deep. A pack of wolves raced through black trees, chasing after a large buck. The deer's eyes glistened in terror as it rose on its hind legs, trying to free itself from a mess of briars. Real wrought-iron vines twisted across the painted ceiling's length. Some draped down, curling above our heads. Others knotted in on themselves, holding little orbs of bright red light.

"Poor deer," Verity said, following my gaze.

"Why is the prettiest girl in the room sitting this dance out?" Fisher interrupted, coming up beside us.

Camille swirled by on the arms of a man wearing a mask of red leather, like a phoenix bursting from the flames. It matched her dress perfectly. Her head tilted toward him as she listened intently to every word he said. They looked radiant together, a king and queen presiding over their fiery court.

Fisher grabbed Verity and guided her out onto the floor, spinning her around and around until she snorted with laughter. He threw a wink back at me, promising I was next.

I made my way along the sides of the dance floor, amazed by the sheer spectacle. At the far end of the hall, a fireplace took up nearly the entire width of the wall. A massive blaze roared in the obsidian chamber, where a whole hog roasted on a spit. More metal vines crept around columns and along archways. Brilliant cherry-colored flowers, each with a small votive candle in the center, sprinkled down them. The petals had been painstakingly pieced together with stained glass.

"Quite a feat of engineering, wouldn't you say?" I heard from behind me. "And I've not seen a single candle burn out. The staff must be going crazy replacing all those flames."

I turned and my heart thudded wildly in my chest.

"Cassius!" I wanted to exclaim it, to loudly express the surprise of seeing him here, but my words came out with no more power than a breathless whisper.

He was dressed in a fine suit of blackest wool, impeccably tailored to his frame. A dark mask obscured his face from forehead to nose. Tiny jet beads sparkled at the edges.

He offered a quick smile. "Are you so certain? I *am* wearing a mask."

Though he teased, I would recognize those blue eyes anywhere. Dark as the sea, with specks of silver, they'd haunted my dreams every night since our encounter on Selkirk.

"What are you doing here?"

"The same as you, I'd imagine. The same as all of them." He swept his arm across the room.

"They're all dancing," I pointed out. I didn't know if it was the anonymity of the mask or the opulent and seductive pull of the castle, but I'd never felt so brazen in all my life. I was practically daring him to ask me to dance.

"Are we not?" he asked, looking down at our feet as if surprised to find them standing still. "We should rectify that."

My fingers slid into his outstretched hand like water over rocks. He led me out to the center of the room as a new tune began. I snaked my free arm up his shoulder and felt my breath stop as his other hand came to rest at my waist. A warm ribbon of desire unraveled inside me, and I dared to wonder what those fingers would feel like against my bare skin.

I soon found out.

It was a lively jig, full of complicated spins and twists. Cassius skillfully led me through the unfamiliar steps, his smile bright. As the song came to an end, he drew me in, so close I could feel the heat of his chest singeing my thin satin, before twisting me into a spectacular dip. His palm splayed across my back, supporting my weight with a deft grace. Behind the mask, his eyes burned down at me.

The crowd broke into applause for the orchestra, and I felt a tap on my shoulder.

"Ready for that dance now, Minnow?" Fisher asked. "Unless you've already made plans with . . ."

I inhaled deeply, catching my breath. "Fisher, this is Cassius. His father is a captain on Selkirk." I turned back to Cassius. "Fisher is—"

"A family friend," he interjected. He grazed my elbow, gently drawing me to his side. "A very close friend."

They sized each other up, their glances heated and decidedly masculine. It was a strange sensation, being caught between the two of them. Though it was flattering, I couldn't help but feel like a swimmer circled by two sharks, wondering which would strike first.

After a pause, Cassius shifted his eyes toward me, his face relaxing. "Save me your next waltz?"

"I'd be delighted—" I started, but Fisher spun me away as a new song began, and I didn't know if Cassius had heard me.

Fisher's hand at my waist was warm and sure, and he guided us through the steps with far more confidence than he'd shown at the triplets' ball. Though we faced each other for most of the dance, his eyes never quite met mine, always resting just above my shoulders as if searching the room to make certain Cassius was watching.

"Fisher?"

His face broke into a triumphant smirk, and as we turned, I caught Cassius leaving the ballroom.

"What?" He laughed, seeing my raised eyebrow.

"What was that all about?"

He shrugged, then spun me out as the music built in a swooping crescendo.

"Fisher!"

"I don't know. I saw you across the room, dancing with him, and I just . . . I knew I needed to come cut in."

I paused. "Why?"

The tips of his ears flared red, and he looked away. "It's hard to admit, Annaleigh."

"We've always been able to tell each other anything," I said, drawing his gaze back. "Haven't we?"

"Well, yes, but . . . It's just . . ." He let out a sigh of frustration. "I truly did not like seeing you in another man's arms."

My steps faltered, and Fisher rubbed his neck, looking exactly like the twelve-year-old boy I'd been smitten with.

"Is that strange to hear? It feels strange to say. All my life I thought of you as a sister . . . a sometimes exasperating but always beloved little sister. But when I came back to Salten and saw you so grown up and beautiful . . . I didn't want you to feel like a sister any longer."

"Oh."

I should have said more, I could feel him silently begging me to say more, but the words weren't there. Fisher stood frozen in a crowd of swirling couples. His eyes swept over me, worried amber fervently searching for something in mine. But they didn't find what they wanted, and he abruptly left the dance floor.

I trailed after him, my stomach in a twist of fluttering knots. As a girl, I'd dreamt of this moment, wished and prayed for its arrival, but now that it was here, it felt flat. Even after his admission, I longed to search the room for Cassius instead, worried he might have overheard.

"Fisher, wait!" I exclaimed, following him to the outskirts of the room.

"Forget it, Annaleigh. Just forget I said anything."

I grabbed at his hand, forcing him to stop. "Where are you going?"

He waved his arm, freeing himself from my grasp. "Anywhere but here. Don't follow me."

"You . . . surprised me." My words fell out, feeble and weak.

He raked his fingers through his hair. "I should have stayed quiet—especially after everything Camille said about that watchmaker."

"What does Edgar have to do with anything?"

Fisher tilted his head, incredulity sharp across his face. "You're not going to end up with a Keeper of the Light. I know that. I knew that. But when I saw you in that dress tonight . . ." He reached out and pushed aside a loose curl behind my ear. His thumb traced across my cheek. "I just dared to dream otherwise." He shook his head. "Forgive me. I've made a mess of this evening. I just . . . I need to just . . ." He turned and raced out of the room.

"Fisher!" I called after him, but he was gone.

"Lovers' quarrel?" A stranger loomed over me, impossibly tall and gaunt. His tailcoat had been cut from a gorgeously thick emerald silk. Embroidered across the lapels was a three-headed dragon, claws raised as if to attack. Its eyes seemed to wink in the strange floral candlelight, but it was the man's mask that wholly disconcerted me. Made of a clear resin, it covered his entire face, hiding the man beneath. Enormous eyes were painted across his own, allowing visibility only through tiny pinpricks in the false irises. Their brushstrokes were full of jealousy, mad with want.

"Not exactly."

"Excellent. Then if you're not otherwise engaged . . ." He held up an unusually long finger. "A dance?"

I glanced back toward the door Fisher had run out of but saw no sign of him. Feeling miserable, I accepted the stranger's arm.

"It's a lovely evening, don't you think?" the dragon man asked after a long moment of silent dancing.

"I've had better," I admitted.

He laughed. "Come, come. Cheer up. This is a party, is it not?"

"I suppose you're right," I said, following him through a series of steps. "Who do I have the pleasure of dancing with?"

He raised up that long finger again, shaking it with a dark smile. "Ah, ah, ah. The very delight of such an evening is being your complete self with a total stranger, don't you think? Spilling your innermost thoughts—ones too dark and deep to ever speak in the light of day, confessing sins of passion and pleasure, maybe even misbehaving, and none of it matters, because if you don't know who you're toying with, then what's the harm in it?" His arm snaked up my back, flush and exposed, pulling me against him. "Tell me, pretty lady, what are your darkest secrets?"

Though I couldn't see his actual eyes, I felt them crawling all over my body.

As the song wound to an end, a string on one of the violins broke, ending the final note on a strange chord. I used the moment to squirm free of the dragon man's grasp.

"I'm afraid I must go find my friend," I stammered.

After a tense moment, he chuckled as if I'd said something amusing. "I'll be back for you later." He tapped his long finger against my wrist. "Count on it."

I wanted to watch where he went, to keep track of him, but there were too many shades of green, and he melted into the crowd, gone in an instant. The orchestra rifled through sheets of music before finding a cheerful fox-trot.

"There you are!" Cassius exclaimed, suddenly at my side. He offered his hand for the next dance.

"Could we sit this one out?" I waved my lace fan back and

forth. My mind was jumbled with too many thoughts, too weighed down to dance.

"Would you care for a stroll? I recall seeing a courtyard as I came in."

I nodded gratefully.

"This way."

Cassius led me through the huge arches lining the side of the ballroom and down the corridor, taking more turns than I could remember. Finally, we stepped out into a quiet courtyard, surrounded on three sides by towering cloisters.

The wind whipped by, blowing strands of hair across my face. It still smelled like autumn here. Pine needles and cold, crisp air, bonfires and moldering leaves, the world dying as it readied to be reborn. I took a deep breath, savoring the sharp tang.

An eerie cry ripped through the air. Another joined it, and another, and suddenly the night was alive with wavering howls.

"The Pelage wolves," Cassius explained as I tensed. "They roam the forests at night, always on the hunt."

Pelage. We were in Pelage. I tried picturing the map that hung in Papa's study, showing all of the regions of Arcannia. Pelage was in the northeast section of the kingdom, about as far from Salann as you could get.

"It almost sounds like the whales at home. You can hear them singing on summer nights when the waters are still." Thinking of Salann made my mind circle back to the one question it had avoided since running into Cassius. But I needed to know. "The last time I saw you, you were on Selkirk. . . ."

His eyes twinkled under the mask. "I remember. You were the prettiest girl on the docks."

I paused, taken aback by his open flirtation. "What on earth are you doing here?"

He looked to the sky as another volley of howls started up. "I could point out you're just as far from home."

"You're right, but—"

"I came for the same reason as you," Cassius continued, nodding back toward the castle. "The dancing."

"Dancing?" I echoed. "You came all this way to Pelage for dancing?"

"Didn't you?"

Our eyes met, and I got the distinct impression he somehow saw more of me than he ought to.

"You're blushing," he murmured, touching my cheek below the tulle mask. "I wouldn't have expected that." He traced one of the stars on my sleeve, curious. "What exactly are you meant to be?"

I ran my hands down the gown, heat sweeping from my cheeks throughout my body. "I . . . I just liked the stars. I thought they looked like a summer's night sky."

His stare weighed heavily across my skin. "They suit you."

"And what about you?" I asked, gesturing to his all-black attire. "Are you scared of the dark?"

"Me?" He looked down. "I'm the most terrifying nightmare of them all."

I raised my eyebrows, waiting for him to elaborate.

"Regret."

I smiled, though it wasn't funny. "Is that really a nightmare?"

"Can you think of anything more frightening?"

Another sharp howl split the night, followed by a barrage of snarls. The wolves must have caught the scent of something. They were on the hunt.

We stared out over the forest, trying to spot the pack, but there were too many shadows.

His fingertips brushed against the back of my hand, no more than a whispered question, sending a dance of shivers down my spine. When I glanced up, I saw Cassius looking at me, but it was too dark to see the intent in his eyes. For a moment, the world seemed to be willing us closer and closer together. I felt his breath on my cheek and knew if I took one small step toward him, he would kiss me.

"Do you want to know what my biggest regret tonight will be, pretty Annaleigh?" he murmured, his lips brushing the skin of my temple.

Every fiber in my being was paused on tiptoe, aching for him to bridge the gap between us. My tongue felt too tied up to properly answer, and as his hand slipped over mine, I thought my heart would shatter with happiness.

"If I don't spend the rest of this ball with you on the dance floor."

He gently tugged me back inside, toward the ballroom. As a new waltz began, I suddenly remembered Cassius had never actually answered my question about what he was doing there.

17

I WOKE UP SCREAMING AND FIGHTING TO FREE MYself from tangled sheets.

Blinking against the early-afternoon light pushing in through half-closed curtains, I struggled to sit up, feeling sick and ready to vomit. My stomach lurched. The sheets were soaked in sweat, and my nightgown clung to me like a clammy shroud. A sour funk permeated the room, coating my mouth and choking me. I stumbled to the windows and pressed my flushed cheeks to the cold glass panes, gulping in the salty breeze and slowly coming back to myself.

It was the third night in a row I'd had the nightmare.

After returning from our night in Pelage, sneaking back into Highmoor just before the kitchen staff woke, I managed to stay awake until breakfast, then collapsed in an exhausted stupor. While I slept, Camille and the triplets returned to the Grotto, seeking invitations for the next ball. And the next ball. And the one after that.

We'd gone dancing every night for a week.

Not all of us, though. The Graces couldn't stay up so late. They had lessons with Berta, and she'd fretted over the dark circles under their eyes, worrying Hanna and Morella. They stayed behind, quite grumpily, while the rest of us primped and powdered, dressing for whatever the night's theme was in Mama's gowns. Cobbler Gerver's claims of the fairy shoes lasting for a whole season were wildly exaggerated. After a week of dancing, the stitching was unraveling and the soles were worn bare. We were forced to squeeze our big toes into Mama's golden slippers and sandals. The aged leather frayed even faster, and stacks of spent shoes grew beneath our beds.

I found the dances great fun at first, seeing new places, meeting new people. A thrill raced down my spine as I stepped into a new ballroom, hoping Cassius would be there. But he never was, and the sleepless nights were catching up with me. I slept in later and later, but my slumber was interrupted by strange dreams, extensions of the dances themselves.

They always started normally enough, with gorgeous dresses in beautiful halls. A handsome man would emerge from the crowd and hold out his hand.

"Dance with me?" he'd ask, and we'd be off, twirling through a series of steps.

But as the dream wore on, the music would take on a different pitch, the notes turning flat and sour. We'd spin around again and again, and a strange light would appear, tinting the room sickly and greenish. No one but me ever seemed to notice. The crowds just kept on dancing. No one ever stopped.

I'd try to, forcing myself to lose momentum, begging my partner for a reprieve, but my feet would never listen. They'd continue following his steps, no matter what I did.

"Dance with me," my partner would plead, but the voice never matched his body. It was raspy and harsh, as though multiple voices spoke the words, wanting to blend into one but not completely synced.

I'd shake my head, backing away. This wasn't right. Something was terribly wrong. I wanted to leave the dance floor now—right now—and that's when she'd grab me.

Her skin was pale and mottled, like a mushroom grown too large and soft. Black hair swirled about her, tangling in her layers of gray chiffon, weightless and writhing. Worst of all were her eyes, dark as night, hostile, and shedding pitch-black tears. They ran down her face, leaving behind oily tracks that dripped to her bare gray feet. Sharp, pointed teeth winked from a sly grin as she pulled me closer.

"Dance with me," the Weeping Woman would whisper, and I'd wake up, gasping for air.

"Don't tell me you're still in your nightgown," Hanna said, bustling into my room. She carried a basket of mending and set it down with a whoosh of breath.

"I had a bad night."

"You and everyone else, it seems. Camille is still asleep. Short of stomping into her room with a pair of brass cymbals, I'm not sure how to wake her." She turned to my bureau, sorting stockings from the basket.

I flexed my aching feet back and forth. I'd broken my last pair of Mama's slippers and could feel hot blisters on the side of my little toes. We needed new shoes.

"Your father is coming home today," Hanna continued.

"Today?" I brightened. Perhaps he'd arrive back from court

in high spirits and I could finally tell him all I'd learned about Eulalie's final night.

"Madame Morella received a letter after supper yesterday. She's been up for hours, waltzing about the house and singing the news to anyone who will listen." She sighed. "And if I have to hear about those babies one more time . . . Do you really think they're boys?"

I pushed the last traces of sleep from my eyes. "I don't know. Mama said she thought we'd all be boys too."

Hanna crossed to my armoire and pulled out a blue gown. "She's carrying so high, I think it must be girls. But she's so sure. . . ." She shook her head. "I fear she's bound to be disappointed." She caught herself and smiled at me. "Not that any of you were ever a disappointment."

I pulled the sodden nightgown over my head before stepping into the dress she held out.

"Speaking of sons . . ." Her smile flattened with a wisp of sadness. "You've spent some time with Fisher since he got back, haven't you?"

"A little," I murmured uneasily.

In truth, I'd not spoken with him since that night in Pelage. When our paths did cross, he'd abruptly turn down another hall, ignoring my pleas. I tried sneaking into the servants' wing to corner him in his bedroom, but he seemed to hear me coming every time. I always found the room dark and empty.

He'd even stopped coming to the balls, despite the triplets' most fervent begging.

Using the vanity mirror, I watched her expression as she buttoned up the dress. Her forehead seemed to have more worry lines than usual. "Is everything all right, Hanna?"

"Oh, fine, fine. It's to be expected, I suppose. It's the first bit of free time he's had in ages. It was silly to think he'd want to spend every spare second with me."

I frowned. If he wasn't at the balls and he wasn't with Hanna, where was he spending all his time?

Hanna ran a hand down my back, smoothing out the bodice. "But I forget he's not a little boy anymore." She patted my cheek once. "Your mother was lucky to have so many girls. Morella ought to pray Pontus gives her daughters instead."

"You're home! You're home!"

Verity, Mercy, and Rosalie raced down the stairs and straight into Papa's arms, tumbling over each other.

"Can we use the catboat today?" Rosalie asked without preamble.

"Not in this soup. Haven't you been outside?" He paused, looking Rosalie over. "You're still in your nightgown." He turned to me. "Is she sick?"

I opened my mouth but froze. I was terrible at lying.

"Just had a bit of a slow start this morning," Rosalie filled in.

"This morning? It's after three. At least you two are dressed," he replied, picking up the little girls by their sashes as they squealed and giggled. "What do you need the cat for?"

Rosalie blanched. "We need to go into town for . . . supplies."

"Supplies?"

"Shoes!" Mercy gasped, shrieking as he swung her.

He set them down, as out of breath as they were. "Shoes? For who?"

"All of us!" Verity spun down the hall, her excitement too big to be contained by a body so small. Mercy and Rosalie were fast on her heels, leaving echoes of laughter in their wake.

I glanced up at my father's profile, pleased it was finally just the two of us. "Papa, there's something I wanted to speak to you about."

He seemed surprised to see me still beside him. "Surely you don't need shoes too?"

My toes squirmed barefoot against the mosaic tiles. "I do, but that's not what— It's about Eulalie. . . ."

Papa's face hardened. I'd have to tread carefully. This wasn't something he'd want to hear about.

"What about her?"

My fingernails dug sharply into my palms. I needed to come out and say it. "It's about her suitors."

"Welcome home, Papa!" Camille said, emerging from the Blue Room as though she'd been practicing at the piano for hours and had not just raced out of bed.

"Just a minute, Camille. Papa and I were talking about—"

"I just wanted to say hello." She stood on tiptoe to give him a hug. "How was the trip? How is the King? Did you—"

"Camille!" I exclaimed.

Papa held up his hands, stopping the quarrel before it could start. "The trip was fine. King Alderon hopes you'll join our next council meeting, Camille. I'll fill you in on the details once I'm settled."

She beamed, pleased to have gotten her way.

He turned back to me. "What's this about suitors, Annaleigh?"

Camille's smile faded. "Suitors? For whom?"

"Eulalie," Papa said, his tone darkening.

The weight of their gazes fell heavily on me.

"Is this about that watchmaker? I told you it was just some stupid fantasy he made up to—"

"Watchmaker?" Papa interrupted.

"It's not about Edgar, and please, Camille, will you leave us alone?" I pleaded, raising my voice to be heard above them.

Though she stalked into the Blue Room, a bit of her skirt protruded from the archway. She was obviously eavesdropping.

"I keep wondering about Eulalie," I said, turning to Papa. "I think someone was with her on the cliff walk that night."

Papa sighed. "When someone dies unexpectedly, it's normal to want to find someone to blame."

"That's not— This isn't just grief, Papa. I truly think someone hurt Eulalie. On purpose." I gathered my courage, and the story flowed out in a rush. "Eulalie was running away from home that night. She was going to elope with Edgar, the clockmaker's apprentice, but someone else was waiting for her."

Papa stifled a laugh, and my heart sank.

"Edgar Morris? That little man with the spectacles?" His lips twitched in amusement. "He wouldn't have the gumption to pick up a copper florette left in the cobblestones, let alone elope with my eldest daughter."

He breezed into the Blue Room, joining my sisters.

"Papa, listen to me, please!" I cried, running after him. "Edgar proposed—he gave Eulalie the locket she was buried in, the one with the anchor and the poem inside. He said when he arrived to take her away, he saw a shadow on the cliff, just after she fell. She must have been pushed."

"Nonsense." He swatted his hand, easily dismissing my theory.

"It's not! Someone was there. Someone who didn't want Eulalie to marry Edgar."

"That could be anyone," Camille cut in. "I can't think of a more unlikely match."

Papa sank into his armchair, chuckling. "Quite true. If I half suspected Edgar capable of stealing Eulalie, I'd have pushed *him* off a cliff. Gladly." He rubbed at his eyes. "That's enough of this, Annaleigh."

"But how can you be so sure—"

"I said enough." His voice was sharp and swift, a guillotine axing the conversation. "Now, what's this I hear about shoes?"

Everyone exchanged tense glances. Finally, Honor pushed her way forward and lifted her skirts to reveal very battered slippers. The soles were scuffed, and the navy dye had completely worn away in spots. Most of the silver beads had chipped off, and the ribbons were completely tattered.

Papa slipped a shoe off, mystified. "Are they all like this?"

The triplets glanced at each other before raising their skirts.

"The cobbler promised these would last all season. They look as though they've seen a hundred balls."

Lenore twisted her mouth, visibly uncomfortable. "Maybe there was something wrong with the leather?"

"And you've no other shoes?" Papa asked, his skepticism evident. "I just paid three thousand gold florettes for a set that didn't last a month."

"You burned our others," Camille reminded him. "On the bonfire with the mourning clothes, remember?"

Papa sighed, pressing the pads of his fingers to his forehead.

"I suppose a trip to town will be necessary. But you'll have to wait. I'm leaving for Vasa the day after tomorrow, at first light. There's a problem there with a clipper's hull. I won't pay for shoddy craftsmanship." He glanced back at Honor's slipper. "Not on ships and certainly not on shoes. I could go early next week."

"We can't go barefoot till then," Rosalie exclaimed. "Could we take the rowboat? We could go tomorrow. We all know how to row."

"But not all of you will fit." He glanced behind us. "Ah, Fisher."

"Welcome home, sir," Fisher said, lingering in the doorway. His face was smudged and his hair damp with sweat. He wore a thick navy sweater and carried a bucket of soft blades for cleaning boats. His amber eyes fell on me once before shifting away.

"Enjoying your stay? Must be nice to get a break from Silas's cooking, I imagine," Papa said, settling back into his chair.

"It is, to be sure. And it's wonderful getting to spend so much time with Mother."

I blinked, Hanna's hurt still fresh in my mind.

"She's put me to work today," he continued, raising the bucket.

Papa winced with a laugh. "Scraping off barnacles like a little lad. I'm sorry to hear that." He paused. "Actually, I might have something to help you out. The girls need to go to Astrea tomorrow if the fog lifts. Could you take them out on the cat?"

Fisher nodded. "I'd be happy to."

"Oh, thank you, Papa! Thank you, Fisher!" Ligeia exclaimed, throwing her arms around Papa's neck.

Papa raised a finger of warning to us all. "I will not make a habit of purchasing new pairs every week. Pick something sturdy to get you through the winter at least. No more fairy shoes."

18

"HURRY UP AND CHOOSE SOMETHING, ROSALIE." Honor hopped from one foot to the other, a petulant whine growing in her voice. Papa had given us sailors' boots, found in one of the storerooms near the dock, and they were too big for even us older girls. On the Graces, they were comically absurd.

We'd been in the cobbler's shop for over an hour. Fisher had carried in the boxes of worn slippers and dumped the contents on Reynold Gerver's table, demanding to know why the shoes had worn out so fast.

The poor shoemaker had hemmed and hawed as he examined his creations, sputtering that such fraying should never have occurred so quickly. He'd offered new shoes for us all, at a fraction of the standard price.

"These are awfully nice." Rosalie picked up a pair of satin shoes with a fashionable court heel.

"And impractical," Fisher said, snatching them from her. "Your father made it abundantly clear I'm not to allow you to purchase something delicate and pretty. Just find something like the rest of your sisters."

Our eyes met, and my throat constricted. I'd longed for the chance to pull him aside and smooth over the mess from Pelage, but a rainstorm had rolled in shortly after we left Highmoor. Fisher had waved me away, citing his need for concentration as the rain soaked us to the skin, making the short journey to Astrea miserable.

Honor threw herself into a chair in a swoon worthy of the stage, and Verity was precariously close to knocking over a display of stacked boxes in the window.

"Why don't I take the Graces for a cup of tea while Rosalie makes up her mind?" I suggested.

"Or cider?" Verity asked, pawing at Fisher with a hopeful smile.

He handed me the coins.

"Make sure your hoods are on," I instructed before opening the shop door.

We raced across the cobblestones, skirting puddles of rainwater to huddle in the sanctuary of the tavern's wide awning.

"Here, take these," I said, pressing the coins into Honor's hand. "There's something I need to do—an errand—so you three go inside, and I'll be back as quickly as I can."

"Where are you going?" Verity asked, clearly wanting to come too.

"Nowhere with cider," I said, scooting her toward the large oak door. "It's cold and wet. Hurry in, you don't want to freeze!"

They scurried inside and I darted back into the storm, making my way to Mr. Averson's clock shop.

My stomach twisted with guilt as I remembered how unceremoniously Edgar had been removed from Highmoor. I should have stopped Camille, should have tried harder to contact him. I was ashamed at how easily I'd been distracted.

The balls were consuming more than just my nights. Whole mornings were slept away. Often we didn't wake until it was time to primp for the next party. After so many years of staid blacks and tepid behaviors, the balls were invigorating. Intoxicating. The masks and paste jewels, the whisper of silks and tulles, the promise of handsome dance partners—they'd all dazzled me until I was blinded to my true purpose.

I'd forgotten Eulalie.

And if I was being honest, it hadn't bothered me until now, when I was firmly rooted back at home, back in Salann, back in the Salt.

I needed to track down Edgar and apologize. I didn't care what Camille thought. I believed his story about the shadow on the cliff, and together we'd uncover who it was.

A silver bell tinkled overhead as I stepped into the shop, out of the rain.

"Coming, coming," a cheerful voice called from the workroom. Or perhaps it came from behind the stack of metal hands near the corner. They were taller than me, used for clock towers in town squares.

Cogs and gears littered every available surface in the shop, and rows of clocks lined the walls. The staggered ticks of passing seconds overlapped, forming a symphony of beats. It was a soft, subtle sound, but once you noticed the ticks, they became impossible to ignore.

"How may I help you today—" Edgar emerged from the workroom. When he saw me, he came to a full stop, nearly crashing into a case displaying pocket watches and chains. "What are you doing here?" he demanded, his tone coloring. "Come to kick me out of my own place of employment? You'll find the Thaumas reach does not extend this far. Good day."

"Edgar—wait! I'm so sorry about that. I should have stood up for you, I should have stopped Camille. I came to apologize and . . . and also to talk."

"Talk?" He glared at me through his tiny eyeglasses.

"About Eulalie, about the shadow."

"I already told you everything I know." His hand raised against the swinging door.

"Not everything," I said, stopping him before he could retreat. "I saw the way you reacted when Camille called for Roland." He stiffened as I mentioned the valet's name. "Why?"

Edgar turned back, reluctance on his face. He removed his glasses and polished them on the edge of his canvas apron, biding his time.

"Could he be the shadow?" I guessed.

He squinted through the lenses as though they were still unclean. "I don't know who the shadow was . . . but I must admit, my first guess would be him." His fingertips trembled as if fighting the urge to wipe the spectacles again. "Every time I was at Highmoor—helping Mr. Averson with that grandfather clock, delivering a fixed pocket watch or mantel clock—he was always about, lurking, listening. Eulalie said it was just part of his job, waiting to be needed, but it felt like more than that. . . . It felt . . ."

"Yes?" I whispered, leaning in.

"Like an obsession."

I watched the rain fall on the soggy market outside, thinking about our day-to-day life at Highmoor. It was true, Roland was always nearby, ready to help, but as he was one of Papa's most trusted servants, that seemed only natural to me. I didn't know much about Edgar, but I'd hazard a guess he'd not grown up in a house like ours, full of more servants than family members.

"Did Eulalie keep a diary?" Edgar asked, trying a different approach. "She learned something she wasn't supposed to. Perhaps she wrote about it?"

Eulalie wasn't the type to pour her heart out onto the page, as Lenore and Camille did. She'd hated penmanship lessons when we were girls and had to be cajoled into writing letters to aunts and cousins.

"I never saw her with one."

His pale eyebrows creased together. "The more I think about it, I'm certain the shadow was Roland," he said, circling back. "He never liked me. If he somehow found out we were eloping . . ."

"Wouldn't he try to stop *you*, then, not Eulalie?" I asked. Edgar's accusation didn't feel right to me at all. It had too many holes. Even if Roland had been wildly in love with Eulalie, he must have known nothing would ever come of it. She was the heir to Highmoor. Papa would never have let her court one of its servants.

Besides . . . he was just so old. . . .

One by one, the clocks' gears turned, chiming out the quarter hour. The cacophony set my teeth on edge, reminding me I'd been gone too long already. I reached for the door.

"Miss Thaumas, wait! I—I need to know . . . You do believe me, don't you? About the shadow? Eulalie didn't trip, and she would never have hurt herself. You know that."

After a beat, I nodded.

"I want to find out who did this to her. Who . . . murdered her." His said the word with an intense precision, as if trying not to stammer over it. "Will you help me? Please?" His eyes, suddenly bright with righteous fervor, fixed me in place like a butterfly pinned onto a shadowbox board.

"Yes," I whispered.

He toyed with his spectacles again. "I know you don't think Roland was involved, but promise me you'll look into it? Ask around. Even if it wasn't him, he must have seen something. He sees everything."

The final clock chimed, its notes slightly sharp, giving a strange importance to Edgar's idea.

"He does," I echoed in agreement.

"Good. Thank you. Will your family be coming to any Churning events?"

The festival was only a week away. Soon Highmoor would be turned inside out, readying for the ten-day affair.

"We always go to the pageant after First Night."

A floorboard creaked above us, and our eyes darted to the ceiling. I'd assumed we were alone. Was someone listening in on our conversation?

"What's up there?"

"Just storage . . . Mr. Averson?" Edgar called out.

"Yes, Edgar? Just taking off my cloak," a voice called out from the workshop behind us. "This rain won't be letting up any time soon."

"Meet me here before the play," he whispered.

I promised I would. "I have to get back to my sisters now."

Edgar brushed his hair back, a smile warming his face. "Good. I'm glad that . . . Thank you for believing me, Miss Thaumas."

"Annaleigh," I offered, extending a small token of friendship. "Annaleigh."

I hurried down the road, taking the fastest route back to the tavern, puddles be damned.

I breathed a sigh of relief when I opened the door and spotted the Graces at a table, then stopped in my tracks.

They were not alone.

"Annaleigh!" Honor called out.

A young man stood up from their table and turned at her greeting. Cassius. His face broke into a smile as he spotted me. "We meet again."

His cheeks were pink from the cold, and his dark curls sprang out from beneath a knit cap.

"What are you doing here?" I immediately wished I could take the question back. It sounded too accusatory, too brusque. "How is your father?" I tried again, softening. I'd forgotten to ask at the ball.

"The same, I fear. I actually came to Astrea for some supplies. Roots and herbs. There's a healer down the road who says they'll help."

"Is it true if you catch scarlet fever, you bleed out of your eyes? That's why they call it scarlet, right?" Honor asked, leaning across the table in ghoulish glee.

"Honor!" I exclaimed, mortified.

Cassius seemed unfazed. He bent in close to her. "Even worse!" He straightened, catching my frown as they giggled. "I had a bit of lunch here and was on my way out when I saw these lovely ladies struggling to be seated. I thought I might step in and offer my assistance."

"They couldn't see us over the counter," Mercy explained.

"That's very kind of you."

"The pleasure has been all mine. I had no idea how delightful a— What is this I'm drinking?"

"Caramel cider!" Verity chimed in.

"How delightful a caramel cider could be. You look in need of one yourself," he offered, pulling out a coin.

"Oh, can I order it?" Mercy asked, snatching at the money before he agreed. "Please?"

"Me too!" Honor jumped in. "They let you sit in the big stools while you wait."

"And me!" Verity cried, not to be outdone.

They skipped off in utter delight at being allowed to perform such a very grown-up task.

"How are you?" he asked once the girls were out of earshot. "There's a weariness here," he said, gesturing around my eyes.

I brushed aside his concern. "Nothing a good night's sleep won't solve. And you? How is your father, really?"

"Not good." Cassius offered me a half smile. "It will be a blessing when it's over." He bit his lip. "That came out wrong."

I remembered Ava's last few hours, her gasps for air, her cries for release. "No, I understand what you mean. My sister . . ."

He nodded in my silence. "Your younger sisters are thoroughly charming. The little one—Verity?—she looks quite a lot like you."

"They didn't talk your ear off, did they?"

"Not a bit. I enjoyed the company. The past few weeks have been a rather friendless existence."

I murmured something about relating, then paused. It wasn't exactly as though he'd been stuck on Selkirk the entire time. He had gone to Pelage. To the ball. "I hope not *all* of them have been without pleasure."

When he smiled, his eyes danced, flickering shades of deep blue. "Of course not."

"I wasn't sure if I'd get to see you after . . . I hoped we'd run into each other again."

"Did you?" Cassius bit back a pleased smile.

Without the sparkling bit of mask to hide behind, my words felt too bold, too brazen, but I remembered what he'd said at the ball. Regret was the darkest nightmare of all. "I really did."

His smile turned to a full grin. "I'm glad to hear it."

My cheeks burned with pleasure, and I looked away from him, feeling too shy to meet his eyes.

On the wall behind him was a large tapestry of Arcannia. Each section was woven with a different-colored thread.

I pointed to it. "Where's your home?"

He turned to study the map. "A little bit here, a little bit there. I've lived just about everywhere."

"A sailor?" I guessed.

"Something like that."

"Which was your favorite?"

He shifted his chair closer to mine, offering us both a better view of the tapestry. "I liked them all, I suppose." He gestured to a bold yellow swatch in the middle of the kingdom. "That's Lambent. I was there for a bit in my childhood. Have you ever been?" I shook my head. "It's a long, hot desert, with hills of sand as far as the eye can see. The sun beats down, drying everything out."

"How do people live like that? So thoroughly cut off from water?"

"There are oasis springs here and there. And there are great beasts called camels, with giant humps and ungainly legs. They walk like this." He used his fingers to pantomime a four-legged creature walking across the table. "They carry the People of the Light, worshippers of Vaipany, across the sands." He pointed to a mountain range, sewn in stitches jagged and blood red. "When I was eight, we spent a brief time in the Cardanian Mountains."

My breath sucked in. "That's where the Tricksters are, isn't it?"

Cassius nodded. "And the god of unholy bargains, Viscardi."

I winced. Even hearing that name spoken out loud made my head ache. Would the Trickster take it as an invitation to join us? "What was that like?"

"It's a poor community. People there make their living picking the Nyxmist plant. Its flowers are bright red, like cranesbill. It only grows there, very high, near the snow line. The oil is prized by healers and is said to cure nearly any sickness. You can instantly tell who in the village harvests the flowers. Their hands are perpetually stained red by a dye the plant secretes."

"How awful," I murmured, imagining a town full of people with bloodied hands. "Is that what they're called? The People of the Flowers?"

"The People of the Bones," he corrected.

My nose wrinkled. "I don't think that's a place I'd care to visit. Why were you there?"

Cassius laughed. "I wasn't making bargains, if that's what you think!" His voice lowered. "My mother had business to attend to."

I couldn't imagine Mama shepherding us around the kingdom,

actively pursuing her own livelihood, and was instantly intrigued. "What does she d—"

"This was my favorite," he said, cutting me off, and stood up to tap the northernmost section of the map. "Zephyr's domain. Tiny pockets of postulants make their home on rocky outcrops. They decorate their villages with blue streamers and banners and flags. Dozens of windmills spin all day, their spokes making a grand symphony of clatter."

Had he interrupted my question in his excitement, or had he purposefully avoided it? "The People of the Gale," I supplied, studying him.

"Yes, exactly!" A clock hanging over the bar chimed the hour. "Is it really three already?" he asked, squinting. "I'm afraid I must be going. I came over on a neighbor's boat. He swore he'd leave me behind if I was late."

"Cassius, I . . ." As his eyes lit on mine, my thoughts flew from me. I wanted to know more about him, so much more, but as he pulled on his raincoat, my mind was suddenly blank and my mouth empty. "Do you like strudel?"

His eyes twinkled in amusement, and I wanted to cringe. What had gotten into me? I felt bewitched, as if someone else was in control of my body. Someone who wanted nothing more than to run her fingers through Cassius's dark hair. Someone who wanted to pull that head full of curls toward her and finally be kissed. Someone who wanted . . . My cheeks burned as my mind raced with improprieties.

"Well, that depends," he replied, his voice light and teasing. "Are you inviting me out for strudel, Annaleigh?"

"No!" The collar of my dress felt unspeakably tight, and I was certain my cheeks were stained apple red. "I just . . . There's a bakery down the road that's well known for it . . . if you like that kind of thing."

"I love strudel," he confessed. "Cherry is my favorite, and I find it even better when shared in pleasant company. But I really must go today. Could I meet you there tomorrow?"

I opened my mouth, eager to accept, but a scream cut me off. It came from outside, followed by shouts for help.

Cassius leaned over me, peering out the window. For a brief second, I could smell his cologne, warm and amber. As he pulled away, I longed to smell it again.

He and several patrons rushed out of the tavern. There was another scream, and my blood ran cold. It sounded like Camille. Had something happened to one of the triplets? The Graces hopped down from the barstools, looking as if they were going to run into the street as well.

"Stay here," I told them, throwing my cloak over my shoulders. "At the table. I'll be right back."

A group gathered farther down the street outside the clock shop. I let out a sigh of relief as I saw Camille and all three of the triplets on the outer edge. They clung to each other, tears in their eyes.

"What's going on? What happened?" I asked, unable to keep from squeezing their arms, making sure they were all right.

"He's dead," Camille sobbed, trembling hands wrapping around me. "He's really dead."

My heart stopped as I searched the crowd, looking for Fisher. "Where is he?"

She shook her head and folded herself back into Rosalie, brushing away tears.

"Fisher?" I called out, pushing my way through the pressing

crowd. "Fisher?" My voice cracked, turning into a shriek as I shoved my way to the front of the circle.

"Annaleigh, no!" Cassius said, suddenly beside me, pulling me back, away from the rain puddle.

Glancing down, I screamed.

It wasn't rain.

Edgar lay in a growing spread of blood, his body broken and smashed on the cobblestones. His spectacles lay feet away, one of the lenses cracked. Fisher knelt next to him with his ear pressed to Edgar's chest, searching for signs of life. After a long moment, he looked up at the crowd and sadly shook his head.

A woman fainted, falling into a deep swoon and causing a flurried commotion as her companions tried to catch her.

"What happened?"

"He was at the second-story window and just . . . fell," a man near us said, pointing up at the storefront.

Cassius tried shielding me from the chaos, turning me away from the sight of the body, but I squirmed free.

"He jumped?"

The man shrugged. "I don't know."

"I heard his sweetheart died recently," a woman near us mentioned, overhearing our conversation. "It was all too much for the poor man." She made a *tsk* of sadness before returning to her business.

This didn't make any sense. I'd just spoken with him. We had a plan to meet next week. He wanted to find out what happened to Eulalie. To find out who had . . .

Who had killed her.

I looked up to the sharp pitch of the shop's roof and the open window, remembering the creaking floorboard. Someone had been up there with him. Edgar hadn't been alone.

Whoever pushed Eulalie from the cliffs had been with Edgar before he fell. I was certain of it. Breaking free from Cassius, I rushed toward the shop, ignoring his protests. If I didn't get up to the second floor right now, I would miss the killer.

I skirted around where Edgar lay and smashed into Fisher's chest.

"Annaleigh, what are you doing?" he asked, grabbing at my wrists to stop me.

"I need to go in there. To go upstairs. Fisher, you have to help me!"

"Help you what?"

"Find the killer! They're inside!"

"Killer?" he repeated, fumbling to keep hold of me as I writhed from his grasp. "Annaleigh, there's no killer. I saw it happen. He jumped."

"He was pushed!"

"No, he wasn't."

"Let go of me!" I screeched, stomping at his feet.

Fisher's arms surrounded me, holding in my flailing arms. "Calm down, Annaleigh. You're making a scene."

He pulled me against his chest, and I caught sight of my sisters, their eyes wide with horror. Cassius's eyebrows were furrowed with concern. Dozens of onlookers surrounding Edgar's body watched my fit. I let out a shaky breath, feeling myself deflate.

I turned away, unable to stand their gazes upon me. I looked up to meet Fisher's eyes, beseeching. "Fisher, I know you're mad at me, but please? Please come with me and look? I was visiting

Edgar earlier. We heard a floorboard creak upstairs. Someone was there. Someone was listening to us! I have to know who."

"I'm not mad at you, Annaleigh. I—I've been embarrassed about what happened, but not mad. I could never be mad at you."

"Then help me, please? We need to find them before they get away."

He raked his fingers through his hair with a loud sigh. "I'll go look. But I promise, there was no one at the window but Edgar. Stay here."

"Be careful!" I called after him.

Now alone on the steps of the shop, I didn't know what to do. A group of men covered Edgar's body with a sheet and pushed the crowds back onto the sidewalk. I wanted to join my sisters and Cassius, but suddenly I was terrified of getting too close to the body. The white sheet was quickly turning red. I turned away, studying the display of pocket watches in the window as tears sprang to my eyes.

He hadn't jumped. He couldn't have.

Fisher returned moments later, his eyes dark as he shook his head. "I'm sorry, Annaleigh. No one was there."

19

"SOMEONE WAS THERE!" I REPEATED HOURS LATER, nearly shouting in frustration, as Camille sat at her vanity, playing with a new color of blush. She swirled the brush over her cheeks, turning them a creamy shade of peach. "You can't possibly be going dancing tonight."

"Why? Because Edgar killed himself? I never thought of him in life; I should hardly be expected to grieve him in death."

"You were crying this afternoon. I saw you!"

"It was upsetting. It's not as though people hurl to their deaths every time I make a trip to the market."

I took the pot of color from her. "Please don't go. Stay home with me."

She arched her eyebrow. "I will not. And you shouldn't either. Come with us and forget about everything." She smirked, applying a generous swish of color to her lips. "Of course, I suppose you wouldn't want to forget everything about today." She handed me a sparkling necklace. Tonight's theme was the Jewels of Court, and she was wearing the rose-gold dress from the triplets' ball. "Can you fasten that for me? The clasp is so tiny."

"What's that supposed to mean? What shouldn't I forget?"

Her smile was sly and knowing. "I saw you through the tavern windows before . . . Edgar. Alone with that boy."

"The Graces were at the counter, getting cider."

I settled the paste jewels against the hollow of her throat.

"You looked awfully happy to be talking about cider. Who is he, anyway?"

"You're not ready yet?" Ligeia asked, striding in. "We're going to miss the first quadrille!"

"I'm ready," Camille said, standing with a twirl.

"I'm not going."

Ligeia's face fell. "Why not?"

I cast the blush aside. "We saw a man die today. How can you possibly want to go dancing?"

"We didn't really *see* him die. He was already dead. Besides, we finally have new shoes."

I toyed with a little hangnail on my ring finger. A fat drop of blood welled up as I ripped it free. "They're not broken in. You'll get blisters."

Camille handed me a handkerchief. "Then we'll get blisters. Go off to bed, then, spoilsport." She kissed my cheek good night. "You'll feel better in the morning."

I tried one last tactic. "You look as though you could use a good night's sleep as well."

Despite the swipe of color across her cheeks, dark circles remained under her eyes, purple and splotchy against her pale skin.

"I'll do that. Tomorrow."

Camille grabbed her reticule and turned off her sconces, plunging the hall into total darkness, save for my candle's glow.

She and Ligeia slipped down the back stairs, heading to meet Rosalie and Lenore in the garden.

Furtive giggling escaped from Mercy's room. No doubt she, Honor, and Verity were up to some mischief. I listened at the door for a long moment, wondering if I should break up their fun. There was humming and laughter and Mercy counting out beats above it all.

"And one, two, three. One, two, three. One, two, three, turn."

Even they were dancing tonight.

After lighting the candelabras on either side of my bed, I hung up my dinner dress and put on a clean nightgown. It was soft voile, dotted along the neckline and sleeves with bands of embroidered snowdrops.

At my own vanity, I took out a handful of hairpins and combed through my twisted locks. Mama said brushing your hair before bed not only left it radiant but also helped untangle pent-up thoughts from the day, ensuring relaxed and peaceful slumber. I wasn't sure how many strokes it would take to unravel this particular tangle. I feared I'd never get the image of Edgar's broken spectacles from my mind.

The silver brush caught the candlelight, hypnotizing me through the mirror as it swooped over my dark locks. Had I made a mistake, not going with my sisters? I was too alone with my thoughts here. If I'd gone dancing, I'd at least have been too busy to stew.

Someone ran past my door, snapping me from my reverie.

I poked my head out, looking down the dark corridor. A burst of giggles sounded from the back stairs. With a tired sigh, I headed toward them. I'd catch the Graces in whatever game they were playing, send them to bed, then go to sleep myself. It was far too late for such nonsense.

I scurried down the hall, hoping to stop them before they woke the whole house. As I stepped on the first tread, I heard laughter from behind me. I whirled around, holding my candle out, but no one was there. Peering into the darkness, I squinted, but the shadows remained still.

"Verity?" I could always count on her to crack first.

Silence.

"Mercy? Honor? This isn't funny."

Solid thumps, like bare feet running down steps, came from below. How had they doubled back to the stairs without my catching them? Irritation mounting, I raced after them.

Everything seemed in order as I stepped onto the first floor. Potted ferns flanked the archway to the kitchens. No one could go past them without causing their riot of leaves to sway back and forth. They were still. The Graces must have headed toward the front of the house.

As I made my way down the main hallway, checking in the dining room, peeking into the solarium, it occurred to me how dim the main floor was. I couldn't see the telltale glow from the girls' candles. Honor lived in terror of the dark; surely she wouldn't have come down without a light.

I listened for a noise to indicate which way they had gone. It felt as if they also paused, holding their breath, on tiptoe, trying hard not to laugh.

Turning a corner, I smashed into a dark figure. My strangled cry echoed down the corridor.

"Miss Thaumas!" Roland exclaimed, reaching out to steady me.

I jerked from his touch, Edgar's suspicions racing through my mind. "I'm all right," I assured him. "You just surprised me."

Despite the late hour, he still looked impeccably crisp, his uniform carefully pressed and buttoned. Even his cravat was tied with tight precision.

"You're up awfully late," he said, his eyes trained on my own, careful to avoid acknowledging my nightgown. "Is there anything you require? A glass of water? Warm milk? Cook has already gone to bed, but I'm certain I could manage some tea. Some chamomile tea to help you sleep?"

I waved aside his offers. "I was looking for the Graces. Have you seen them?"

"Are they also not asleep?" he asked, peering around my shoulder as if to catch them sneaking up on us.

The taper's flame caught in a draft, causing shadows to dance back and forth across Roland's thin, pointed features. One moment, he was a leering gargoyle; the next, a trusted family confidant.

"They're playing at some game. I was hoping to put them to bed before Papa finds out."

"Should I wake the staff to help?"

I shook my head. "No—no, of course not. I'm sure they're around here somewhere."

Roland's pale eyes dragged back to mine. He was waiting for me to release him, I knew that, but for a moment, it seemed he sensed I had matters other than the Graces on my mind.

"Do you . . . do you remember the night that Eulalie . . ."

He knit his silver brows, guessing at the evening in question. "Very well, my lady."

"Did you see her at all—or see anything unusual about the house?"

Roland's face fell. "Unfortunately not. I . . . I had the evening off for my mother's birthday. Her eightieth, you see. There was a small celebration in Astrea. I left early that afternoon to help with preparations. My brother, Stamish—you know he's the valet for King Alderon—even he was able to attend. It was quite a fete." His mouth twisted. "I blame myself for Eulalie's death. If I hadn't left, if I'd only been here, I might have stopped her."

"Stopped her from what?"

His long fingers flexed at his sides. "I don't believe she was just out for a walk in the moonlight, as your father does. . . . The maids gossip something terrible, you know, and they were convinced she was running away that night. Eloping," he added in so low a whisper, I barely heard it. "I noticed when Eulalie's room was cleaned that a small valise was missing, as were some of her clothes and personal effects." His eyes grew dark. "She was running away, Miss Thaumas, I just know it."

"So her companion . . . pushed her from the cliffs, then?" I asked, careful to avoid clouding his theory with my own knowledge.

Roland cleared his throat, a sudden loud bark down the empty corridor. "Certainly not! It was windy that night . . . too windy to be out on the cliffs with an unwieldy piece of luggage. She should never have been out there in the first place. . . . It's uncharitable to speak ill of the dead, but that watchmaker from Astrea was up to no good. He would have brought shame to this family. Shame to Eulalie. Perhaps it's better he chose to . . ." He trailed off, shaking his head. "Forgive me, Miss Thaumas. I'm speaking out of turn. Do you think we ought to relight the sconces?"

"The sconces?" I repeated.

"To find the little girls more easily."

Apparently, our conversation about Eulalie had ended.

"Oh . . . no. I'm sure they've tired of the game and made their way to bed. Perhaps you ought to do the same?" I offered.

"You're sure there's nothing more I can do for you?"

I shook my head. "You do so much already. Good night, Roland."

"Pleasant dreams, Miss Thaumas."

I turned down another hallway, as though heading for the stairs, but stopped where my candle's light would not be seen.

Despite Edgar's certainty, Roland hadn't been at Highmoor the night of Eulalie's murder. I felt like crying. I was no further along than I'd been the night of her wake, but now I was wholly on my own, with Edgar's death to consider as well. Where was I to go from here?

Wiping my eyes, I pushed off the wall. I needed to go to bed. Everything would seem better after a good night's sleep.

As I passed the gallery, a rustle caught my attention.

Clearly, the Graces hadn't made their way upstairs after all.

I entered the long room. Portraits of distant family members stared down at me from elaborate, heavy frames. No amount of passing years could erase the sharp scent of oil paints and varnishes burning my nose. Small statues, busts of previous dukes on marble plinths, dotted the room.

Coming around a particularly large bust, I stopped in my tracks. "Verity?"

She didn't respond, and I glanced around the room, wondering if Mercy and Honor had planted her there to surprise me.

She sat in the middle of a moonbeam, tracing pictures across the floor with her fingertips.

"Verity?" I repeated, struck cold and suddenly convinced this wasn't my little sister at all. When I finally reached her side, I feared a stranger would be in her place.

A stranger with black tears running down her face.

But it was Verity, all curls and round cheeks.

"Look at my drawing, Annaleigh!" she exclaimed.

I glanced at the floor. There was no paper, no pastels.

"I think you were sleepwalking, dear heart," I murmured gently.

She shook her head, her eyes lucid and bright. "Come here." She patted the floor in front of her.

I knelt down, certain Mercy and Honor were poised to rush out from a dark corner to startle me. When they didn't, I gestured to the checkered tiles between us. "Tell me about your picture."

"It's Edgar," she said, pointing to a blank square as my heart thudded to a stop.

"What?"

"See, here's where he fell . . ." Her finger mimed a pool of blood.

I shook my head. "You didn't see that."

". . . and here are his glasses. . . ."

"You didn't see any of that."

Verity glanced up, surprised. "I didn't need to. Eulalie told me." She placed her warm hand over mine, misjudging the look of horror on my face. "Don't be sad for Edgar, Annaleigh. He's with Eulalie now. They're together."

"Eulalie told you this?" I echoed, my stomach twisting into

painful knots. This was not normal. This was not a phase. Something was terribly, terribly wrong with my little sister.

She nodded, unconcerned, and a memory sparked within me. Something Fisher had said.

She was never one for a short story, was she?

"Verity . . . when Eulalie comes to visit, how do you talk to her? If there was something we wanted to ask her . . . could we?"

"Of course."

"How do you find her? Do you have to wait for her to show up?"

"Do you want to talk with Eulalie?"

I paused. This was utter madness. I shouldn't be encouraging it.

I nodded all the same.

Verity's eyes flitted from mine, staring just past my shoulder. "You can ask her now if you like."

The hairs on the back of my neck prickled. "What do you mean?"

"She's right there. They both are."

I followed her finger, spotting two dark silhouettes in the window before I snapped my neck back, facing Verity. It was a trick of the light, long shadows cast from the plinths around the room. That was not Eulalie.

And then I heard it.

It was a soft rustling, silk skirts raking across the marble tiles, accompanied by the click of a man's dress shoes.

They were heading toward me.

The footsteps stopped behind me, and I suddenly felt them, felt their presence, like a fish trained to sense the movements of its school even before they were made. My chest constricted, pulled too tight to take in a proper breath. Verity smiled up at the visitors, but I couldn't bring myself to turn and do the same. I didn't want to see my sister. Not like that. I leaned forward, resolutely keeping my eyes on the floor.

"She wants to know why you won't look at her," Verity said, her voice soft and distant.

"Eulalie?" I whispered faintly, feeling as though I'd gone mad. I tried to imagine I was in the crypt, sitting before her statue. What would I say then? "I . . . I miss you so much."

"She misses you too."

"Can you tell me about that night, out on the cliff walk? Edgar said he was supposed to meet you—but someone else was there instead?"

From the corner of my vision, I saw Verity slowly nod, her own eyes unspeakably large.

"Who was it? Who murdered you?"

My skin tingled, sensing Eulalie step even closer to me. A foul odor flooded my nostrils, like the funk of a fish market at the end of a hot day, the meat turned and spoiled.

A pair of cold hands grabbed my shoulder, and I sank my teeth into my lower lip, jerked backward. Her fingernails had been painted a cheerful coral, but the ends were scratched ragged, and two nails were missing from the waterlogged flesh. My eyes squeezed shut as a keening whimper escaped me.

"You!" Eulalie screeched, then shoved me forward with such force, I struck my head on the marble tiles.

I blinked away stars, ready to grab Verity and run, but the room was empty.

"Verity!" I called out, then lowered my voice. "Eulalie?"

From the far end of the room came the rustle of skirts again, near the windows. She must have snatched Verity and spirited her behind the drapes. Eulalie had always loved playing hide-and-seek.

I swallowed deep and approached the heavy velvet curtains. My imagination was flooded with a barrage of gruesome images as I anticipated what I was about to find.

Moonlight poured into the room, silvery and so thick I could almost touch it. With shaking hands, I yanked one panel back, then the other, but my sisters were not there.

Movement caught my attention. A butterfly, nearly as large as my hand, clung to a windowpane. It fluttered its wings, rustling up against the glass.

A second butterfly crept out from the folds of the curtains, crawling along the toothy surface. Strange markings like tiny, leering skulls dotted the wings. A third came down. Then a fourth. I backed away from the window, and one landed on my shoulder with surprising heft. It caught in my hair, tangled and twisting. I ran my fingers through the spot, hoping to rescue it, and my hand brushed against something furry.

In disgust, I shook my hair out. The insect landed on the floor with a thud much greater than a bug should make. Leaning in to examine it, I was disgusted to find the biggest moth I'd ever seen. Its wings were tattered and powdery, and it flopped against the tiles, struggling to right itself. Six legs, muscular and writhing, squirmed with rage. Huge antennae crowned the moth's head, just above its bulging black eyes.

"Verity?" I cried again, but there was no response. My little sister was not here, and I was beginning to think she never had been. My head felt loose and disjointed as I struggled to put together what was happening to me.

Another moth sailed in from above, landing next to the first. Backing away, I stepped on one. Feeling the wings crunch beneath my toes, I panicked and bolted from the room before any could come after me.

Daring to look back, I saw a swarm of moths, many hundreds strong, settled on the statues, the paintings, the fireplace mantel—anywhere they wanted. I charged up the stairs to the fourth floor.

"Papa! You have to wake up!" I cried, bursting into his bedroom.

From the noises coming out of the bed—its drapes blessedly closed—it was suddenly painfully obvious that Papa was not sleeping. Morella's cries of ecstasy turned into a strangled howl of frustration.

"Go away, Annaleigh," she commanded through gritted teeth.

"But there's . . ." I trailed off. My chest felt a painful jumble of warring emotions. The terror I'd felt downstairs was momentarily drowned out by the boiling-hot acid of sheer mortification.

Bedsheets untangled with another loud sigh. Papa's head poked out from the curtains, flushed red by exertions I never cared to think about. "What is it, child?"

"I can't find Verity, and there are moths. Hundreds of them. All over the gallery."

There was a long moment of silence. I tried not to imagine what had been going on before I stormed in, but I couldn't erase the sounds from my head. A hand pushed aside the curtains, and Papa pulled a robe off the bedpost, muttering something I couldn't hear. I saw a quick flash of Morella's white body before he drew the curtains shut around her.

"Show me," he ordered, tying a knot in place.

His face was terrifyingly stern as we reached the main floor. I stopped outside the doors of the gallery, too frightened to go in. I couldn't bear to see their furry bodies crawling over everything.

"Annaleigh, explain yourself."

I dared to peek in. The gallery was empty. Papa turned on several of the gas lamps, looking for evidence of the swarm, but there was nothing.

"I don't understand." I shook out the drapes. Perhaps some had hidden away in the folds. "They were here. Everywhere. I stepped on one right there."

I crossed to the fireplace. Had they all flown up the flue and clung to the darkened bricks like bats in a cave? I looked up, certain I would be attacked by large, moldering wings.

It was clean.

Papa stared out the window, limned by moonlight. Waves of tangible fury radiated from him. "This wasn't funny, Annaleigh."

"But, Papa, they really were—"

"I know you older girls are not keen on my relationship with Morella, but she is my wife, and I will not have you interrupting our nights like this again."

My mouth dropped open. Did he really believe this was a mean-spirited prank? "That wasn't what— I didn't even know you were . . ." I stopped, my cheeks burning. No amount of remorse could make me finish that sentence.

"Go to bed, Annaleigh."

"But Verity—"

"Verity is asleep in her room. We'll deal with this when I return from Vasa." I opened my mouth to protest, but he immediately cut me off. "Not another word."

I trudged out of the room when it became clear he wasn't going to listen to me any longer. He crossed to the foyer, taking the long way up to avoid me. My stomach twisted as I watched him go.

What had just happened? First Verity and Eulalie, then the moths. I paused at the foot of the stairs, then turned and went back to the gallery, certain I'd find it crawling with the flying monsters.

It was empty.

I left, rubbing my temple and feeling not altogether there. I'd never been prone to sleepwalking before, but perhaps I'd dreamt the nightmare up.

But it had felt so real.

Elizabeth had spoken of seeing ghastly things before she took her fateful bath. Shadows that weren't there. Omens in tea leaves. She once spent a whole afternoon trapped in her room, too frightened to leave because she'd seen an owl fly by in broad daylight and claimed it was a sign foreshadowing death. Servants whispered she'd gone mad.

When I reached the third floor, I immediately went to Verity's room, convinced it would be empty. But I found her, just as Papa had predicted I would, in bed and fast asleep.

I watched her chest rise and fall with slow regularity. She'd been sleeping for quite some time, not downstairs speaking to our dead sister. I rubbed my eyes, pushing back a horde of unhelpful thoughts.

I was tired. That's all it was. An exhausted mind was apt to play tricks—there were certainly enough stories of sleepy sailors spotting ghost ships or mermaids on the midnight watch.

That's all it was.

I turned away, heading for my room. After a good night's rest, everything would look better.

20

I HEARD THE SCREAMS BEFORE I WOKE UP. BUT THIS time it wasn't my nightmare.

It was Morella.

On the fourth floor, Roland paced outside the bedroom, barred from coming in by some ridiculous notion about where men ought to be during moments of womanly crisis. My sisters surrounded her canopied bed, their faces helpless against the wailing figure in the middle of it.

"Make it stop! Oh, please, Annaleigh, make it stop!"

Morella's nightgown rode up over her bump, twisting around her body like an eel as she thrashed back and forth in pain. She dripped with sweat and was burning to the touch. I joined her on the bed, trying to calm her writhing.

"Where does it hurt?"

She rubbed her burgeoning belly. "It feels as though I will rip apart!"

"*Shhh,*" I soothed, stroking her forehead. "You need to calm down. This panic isn't good for the babies. Rosalie, get a bowl of water and some fresh towels," I ordered, taking control since no one else had. "Lenore, bring some lotion and lavender oil. Verity and Mercy, see if Cook has some chamomile tea. Honor, find a fresh nightgown, will you?"

They nodded and dashed off. Camille leaned against a bedpost, her fingers knotted together. "What should I do?"

I stripped Morella out of the sodden nightdress and handed it to Camille. She carried it away, holding it out as though it contained the plague.

"What happened?"

"The pain woke me. I could feel them kicking, but it turned into something worse. Almost as if they were fighting. And my skin feels so tight, like a drum. They're tearing me in two." She started to sob.

Rosalie returned, carrying a tray. I wiped a towel across Morella's forehead, making soft noises to calm her.

"Something's wrong. Something must be wrong," she howled.

I racked my brain, trying to think what Ava and Octavia would do if they were here now. "It sounds like they're growing faster than you," I guessed. "Has anyone sent for a midwife?"

Someone must have thought to do this . . . but no one replied.

"Hanna!" I cried out. She rushed into the room, her arms full of fresh bed linens. "Have Roland send for the midwife *now*!" It would be at least half a day before a midwife could get here from Astrea.

Hanna raced out of the room, nearly knocking over Lenore as she entered. She passed me the vial of oil.

"Keep a cool towel on the back of her neck," I instructed, handing Lenore the water. I warmed the oil between my hands before spreading it across Morella's stomach. "Lavender will help you relax," I told her. "Breathe it in. Doesn't it remind you of a beautiful spring day?"

"There were flower fields near my house when I was a little girl," Morella whispered, a trace of a smile on her face. "I loved to run through all those petals."

As I massaged the oil in, a sharp kick jabbed at my hand, and she groaned again.

"Are they fighting to the death?" she asked.

"They're probably just squabbling for space. It must be rather cozy in there, don't you think?"

She doubled over, wheezing.

"Shhh, shhh, shhh." I continued massaging. Something long and sleek, perhaps a back or maybe a leg, rippled out under my hand, and I pushed away the idea that it was a swish of something serpentine.

The babies are healthy, the babies are normal, I silently repeated over and over.

Scooping out a generous dollop of lotion, I rubbed it into the tight skin, softening it and relaxing her in the process. Verity opened the door, and Mercy carried in a tea tray.

"We brought some of the ginger scones you like, Morella," Mercy said, sliding the tray onto the nightstand. The soothing scent of chamomile wafted from the little kettle. "We thought maybe the babies were hungry."

"That's very thoughtful of you both," Morella murmured around another sharp movement from the twins. "Thank you."

Once her abdomen was well and truly moisturized, we dressed her in a clean gown and moved her over to the sitting area so Hanna and the triplets could change the bedsheets. Morella nibbled on a scone while watching them work. Honor brushed out her hair with long, comforting strokes.

I noticed tears welled in the corners of her eyes. They were fat and clung to her eyelashes, not like the ones of pain that had raced down her cheeks earlier, eager to be free and spread their misery.

"Morella, what's wrong?"

"You've just been so kind. I never expected that."

I squeezed her hand. "We're family, we take care of each other. We want you feeling as good as you can right now. All of us."

Morella's breath caught in her throat, and she nodded, averting her gaze to the window. "I wish Ortun was here."

"He'll be home tomorrow, I think."

When he'd left for Vasa, we'd all lined up in the foyer to wish him goodbye. He'd walked right by me, his jaw set in a tense clench.

Morella's eyes grew pained. "He feels so far away."

"Even if he was at home, I bet he'd be in the hallway, hiding with Roland," I told her. "He gets rather squeamish about pregnancy things. I remember Mama teasing him he could stare down a forty-foot wave in nothing but a dinghy without a tremble, but a little bout of morning sickness was enough to send him racing for cover."

She smoothed her hair back. "I'm just so tired. Would one of you mind helping me back to bed?"

Rosalie wrapped her arms around Morella as they shuffled back to the canopied bed. Morella crawled into the fresh sheets, pulling the duvet up to her chin.

"I just need to rest," she murmured.

"Do you want us to stay with you while you fall asleep?" Though most of her color was back, her eyes were bright, and I worried there was a fever.

Her eyes fluttered up to the top of the canopy, staring at the great octopus making up the bed frame. Her jaw quivered as she studied it.

"Morella?" I prompted.

"I don't need you all to stay, but . . . there is something I wonder if I could ask you to do?"

I sat beside her, careful not to jostle her stomach. "Anything."

"The Churning Festival is only days away." She pressed her lips together. "There's still so much work to be done. I planned on getting to it once I felt better, but I've just been so tired the last few weeks. I . . . I feel as if it's going to be a disaster. I don't know how to do any of this. Plan the meals, plan the entertainment. I haven't even assigned rooms for the guests yet." She took my hand in hers. "Annaleigh . . . I just don't know what to do."

I heard a low *tsk*ing sound from the door. Camille had returned and was leaning against the frame, listening.

"We'll help, of course. Do you have a list of the guests?"

She nodded. "On my writing desk."

Honor scurried after it and brought the sheets of paper to the bed.

"Cook and I have gone over the dinner for First Night itself, but there are still the other meals to plan. I'm in over my head, I'm afraid. I've never planned anything on this scale." Morella laughed, but it sounded small and sad. "I've never been to anything like this before. I don't know what's expected. I don't want to embarrass Ortun."

"Don't worry a thing about it," I said with more confidence than I felt. "You get some rest now. We'll go downstairs and take care of everything."

Camille immediately turned on her heel and left. One by one, everyone else nodded and offered little words of encouragement before heading out. Verity backtracked to the bed to give Morella a kiss on the cheek. I gathered up the papers and her notes and turned to leave.

Glancing over my shoulder, I smiled, seeing Morella ensconced in the bed, holding her belly and talking to the babies. How terrifying to feel as though you might lose something so precious.

"Annaleigh?" Verity called after me.

Morella looked up, surprised she wasn't alone. She offered me a small smile, bidding me farewell.

After retrieving my robe and running a comb quickly through my hair, I headed down to the Blue Room. There were several familiar names in Morella's notes. Sterland Henricks and Regnard Forth topped the guest list.

They were two of Papa's oldest friends and captains under the Thaumas banner. All three attended the naval academy together as young men. It would be good to see them. They were like uncles to us.

There were a few other captains, whom I knew in name only, and a pair of Papa's clerks from the Vasa offices. I wondered if they would still be welcome after the incident Papa was currently trying to fix.

Running my fingers over the last name on the list, I froze. "Captain Walter Corum."

Cassius's father! He must have sent in his response before getting sick. But perhaps the tinctures Cassius picked up had worked and he'd be ready to travel next week. Cassius might even have to accompany him as caretaker.

I looked up and down the corridor, imagining Cassius walking it. Cassius roaming the grounds of Highmoor. Cassius and I sneaking into the solarium to steal kisses under the cover of an enormous frond...

I pushed the thoughts aside. There was a stack of papers to go through, and we'd need all the time we could get. I could lose myself in fevered daydreams later, once everything was managed.

Turning into the Blue Room, I stopped short. My sisters were scattered throughout the room, as if arranged by a portraitist trying to capture everyone in the very best light.

All of them.

Camille stood by the piano, her hand resting on the lid. Rosalie and Ligeia were on the love seat, with arms cozily linked behind their backs. Lenore stood behind them, her fingers perched on Rosalie's shoulder. Honor posed at the window with an open book in hand, though it was upside down. Mercy and Verity were sprawled out near the fire on a thick rug. They appeared to be deep in a game of jacks, but nothing lay before them.

Everyone looked up as I entered, their heads turning in jerky unison. I blinked at the unnatural movement, and for a terrible second, my other sisters materialized into the scene. Octavia stood in front of Honor, reading the book right side up. Elizabeth sat at the piano, playing a song for Camille to sing. Eulalie was between Verity and Mercy, snatching up a handful of jacks, and Ava was next to Lenore, completing their eerie tableau with her fingertips on Ligeia's shoulder.

"We'll take care of everything, Morella," Camille mimicked, breaking the moment.

Everything returned to normal. Only seven of my sisters were now in the room. I squinted, trying to re-create the monstrous image, but the vision was gone.

"Aren't you the dutiful daughter today? Taking care of your poor, ailing stepmother, stepping in to oversee First Night. You'll be volunteering as the Thaumas masthead before we know it."

I ignored her barbs, joining the triplets in sorting through the notes on the coffee table. "I didn't see you racing in to help."

"Nor will I," she quipped. "She brought this on herself."

"She can't help what the babies are doing."

Camille shrugged. "Such ambitions and all for naught. She dreamt of running this estate, and she can't even handle putting together Churning. I'm not helping her. Let her fail, and Papa will see what a miserable and useless creature he married."

"Camille!" Rosalie exclaimed. "Whether you like her or not, that's hardly a way to speak about our stepmother."

"She's no mother of mine." She stormed out of the parlor. Her pounding footsteps echoed through the hall.

Rosalie blew a strand of hair from her face, glaring at the doorway.

"What set her off?"

"She's not been getting much sleep," Lenore murmured.

I sniffed. "Because of the dancing? Why doesn't she take a night off?"

Lenore picked at her skirt. "She's desperate to find a beau. Last night, she kept going on and on about how you'd already found someone on Astrea and she was going to be a spinster for the rest of her life."

"Oh, Camille." I chewed on the inside of my mouth. Right now there were bigger issues to deal with. I thought of Morella, left alone in that big bed, waiting for Papa's return. I'd never seen her look so small and lost.

I shook my head. "Churning begins next week. We only have six days to make sure everything is prepared for First Night."

Ligeia shrugged. "So?"

"Let's take a break from the dancing—"

"What? No!" Rosalie exploded.

"Just this week, so we can be well rested and focus on making this run as smoothly as possible. You saw how much pain Morella was in. She can't take on such a large project."

"We can do all that and still go dancing," Ligeia protested.

One eyebrow rose up. "Can you really? We all slept past noon today. Again."

Even Lenore looked upset, crossing her arms over her chest. "So?"

"We need our rest. We've all got circles under our eyes and are snapping at each other. It's not the end of the world. Just one week."

Rosalie narrowed her eyes. "And we'll all go dancing after Churning?"

I promised we would.

The triplets exchanged glances.

"Fine," Rosalie said with a huff that didn't leave me wholly convinced she meant it.

"What do you need us to do?" Lenore asked.

"If First Night is planned, that leaves nine more dinners for our guests, assuming they don't spend any nights on Astrea. We'll need to write up menus. Mercy, Honor, you spend so much time in the kitchen with Cook. Can you take this on?"

They nodded eagerly.

"What about me?" Verity asked.

"You can help me with the East Wing. We'll make sure the rooms are ready. There ought to be some winter pansies blooming in the solarium. You could make little posies to greet the families when they arrive."

"I could draw them something too!" she exclaimed.

Remembering the last series of pictures Verity had created, I gave her an encouraging smile but promised nothing.

What else was there? I filtered through memories of Churnings past. "We'll need some sort of entertainment. Perhaps we could organize some rides through the forest? It looks so lovely in the snow. We'll also need to be sure to have boats and crew on hand to ferry the guests back and forth to Astrea for all the activities at the festival."

Every Churning, there was a play showing Pontus mixing the oceans with his great trident. The players created waves using yards and yards of iridescent fabrics. One year, a wave flowed too close to the footlights and caught fire. That was the year Acacia had come to Churning. One of Pontus's daughters, she summoned a waterspout to rain down its fury upon the flames. When the fire was out, the stage was a mess of puddles and soot, but everyone cheered for the goddess's quick thinking.

"Can you think of anything else?" Lenore asked.

I twisted the silver ring on my pointer finger. "Remember

when we were small and Mama held a Churning contest for the best snow castle?"

"Snow castle?" Honor asked, too little to have taken part. "Like a sandcastle?"

"It was in the garden," Lenore said with a laugh. "The castles, the seashells, the decorations, everything had to be made of snow!"

"My hands nearly fell off trying to create that moat," Rosalie reminisced. "Remember all my water kept freezing?"

Ligeia nodded. "And then Greigoff crashed into it and the whole fortress fell apart!"

"Who?" Verity asked.

"Greigoff. He was Mama's wolfhound. His legs were nearly as long as mine, and he was always tripping over those monster paws," Rosalie said, giggling. "I've never seen a clumsier dog."

"What happened to him?"

"He died just before Mercy was born. He was nearly fifteen by then and all gray whiskers and beard."

The room grew somber, tallying another death.

Verity spoke up first. "I would like to build sandcastles in the snow."

"So would we," Ligeia said, speaking on behalf of the triplets.

Mercy and Honor nodded.

I smiled. "Good. Why don't we get breakfast, and then we can start on all the planning afterward?"

"Do you think Morella will be okay?" Honor's voice sounded pinched, and she dug fingernails into the palm of her hand, worrying.

"She just needs to rest. Growing one baby is hard enough, and she's got two."

"I just don't want her to die," she admitted quietly. "I don't want any more of us to die."

"The midwife will be here soon," Lenore reminded her. "I'm sure she'll have something to help with Morella's pain. And the rest of us are fine."

"Eulalie was fine, until she wasn't."

"That was just a fluke. One terrible, horrible, awful fluke."

"And the others?" Her voice rang out sharply.

Lenore shrugged at me, asking for help.

Before I could respond, Verity looked down into her lap, twisting her hands till her fingers turned red. "Maybe I should go away."

I frowned. "Why would you say that?"

When she glanced up, tears shone in her eyes. "I'm the curse. Everything started with me. I killed Mama."

The triplets rushed to her, kneeling at her feet.

"You did no such thing."

"That wasn't your fault, dear heart."

"There is no curse. Don't think that way."

She clasped her hands tighter, her tiny fingernails growing white with pressure. "But if it hadn't been for me, she'd still be here."

"We don't know that," I said, stroking her hair. "Pontus called her back to the sea then. He would have done that no matter what. And even though we were all very sad about Mama, everyone was so happy to meet you. Papa used to pick you up out of your crib and say, 'Look at my happy girl, look at that beautiful smile.' Without you, Verity, we'd just have this awful sadness in our lives. You brought us joy."

Her lips quivered, and she seemed desperate to believe these words. "I'm glad I was born," she finally said. "And I'm glad you're my sisters."

We all came together in a big group hug. I closed my eyes as my arms folded over Verity, praying nothing would happen to any of us again.

21

CHURNING ARRIVED IN A FLURRY OF SNOWFLAKES.

Papa was in the foyer, waiting for the guests to arrive. Morella rested upstairs, mustering the energy to make it through dinner. She longed to be seen as the true and proper hostess, but the twins had other ideas.

The midwife had found nothing wrong with her. Though the twins did feel large, she blamed the fresh sea air and our healthy diet for that. She showed me stretches to help ease the tension in Morella's lower back and said to keep using the oil and lotion. Verity watched, enthralled and eager to help as she could.

Papa looked down our receiving line, counting with a frown. "Where is Camille?"

"Coming, coming." Camille breezed in, slipping into place. Her hair was windswept, and try as she might, she couldn't keep smiling.

I raised my eyebrows at her. Was she coming in from the Grotto just now? She'd remained staunchly true to her threat to not help with Churning activities. She went dancing every night instead and slept in later and later, often not waking until well after three in the afternoon. Papa had been too occupied with business and Morella to notice, but the rest of us had felt her absence keenly.

The door opened, bringing in a shower of snow and our guests. Captain Morganstin, his wife, Rebecca, and their two daughters were first. The Graces instantly took the girls into their mix with promises of dolls and jacks later that afternoon.

Captain Bashemk was next. His wife was in confinement and unable to travel, but he brought along his first mate, Ethan. Rosalie batted her eyes at the younger man, then looked down with a coy smile as the officer's face flushed red.

Sterland and Regnard came in together, swapping stories and greeting Papa with boisterous hugs. Regnard's wife, Amelia, trailed behind them, asking after Morella.

Two young men stepped in from the cold, looking up at Highmoor's grand foyer with open awe. One was short and trim, with hair so blond, it looked nearly white. He nudged his friend in the ribs as he spotted my sisters and me. The other was his total opposite, towering over him, with jet-black hair and a nose so crooked, it must have been broken at least twice in his life. He caught me staring, but rather than smile, he let his eyes wander up and down my body. It felt like a beetle crawling across my skin, and I looked away.

"Jules, Ivor!" Papa exclaimed, greeting his clerks. "Have you met my daughters yet?" He scanned the room for someone who was free to chat, and I ducked into the entryway, making myself look busy overseeing the livery boys unloading trunks. I wanted to be available the moment Captain Corum arrived.

I frowned. The sleighs were empty, the guests apparently all inside. Had I missed seeing him come in? I turned back into the foyer, counting heads.

"Was Captain Corum with you on the boat?" I asked, sidling over to Amelia. Poor Lenore was caught in conversation with the taller clerk. I vowed to rescue her after I met Corum.

Amelia removed her hat, running her fingers over her silvering hair. "Oh! You haven't heard the news, then? He passed away just a few days ago."

"Oh no!" Poor Cassius. Even if he hadn't known his father for very long, losing him still had to sting.

She leaned in with a whisper. "Apparently, it was scarlet fever. Dreadful disease. His son came, though. He should be around here somewhere." She looked around the entryway. "There he is."

I turned and my heart seemed to stop.

"Oh."

It was Cassius. Here at Highmoor, speaking with Papa. When his eyes caught mine, he brightened.

A wave of warmth washed over me. I opened my mouth, ready to form a hostess's greeting, but nothing came out. Papa saw my floundering and brought him over for introductions.

"This is my second eldest—"

"Annaleigh," they finished together.

Papa ran a quick appraising eye over us. "Annaleigh, this is Captain Corum's son, Cassius. He'll be joining us for the week in his father's stead."

"We've met before," I admitted, surprising both Papa and Cassius. "In the marketplace on Selkirk. I'm so sorry to hear about your father's passing."

"Indeed," Papa said, patting him on the shoulder with a

reassuring slap. "Your father was a great man and will be sorely missed."

He turned to the room, clearing his throat. "Ladies and gentlemen, welcome to Highmoor. My family is so pleased you could be with us on this occasion. First Night has always been special to our house. Our valet, Roland, will show you to the East Wing so you may settle in before the feast begins."

As the room stirred into action, Cassius took my elbow, holding me back from the bustle. Away from Papa, he seemed to have relaxed, his voice low and his cadence easy. "When I saw the Thaumas crest on the envelope, I knew I had to come, if only to see you again. I hated leaving you like that in the marketplace last week, but I had to get back to my father." He swallowed once. "For all the good it did. He died just hours after I returned."

"Oh, Cassius, I'm so sorry. I'm glad you were with him at the end."

He looked up, his blue eyes searching mine before spotting someone across the room. "That's the man from the marketplace. The one who discovered the watchmaker's body."

I turned and saw Fisher speaking with Camille. He looked up and caught me watching. Holding my gaze for a long beat, he murmured something in my sister's ear. Camille smirked.

"That's Fisher. He's training as an apprentice at the lighthouse on Hesperus."

Cassius studied him, watching Fisher's hand snake around Camille's shoulder. "Funny way to train, so far from a lighthouse."

I couldn't help my smile, remembering their confrontation at the ball in Pelage. "You sound jealous!"

"Hardly. And do you know why?" I shook my head. "Because

I'm the one whispering in the corner with the prettiest girl in the room."

Then Cassius was off, saying hello to the triplets before following the rest of the party upstairs. As he reached the top step, he turned and caught me staring at him. With a quick wink, he was around the corner and out of sight.

Never one to miss a thing, Rosalie dashed over. "Who was that?" Ligeia and Lenore were not far behind.

"Cassius Corum."

"And he sails for Papa?"

I shook my head. "His father used to."

"Well, he's certainly an upgrade from the clerks Papa invited," Ligeia murmured once the guests had cleared the room. "That little one comes right to my bosom. He spent the whole conversation staring directly into my cleavage."

"Not that there's much there to stare at," Rosalie said, tickling her.

"Better than the other one. Ivor, I think it was?" Lenore added. "He just leered over me like a great gargoyle." She pantomimed a frightening face and hooked claws. "I feared he'd eat me up right then and there."

"But Cassius," Ligeia said. "Cassius certainly has potential."

Rosalie made a face. "Pass. Give me a man with a big, bushy mustache, like that sailor Captain Bashemk brought. Now, he's a catch! I need a man at home on the ocean. One who can handle the curves and swells of the waves." She ran one hand down the curve of her own hip, dipping theatrically, her voice growing husky. "One who can maneuver his ship into any port, however tempestuous."

Ligeia snorted, covering her mouth.

"One with a very large, very thick, very hard . . . mizzenmast."

The triplets burst into a fit of giggles, and I rolled my eyes.

"If Papa hears you talking like that, he's going to take away every one of your romance novels and burn them."

"Don't be crabby, Annaleigh. It's Churning. We're allowed to be a little brazen, aren't we?" said Rosalie. "Besides, you might be fending off a mizzenmast of your own. Cassius may be no sailor, but he's not awful to look at."

"I don't think he's—"

"No, he definitely is interested in you," Ligeia jumped in. "You didn't see it because you were talking with Amelia, but the whole time he was with Papa, he couldn't keep his eyes off you."

"Who's he sitting next to at dinner?"

"Me," Camille said, sidling in. "I assume you're all in a tizzy over Captain Corum's son? I saw the seating chart. Annaleigh placed me next to the captain. You're not going to swap things around now that it's his son instead, are you?"

She arched an eyebrow at me, daring me to say I would, and I found myself longing to give her braid a good yank, like when we were girls. I didn't care how tired she was. She'd done it to herself while leaving all the hard work to us.

"I wouldn't dream of it," I muttered.

"Wonderful. Now that that's settled, I need to start getting ready for dinner. I'll certainly want to look my best." She waltzed up the stairs, humming a little song to herself.

"Don't let her get to you," Lenore said. "She's been upset she didn't help more."

"She didn't help at all."

Lenore tucked a stray piece of hair behind her ear. "And she knows that as first daughter, she should have. She's worried Papa will think badly of her."

Ligeia nodded as we reached the second landing. "Do you want to get ready with us? So you don't have to deal with her?"

"No. I'm not letting her bother me. Besides, I need to make sure the Graces are getting ready too."

"You should wear your green dress tonight," Rosalie said.

"The one from your ball?"

She nodded. "It's just the right shade, and you look like a mermaid in it. What could be more perfect for Churning?"

My mind raced, conjuring up Cassius's face as I glided into the great hall wearing that dress. My chest grew warm, and the flush raced up my cheeks as I pictured his eyes working over me. "You don't think it's too much?"

"Not for First Night," Ligeia said. "Cassius won't even notice whatever Camille comes down in."

I sputtered. "That's not what I—"

"Just put on the dress, Annaleigh," Lenore said, pushing me toward the stairs.

22

"WE, THE PEOPLE OF THE SALT, COME TOGETHER ON this special night," the High Mariner intoned, "to give our thanks to mighty Pontus for his great benevolence, blessing us with a season of bountiful plenty. Our fishermen's nets—filled to bursting. Our winds—strong and sure. And the stars—clear and true. Now he churns the waters, changing the season over to a time of rest, replenishing the sea, taking care of us as he has for thousands of years."

"Pontus, we thank you," we echoed together.

We sat at the long table in the great hall, waiting for the ceremony to end and the seventh course to be served. Papa and Morella were at the head of the table, and my sisters and I were sprinkled among the guests. Unfortunately for me, Ivor sat at my left. I'd caught him sneaking looks down my neckline twice already.

The High Mariner stood behind his own table. Across it lay an assortment of items. I recognized his abalone chalice, filled once again with seawater. A conch rested on its wicked points, showing off its polished pink core. There were urchins, purple and spiny, and great sea stars, long since dead but preserved and buffed till their orange arms glowed.

"We, the People of the Salt, come together on this special night to commemorate the souls of those snatched too soon from us, who now rest in the waves' powerful embrace."

He meant sailors lost in storms or fishing accidents, but as I glanced over at my family, I knew we were all thinking of our missing sisters.

"Dear ones, you are commemorated."

"We, the People of the Salt, come together on this special night," he repeated, bringing home his oration, "to remember who we are. We who make our homes on the Salann Islands are a proud people, ruled over by a proud god. We are born of salt and starlight. Let us now drink to that, to remember where we come from and where—Pontus willing—we shall return."

This was the only part of First Night I hated.

Everyone took up the small snifter nestled inconspicuously among the water goblets and wineglasses. Cassius, across from me but two people down, delayed his response to the High Mariner's invitation. He was clearly not an islander.

I tossed back the thimbleful of salt water and swallowed fast, trying to keep the brackish taste off my tongue. It lingered, tart and biting. I set the snifter back down with a grimace, as did most of the table. Cassius wiped his mouth with a napkin and appeared to spit the water into it. He caught me staring and put a swift finger to his lips, warning me to keep his secret. I nearly forgot to say the last of our lines.

"We remember."

"And now we, the People of the Salt, celebrate!" the High Mariner exclaimed.

Perfectly timed, the doors opened and four butlers entered, hoisting a tray high above their shoulders. A sailfish, almost ten feet long and roasted, was on the silver platter, propped up on its pectorals. The navy dorsal fin fanned wide, showcasing Cook's talents. The silver body gleamed, and for a moment, everyone could imagine this great predator in the wild, flying out of the water with muscular grace.

Cook came out to take a little bow. Once Papa had carved out the first ceremonial fillet, Captain Bashemk pantomimed challenging the fish to a duel, striking its long sword with his butter knife. Wine flowed freely all evening. The women sipped with restraint, but the men were already a little worse for wear, and we still had six courses to go.

Father placed the fillet on Morella's plate with a loving look. Offering her the first piece was a sign he esteemed her above everyone else in the room. Camille's lower lip pushed out, dangerously close to petulance. She turned toward Cassius and muttered something that made him laugh.

Cook carved up the other servings as everyone exclaimed over the fish's beauty. It was a complete extravagance, roasting an entire sailfish for a party of just twenty-four. I knew the remainder of the fish would be served to the staff for their First Night celebration later that evening, but looking at the proud beast, I was sorry he'd been caught. He should have been out in the Salt, not between gleaming vegetables and fruits.

As the High Mariner sat down to eat, the table's conversation picked up again.

"Some of your girls had a birthday ball recently, eh, Ortun?" Regnard asked, swirling his glass of wine with unnecessary panache.

"My triplets," he said. "It was a lovely party. We were sorry you missed it."

"We ran into a squall coming back from Antinopally. Damned storm took us three days off course." He peered down the table. "You're all, what now, fourteen?"

"Sixteen, Uncle Regnard," Rosalie corrected, flashing him a smile.

"Sixteen! And all still at Highmoor?"

His voice held a note of teasing, but a prickle rippled down my spine all the same.

"None of you are spoken for, then?" Jules asked, shooting a quick glance at Camille.

Ivor raised his eyebrows, looking me over again.

Sterland chuckled. "Ortun, you need to marry these beauties off before they run you out of house and home!"

"You've no idea, good sir. No idea at all. The cost that . . . You know, there's a story about that." Papa stood, commanding the attention of the room. "A mystery, actually." His voice was colored by the wine, more relaxed than he'd been in days. "As you know, I have eight beautiful, lovely, talented daughters. And it's true, they do cost quite a bit to keep up with, but it's never bothered me before. Pontus has blessed our family with wealth, and it's a privilege spending it to keep my girls happy and beautiful. However, recent events have given me pause. You see, there's something wrong with my girls' feet."

"Their . . . feet?" the High Mariner asked, looking to each of my sisters in turn.

The guests eyed each other nervously, everyone wanting to peek under the table to see what horrible talons hid under our skirts.

"They go through shoes faster than anyone I've ever known. I bought them new shoes, costly slippers, just before the triplets' birthday. All worn out. I let them go to town to buy new ones—already, those are frayed and unraveling. Every other day, they're begging to go into town for new shoes, and now I hear from my own staff that the triplets have been asking to borrow the maids' extra shoes."

I shot a quick glance at Rosalie. They'd all promised to stop dancing for Churning. She looked into her lap, avoiding my gaze. Even the Graces looked cagey.

"At first, I thought it was to keep up with the latest fashions, acquiring more and more for their collections, but no. The leather is cracked and worn thin, splitting at the seams."

"How odd," Amelia said. "Perhaps something is wrong with the cobbler's goods?"

"That's what I thought, that's what I thought!" Papa cried, taking a great gulp of wine.

Morella reached up to pull him to his seat, but he squirmed from her grasp, eager to continue his tale.

"I arrived home from Vasa just days ago and had to make an immediate trip to Astrea to berate and rail against this poor cobbler for selling my daughters bad shoes. But it wasn't him. The fault, you see, lies with the girls."

The guests shifted toward us. Cassius stared at me, pondering Papa's words. I looked down, a rush of heat flaring across my cheeks. Pressing a fork into my fillet, I pulled the fish apart until it was nothing more than a pile of flakes.

The cold, dead eyes of the sailfish seemed to glare at me too.

"'No other customers have complained,' the cobbler says. Not one. Just my girls. They must be sabotaging them, but I'm at a loss to say how or why. Perhaps you can get it from them."

"Let's see these shoes!" Captain Bashemk exclaimed.

"Yes!" his first mate cheered, emboldened by drink. "Show us the shoes!"

"Ladies?" Papa asked.

We stared at him blankly. This was not how First Night was supposed to go. He swished his arm, indicating we stand up. After a moment of hesitation, we pulled the skirts of our dresses to the side, showing our shoes. I was wearing my second pair of slippers from Astrea. I'd not gone dancing since Edgar died, and the leather was still strong and free of scuffs.

Regnard bent over, examining Lenore's feet. "Ortun, you're right. These shoes are thoroughly worn out. How do you even keep them on your feet, child?"

Lenore froze, terrified to be called out in front of so many people. "Papa won't buy us any others," she admitted, cringing.

"Ortun, surely you're joking," Amelia asked. "It's winter now. You can't have your daughters traipsing around barefoot in the snow."

Papa seemed more amused than angry. "Find out what mischief they're up to and I'll fix that. I'll even buy you a pair, Millie! The prettiest slippers in all of Salann!"

Everyone laughed.

"No, I mean it, I mean it!" he cried gaily. "I'll buy pairs for the whole table if you can figure out what is going on!"

"I don't think I'd do well with shoes as dainty as Miss Annaleigh's," Captain Morganstin said, chuckling, as he leaned over to study mine. "But, Ortun, you've been exaggerating. These shoes look fine to me. There's not a scratch on them."

"That's true, that's true. Annaleigh is the only one who hasn't come around asking for more," Papa agreed, his eyes increasingly glassy. Morella set a glass of water in front of him, but he patently ignored it.

"How curious!" Amelia said. "What are you doing differently, Annaleigh?"

Camille's stare weighed on me, and I raised my shoulders, admitting nothing.

"See? Can't get a word from any of them!" To Morella's relief, Papa sat down, resting his elbows on the table. "It's maddening. I'm almost willing to offer up my estate to find out what's behind all this!"

"Say, now, there's an idea!" Captain Bashemk exclaimed, needling Ethan in the ribs. "Kill two birds with one stone! Whoever solves the mystery wins your blessing to marry one of the girls! And I'm sure we all know who he'd pick!"

He didn't need to tilt his head to his right to indicate his choice, but he did. Camille. Obviously. She was the prettiest and the cleverest. And she was the daughter set to inherit Papa's fortunes. Though the Salann Islands were small, we were mighty, and that could prove to be an enticement too great to ignore.

Papa downed the last of his wine and waved for a refill. Half of it was drunk in one large swallow. He blinked heavily, struggling to put the connections together. Finally, he looked up, smiling. "It's not a bad idea, is it?"

I peeked down toward the triplets. They looked as bemused as I felt. What was going on? Surely Papa couldn't be serious.

"Darling, perhaps we ought to save this idea for another time," Morella suggested lightly. "We're meant to be celebrating

Pontus and First Night, aren't we? I'd hate to offend our esteemed High Mariner...."

The priest waved her off, eager to watch this drama play out.

"We could send a messenger to the other lords of Arcannia," Papa said, still thinking. "They could help spread the word. We'll let anyone in the kingdom who wants to try his hand come and see."

"Anyone at all?" Fisher asked, setting his wineglass on the table with a heavy thunk. He was the only one who knew our secret. "They wouldn't have to be titled?" He waggled his eyebrows at Camille.

Ligeia elbowed him hard in the ribs.

Regnard nodded, his head going up and down with great care. Amelia shot Morella a look of apology. Was there any man at the table who wasn't drunk now? Cassius sat perfectly still, but his eyes bounced around the table, following the discussion with interest.

"Better yet, better yet!" Captain Bashemk said, shouting in excitement. "Five strapping lads sit at this table. Let them have the first crack at it!"

"Six," Sterland corrected from the depths of his wineglass.

"Come now, Henricks, don't you think you're a bit old to be chasing after young ladies?" Captain Bashemk said with a laugh.

Sterland leaned back in his chair, his mouth slack with inebriation, staring down the row of us. I looked away as his eyes met mine. Though he wasn't a true uncle to us, not by blood, it still felt wrong.

"Hardly. In fact, if Highmoor is truly on the line, it's only fitting I try my hand for her first. You owe me that much, Ortun."

Regnard momentarily sobered, glancing between his friends. "Sterland," he warned. "Not tonight."

"I . . . owe you?" Papa bristled, his hand tightening around the stem of his wineglass. "I owe you nothing."

"Here we go again," Regnard muttered.

But Sterland wasn't one to back down from a fight. "If not for you—"

"If not for me, what?" Papa snapped, his voice rising with the color in his cheeks. "If not for me, you'd have nothing. No education, no career. My family created you, and this is how you repay me? Harping on perceived injustices? Living in a delusional past? I've had enough!"

His knuckles turned white, squeezing the glass until it shattered, raining glittering shards. Blood welled up across Papa's face. One of the flying pieces had struck his cheek, slicing deep.

"Ortun!" Morella exclaimed, dipping her napkin into water and trying to wipe the cut.

"Stop meddling with me!" he roared, lashing his arm out to knock hers aside. Heavy plates were swiped off the table and smashed to the floor.

"I . . . I'm sorry," Morella said, sinking into her chair, looking small and so much younger than she was.

"Ortun, calm down," Amelia ordered. "You're drunk."

"And if I am? This is my house. My home! You can all be turned out into the cold if you don't like it." He pointed an unsteady finger at Morella. "Including you." He drained his wineglass in two slugs. "More!" he demanded.

As a footman raced over to oblige, Morella dabbed at her eyes, swallowing back tears. Though it didn't happen often, Papa could fly into dangerous rages after drinking too much. They were like storms on the Kaleic Sea, ruining a perfectly sunny day with gale-force winds and biting rain, only to be over moments later. My heart went out to Morella, but it was better to just stay low and let his anger pass.

After a painfully long moment of tactful silence, Ethan spoke up, his voice cracking with bravado. "If you're serious, my lord, I'd love to try and solve the mystery."

No surprise there. I'd seen him taking in the beauty of Highmoor since his arrival, with eyes so wide, they practically bugged out of his skull.

"As would I," Ivor said, his voice as gravelly as a crocodile. He winked at me, and I turned my head away.

"Splendid!" Papa's voice rang out drunkenly above the guests.

Jules clapped his hands in glee. "When do we start?"

And just like that, Papa's festive mood returned. He patted Morella on the back, whispering to her with apologetic, watery eyes. She dabbed at the cut on his cheek, all apparently forgiven.

"Ah, son, what fortunes could be yours," Captain Bashemk said, wrapping his arm around Ethan to give conspiratorial advice.

Rosalie slammed her goblet down hard enough to silence the room. "Don't we get any say in this?"

Papa's eyes narrowed. "You had your chance and remained silent."

"I don't see why you're upset," Camille snapped. "I'm the one who has to marry whoever wins. Papa, you can't be serious! Tell them all it's a joke."

"Why are you so sure you'll be chosen?" Ligeia interrupted,

fury flashing in her eyes. "I'd imagine someone ingenious enough to solve such a mystery might be interested in any one of us."

As my sisters erupted into bickering, hurling insults and outrage at one another, I leaned back in my chair, wishing the padded seat would swallow me whole. First Night was a disaster. The captains' wives watched the circus play out in horrified silence while their husbands shouted and cheered. In all the madness, Ivor crawled under the table to further examine the shoes. When his hand brushed across my ankle and ran up my calf, I kicked out hard, not caring if it was his chest or face I struck.

Papa sat back in his chair and began to chuckle. His laughter grew louder until his expression appeared entirely deranged. Morella placed a hand on his arm, but he swatted it away, slapping at the table.

Verity caught my eye, confusion written across her face, springing me into action. I hurried to the far end of the table, where the Graces and the Morganstin girls sat. They didn't need to witness such absurdity from so many adults.

"Come on, ladies." I tried keeping my voice even. "We'll have a special treat tonight."

"What is it?" Verity asked, perking up as she slid from the tall chair.

"Sweets in the classroom," I made up, praying Papa and the guests wouldn't think to carry their festivities into that area of the house.

"Oooh!" Honor breathed, her eyes sparkling. "Come on, I'll show you where!" She grabbed one of the girls by the hand, and they all raced out.

Following them, I spotted a butler hurrying down the hall with a decanter of brandy.

"Can you let Cook know the children will be eating dessert in the classroom tonight?"

He grasped at the decanter's neck, looking a bit panicky. "Brandy isn't meant to be served until after dinner, in the library." He bit his lip.

"Did Papa ask for that?" He nodded and I sighed. The last thing the room needed was liquor on top of all that wine. "Why don't you let me take care of it," I said, grabbing the bottle. "Ask Cook if she can ready coffee and madeleines for the guests in the hall. Tell her to make it especially strong."

He hurried back to the kitchen. I stood in the hall for a moment, tapping at the bottle as I pondered my next move.

"That was expertly handled," said a voice from behind me. Cassius stood under an arched window. "You're not going to take that and run, are you?" he asked, indicating the brandy.

I let out a small laugh, but it contained no joy. "No. I was wondering how to keep Papa from noticing its absence."

"It has gotten a little . . . spirited in there."

This time my laugh was real.

"Will Sterland be all right, do you think?"

I nodded. "Something like this always happens whenever he visits Highmoor."

Cassius offered me an easy smile. "It's a wonder he ever dares show up."

Memories of past fights—Sterland's eyes bright with indignant anger, Papa's face red and quivering with rage—surfaced.

"He and Papa have been friends for a very long time, ever

since they were young boys. It's just . . . something they do. Sterland was even engaged to my aunt Evangeline."

"I didn't realize he was married—"

"He's not. Evangeline died before they were wed. He never got over it. Highmoor has always been like a second home to him. . . . I'm sorry for all that nonsense with the contest and the shoes."

He waved aside my concern. "People need ways of entertaining themselves. This isn't the worst thing they could be doing during Churning, or so I've heard."

"Is this your first?"

A roar of laughter burst from the dining room, and Cassius drew me to a bench down the hall, away from the noise. I sat, leaving the bottle between us, but then wished I hadn't. Without it to hold, my hands felt too free and I didn't know what I ought to be doing with them. I studied his, so loose and relaxed against his knees, and placed mine in an approximation. They still felt wrong.

"It is. Camille said the true festivities begin tomorrow?"

"Yes. We'll go over to Astrea in the afternoon. There's a bazaar and contests. Lots of vendors selling food. The pageant begins after nightfall. It's so beautiful. There are puppets that look like jellyfish and great paper lantern whales that float through the theatre. Words can't do it justice."

"And after that?"

"More celebrating. I'm not sure how long Papa will want to stay. . . . It gets a bit out of hand, but it's the first break the fishermen and mariners have had since Westerlies."

"That's the start of the fishing season?"

"When Zephyr wakes Pontus, bringing warm winds to thaw the ice. Pontus uses his trident to shift warm currents back to us. The fish return, and the kelp grows green and thick."

Cassius leaned in, one of his hands bumping against mine. "You know, most people call that spring."

"Not in Salann," I managed to stammer. When his hand returned to his knee, my knuckles felt its absence keenly.

"I've noticed things are done quite differently here." He looked at the architecture above us. When he studied Highmoor, it wasn't with the same open hunger as Ethan. "Camille will inherit all this, isn't that right?"

The last person I wanted to be talking about in a darkened hallway with Cassius was Camille.

Papa's voice rose, booming down the hallway. "Damn this coffee and damn these madeleines! Where's my brandy? I asked for brandy!"

With an inner sigh, I stood up. I didn't want to end our conversation, but I also didn't want the staff being blamed for something I'd done. "Looks like I've stalled long enough."

He stretched his long legs out in front of him. "I'll be back in a minute."

"Haven't you heard enough about shoes for one evening?"

He smiled and I wanted to race back to him. "Why *are* yours the only ones undamaged?"

I arched an eyebrow. "Why? You're not planning on taking Papa up on his challenge, are you?"

He looked back up at the ceiling. "I might. It is an awfully beautiful house."

"Oh."

It was a punch to my stomach. Of course he'd go after Camille. It was foolish to assume otherwise. There was an attraction between us, I knew it, but it couldn't hold a candle to the allure of the Highmoor estate and the Salann title.

"Where's the brandy?" Papa roared. There was a great clatter and crash. The poor butler was probably surrounded by broken saucers dripping in hot liquid.

"I need to go." I snatched the bottle from the bench and hurried down the hall.

23

"THAT DIDN'T GO QUITE AS I ENVISIONED," MORELLA admitted, twisting her fingers in the fullness of her nightgown.

After dinner, Papa and the captains went on a drunken tour of the house, looking for clues to help the lads solve the mystery of the shoes. A butler said they'd fallen asleep in Papa's study, sprawled across any surface remotely comfortable enough to lie upon.

I knelt beside the chaise, setting out the lotion and oil for her nightly massage. "Not at all."

She leaned back on the chaise, thrusting her belly out to a more comfortable angle. I could feel the hard bodies of the twins beneath her tight skin and took care not to prod at them too much. For the moment, they appeared to be asleep.

"I'm sure all will be well in the morning."

Dipping my fingers into the pot of lotion, I concentrated on her calves, wondering how to bring up Papa's outburst without causing her more distress. Her legs were swollen fatter than stuffed sausages, her ankles nearly unidentifiable.

"I don't think Papa was serious about that contest, do you?"

My initial instinct was to write it off as a joke. It was insane to think Papa would give away his entire estate to the one who could tell him we were dancing through our slippers. But he'd changed so much in the last few months. His emotions swung from excessive highs to raging lows, like a bobber caught on waves far too large.

"You know him better than I do, I fear."

Her voice sounded so sad, I raised my eyes to study her face. "Is everything all right, Morella? Between you two, I mean. Papa didn't mean anything he said when . . ."

I wasn't sure what to say to make any of it better. I wished Octavia were here. She'd been so much better at these sorts of things, always ready with the right words.

Morella played with the end of her braid, weaving it through her fingers. "I think so. Everything has been so out of sorts since Eulalie . . . Ortun hasn't exactly been himself. He has outbursts . . . says things he doesn't mean. It's his way of grieving, I suppose. That's all." She smiled and repeated her last sentence quietly, reassuring herself.

"If you ever wanted to talk about it . . ." I picked up the other leg, beginning tender ministrations on her foot.

"You're very kind, Annaleigh. So very different from your sisters."

"They're not—"

"I didn't mean they're not nice. They are—mostly—but you've got a softer heart than any of them. I know we're not particularly close, you and I, and I'm sure there are times you don't even like me . . . but you've stepped up so many times for me . . . the kelp lotion, the massages, planning out this week when it should have been me doing it."

"You needed your rest."

She placed her hand on the top of my head, stroking my hair. For the briefest moment, I remembered Mama doing that, and my heart grew tight. "Thank you."

"I knew it was important to you. I'm sorry tonight was such a disaster."

Morella shook her head. "I imagine it will be one of those stories we laugh about many years from now."

"Many, many years from now."

She closed her eyes, settling further into the pillows as I worked on her foot.

"I wish things could be different," she admitted softly.

"What do you mean?"

"I know I'll probably only ever be a stepmother to you, but I wish . . . You're the kind of person I wish I could be friends with."

I stopped the massage. I'd never considered what a lonely life Morella led. She married Papa and moved so far away from all the friends and family she'd ever had. The only people to keep company with now were her servants or stepdaughters. We were too isolated to go into town every day for teas or dinners, but even if we weren't, who would she visit? Eulalie died so shortly after her arrival, Morella had no time to make friends in Astrea.

"We're friends," I tried, but knew we weren't, not really. Not the kind of friend she obviously yearned for.

She offered me a small, tight smile. "Good."

I rubbed small drops of the lavender oil into her wrists, then her temples, then her feet. Finally, I brought my hands to her nose, cupping them as the midwife had shown me. "Breathe in," I instructed.

She took three long breaths, her eyes soft and sleepy. "I will rest very well tonight. I might even be up for going to Astrea tomorrow with the group."

I was surprised Morella would want to make the trip over. She'd not left the house since the triplets' ball, and I would have thought all the festival's activities would have been too much for her.

"Do you want me to help you over to the bed?"

"No, I think I'll stay here awhile longer. Ortun may still come up."

I arranged the balms back on the tray and carried it to the vanity. It bumped into a little glass bauble, and I scrambled to catch it before it shattered. It was a nearly perfect sphere of glass, with one side filed down so it wouldn't roll. Encased within it, suspended in ageless perfection, was a little red flower, a puff of tiny frilled petals.

I twisted it around. "Pretty."

"My father gave that to me for my fifth birthday. I've always kept it with me wherever I've gone."

It was a wonder the little ornament was still intact. Suseally—Morella's birthplace—was hundreds of miles inland. She had given up all she knew to follow Papa to Salann, trading in fields of flowers and wooded brambles for our unending waves and rocky shores. I couldn't imagine ever moving so far from my sisters, no matter how besotted I might be.

I set the sphere back on the vanity and spotted Morella's wedding bands sitting in a ring dish. Her fingers had grown too swollen to wear them. I tapped my finger against the engagement ring. "How did you know that Papa was the one for you?"

Morella looked uneasy.

"When you first . . . before you were courting. How did you know if he was interested in you?"

She smiled. "Has one of the gentlemen from tonight caught your eye?"

I pushed aside thoughts of Cassius's smile with a shrug. "Maybe. I don't know. I thought . . . I'd hoped he might be interested in me. Romantically, you know. But now I'm not sure at all."

She shifted her legs, patting a spot on the chaise for me to join her. "Tell me all about it."

My face fell. "I'm not really sure how much there is to tell. He . . . he paid me a few compliments, but when Papa announced that contest—"

She shook her head, smirking. "That stupid, stupid contest."

"Camille is far prettier than me, and she'll inherit the estate someday. And I'm just . . . me."

Morella rubbed my hand in hers. "Then he's a fool."

I was strangely pleased she thought well of me. "What was your courtship with Papa like?"

Her smile froze for a moment, and I feared I'd pried too deeply, too fast.

"Well, our courtship was a bit unconventional. He was in Suseally for such a short period of time. It happened very fast."

I nodded, unsure if she'd share any further.

"But . . . there was a man, before all that, who I fancied quite a lot. Our eyes would catch across a crowded room and send such delicious shivers down my spine. I was much younger, not more than a blushing schoolgirl, really, but I knew I wanted him."

I leaned in. "And did he return your feelings?"

She nodded, a red stain creeping into her cheeks even now.

"I probably shouldn't go into those details with my husband's daughter."

I bit the inside of my cheek and decided to be brave. "But if you weren't with your husband's daughter . . . if you were just talking with your friend?"

Her eyes lit up, and she looked happier than I'd seen her in weeks. "If I was talking with my friend, I'd tell her if she wants something, she should go after it with all her heart."

I nodded, matching her smile. "Good. I'll make sure to tell her that. Your friend."

"Oh, Annaleigh," she called out as I was leaving. "There's a book on my nightstand."

I found the novel and offered it to her, but she pushed it back into my hands.

"I finished it already. It was so wonderful, I stayed up for hours reading it. You would enjoy it. Maybe when you're done, we could discuss it? I . . . I really enjoyed talking with my friend tonight."

I wasn't sure how to respond. After all the preparations for Churning, then the unfortunate First Night dinner itself, I was exhausted and wanted nothing more than to curl up in bed and go to sleep.

But her eyes looked so hopeful. She wanted a friend. Needed one badly. And this book was her way of extending an olive branch. I could make it through one chapter, surely.

"I'd like that," I murmured. "I hope you have a good night, Morella." As I crossed the threshold, I turned, certain she'd said something, but her eyes were closed.

24

THEY RELEASED THE WHALES FIRST AS THE CHURNING pageant began.

The floating silk lanterns, shaped as orcas and belugas, lit the stage with a luminous golden glow. Somewhere in the wings, a mangled horn bellowed out notes, sounding eerily similar to a humpback's calls. Actors tied the lanterns' ropes to bits of scenery painted like a coral reef.

Next came puppets of sharks and sailfish, then squid and starfish dyed red and orange and elaborately articulated. Waves of fish, each tied to an individual line, swam out. The puppeteers were true artists, making the fish shift at the same time, just as a real school would. The glittering silver fins reflected the light of the silk balloons above.

A drumbeat sounded, booming so loudly I thought my sternum might shatter. Another and another built toward a raucous climax. I felt the audience shift its attention to the ducal box, stealing quick peeks at our family's reaction as the final sea creature emerged onstage.

Purple tentacles shot out of a small rock, each manipulated by children dressed in black. The head popped free, buoyant with hot air and steam. The Thaumas octopus spread across the stage, performing an elaborate dance timed to the music. At the end, on the final beat, its eyes lit up, piercing and bright.

The audience erupted in applause. As the puppeteers shifted to the next scene in the pageant, I glanced at the Graces. They were enraptured, leaning on the box railing so they wouldn't miss a moment.

"How impressive," whispered Morella, next to me.

Our guests murmured their agreement, and I was pleased to see Papa put his hand on her knee and give it an affectionate squeeze.

It had been a wonderful day. We sailed to Astrea after breakfast and spent the afternoon taking part in the festival's many delights. We watched local fishermen bring silver hooks to Pontus's altar as thanks for a bounteous season. Throughout the week, the hooks would be made into nautical sculptures by artists and displayed in the streets during Churnings to come. At night, they shone in the dark, brushed with glowing algae harvested from the bay.

We stuffed ourselves with treats from street vendors. Spun-sugar sea glass, glazed almond cookies shaped like sand dollars, roasted corn, and bowls of thick clam chowder were offered on every corner, along with more exotic fare: red frog crabs and whelks, jellyfish jerky and sea urchins. The children raced up and down the beach with silk kites painted like stingrays and seahorses. Glass orbs were strung across the town square like humpbacks' bubble nets.

At the end of the pageant, the actor playing Pontus stepped forward and announced there would be a grand fireworks display at midnight, just two hours away.

"May we stay, Papa?" Mercy asked, shifting in her seat. "Oh, please?"

The rest of the girls joined in, begging and beguiling. Their voices rose to a clamor before Papa raised his hands and looked to the other adults for their thoughts. Seeing the round of nods, he smiled at the group. "Fireworks it is!"

"It's getting a bit chilly, don't you think, Ortun?" Regnard asked, slapping him across the back. "What say we while the time away in that tavern I saw just down the road? A round of Tangled Sirens for everyone!"

Tangled Sirens were special drinks, served only at Churning. A mixture of spirits and bitters, they boasted a tangy kick of salted kelp.

"I never could stomach those. You men go off and enjoy yourselves," Amelia suggested. "Come, ladies, isn't there a bakery not far from here?"

The little girls groaned, wanting to be out in the spectacle of Churning for as long as they could.

I caught the look in Morella's eyes. It had been a long day for her, and though she'd not complained, her feet must be aching. "I saw a vendor selling flavored ices near the sculptures in the park. Who wants stuffy cake and tea when we can have shaved ice and cream? My treat!"

With a squeal, the girls darted off down a side street. Lenore and Ligeia ran after them, trying to keep the five in line. Camille followed several paces behind, more interested in the brightly lit shopwindows than the celebration around her. Rosalie winked at Ethan before sauntering away, clearly hoping he'd trail after her.

"We'll join you later," I promised the older women. "Just before the fireworks start."

Morella linked arms with Rebecca as they headed off. I remembered how lonely she'd been the night before, and my heart smiled for her. Maybe she would make friends this week after all.

Papa released a scattering of coins into my hand. "For your ices."

My mouth dropped open. "This would buy shaved ice for years." I tried to give the gold florettes back, but he waved me off. His eyes looked wild in the moonlight.

"Then spend it on something else, my sweet. It's a celebration. Tonight is for extravagance."

The captains and clerks hollered a bawdy cry behind him. Papa swung a brotherly arm around Sterland, heading inside. Cassius was the last one out. At the threshold, he looked over his shoulder.

"What am I about to get into?"

His eyes danced, and I swear he winked at me. I wanted to believe it was more than a trick of the light, but his comment about the contest last night still stung.

"Don't let the Sirens lure you too far. I've heard they're potent."

I turned and hurried after my sisters. The men's shouts echoed through the streets. They weren't the only revelers this night, but they were certainly the loudest.

The park had been transformed into the staging area for an ice sculpture contest. Glittering forms rose up into the night, lit with focused lanterns. Most shone a soft white, but others had colored gels in them, casting brilliant tones on the crystal statues.

I found the girls circled around an icy palace in the center of the park, pointing out startling details. Frosted flags spun in the breeze, hinged with little bits of metal. The brick edges were softly rounded, making the architecture flow with a dreamy swirl.

"Look at the tridents on the bridge!" one of the Morganstin girls said. "Just like in the play!"

"This is Pontus's castle," Mercy explained. "He carries a great trident with him wherever he goes."

"I thought he lived in the ocean. There aren't castles in the ocean."

"He lives in the Brine," I said, stepping in. "It's a part of the Sanctum, where the gods live, which is broken into different kingdoms. Pontus gets the Brine, Vaipany the Corona, Arina the Ardor. . . . Didn't your parents teach you this?"

They shook their heads.

"Ooh, look!" Verity cried, pointing behind us and ending the conversation.

Swaths of blue linen hung from a semicircle of trees. In the middle of the grove, an old woman had a series of curious metal boxes. Pinprick holes were hammered into their sides, and as she inserted lanterns into the boxes, dazzling images were projected onto the cloth strips. With a touch of her finger, the boxes spun. Dolphins leapt in and out of waves, seagulls soared by with wings flapping, and great puffs of air plumed from breaching whales.

A crowd gathered around her, applauding, as she created her illusions. Farther down the street, on the veranda of another tavern, a group of fishermen burst into a lusty sea chantey.

"I love Churning," Rosalie whispered, her shoulder bumping into mine as we shared this special moment.

Her eyes caught sight of something in the mob of people. I followed her gaze. Not something. Someone. Ethan waved at her from the corner, and I saw Jules and Captain Morganstin among the crowd. They must have come to see what the commotion was all about.

"I think I'm just going to . . ." She trailed off, unable to come up with a plausible excuse to leave.

"Yes . . . I think you'd better just," I teased her, pushing her away with a knowing smile.

She slipped through the throng and was across the street before I could blink.

There was a titter of giggles to my left, and I turned to see Camille throwing her head back in laughter at something Fisher said. He must have come over from the pub as well.

Just beyond them, a man stood, his slim form cast in dark silhouette against the colorful lights. Though I couldn't be entirely certain, I felt his eyes fall on me, his gaze a tangible pressure. As I stared, a memory clinked loose in the back of my mind.

"I know him," I whispered.

"Hmm?" Ligeia asked, drawing her attention from the light box show.

"That man over there. I recognize him, but I'm not sure from where."

As if he sensed I was talking about him, he raised his chin, beckoning me over.

"What man? There're men everywhere," Ligeia said, sweeping her eyes over the crowd. "Oh, look at the waves!" she exclaimed, turning back to the performance.

"It's gotten too crowded for me," I said, pressing one of the coins into her hand. "Can you watch the girls? I need to get some fresh air."

She nodded, and I weaved my way through the crowds, fighting through even more onlookers as they joined the show. When I reached the spot in the park where the dark figure had stood, he was gone.

I turned in a circle, trying to spot anyone with his unusually tall carriage. A shadow moved against the trees at the edge of the park, the figure's silver hair catching in the moonlight. He looked back once as if to make certain I was following him.

As he turned, the gas lamps briefly illuminated his jacket, reflecting the golden threads embroidered across the right shoulder.

A three-headed dragon.

It was the man from the first ball, in Pelage.

What was he doing in Astrea?

Curious, I ducked down a narrow alley, and then another, unsure of where I was headed. Every time I thought I was catching up, I caught a glimpse of the dragon man's coat disappearing down another street. In the dark, with the decorations for Churning, I soon became completely turned around. I pushed through the long strands of sea glass beads and ropes of fake pearls that formed a curtain across the alley's exit.

The street I emerged onto looked different from the harbor or the town square.

Darker, dirtier.

Danker too.

The first storefront I saw was bathed in a pink glow, and my stomach turned as I guessed at what merchandise was sold behind such lurid trappings. Several other pink houses lined the street. Some had girls in the windows, waving and posing. Others were awash with tinsel and gaudy paste jewels.

The dragon man was gone, vanished into thin air, and as I glanced about, trying to get my bearings, I wondered why I'd ever followed him in the first place.

As I turned to head back, a pack of young women traipsed out from one of the pink houses, stopping just in front of the alleyway. They were made up as Sirens. Long curls cascaded down bare backs, their goose-bumped skin painted with bronze and silver glitter. Sand dollars and starfish covered their breasts, but just barely, and too few gauzy green ribbons made up their skirts. Some wore heels with impossibly high platforms. Others carried parasols done up as illuminated jellyfish over their shoulders.

"You there!" one called out, and I instantly felt my face flush, horrified she was speaking to me. "Come to drop anchor, sailor?"

A trio of laughter sounded behind me, and the women broke ranks to stare down these potential customers. I ducked back into the alley, my heart pounding in my throat.

"You're a long way from the park, aren't you?" a voice murmured in my ear.

I let out a startled shriek, certain the dragon man had doubled back to surprise me, but instead Cassius stood in the alleyway, his blue eyes shrouded in shadows.

"I could say the same for you. I thought you were with Papa."

He pushed a lock of hair from his eyes, his nose wrinkling even as he smiled. "Tangled Sirens aren't exactly to my taste. Ivor and Jules started in on the mystery of the shoes again, and I got out while I could. I saw you leaving the park in a rush and thought you might need help."

I glanced down the alleyway, but the dragon man was truly gone. "Do you know how to get back to the park? I'm afraid I'm all muddled."

His smile warmed. "Let's find our way together."

We headed down the alley, escaping from the street of pink houses. Coming out onto the next road, Cassius stepped on a sheet of black ice and slipped. He grabbed at me instinctively, and I struggled to hold him up, but we both spun, then crashed to the ground in a tangle of cloaks and limbs.

"Are you all right?"

His voice was tinged with real concern, but I brushed it aside with a laugh. We'd been far more graceful on the dance floor. "I'm fine. Are you hurt?"

"Just my pride."

He helped me back to my feet, and with a teasing smile, I offered my arm to him as a gentlemen might to a lady. He rubbed his bruised hip, then accepted with a snort of laughter.

"Have you enjoyed the day?" I asked as we walked the street, trying to find the quickest route back to the town square. I'd spent most of the time with my sisters. Whenever I snuck a look toward Cassius, he'd been in deep conversation with Regnard or Papa.

"Very much. It's quite different from the festivals I'm used to."

"I never asked what you are . . . Who do you—"

"The People of the Stars," he supplied, amusement written across his face as I struggled with my question. "Versia."

"The Night Queen." I looked up at the sky, the stars dazzling across the inky expanse. "It seems like she's enjoying the festivities as well."

"I think so."

"Where will you go after Churning is over?"

"I still have a bit of work in Selkirk, clearing out the last of my father's papers, settling some of his final business, but I haven't given much thought to what happens after that. Walter left me some money and his house. Perhaps I'll stay there, learn to sail, learn to fish, or—"

"It sounds wonderful," I interrupted, picturing a small house and dock, quiet mornings waking before the sun, readying the nets for the day's work. Real work.

One of Cassius's eyebrows quirked up. "Stinky fish bait and traps?"

"You have the whole world open to you. That's wonderful."

He studied me. "What are your grand dreams, Annaleigh? If you could go anywhere, do anything you wanted, what would it be?"

"There's a lighthouse out to the west. We call her Old Maude. Ever since I was a little girl, I've wanted to live there, to keep her clean and take care of the light. When the apprentice position came up, oh, how I hoped and prayed it would be mine. But Papa sent Fisher instead."

"The whole world is open to you and you want to hop a few islands over?" Though his question was clearly meant to tease me, true curiosity shone in his eyes.

"I'd never want to leave the sea. It's my home."

We turned down another street and heard the murmurs of a crowd. A small stand at the far end of the road sold hot chocolate and tea. Steam rose from the little clapboard stall, a welcome sight as the night grew colder.

"Would you like one?" Cassius asked, rummaging through his pocket for coins.

"Please."

"There's no seaweed or anything like that in this, is there?"

he joked with the man, pointing toward the copper pots. "Just chocolate?"

"Best in all the islands," the vendor boasted with a grin.

"Excellent. We'll take two."

"Thank you," I said, accepting the tin mug.

Cassius took a sip and made a face. "I can still taste salt. Does it go into everything here?" The vendor laughed, and he tried it again. "With the caramel, it's not as bad, but seriously! In every drink!"

We wandered into the park, weaving our way through the ice sculptures until we found a quiet section with an open bench. It was right beside a flotilla of sea turtles, the ice tinted green and lit with blue light.

"Those are my favorites."

"I know," he said, taking another sip of the chocolate.

I studied him. "Do you?" I thought back over every conversation we'd had but couldn't recall mentioning sea turtles before.

His face froze for a split second before breaking into a smile. "Verity told me. Earlier this afternoon—at the kite contest. She's quite enamored of her older sister, you know."

I traced the rim of my cup thoughtfully. He'd been talking to Verity about me! It pleased me more than I cared to admit. "I'm awfully fond of her as well."

"I can see why. She's charming. All your sisters are. But I ought to tell you . . ." He reached out and tapped my thumbnail. It was a strangely intimate touch, drawing me closer to him. "I think I like you best of all."

I couldn't help my heated grin as his words washed over me, pulling me under and heading straight for my heart. "You do? I was certain . . ." I trailed off, not wanting to admit my worries from the night before.

He nodded seriously. "Oh yes. Best of all." He tapped my thumb again, lingering for a moment. "No house or title or lands could ever possibly persuade me otherwise."

Ashamed at being so easily read, I felt my cheeks color. "But last night you said . . ."

"I felt terrible about that! I saw how the others were salivating over Highmoor and wanted to make a joke—not an especially good one—but you scurried off before we could laugh at it."

I looked down at my lap, squirming. "It's just that so many others are after exactly that. It was easy to believe you were as well."

"Oh, Annaleigh, forgive me, please. I hate to think I upset you." He cupped my cheek, his fingertips dancing across my jawline and sending the most delicious flutters down into my chest. "Especially when it's so patently untrue. I meant what I said—best of all."

My mouth was too dry to speak, so I bobbed my head, accepting his apology.

Cassius turned back to the statue, smiling and utterly at ease. "Now, tell me about these turtles of yours."

I sifted through my memories, trying to grab a bright, shining one with all my sisters together, happy and whole.

"It was the summer before Mama passed away. She was pregnant with Verity. We liked to go down to the beach to watch the baby sea turtles hatch and make their way to the sea. That year, one of the nests didn't hatch with the rest. A big frost came in early. Usually hatchlings head straight for water, but the chill must have disoriented them. They went in the wrong direction, fighting their way up the sand dune. No matter how many times we'd turn them around, up the beach they went. My sisters eventually wanted to head home. The wind cut through our dresses. It felt more like November than August.

"Nine of us were playing on the beach that day—Mercy and Honor were too little. They all marched back to the house without a second glance, tired of trying to help creatures who didn't seem to want saving.

"I gathered the hatchlings up in my skirt, like a basket, and carried them home. There were so many of them, and they kept trying to fling themselves free. I filled a bathtub with seawater and put them all in it." My voice was distant, caught in the memories. "The maids were furious I'd brought the little turtles in, but Mama told them to leave me be. She'd come downstairs to watch them flip about in the water, gaining their strength."

Cassius shifted on the bench, angling his body more toward me instead of facing out. "How long did you keep them there?"

"Nearly a week. I fed them seaweed and little fish eggs. When the weather turned warm again, I brought them back to the beach."

"And they all raced for the water?" he guessed.

I'd known I couldn't keep them, they were wild and meant to be in the sea, but how I hoped one or two might linger behind, still needing me. "Every last one. They were so strong." I smiled, remembering how quickly their little fins flipped forward, eager to meet the ocean. "I'd sat with them in the bathtub, kicking and churning the water for hours at a time."

As he laughed, his hand fell on mine. It happened casually, as if it were perfectly natural for our hands to be in such intimate contact. "Why?"

It took everything in my power to drag my eyes from the knot our hands formed. "They needed to learn to swim with the waves."

A flicker of hope burned deep inside me, sparked by the friction of his thumb across my palm, like a bit of flint against a pile of kindling.

"Annaleigh Thaumas, brave hero to sea turtles great and small," he murmured, and then tilted my chin and kissed me.

Though I'd never been kissed before, I'd daydreamt about what it would be like, the meeting of two pairs of lips. Would there be exploding fireworks or a fluttering rush of wings unseen? I was certain Eulalie's romance novels trumped up such contact to turn pages. Surely it was nothing more than the brush of flesh on flesh, like a pat on the back or the shaking of hands.

This was so much better.

His mouth was warm against mine and softer than I'd ever imagined a man's could be. My skin sizzled as his hands cupped my cheeks and he pressed a kiss to my forehead before returning to my mouth. I dared to bring my fingers up to explore his jawline. It was rough with stubble and felt so completely different from me that I ran my fingertips over it, memorizing the lines.

Finally, I pulled away, giddy and breathless.

"Your blushes are so very beautiful." He grinned and kissed my cheek, rubbing his fingers over its rosy glow.

"So are yours," I murmured, then shook my head, my cheeks deepening in color. "That's not what I meant. I'm sorry, I—"

He looked pleased. "Have I flustered you?"

"A little," I admitted. I shifted on the bench, allowing the cool space between us to clear my mind.

"Oh, look, the fireworks are starting," he said, his knee pressed into mine as he looked up.

I followed his gaze, searching the sky, but it remained dark. "Where? I don't see any—"

And then he kissed me again.

25

I SAT UP ABRUPTLY, STARTLED FROM SLEEP. BLINKING groggily, I pushed aside my hair, my bedclothes, and the sleep from my eyes. Memories of last night came floating back to me through a deep fog. The Churning Festival . . . the play and sculptures . . . Cassius kissing me . . .

On the boat ride back, snow had begun to fall, more and more heavily. Cassius and I used the cold as an excuse to sit too near to one another, our knees pressed daringly close. By the time we reached Salten, the sky had whipped into a cold fury, blasting the island with howling mistrals. Before I went to bed, I watched waves crash against the cliffs like battering rams.

A shriek pulled me from my heated thoughts. Shouts followed, then a keening wail, like an animal in torment. What on earth was going on? Wrapping my gray robe around me, I wandered out into the hall. The sounds came from downstairs. I broke into a headlong sprint, recognizing Lenore's wails.

"They're gone," she cried as I entered her room. "They're gone, Annaleigh!"

Camille and Hanna were already there, talking over each

other with such force, I couldn't make sense of it. Lenore flung herself into my arms, her cold, wet cheeks pressing into mine. Her body was a chaotic swirl of flowing hair and layers of ripped nightgown.

"What happened? Where are Ligeia and Rosalie?" I ran my hand over her hair, trying to soothe her. My fingers caught on something snagged in her locks. Working it free, I found a small twig. Red berry buds dotted the little brown branch.

"Were you outside?" I asked, showing her the twig.

"I don't know, I don't know," she howled as Hanna raced off to find Papa. "But they're gone!"

I barely missed being hit by her flailing arms. "Camille, what happened?"

She helped me guide Lenore to her bed. "From what I can make out, she woke up and Rosalie and Ligeia weren't in their beds. She's been raving ever since."

"It's the curse!" Lenore sobbed, muffling her cries in the pillows.

I rubbed her back. "Couldn't they be down at breakfast? Or out on a morning walk? Has anyone checked?"

Camille shook her head. "I don't know. I can't get anything coherent out of her."

"Lenore, you need to calm down." I kept my voice firm but soft, pushing back a quiver of fear at the mention of the curse. I couldn't bury any more sisters.

"They're dead. I know they are!"

"Tell us what happened. Did you see something?"

She shook her head, miserable, and flung back the duvet I'd wrapped around her, eyes feverishly bright. "I'm them. They're me. And they're gone. I just feel it!"

I raised my hands, showing her I meant no harm. "It's okay. We'll find them. Do you know where they might have gone?"

Lenore sat up straight, making eye contact with Camille. "She does." Her voice was dangerously laced with accusation.

Camille's eyes flashed up to the ceiling as a look of rage passed over her. "She's hysterical."

I pushed a lock of hair from Lenore's face, stroking her cheek. "What do you mean by that? Tell me, Lenore." She fell back, sobbing, and I suddenly guessed her meaning. I turned on Camille. "Did you go out dancing last night?"

"What? No! We got back from Astrea so late, and there was the storm. No one would want to go out in that."

Lenore's jaw quivered. "They did!"

My eyes darted back and forth as they hurled volleys at each other.

"I had nothing to do with that."

"You told them where the ball would be!"

Camille's mouth dropped open in surprise. "I didn't."

"I saw you!"

She turned to me. "Annaleigh, I swear I don't know what she's talking about. I went straight to bed last night."

Papa entered the room, bringing all talk of dancing to an end.

"The house is in total chaos. Servants are running around in tears, wailing about the triplets. What is going on?" He spotted Lenore. "Where are your sisters?"

"Rosalie and Ligeia weren't in their beds when Lenore woke up," I interceded, to keep Lenore from relapsing. I pulled him to the side, trying not to recoil—he still smelled like a tavern.

"She thinks they're missing."

Papa groaned, wiping a hand over his brow.

"They've got to be somewhere. I'll start the search. Perhaps you could join us . . . after some coffee? They'll be found soon."

I would make sure of it.

Hours passed as the house was searched without finding a trace of my sisters.

"We've looked through the entire hedge maze, my lady," Jules reported, coming in from the blizzard. Sterland and Fisher were with him. "We found nothing."

As news of my sisters' disappearance spread throughout Highmoor, our guests volunteered to help in the search.

"Where could they be?" Morella asked. She'd holed up in the Blue Room, entertaining the youngest girls and staying warm by a roaring fire. She looked pale and drawn. I worried what the day's stress was doing to her and the babies.

I crossed the maze off the list of places to be searched. "Has anyone tried the crypt?"

"There's at least a foot of snow outside," Sterland said. "We would have seen their tracks."

"The wind could have blown them away. I think we should search it. Tell Papa where I've gone."

Cassius entered the room, snow dusting his shoulders. He'd been out searching the stables. His cheeks were bright red, burned from the cold and the winds. My swell of hope crashed as he shook his head.

"You said you're going out?"

I nodded. "To the family crypt."

"I'll come with you. The storm is picking up. I can't in good conscience let you go out alone. It wouldn't be safe."

All morning long, I'd avoided him, trying not to think about last night, about our kiss. I needed to stay focused. But he was right. If I went out in the storm on my own, there'd be another search party just for me.

"I need my cloak," I said, scurrying up the stairs. "I'll just be a moment."

His footsteps trailed after me. As our eyes met, I felt my jaw tremble.

"How are you?"

His voice was low and warm and threatened to undo the hardened facade I'd tried to maintain all morning. I pushed a tear from my eye, as if it was no more than a speck of dust. "Today is most decidedly not about me."

He bounded up the stairs between us. "You look exhausted. Let me search the crypt."

I kept climbing. "You don't know how to get there."

"Send a servant with me. We'll be there in no time." His fingers brushed the hollow of my back. "Annaleigh . . ."

I stepped onto the landing. "I need to do this, Cassius. I can't stay here looking through the same rooms over and over while everyone else is out searching. I feel like I'm going mad. Let me do this."

"We'll find them," he promised, squeezing my hand. "There must be a room we missed, or perhaps they're playing a prank?"

I shook my head. "They wouldn't do that. They know what we'd think."

Cassius stopped at the portrait just across from my bedroom, studying it. It had been painted before the triplets were born, back when there were just six of us.

"Those are my older sisters."

"Ava, Octavia, Elizabeth, and Eulalie."

I paused. "How did you know their names?"

He froze, his blue eyes dark. For a moment, he looked worried, caught in something. "On the plaque."

I squinted at the little bit of brass under the picture frame. I couldn't make out their names in the dim light. "There were twelve of us originally. But one by one, we've been picked off. The villagers think there's a curse on our house. So you see, Rosalie and Ligeia would never pretend to go missing. It would be too cruel."

"So much loss," he said, his eyes focused on the painting.

I turned away from my sisters' gazes. "Oh."

"What is it?"

I studied the door handle. "I'm certain I left my door shut."

But it was now several inches ajar. I pushed it wide open, hoping to find Ligeia and Rosalie inside. When I spotted a dark form near my bureau, a startled cry burst from my throat.

Ivor looked up in surprise, his face cloudy but panicked.

"What are you doing in here?" I demanded, and felt Cassius at my back, peering in.

Ivor slowly shut the drawer. One of my silk stockings caught in the latch. "Looking for the twins."

"In Annaleigh's dresser?" Cassius's voice was dark with warning. "And they're triplets."

He shrugged. "Thought with everyone busy, I might search for clues."

"Clues?"

"About the shoes."

"My sisters are missing and you're worried about our shoes?" I flew at him, grabbing his arm and pushing him toward the door with all the strength I could muster. It was like trying to move a mountain. "This is my private room. Get out of here!"

Ivor ducked out of my grasp. "I was just trying to help."

"Help yourself, more like it."

"The lady has asked you to leave her room," Cassius reminded him, stretching out his frame.

Ivor glanced back and forth between us, one eyebrow raised. "And just what exactly are you doing in the lady's room?"

Cassius's eyes narrowed. He stared him down, silent and unmoving, until Ivor shuffled off. "There's a trinket in your pocket I'm certain belongs to Miss Thaumas," he called after him. "Leave it."

Without looking back, Ivor dropped one of my hair ribbons to the ground, trampling it as he left. Cassius followed after him to make sure he didn't wander into any of the other rooms.

As I picked up the ribbon, a memory stirred deep within me.

Hair.

I'd pulled a twig from Lenore's hair this morning. A berry twig. I knew where those bushes were. They grew in a thicket in the forest not far from Highmoor. Lenore must have been there. And the triplets never did anything by themselves. . . .

"I think I know where they might be," I said as Cassius returned.

"Where?"

I raced down the stairwell, throwing a scarf around my neck. "Follow me."

26

I TOOK THE QUICKEST ROUTE THROUGH THE GARdens, but we were still half frozen by the time we entered the forest's edge. Along the way, I kept an eye out for any signs my sisters had come this direction, but the howling winds obscured any traces they might have left. I tried to ignore the growing fears in the pit of my stomach as they twisted my hopes with grim pragmatism.

It was too cold.

They'd been gone too long.

There was no way we'd find them alive.

No!

I pictured Rosalie and Ligeia huddled in the thicket, cold and disoriented, but we'd cover them in our cloaks and bring them home. They'd warm up in front of the fire, cheered with cups of hot cider and a good meal, and we would all laugh about this one day.

We raced through the woods as fast as the snow would allow. In some parts, there was hardly a dusting, but our ankles snagged on frozen roots and vines. In others, the drifts came up over my knees. Within the protection of the trees, the wind wasn't as sharp, and our visibility increased tenfold.

Cassius caught himself before tripping on a fox hole. "What would they be doing out here?"

I pushed aside a low-hanging limb, but it swung back, catching my face. My cheeks were too numb to feel the sting. My feet ached, frozen and tingling, as they trudged through the heavy snow.

Up ahead was a flash of red, the first true color we'd seen since stumbling into the tree line. The berry bushes!

They clustered together, forming a thick, circular hedge. There was a break farther along the bushes, opening on a small clearing in the center. In the summer months, we often packed picnics and spent whole afternoons hidden in the verdant thicket.

I spotted footprints in the untouched snow.

My heart soared, so full of hope I thought it might burst. They'd been here! "Rosalie! Ligeia!"

Cassius was ahead of me now, following the prints around the hedge. I wanted to push him out of the way and run faster, but snowbanks pulled at my skirts, keeping me several feet behind.

I counted three sets of tracks. "Look! Do you see? They might still be here!"

He halted abruptly at the opening of the thicket, blocking me. Cassius grabbed at me as I ducked around him. His fingers briefly slipped over mine, but it wasn't enough to stop me.

"Annaleigh, don't!"

I stopped in my tracks. Everything in the world froze except the beating of my heart. It pounded harder and harder, faster and faster, until I felt its tempo in the hollow of my throat, cutting off my breath.

I think I screamed but I heard nothing, just the sharp whine of a silence grown too strong.

I wanted to go to them, but the only way I could move was down as my knees collapsed from under me and I fell into the snow.

I don't remember how I reached them—I must have crawled—but suddenly I was there, with my sisters, my hands feeling for a pulse in their frozen throats, their pale blue wrists. I pushed my ear to silent chests, desperate to hear a heartbeat, but there was none.

"Rosalie?" My voice constricted into a sob as I cupped her cheek. Tears streamed down my face. She was cold. She was so cold. They'd been out here far too long. "Ligeia? Ligeia, Rosalie, please wake up," I begged the cold shells of my sisters before throwing my arms around them and howling.

They lay in the center of the thicket on their backs, their frozen eyes looking up at the sky. If you could see past the icicles on their lashes, the frost beneath their nostrils, and the blue of their lips, they could have been watching clouds go by, pointing out funny shapes they saw.

Cassius was at my back, trying to pull me off the bodies. No. Not bodies. Rosalie. Ligeia. My beautiful, carefree sisters. They weren't bodies. They couldn't be dead. They couldn't be. . . .

I allowed his arms to enfold me as he tried to absorb my grief. Sobs ripped from my chest as if they would splinter my sternum in two, but he held me tight, pressing kisses in my hair, stroking my back, keeping me together and whole.

When I turned back to my sisters, I noticed their hands were clasped together, and I recalled the story Mama loved to tell about the day the triplets were born. Having spent so many months crammed and squished tightly together, none of them could bear to venture out into the great unknown world on their own, so they formed a chain, holding on to each other's hands, their bond broken only as the midwife pulled them free. First Rosalie, then Ligeia, then Lenore.

Ligeia had reached her free arm out into the snow, searching for the hand of her sister, looking for Lenore, desperate to leave the world as they had entered it. Together.

Tears filled my eyes, blinding me, and I knew no more.

27

"WE, THE PEOPLE OF THE SALT, COMMIT THESE BODIES back to the sea."

The High Mariner's voice held a trace of sadness I had not detected in my other sisters' burials. He nodded to Sterland, Regnard, Fisher, and Cassius.

Our makeshift pallbearers.

The storm still raged outside, cutting off access to the mainland and any relatives willing to brave this further confirmation of the Thaumas curse. Most of the guests had wanted to leave Highmoor after my sisters were found. All but Papa's oldest friends and Cassius had left for Astrea, intending to wait out the storm as far from our grief as they could get.

The men slid the coffin into the tomb, trying not to grunt with their efforts.

Coffin. Singular.

The crypt was only big enough to hold one box at a time. Prior Thaumases apparently never died in pairs. I didn't want to know what had been done to make both Rosalie and Ligeia fit into one coffin, but it did make me feel better somehow that they were in there together.

"We are born of the Salt, we live by the Salt, and to the Salt we return," the High Mariner continued.

"To the Salt," we repeated listlessly.

He poured the goblet of salt water onto the box, doused the candles, and it was over.

There was no speech from Papa this time. No wake. This was not a time to celebrate their lives. Mourning settled back upon us like a second skin.

It took three carriages to return everyone to Highmoor. Papa, Sterland, Regnard, and the High Mariner were in the lead. I sat in one with Verity, Mercy, and Fisher. Camille, Honor, and Cassius followed behind. Morella had stayed at home, unable to be out in such cold, and Lenore . . .

Lenore.

She'd taken to her bed since Cassius and I returned to Highmoor with the sad news. I couldn't remember much of the trip back. I'd never swooned before. It was nothing like what I'd read in those ridiculous romance novels the triplets swapped back and forth.

Had swapped.

When Lenore heard the news, she nodded once, our words affirming what she already knew, and left the room with an eerie grace. Hanna hurried after her, certain she would harm herself.

But there was no violence. There were no tears, no screams or moans or wailing. It was as if the spark of life animating Lenore followed after her sisters, leaving behind an empty shell. She woke and slept and ate and bathed, but she wasn't really there. Even when I curled up next to her at night—I couldn't stand leaving her alone, knowing the pain I suffered was magnified ten thousand times for her—she said nothing. I almost wished for the frantic, wild state she'd been in before. This detached, silent grief was too terrible to bear witness to.

"You saw them, didn't you?" Verity asked, bringing me back to the jostling carriage ride. Even with the windows closed and covered, our breath steamed in the air, and we all huddled together under thick blankets and furs.

I nodded.

"What killed them? Papa won't say. Roland told me it was a bear."

"There are no bears on the island," Fisher reminded her.

"It wasn't a bear," I said. My voice felt rusty, corroded from tears.

"Then what was it? He said they were ripped to shreds. There was blood everywhere."

"Roland is going to find himself without a job. He should never have said such things to you. They're not even true. When we . . . found them . . . they were just in the thicket, on their backs."

"Did someone poison them?" Mercy asked.

"Of course not!"

"Then how?"

I shrugged. "It looked like they wandered out into the storm and just got too cold. It was very peaceful. And they were together. I don't think they were scared or sad."

"Then why didn't they come back?"

I wondered the same thing myself. Lenore had made it through the storm. When I pressed her for details, trying to find out what had happened that night, she turned to me with her strange and empty stare and simply walked away.

"I don't know," I admitted. "There're lots of things I just don't know."

"The curse," Verity said, her voice soft and small.

"There is no curse. Just bad luck."

"Couldn't bad luck be a curse?" Mercy asked.

"No. It's just coincidence."

"The curse could make itself look like coincidence."

"There is no curse!" I shouted, much louder than I meant to. The girls jumped in surprise. It wasn't nice to have startled them, but the carriage was blissfully silent for the rest of the ride.

When we reached Highmoor, Mercy and Verity hopped out of the carriage, anxious to get away from me, but Fisher remained behind, his eyebrows furrowed into one straight line.

"What?" I prompted when it was clear he had something on the tip of his tongue. He shook his head, reaching for the door. I grabbed his hand, stopping him. "Fisher, what is it?"

"Cassius was with you when you found Rosalie and Ligeia?"

"He was."

His brown eyes flickered over mine for a moment before returning to the window.

"It's nothing."

"It's obviously something."

His breath billowed around him in the cold air. "It's just . . . I went through those woods myself. During the search . . . I know my memory of that day is a blur, but I feel like I'd have seen the girls when I went past the berry bushes."

"What are you getting at?"

He rubbed his forehead as if his fingers could erase the dark thoughts piling up. When his eyes met mine, they were as sharp as tacks. "I'm saying they weren't there. I'm saying someone put them there later on."

"Put them there?" I repeated. A bit of cold sparked in my heart, running through my veins like icy water, freezing me in place. "What do you mean? You think . . . you think they were murdered?"

"Don't you? You told me someone killed Eulalie. You shouted at me and all of Astrea that Edgar was pushed. Don't you suspect foul play here?"

I frowned, horrified. "No . . . Eulalie . . . that was someone else. Someone who was jealous of Edgar and . . . But Rosalie and Ligeia . . . they'd gone dancing. They were just caught in the storm. . . ."

"Were they?" Fisher asked, his voice brusque but not unkind. "You said you saw three sets of tracks in the snow. . . ."

"That was Lenore," I said readily before realizing how feeble it sounded.

"Why would only Lenore make it back?" Fisher leaned in close. "You know she wouldn't have left them."

"But the berry branch in her hair—"

"Could have been planted later."

I imagined a great, hulking shadow stealing into my sister's room as she slept, leaving behind a single twig, and shuddered.

"You think the third set of footprints were from the killer? Eulalie's killer?"

He nodded.

My mind spun, trying to remember all the reasons I'd thought

Eulalie's murderer had been an unrequited love. If it hadn't, if my theory had been wrong . . .

"If Rosalie and Ligeia really were murdered . . . that means none of us are safe," I whispered.

Glancing out the window, I saw Verity and Mercy patiently listening to Papa talk with the High Mariner, and my stomach plummeted. Someone could be after them. Someone who . . .

The final carriage pulled into the courtyard. Cassius stepped down, offering his hand to assist Camille and Honor. He gave our coach a lingering look before escorting them inside.

"How much do we really even know about him?" Fisher asked unhappily. "I mean, your father didn't even know Corum had a son until he showed up. Doesn't that strike you as odd?"

My head hurt, a sudden migraine brought on by the icy chill and the accusations swirling in the air. "It's a little suspicious, I admit. But it doesn't mean he's a killer."

"True, but . . ."

I held up my hand, stopping him. "I have to ask this, Fisher. . . . You're not saying any of this because . . . because I chose him over you?"

His mouth dropped open. "Of course not! How can you even think I would . . ." He put his hand on the door of the carriage, ready to throw it open and leave me.

"Wait! I'm just saying . . ." I blew out a long breath, shaking my head. "I don't know what I'm saying. I'm sorry. I haven't been sleeping well, and I . . . I'll think it over, all right?"

Fisher's eyes burned into mine.

"What? Right now?"

He shrugged. "Do you have something else more pressing?"

Sighing, I tried to remember that day. "You and Sterland were in the maze with Regnard and Ethan, weren't you?"

"For most of the morning."

I counted them off on my fingers. Ivor had been upstairs, searching for clues about our worn-out slippers. Another tick.

"Jules was in the stables with Cassius, I think," I said. Even as I said it, my mind flashed to Cassius coming in alone. His cheeks had been bright red, as though he'd been out in the cold for quite some time.

Why?

The stables weren't a far walk from the house, and they were heated with banks of coals for the horses.

"You're certain you went by the berry bushes?"

The hollow of my throat tightened. I felt as though I was standing on the edge of a cliff, with pebbles and gravel shifting under my feet. I knew I was about to fall, but I couldn't stop and save myself.

Fisher nodded. "The thicket was empty. No one was there."

I stared out the window but couldn't see anything except Cassius's red cheeks.

The glass panes fogged over with condensation from our breath as Fisher waited in silence, letting me process his words.

"Come on, let's get you inside," he said finally, pushing open the door and helping me out.

I stood in the courtyard in a dazed fog. I didn't even flinch as the driver cracked his whip, startling the horses into action. Though I ran my hands up and down my arms for warmth, it didn't help. I couldn't feel anything. I'd gone completely numb.

"Someone on this island killed my sisters."

Fisher's face was lined with sadness as he took my elbow, guiding me inside.

Just before ducking beneath the portico, I looked up and caught sight of a figure, perfectly framed within one of the Blue Room's windows. Cassius stood looking down at us, lines of worry across his brow.

28

THE ROOM WAS HOT.

I lay next to Lenore, unable to sleep. Sheets stuck to my legs, twisting and pulling. I tried to flatten them with my foot, but it only tangled them more.

How much do we really even know about him?

Fisher's voice welled up, repeating the question over and over again until each word ceased to have meaning, leaving only a jumbled echo of consonants ringing in my mind.

It didn't make any sense.

It couldn't.

But his cheeks had been so red. . . .

I bunched the pillow up beneath me, trying to get more comfortable, but it only served to further agitate me. I slammed my fist into the downy softness, wishing I could pummel my thoughts into such submission.

"He wasn't even in Salann when Eulalie fell," I reminded myself.

You mean you only met him after she'd died. . . .

I shook my head, longing to silence the little voice. Cassius had no motive to kill Rosalie or Ligeia, and he'd been with me when Edgar died. It couldn't be him.

But Eulalie . . .

I took a sharp breath, remembering the oil painting in the hall the morning we'd gone to the berry bushes.

He'd known Eulalie's name.

He'd known all my sisters' names.

There was no way he'd been able to read the small, smudged plaque beneath the portrait. So how, then?

With a hiss of frustration, I flipped over. Moonlight cast the room into stark highlights and shadows. Catching sight of the two empty beds, I turned away, coming face to face with Lenore.

Her eyes were open, staring at me. It was the first time we'd made direct eye contact since I'd returned from the thicket.

"You're awake," I said needlessly. "I'm sorry, I couldn't sleep. Did I wake you?"

Predictably, she didn't respond.

"Is it always so hot in here?" Silence. "Perhaps the fire was built too high." I sat up, struggling to free myself from the bedsheets. "Can I get you anything? You didn't come down for dinner. What about tea? Would you like tea?"

I was used to one-sided conversations in the mausoleum with Mama but found it unnerving to carry one on when there was a living, breathing person next to me, never answering.

She rolled over and studied the canopy. Minutes passed.

Finally, I swung my legs over the side of the bed. My nightgown clung to me, clammy and suffocating. "I'm going to take a bath to cool off. I'll bring up some tea after, if you're still awake?"

I didn't wait for her to not respond.

It would have been easier to use my own tub on the third floor, but the pipes were loud and I didn't want to wake the Graces. Lenore was the only one who would hear me down here.

As the bathtub filled, I stripped out of the sodden nightdress, leaving it in a pile near the sinks. It was well after midnight—too late to wash my hair and have any hope of its drying before sunrise—so I twisted up my braid, pinning it off my shoulders.

The bathroom, all marble tiles and porcelain, held a sharp chill at odds with Lenore's room. I stepped into the bathtub, appreciating the warmth of the water. This tub was so much bigger than ours, I could float on my back without touching the sides.

I closed my eyes, listening to the last drops of water trickle from the spout and echo in the arch overhead.

Drip. Drop.

Drip. Drip. Drop.

It fell with a hypnotic pitch, lulling me toward tranquility. For the first time that day, my muscles felt as though they could truly relax, my mind felt empty and at peace.

How much do we really even know about him?

Eyes flashing open, I jerked back with a curse of surprise. Lenore stood beside the tub, peering at me in glassy-eyed silence.

Water splashed over the sides and onto her, but she didn't acknowledge it, only continued to stare at me with a curious blank expression. Her face was shrouded in shadows, long and drawn, and her hair hung in obscuring strands, having come undone from the braid I plaited for her that evening.

"Did you change your nightgown?" I asked, studying the unfamiliar lace trim. "What's the matter? Did you want tea? I'll bring it to you when I'm out," I promised, sinking into the water, angling to cover up as much of myself as I could. I'd never felt the need for modesty around my sisters—we spent half our lives changing in front of each other—but something in her eyes made me long for a bath towel to hide behind.

She blinked once, then slowly turned around and stumbled toward the doorway, moving as though her legs had fallen asleep.

"Lenore!" I called after her.

When she didn't return, I pushed myself from the steaming water and toweled off. Wrapping my dressing robe around me, I hurried after her.

Lenore was already at the landing of the front staircase.

"What are you doing? I'll bring you the tea. You should be in bed."

She turned back to me but then started down the steps, still moving with an awkward gait. With a sigh, I pulled the robe more securely around me and followed her.

Reaching the first floor, I could only guess at where she'd gone. I tried the kitchen, but it was empty, as was the larder.

"Lenore?"

Returning to the main hallway, I caught a flash of a white dress and red hair crossing into the library. I hurried to catch up, but the door across the room was already closing as I entered.

"Lenore, wait for me!"

Down the corridor, a door clicked shut. It sounded like the glass door of the solarium. What could she possibly be doing in there at this hour?

I stepped into the thick and humid air. When we were little girls, we loved to while away winter afternoons in the solarium.

Sitting in the midst of a jungle with snow swirling outside the tinted glass windows felt magical.

"Lenore?" I called out again, taking a step forward. "Where are you?"

There was no answer, but a fern frond swayed back and forth. I closed my eyes and listened carefully. The trickle of the indoor pond couldn't quite obscure the rustle of long skirts dragging on the stone pavers.

Turning, I followed. The gardeners were given the first month of winter off, and the palms grew wild in their absence, spreading out across the paths with no regard for those who needed to walk by. I shifted a particularly large leaf out of the way but nearly tripped on something in the middle of the path.

It was Verity's sketchbook.

I'd not seen it since that day in Elizabeth's bedroom. What was it doing in the solarium? Had Lenore somehow brought it with her?

The paper cover flipped open as if caught in a breeze, revealing the drawing of Eulalie ripping the bedclothes from Verity while she slept.

As I bent over to retrieve the morbid book, the pages turned again, though I felt no draft. Images of my sisters, horribly twisted and decayed, flashed before me in rapid succession. Sketches of Eulalie, Ava, Octavia, Elizabeth, and even Rosalie and Ligeia flipped over and over, turned by unseen hands. The book came to an abrupt stop at the final drawing.

It was me.

I lay in the middle of a grand ballroom, with crowds of partygoers leering behind masks. My satin skirts spread around me like a puddle, revealing the unnatural angles of my splayed ankles. Every one of my joints faced a wrong direction, like a puppet with severed strings.

My head was tipped back, and I stared directly off the page with dead eyes. My mouth hung open, soft and slack. One hand reached out, curved as if beckoning the viewer in.

Swallowing a cry of horror, I slammed the horrid book shut, kicking it away from me.

Why would Verity draw such a thing?

Or had she?

"Lenore?" I called out, my voice creaking as my throat closed in fear.

My drawing looked different from the others, its style more subtle and refined. Had Lenore drawn it? She'd been silent ever since our sisters were found. We'd all assumed it was her way of grieving, but what if we were wrong? What if she'd snapped?

I glanced around at the palms surrounding me. Distracted by the book, I now had no idea where she was. She could be anywhere in the solarium, watching me, stalking me with those haunted eyes.

A chill raced down my neck, and I bolted down the path, zigzagging through the plants to avoid being an easy target. Rounding the bend, I stopped short, seeing her silhouetted in moonlight by the window. Her hand pressed against the glass, as if trying to grab at something just out of her reach. She looked back at me, then headed to the left.

I peered out to see what she'd been looking at. The West Wing was clearly visible from this vantage, jutting out across the front lawn. It was dark, save for the light coming from one window on the second floor.

Lenore's room.

My breath caught in my throat, nearly choking me, as I spotted a dark shape looking out from the window.

It was Lenore.

I froze, the hairs on my arms rising. The palms shifted again, and the rustle of a skirt that was not Lenore's approached me. Mouth dry with dread, I turned and saw not Lenore but Rosalie and Ligeia, standing side by side, hands clasped together, with matching blue lips and frost in their hair. Their eyes were like milky marbles.

"Rosalie?" I dared to ask. She swayed back and forth, giving no indication she heard me. "Ligeia?"

Rosalie extended her free arm, pointing a finger at me. No, not me. At something just past me, over my shoulder. Slowly, as if pulled by an unseen string, their heads turned toward the right. Their bodies followed, crossing down the path, drawn by something I couldn't see or hear.

I turned to see if Lenore had spotted her sisters, but her window was now empty and dark. Was she on her way down here? My heart jumped as I put it together.

They were on their way to *her*.

I broke into a run, pushing aside palm fronds, my bare feet slipping against the slick stones. I fell once, bashing my knee against a statue. Blood ran down my leg, trickling between my toes, but I didn't care. The only thing that mattered was getting to Lenore before my sisters did.

Every time I seemed to gain ground, they sped up, their movements a jerky blur, a vibrating haze painful to watch. The air buzzed as they shivered, and my eardrums felt as if they might burst.

My sisters reached the door. One moment, they were in the solarium with me, and the next, they were on the other side of the glass. I shook my head, certain it was a trick of the light, but Rosalie put her hand up to the pane of glass, pushing the door shut. It caught with a loud click.

I tried the handle, but they'd locked me in. I beat on the windows with my fists. When they grew too tender, I used my palms, then my feet, trying to shatter the glass.

My sisters watched me with a flat curiosity. Ligeia tilted her head to study the streak of blood across the glass after my knuckles split open. She pressed her fingers across the scarlet smudge.

"Let me out, please," I begged. "You can't leave me in here!"

She tapped at the spot once, then clasped Rosalie again. Her free hand reached out reflexively for Lenore, but it swung free, missing its mark. She looked down at the air beside her, clearly perturbed her hand remained empty.

With a nod from Rosalie, they were gone, buzzing down the hallway again with that awful vibrating movement. It was a relief to see their nightmarish visages go, but then I remembered Lenore and began banging on the doors again, crying out for help. I didn't care if I woke the entire manor and everyone thought me mad. My sisters' ghosts had to be stopped.

A series of soft clicks on the other side of the door woke me.

I lay crumpled against the glass panes, completely spent. My hands were raw and bloody, and I'd gone hoarse from screaming. After my sisters had blurred away, my eyes hadn't seemed to work right, couldn't focus on anything. I'd let them flutter shut, intending to rest them for just a moment, maybe two.

Suddenly the door opened and I fell, my head striking the wooden floor of the hallway with a painful crack. Gazing up, nearly cross-eyed, I saw the dark silhouette of Cassius peering over me with a candle, his face masked in concern.

"Annaleigh, what are you doing down here? You're injured," he said, taking my hands in his.

"Get away from me!" I jerked from his touch, tumbling down the steps into the solarium. My head spun as the room tilted sharply to the right, blurring to a fuzzy haze before sharpening with too much clarity, too many colors. My stomach lurched, fighting with the room's off-kilter equilibrium. I grabbed at a potted palm to keep from turning upside down with it.

He straightened. "I didn't mean to frighten you. Are you all right? I heard screaming."

"Just stay back!"

I brushed bits of dirt and leaves from me, suppressing a whimper. Each sweep of my swollen hands was agonizing, but I couldn't let him know I was in pain.

Seeing my sisters' ghosts had convinced me Fisher's theory was true. They had been murdered and had come back, haunting us until their killer was found. And though it broke my heart to think it, Cassius was the most likely suspect.

His every move now seemed deeply calculated to me. A sly hardness glinted behind his eyes, appraising the situation with care, taking in every possible detail.

My vision rushed in and out of focus again, and I briefly entertained the thought of a concussion before realizing Cassius was using my distraction to slowly cross into the solarium.

"Annaleigh, what happened? Your hands look awful."

"I told you to stay away from me!"

He paused on the final stair, and I tripped over the hem of my robe, stumbling into the foliage. If Cassius truly had killed my sisters, I could only assume he would come after me as well.

Awful visions crowded my mind. Verity discovering my body floating facedown in the pond. Camille tumbling over my half-hidden ankle as they searched the house. Lenore waking up to see my corpse laid out beside her. Another funeral.

What would they do with my body? I couldn't fit in the crypt with Rosalie and Ligeia still there. Would they dump me out at sea? Would I end up in the Brine with the rest of my family, or would I be doomed to toss about on the waves for all eternity, like a ghost ship never reaching port?

The room flipped on its axis again, and I struggled to keep sight of Cassius.

"You poisoned me," I accused as black dots swam into my vision. This couldn't be a concussion. I'd been drugged.

His face was a perfect mask of incredulity. "Poisoned? What are you talking about? Annaleigh, tell me what happened!"

He rushed toward me, and I wheeled around and raced down the path. I knocked over potted plants and small statues, anything I could to slow his pursuit, but his footsteps trailed closer and closer.

Bursting through the ferns onto the tiled area by the pond, I grabbed a little metal table and wielded it between us.

"Stay away from me! I know what you did."

Even as I hurled the accusation at him, I knew I wasn't making sense. Poisoned? How? When? But what else could explain my disoriented state?

Cassius's eyes were wild with confusion, and he held his

hands up, presumably to show he meant no harm. "What I did? Annaleigh—I've done nothing!"

"Then why are my sisters dead?"

Once the words were out, they couldn't be taken back. They cut through the air, sharper than a serrated blade, slicing deeper still.

I'd never forget the look of horror on Cassius's face.

"You think I killed your sisters?" He let out a short, dry laugh.

"Someone did. Someone on the island."

His jaw clenched. "So you assumed it was me, the outsider."

He turned to go, and a cold wave of dismay crashed over me. Why was he leaving? A killer wouldn't walk away from a witness. A killer would make certain they were silenced. His retreating footsteps hammered doubt after doubt into my heart.

Had I been wrong again?

"You knew my sisters' names!" I shouted after him.

Cassius whirled around, wounded outrage constricting his face. "What is going on, Annaleigh? Is it your head? When you fell?"

"Ava and Eulalie. Octavia and Elizabeth. I never told you their names. You knew them in the portrait."

"And this makes me a murderer?"

"It doesn't make you look good. And there are other things. . . . Verity never told you about the sea turtles," I guessed, grasping.

"She didn't, but . . ." He blanched, losing his composure for just a moment, but I saw it.

"How long have you been watching my family?"

The table clattered from my hands as a fresh horror swept in, spreading across my mind like a red tide, poisoning everything it touched.

"Eulalie wasn't the first, was she?" My lips trembled. "Elizabeth didn't kill herself. And Octavia didn't fall." A sob burst from my chest. "You've been behind all their deaths."

I fell to my knees, the room shrinking around me. My head spun in dark chaos, throbbing with terror. A low hum, similar to the noise Ligeia's and Rosalie's ghosts had made, buzzed from the corners of the solarium. I shriveled against it, pressing my hands over my ears, but nothing could muffle the roar. It grew louder and louder, and I cried out, screaming against the chaos. I was certain my eardrums would burst.

And then it was suddenly gone, and the only noise I heard was Cassius's footsteps as he approached me.

"Get up."

I remained where I was, wishing the ground would swallow me whole.

"Annaleigh," he warned.

Certain I was about to take my life's final breaths, I rose to my knees, shivering before him.

"You honestly believe I killed your sisters?" His eyes roamed over me, his disappointment a tangible weight.

The pressure in my head tightened, like a fist clenching around my brain, knuckles unmercifully white. I turned to the side, retching. Cassius was immediately at my side, supporting my frame, holding back my hair. He murmured meaningless noises of assurance, his fingers tracing soothing patterns across my back as I threw up. When I dared to meet his gaze, it was as though I'd been lost on the water in a soupy fog, unsure of which way I was heading, before a swift wind picked up, revealing the shoreline had been in front of me all along.

As clarity rushed over me, my confusion turned to horror. What had I done?

"Cassius, I'm so sorry. I don't . . . I don't know what's happening to me." I wiped my mouth, wishing for water.

"It could be a concussion," he muttered, probing the growing knot at the back of my head. "Let me see your hands."

With far more tenderness than I deserved, he took them, examining the sides, swollen and split, the nails broken from trying to pry the doorframe free.

"What caused this?"

"I . . . I thought I'd been locked in."

I could see in his eyes he didn't believe me.

"And you couldn't wait until someone came for help?"

We were much too close to one another. Color stained my cheeks and chest, and I looked down, ashamed to meet his eyes. "I saw my sisters."

"Camille and Lenore locked you in here?"

I shook my head.

He frowned. "The little ones?"

Another shake.

"Oh."

The jagged ends of my fingernails dug deep into the palm of my hand. "Do you believe in ghosts?"

He paused for such a long moment, I worried he thought me mad, but he nodded. "I do. We need to do something about your hands."

"My hands?" I echoed. My hands were the least of my problems.

But Cassius drew me from the solarium and down the hall

before I could protest. The sconces were unlit; the corridor was silent. It felt as if we were the only two people awake in the house, in Salann, in the whole of Arcannia.

"Hanna keeps a little box of gauze and ointments in a kit in the laundry room," I offered, but he walked past the hall without pause. "Where are we going?"

He stopped at the door leading into the garden. Cassius traced his fingers down the wood's grain, unable to look at me. "You need to know I was going to tell you all of this eventually, Annaleigh, truly I was."

My guard flared up, gooseflesh scouring my arms. "Tell me what?"

He pushed the door open, letting in a blast of icy wind. "Come with me."

I dug my feet into the carpet runner. "We can't go out there like this. We'll freeze to death in minutes."

"It won't take minutes. But I have to be outside."

"For what?"

He pulled me out after him into the snow. I gasped, my breath squeezed from me as a thousand frozen knives bit in. My feet rebelled, painfully numb with every step I took. The winds sliced through the thin silk of my robe, and my body trembled against his as he dragged me after him.

"Cassius, this is insane!" I protested, shouting to be heard over the gusts.

"I need to be away from the trees. We can't be under any branches."

Once in the open, he pressed me flush against the length of his body. I burrowed into his embrace, seeking all the heat he had to offer, propriety be damned. With my head tucked beneath his chin, nestled close to his chest, I couldn't see what was happening, but it felt as if we were in a sudden waterspout, all wind and icy water droplets. Pressure built in my ears, making my head spin. I sank to my knees, feeling light-headed and sick.

The air was suddenly warm. Balmy, even, and scented with honeysuckle.

I opened my eyes and let out a shriek of disbelief.

29

WE WERE IN AN ABBEY. SOMBER GRAY STONES SOARED stories above us, creating a maze of arched colonnades and corridors. The surrounding forest—lush and verdant—crept inside, claiming the pillars as its own. The roof was gone, letting strange pale light filter in. The shadows seemed sharper, as if two sets were imprinted on top of one another. The sky felt just moments before sunrise, even though I knew it to be late at night in Salann.

"What is this place? Where are we?" My voice was no louder than a whisper. The air felt knocked from my chest, and my hands were shaking.

I rubbed my eyes, certain I was still asleep, collapsed near the door of the solarium. This couldn't be real.

Cassius stepped back from me, looking toward the sky. "This is the House of Seven Moons. We're in Versia's abbey."

Versia. No goddess was more powerful than she. She ruled the night and its skies, bringing darkness across the kingdoms. The stars trailed behind her like jewels on a velvet train. Pontus himself followed after her, a lovesick swain, his waves ever drawn to the beauty of her moon.

"In the Sanctum? That's not possible. Mortals can't enter the—"

He quickly shook his head. "No, no, we're not in the Sanctum. We're on the island of Lor, in the southeastern corner of Arcannia. This is where the People of the Stars live."

"Why are— How did we— How did you . . ." I trailed off, suddenly terrified I was asking the wrong questions. I backed away from him into a stone archway. "What are you?"

His eyes were dark, unreadable. "I'll answer everything, but first, just trust me. . . ."

Trust him?

I shouldn't.

But I wanted to.

Cassius moved deeper into the abbey, beckoning me to follow. Directly in front of us, at the end of a long sanctuary, was the altar. There wasn't a table or shrine to mark it, but the back wall was far too impressive for it to be anything else.

Three wide peaked arches rose from the ground, holding up the wall above them. Seven identical circles formed an empty rose window. Had stained glass once filled them? Now all they framed was a sliver of the moon, perfectly balanced in the top right circle.

Rivulets of water wept down the stone wall like quicksilver, as if beads of moonlit dew flowed out of the very bricks themselves. They trickled into a large crescent-shaped basin behind the altar. It sounded as though we'd been transported into a summer rainstorm.

I stared up at the windows, hypnotized by their perfect symmetry.

"Annaleigh?" Cassius prompted, breaking my gaze. He took out a crystal chalice and dipped it into the silver water. "Hold out your hands."

The water smelled like fields of wild mint, tickling my nose and making me want to sneeze. As it spilled out onto my swollen knuckles, it left tingling tracks over my skin, sinking in and chilling me, though it wasn't cold to the touch. Even the thick, humid air couldn't stop a shiver from racing down my spine.

I flexed my fingers in amazement. The bruises faded as the swelling subsided. Broken, cracked nails were repaired. The pain was suddenly entirely gone.

"Tip forward," he instructed.

Scooping out another cupful of the silver water, he poured it over the bump at the back of my head. As it sank in, I could feel the last bits of confusion and panic ebb away. He placed the cup back in its carved niche and disappeared behind one of the archways. I rubbed at the fading knot, amazed at how like myself I suddenly felt, as if the water had chased away a phantom presence, leaving just me behind. When he returned with a glass of water, I drank it gratefully.

"What is that?" I asked, pointing to the waterfall wall.

"Have you ever made a wish on the first evening star?"

"Of course."

"Versia gathers them up, and they rain down here."

I studied the water, searching for a sign of its magical properties, but all I saw was my reflection staring back at me. "You speak as if you've met her."

"I have," he said, and pulled me over to a series of benches.

I sank down on the stone seat, toying with the skirt of my

nightgown as I tried to make sense of all this. Back before we knew of the door in Pontus's shrine, Fisher said gods once dealt directly with mortals, stepping in to mediate disputes, help with crops and harvests. Along the way, most retreated further and further into the Sanctum, content to leave mortal affairs to the mortals.

But I knew some gods still used emissaries to carry out tasks for them. Was Cassius one of Versia's messengers? It would explain his vague responses about his life before showing up that morning on Selkirk.

"Do you work for her?" I asked, stumbling over my words. "As a messenger?"

His eyes crinkled into a smile. "No . . . I'm her son."

My mouth fell open in astonishment. "Son? But that would make you . . ."

"Half god."

I twisted my fingers together. It was hard to understand and almost impossible to believe, but I was sitting here, in his mother's abbey. I felt the heat of the air and the stones beneath my feet. Her magic healed my hands. This couldn't be made up.

"Why didn't you tell me this earlier?"

He ran his fingers through his dark curls, tugging on the ends. "Do you remember what you told me in the park at Churning? About how so many of the men you meet are after your position and money?" I nodded. "I too want to be liked for who I really am. Not all this." He raised his hand, gesturing at the moon wall.

"Why are you telling me now?"

"You said you were being haunted. By your sisters."

My hands balled into fists as I remembered opening my eyes

in the bathtub and seeing not Lenore but Rosalie staring down at me. Cassius placed his fingers over mine, covering them with earnest care.

"I know you're not."

He squeezed my hands once, effectively crushing any bit of hope I had within me.

"You were right, back in the solarium. I shouldn't have known your sisters' names. No one ever speaks of them. But . . . I've met them . . . and I can promise you—they are not ghosts."

I stilled. "You what?"

He cleared his throat. "The Sanctum is divided into different regions, each place a separate haven for the god or goddess it houses. To show Mother his devotion, Pontus built her a palace of moonstone in the Brine with him. It's where I grew up, thoroughly doted upon, a strange half-mortal child. But as I got older, and it became obvious that I didn't have the same talents as my other half siblings, some of that charm wore off."

He rubbed at the back of his neck.

"It sounds lonely," I said, wanting to commiserate but also desperate to hear more about my sisters.

"It was. Mother was gone quite a bit, looking after all this. And there was no one there who was like me. All I had for company was the souls of the departed." He offered a little smile. "I explored every inch of the Brine, talking to whomever I came across, listening to their stories, and one day I found Ava. She's so striking, with her black hair and pale skin. She told me about her life before. About her sisters. About you. Later on, when Octavia came, she brought new stories with her. Then Elizabeth."

I tried to wrap my head around the sheer incredibility of the conversation. "So . . . when you met me at the wharf, you already knew who I was?"

He nodded. "I hoped so. You look just like Ava. Then you said your name and confirmed it."

"What else did they tell you about me?"

"Ava said you were about my age, a little younger, maybe. She said you loved to play the piano and run about the estate, pretending to be a sea captain on your boat."

A blush crept across my cheeks, warm and pink. "I wasn't more than six then."

"Elizabeth told me all about the sea turtles."

"That's how you knew."

He had the decency to look chagrined. "Yes . . . But this is how I know you're not being haunted. Your sisters are in the Brine, happy and at peace. They're not trapped here, with unfinished business. Whatever you've been seeing, it isn't ghosts."

"But tonight it was Rosalie and Ligeia—you don't know if they're in the Brine. And Verity, she's seen them too. She's made the most terrible pictures. And they look just like them. How do you explain that? She's too young to remember Ava and Octavia."

He leaned back against the stone wall. "It could be something else."

I focused on his choice of word: some*thing*.

A line of women entered the abbey, interrupting us. They wore long ice-blue robes, the color of moonlight, with hoods up to conceal their faces. There were an even dozen, holding out lanterns of mercury glass. Charms of silver stars and golden moons hung from their corded belts, tinkling like chimes as they passed. Though most were focused on the altar, one girl at the end, younger than the rest of the group, glanced over at us with curiosity. Recognizing Cassius, she immediately dipped her head in reverence.

"Versia's postulants. The Sisters of the Night. They live at the abbey, tending to the wishing wall and paying homage to my mother. They're about to begin their first service of the day. Come with me." Cassius drew me away from their ceremony.

"Why seven?" I asked, gazing back to the moon windows as we paused on the steps leading out into a courtyard.

"What do you mean?"

"House of Seven Moons. Seven windows. I assume each one holds a different phase of the moon?" He nodded. "But there are eight phases."

"There's no window for the full moon. See how they are arranged? Those are the quarter moons," he said, pointing, "and the gibbous and crescents. And in the middle—that's the new moon. At the full moon, Versia's postulants blow out every candle in the abbey to let the light wash over everything from up there." He gestured to the open roof.

I imagined it at night, with silvery moonlight raining down on the pale gray stones sprinkled with metallic flecks. How they must shimmer.

"What a lovely sight."

"I'll take you, if you like. At the two solstices, crowds come to the abbey to celebrate the night. It's much like Churning, but for Versia and the People of the Stars. There's a wall deeper in the abbey that holds hundreds of tiny candles. Each person takes one and makes a wish."

"What happens then?"

"Later that night, everyone gathers here with their wish candles. They light paper lanterns, sending them floating into the sky. They glow and sparkle, drifting higher and higher until they join the heavens. The People of the Stars believe that in the coming months, if they see a shooting star, it's their wish on its way back to them."

My mouth curled up, picturing the sky lit with hundreds of tiny flames. "I'd love to see that."

"The next solstice is only a month away. You must start thinking of a very important wish."

He led me through a set of arches, showing me the view beyond the abbey. A rocky point stretched into the sea, sharp and jagged. The water below was warm green topped with foamy whitecaps. So different from the dark and deep Kaleic.

"That's where I release my lantern. It keeps it away from the rest of the group so I don't lose sight of it. I like keeping an eye on my lantern for as long as I can." He looked back at me with a shy smile. "If you come with me, you can release yours there too. I wouldn't mind if our wishes got twisted up in each other."

Two lanterns twirling together in the dark night to join the stars. It made such a beautiful image in my mind, I wanted to send them up right now. I'd wish for . . . What would I wish for?

I wanted the killer to be found and for my sisters to stop dying. I wanted Morella to have a safe delivery and healthy twins. I wanted Camille to marry someone and start a family. If I wasn't second in line anymore, I could figure out what I was meant to do with my life. I studied Cassius's profile, enjoying the way the strange light played off his cheekbones.

In that moment, more than anything, I wanted him to kiss me again.

"Have any of your wishes ever come back?"

His smile suddenly turned bashful, and the tips of his ears glowed pink. "I met the girl who taught turtles to swim with the waves, didn't I?"

Cassius brought his hands up, cradling my cheeks, and pressed a tender kiss to my forehead. I tilted my chin, and his lips were on mine, soft and achingly sweet. I ran my fingers up his chest, letting them linger on the back of his neck and twist into his dark curls.

"All my years of imagining you," he murmured, leaving a trail of kisses across my face, "and you are so much more than I ever could have dreamt of.... You smell like sunlight," he whispered against my mouth.

"Sunlight has a smell?" I asked, gasping as he planted a kiss in the hollow of my throat.

"Oh yes," he assured me. "All my life has been moonlight and the stars. I can smell the sunlight racing through your veins from across a room. Sunlight and heat and salt. Always the salt."

I cupped my hands around his cheeks, bringing his mouth to mine and silencing him. I nipped at his lower lip, surprised by my own daring. The kiss intensified then, and I opened my mouth, letting my tongue venture out to find his. He tasted crisp and cool, like the night's dew across the garden or the first bite of a shiny green apple.

A shot of desire raced through me, burning my limbs like lightning. His hands snaked around my waist, pulling me flush against him, as when he first brought us here.

Fighting against every impulse sailing through my body, I pulled away, breaking the kiss, thoroughly breathless. "How did we get here?" I asked, desperately trying to rein in my heartbeat. It pounded, singing Cassius's name through my veins so loudly, I was sure he could hear it. "Did we ... did we fly?"

Cassius let out a bark of laughter and turned, showing me his back. "Do you see wings?"

"I don't know what else to call it. You didn't even have to use a door."

His eyebrow quirked. "A door?"

"We use the one in the Grotto. To get to the balls."

His head tilted. "I don't . . . I don't understand."

"There's a door we discovered on Salten. Pontus uses it to travel quickly through our world. We've been using it to leave the island."

A flock of birds burst from the facade above us, a flutter of wings and chirps, breaking the intensity of Cassius's stare.

"What's it like, this door?"

I stepped down into the courtyard, feeling as though I'd said something wrong. "It's at Pontus's shrine. You twist his trident and the door just . . . appears."

"Where does it take you?"

I raised my shoulders. "Anywhere you want. You just have to think very hard of the place as you walk into the passage. It's how we got to Pelage that night." I inhaled sharply, piecing everything together. "And that's how *you* were able to get there so quickly but be back in Astrea days later! You . . . flew," I said, still unsure of what to call it.

"I've been in Salann since I arrived to take care of my father. I don't know what you're talking about."

I blinked. "You were there. At the castle with the wolves and the People of the Hunt."

He nodded. "I know where Pelage is, but I'm telling you, I've never been. It wasn't me."

I frowned, recalling that night, that first ball. A smile rose to my lips as I remembered his hands at my waist. "I'm certain it was. You had on a mask but—"

His eyes narrowed. "It wasn't me." Cassius turned away, pacing across a mosaic of the night sky. The stars twinkled beneath his feet. He suddenly whirled around. "Your shoes!"

"My shoes?"

"I just realized—you've been using this door to go to parties . . . you're dancing through the shoes!"

I nodded. "We were all going at first, but I stopped that day in Astrea with Edgar. . . . I didn't feel like dancing after that."

"That's why yours was the only pair not worn out at First Night."

"Yes, but . . . the shoes don't have anything to do with my sisters' deaths."

"Don't they?" he asked, peering at me. "You truly think the killer is from Salten?"

"It has to be someone at Highmoor," I murmured unhappily. "There was that awful storm the night Ligeia and Rosalie went missing. No one could have left the island during that."

"Not by boat, certainly," Cassius said. "But what if you're not the only ones using this door?"

I was caught off guard by his reasoning, and my breath hitched, chilling me. It had never occurred to me the very door we'd been using to visit faraway castles and estates could be used by others to get to us. If anyone in Arcannia could gain admittance onto Salten, how would I ever be able to narrow down the suspects?

The train of postulants left the abbey, cutting across the courtyard and stalling our conversation. This time they were all aware of Cassius's presence, dipping into solemn curtsies as they passed. He lowered his head, giving a short bow in response.

Too keyed up to remain still, I made my way past the archways and out into the tall grasses leading to the cliff. A temperate breeze swished by, rippling the skirt of my robe out behind me.

"I want to see this door," Cassius said, coming up from behind me. "And one of these balls. Something about them isn't right. I was never in Pelage. Someone . . . something might have been using my face to get closer to you."

That choice of word again: some*thing*.

"You think the killer has been at the balls?" My stomach squirmed with a painful twist.

"Perhaps. Perhaps he saw your sisters there and . . ." He trailed off with a shrug.

"But Eulalie died before the balls started. . . . He would have to have known her from somewhere else."

Cassius nodded, considering that. "I still want to go to one myself, look around and see what I can learn. They're connected somehow, I'm sure of it. See if Camille is going out tomorrow night." He wrapped his arms around my waist, leaning his chin on my shoulder. "We'll figure this out, all right? You and I. You're not on your own, Annaleigh."

A warm, peaceful stillness fell over me. For a moment, the gray clouds above us parted, but rather than reveal a sunlit sky, the dark swirling cosmos of stars winked at us. A shooting star danced across the opening, but before I could point it out, Cassius's lips descended on mine, and I forgot all about the sky.

30

"WOULD THIS WORK?" I ASKED, PULLING OUT THE SEA-green ball gown from my armoire and holding it up for Camille's inspection.

She wrinkled her nose. "No! You've worn that twice now, plus at Churning. This is a ball at Lambent! With the People of the Light! Fisher said everyone is meant to wear pale shades to honor Vaipany. You'll stick out like a sore thumb in green."

I settled the dress back onto the rack and shut the door. "Then I can't go. I don't have anything like that."

She grabbed my hand. "Come with me." Camille raced us down to her room and knelt beside her bed. She slid two enormous boxes out from under her duvet and handed me one. "Surprise!"

"What is this?" I gasped as I removed the lid. "Oh, Camille!" Nestled inside, on a bed of pale pink tissue paper, was the most exquisite gown I had ever seen. "Where did you get this?"

"Do you remember the ball at Bloem? With the People of the Petals?"

Of course I did. It was the single most opulent evening of our lives. There wasn't an item in the whole of the castle not bedecked in pearls, jewels, or silver leaf.

"I had Mrs. Drexel make us dresses just like the ones I saw there. I picked them up in Astrea the night of the Churning pageant." She swallowed. "Just before Rosalie and Ligeia . . ." When she met my gaze, her eyes were bright with unshed tears.

"It's beautiful," I assured her, picking up the gown and letting the blush-colored silk fall to the floor. The layers were so light and insubstantial, they seemed to dance on their own. Ropes of pearls coiled around the shoulders and across the back, clinking against one another.

"Try it on! Try it on!" she exclaimed, pushing aside her moment of sorrow with a pasted-on smile.

When I'd told Camille I wanted to go out, she'd squealed with delight, launching into a discussion of what dances were being held. I was surprised she'd kept such close tabs on all the social events, especially in light of our sisters' deaths, but we all grieve in our own way.

I had no desire to go to this ball. I wanted to curl up in bed—warm and safe and surrounded by my sisters, like when we were little—and sleep. Sleep safe from Weeping Women nightmares and curses and killers. Just sleep.

But Cassius was so sure we would discover something. If there was even a chance my sisters' killer would be there, I had to go to learn everything I could.

Camille unhooked the back of my gown, freeing me from the dark twill, and helped me slide the new dress over my head. It settled on my frame like a wispy bit of sea-foam. The pearls still held a chill as they rolled across my bare back, setting my teeth on edge.

"Don't look in the mirror yet!" she ordered, far more excited than I was. "Help me into mine. I want to see what they look like together."

Hers was also sleeveless, with a soft illusion neckline. Icy champagne and silver seed pearls formed intricate designs all along the sheer mesh overlay.

"You look dazzling."

She waved aside my praise, rummaging through a box on her bureau. "I found these among Mama's old things. We should wear them tonight. Everyone needs to know the sisters of the Salt are there."

She handed me a strange piece of jewelry, and I turned it around, trying to make sense of it. It was the Thaumas octopus. Its body, made from the largest pearl I'd ever seen, was a ring. The tentacles formed a bracelet of delicate rose gold, twisting and wrapping up my wrist as I slipped the bauble on. Camille opted for a tiara of jeweled starfish and pale pink drop earrings.

"I gave the Graces other little bits from Mama's jewelry box. Nothing terribly valuable, but they were pleased."

I looked up from the Thaumas bracelet in alarm. "The Graces are coming?"

She nodded, toying with the back of one earring. "Of course. We all ought to go, don't you think?"

"Not Lenore," I clarified, praying Camille hadn't pushed her into this.

She shook her head with a sniff. "It's impossible to talk to her right now. She just sits there, staring over your shoulder as if you're not even there."

"She's grieving."

Camille's lips twisted in a pout. "I know that. It's just . . ." She let out a sharp sigh. "I don't mean to sound callous, but haven't we done this enough? I'm sick of mourning. I just want to live without the fear I'm going to lose another of you."

I raised one eyebrow skeptically at her. "If I died tomorrow, would you mourn me?"

Her face dropped, crestfallen. "Don't even joke about that. Of course I would. But . . . would you really want me swathed away in black taffeta and jet jewelry, another year of my life put on hold just because yours was over?"

I wouldn't, but it seemed unkind to say it so soon after Rosalie's and Ligeia's deaths.

"Come," she said, taking my hand. "We've had enough mourning and grief to last us too many lifetimes. Tonight is about champagne, and caviar, and dancing!"

On the way to the Grotto, I kept an eye out for Cassius to make sure he was following after us. As I trailed Fisher and the Graces down the steep cliff walk, a shadowy form shifted out from behind a grove of trees.

Once inside the cave, Fisher twisted the trident around, and the wave wall slowly broke apart, turning into the open passage.

"So we're going to Lambent," I said loudly, for Cassius's benefit. I'd heard a pebble crunch out on the cliff walk and hoped he could hear me. "For the People of the Light's dance. Remember, we all need to be thinking of that as we go through the tunnel."

Honor gave me a pointed look. "You don't have to remind us. We know how it works."

"We know you do," Fisher said, twirling her through the entrance with a laugh as they vanished. "Minnow just wants to make sure Mercy hasn't forgotten!"

"I didn't!" she cried out, racing through the mouth and disappearing.

Camille and Verity went next, and I dared to look back at the empty Grotto. "Lambent," I repeated before following my sisters.

The tunnel took us straight inside the new palace. The stone walls of this estate were much lighter, almost the color of a sun-stained shell, and the air was warm and dry, perfumed with burnt myrrh and lotus blossoms. I already missed the salty tang of the sea.

Sconces dripped golden wax onto the stone floor below. The smoke from the flickering wicks hung heavy, filling the hallway with a gray haze. I looked back toward the door to Highmoor, but it was shrouded in shadows.

Camille smiled over her shoulder at me as she spun Verity in giddy circles. The smoke lent a dreamy quality to the air, slowing motions and imparting a strange importance to every gesture. I blinked several times, trying to sharpen my thoughts, but felt drugged. My mind struggled to focus.

A grand foyer opened before us. On the right was the ballroom and, from the sounds of the orchestra and chatter, the festivities were already in full swing. To the left was a series of open arches leading out onto a moonlit terrace. I spotted the dark outlines of sand dunes in the distance, blotting out part of the sky. We were a very long way from the seashore.

Across the room was a fountain spouting wine. Couples in formal court fashions mingled around the circular base, sticking out cups to catch the scarlet liquid as it flowed from an ornate bronze battle scene. In it, three men hoisted another as he tried to escape their grasp. Above them flew a horrible winged figure that was slitting the fugitive's throat with a scythe. The wine spilled out from the poor soul's wound.

"Don't look at that," I said, trying to direct the Graces' attention away from the gory tableau. Smoke burned my eyes, and as I blinked, I saw I'd been mistaken. The statue was a cherub aiming an arrow at a group of girls sitting at the fountain's edge. The wine poured out of their pitchers.

I rubbed my eyes, trying to make them see the awful statue again. How had I misinterpreted it so terribly? Before I could take a closer look, Camille tugged me into the hall.

One wall was divided into a triad of enormous frescoes, each depicting a moment from the creation of the world. Vaipany loomed in the center, spinning the sun into existence. On the right was Seland, forming the earth out of mud and clay, his hands brown with primordial ooze. Versia was on the left, floating through a field of stars and planets. I glanced around the room, wondering what Cassius thought of it.

Large waves of golden silk hung across the ceiling, rippling toward a spectacular chandelier. Giant spheres of spinning metal were suspended in midair, protecting a massive ball of flames. I'd never seen anything like it before.

Fisher whisked Verity off to the dance floor, and two younger boys asked Honor and Mercy if they would like to dance. Camille and I watched the couples swirl by. I craned my neck, searching the crowds for Cassius.

"See that man dressed all in silver by the columns?" Camille whispered to me. I squinted through the crowd but couldn't quite make out whom she pointed to. "We danced together last night—a minuet and three waltzes. He's an excellent partner." She nudged me toward him.

"What are you doing?" I asked, fighting to stay in place against her jostling.

"He's not dancing. Go ask him."

I squirmed from her clutch. "I'm not asking a man to dance!"

Camille sighed. "That's so old-fashioned." She left me, wading into the sea of people.

I looked back to the chandelier, studying its kinetic frenzy. I could think of no mechanical means to engineer such fluid movement—and to make it appear as if it were floating, no less. A warning panged deep within me. Dark magic was at work here.

"I don't think we've had the pleasure of meeting."

Jumping, I turned and saw Camille's man in silver.

Up close, I immediately recognized him. Another series of dragons was stitched across the pale velvet of his jacket. Deep-set eyes, so pale blue they were nearly white, ran over me, like the writhing arms of a jellyfish closing around its prey.

He reached out with a brazen hand, cupping my chin and turning my head this way and that. His fingers were too long, too thin, too angular, and I cringed from his grasp.

"No, I certainly wouldn't forget such a face. I'd be honored to have such a pretty partner. Shall we?"

The dragon man held out his hand, grabbing mine when I hesitated. He whirled me toward the dance floor with practiced charm.

"Actually, I believe we have met. Twice, in fact," I commented. I needed to learn as much about this ball as possible, especially as it appeared I was on my own. Cassius had still not made an appearance. "You were at the ball in Pelage."

"I was," he said, leading me into a complicated series of steps. His eyes brightened in recognition. "I remember dancing with you—you're one of the Thaumas girls! I know your sisters well."

"Do you?"

He smiled. "They certainly make for the loveliest dance partners." He spun me away from him, his eyes roaming the hall. "But I don't see the triplets here tonight." His teeth winked with a predatory warning. "I do hope nothing happened to them."

I nearly tripped as alarm bells began to ring deep within me. "Why would you say that?"

He raised his shoulders in an elegant shrug. "What would you have me say?"

With a flick of his wrist, he twisted me back into his arms. "You never asked where our second meeting was," I sputtered, turning my face from his as he maneuvered me into a dip and leaned over, breathing in my scent. I had the horrifying premonition he was about to lick the hollow of my throat.

"On Astrea, of course. The night of the Churning pageant, if I'm not mistaken. The night two of your sisters went missing."

My breath stole away from me. How would he know that? "What were you doing in Astrea?"

He blinked once, his pupils suddenly impossibly large, like the flat, dead eyes of a shark.

"Tell me, Annaleigh, why do you ask me things you already know?"

I pushed him away from me. "I never told you my name."

The dragon man laughed. "No, but she did." He nodded

toward the center of the room, where Fisher swayed back and forth, letting Verity stand on his toes.

Knowing this stranger had spoken to Verity made me want to cry. "Stay away from my sisters."

He grabbed my elbow, drawing me close. "We're taking up space on the floor just standing here. Dance with me."

His grip was too tight, and I couldn't free myself. Before I could raise my voice to protest, Camille and a new partner spun by.

"Isn't this exquisite?" she called out.

My stomach churned as I watched her swirl away. Why couldn't she sense the danger I felt? She looked as carefree as a butterfly, fluttering from partner to partner.

"Dance, Annaleigh," the dragon man urged, bringing me back to the present. He drew his thumb across the curve of my jaw, running it over my lips. Stuck in his grasp, I leaned as far away as I could, but I still felt the heat of his breath on my cheek. "Dance for me."

This man had something to do with my sisters' deaths, I was sure of it. I had to find Cassius. Had to get help. Had to escape this ballroom and the smoke clouding my thoughts. Had to run from the music. It was a half note off, too sharp, setting my teeth on edge and making it impossible to hear, let alone dance to.

"Get away from me!" I screamed, and shoved at his chest with all my might. As I turned to run, I expected noises of surprise and concern, gasps from onlookers as I created quite a loud scene.

But there was no reaction.

I stopped in my tracks, staring at the couples on the floor.

None of them had noticed my outburst. It was like the moths. I'd seen them, but later Papa had not. Tonight, I was seeing and hearing things that crowds of people in the same room as me were not.

First that macabre statue and now this music—no one but me noticed anything wrong with it. I whirled around, searching for Cassius. Why couldn't he see how much I needed him?

A young man in a sparkling gold vest stepped into my path, interrupting my train of thought. "May I have this dance?"

I shook my head, turning in the other direction. "I'm through with dancing."

"But the party has only just begun." He darted in front of me, surprisingly agile.

"I'm tired. Perhaps another time."

"One dance." He linked our elbows, twirling us in a circle.

"I'd really rather—"

"Come."

He navigated us farther into the crowd with a series of steps I struggled to keep up with. The orchestra played a lively mazurka, and the couples around us moved too quickly for me to break free.

The opening note of another song rang out, hitting the wrong pitch. I felt as if my ears were about to bleed.

"Oh, I do love this song. Pretty, pretty lady, might I tempt you into another round with me? It would be my honor."

"I'm afraid she's spoken for," a voice said from the side of the room.

I turned, hoping to see Cassius, but it was a short, stalky man smoking a cigar. He exhaled a strange cloud of lavender-colored smoke into my face, making my eyes water. After one last drag, he stomped it out and whisked me away.

I wiped my eyes, trying to clear them and gather my thoughts.

There was something I'd needed to do, but I couldn't seem to remember what it was. I swept my gaze over the room to jog my memory. The ballroom was so lovely. So sparkly, and sumptuous, and . . . *exquisite.*

The short man and I danced past Camille, and her partner said we ought to switch after the waltz. I readily agreed. I danced two numbers with him before a little boy all in saffron, looking very much like the son of the house, asked if he could cut in.

Charmed by his impeccable manners, I ended up dancing three times with him. He told such funny jokes, the time flew by. Then a blond man tapped my shoulder and asked so nicely, I accepted his offer for a quadrille.

"Do you know where the refreshment tables are?" I asked mid-dance. "I'm not accustomed to such warm weather."

He pointed to the far end of the room.

A beautiful spread of tables boasted rows of crystal cups and three different kinds of punch. There was a miniature castle of stacked petits fours and trays of exotic meats, smoked, roasted, and pickled. At the center of it all, in the place of honor, was a magnificent tiered cake. Thirteen layers tall and surrounded by hand-painted edible flowers, it was stunning.

Before I could partake of this feast, I felt someone behind me. It was the dragon man again. He looked utterly resplendent in his tails. The velvet was thick and luscious and tailored to his form with precision. "May I have this dance?"

I was about to consent—I'd had such a marvelous time with him before—when something shifted inside me.

Had I?

I blinked and he seemed to lose a shade of his splendor. I noticed a patch of stubble he'd missed shaving, and his eyes seemed far more sunken than they had only a moment before.

Odd.

"Thank you, but I believe I'm going to sit this one out."

"Nonsense! It's the last dance before the fireworks. Dance with me, Annaleigh."

I held out my hand, ready to accept, but then noticed the buffet again. I'd been thirsty before. I'd come to the table for something to drink. Such a silly thing to forget.

"I'm going to get a glass of punch, but thank you."

"Wouldn't you rather something stronger?" He pushed back his jacket, revealing a slim flask. He took a long swig from it before offering it to me. I waved it aside. "Get your punch, then," he sneered. "But then we dance."

That sneer. The tone of his voice, husky but holding back such a rank, entitled anger. It sounded so familiar. I suddenly remembered his thumb brushing my mouth, full of dark desire, and snapped to my senses.

Why had I forgotten that? Why had I forgotten everything? I wasn't here to socialize and dance the night away. I was meant to be searching for information on who would want to harm my sisters.

"I'm not dancing with you." I kept my voice strong and decisive and turned on my heel, looking over the buffet, steeling my mind for the task at hand.

Find a cup.

Pick a punch.

But even as I coached myself through such a simple process, my feet worked in open rebellion, itching to dance.

"Which punch, Annaleigh?" I muttered, grounding myself in the moment.

I finally chose the pink one. Dozens of iced strawberries floated on top. We hadn't had any in months, since the cold weather set in, and this looked simply enchanting.

No. Not enchanting. Just punch.

Taking a large sip, I immediately spat it out. Something wasn't right. There was a strong metallic taste, as if a dozen copper florettes were mixed in.

A strawberry seed stuck between my teeth, wedged deep enough that no amount of ladylike prodding with my tongue could dislodge it. I worked it free with a surreptitious swish of my fingernail.

I intended to flick it aside without a second thought, but it was much larger than a strawberry seed should have been. I brought it up for a closer inspection.

It was a fish scale.

I rubbed the silver speck between my fingers, puzzled. How on earth did a fish scale end up in a bowl of party punch? I turned to let a servant know about the contamination, then froze. The festive red floats I'd taken for strawberries weren't fruit at all. Hacked-up bits of seafood bobbed in the punch, a veritable chum stew.

The punch was made of blood.

My stomach rolled over, threatening to toss up every bite of dinner I'd eaten. The cakes and the trays were gone, replaced with butchered carcasses of fish. A fluke here, a dorsal fin there. The yellow satin of the tablecloth was soaked red around these cuts of meat. Tentacles, long and ropy, flailed off the table, spiraling to the floor below.

My nostrils flared against the stench. This seafood had not been freshly caught. It was weeks old and had turned. So many people milled around, clearly unaffected. How did they keep dancing before such a massacre?

Then it hit me. Only I saw this. Only I smelled this. I was the only one who noticed any of this night's horrors. Hundreds of people were here, but I was the only one to see this world for what it was.

How was that possible? How was any of this possible?

There is one way, a tiny, dark voice whispered in my mind.

I shook my head, as if warding off a buzzing mosquito.

None of this is real, it persisted. *No one else sees it because it's not really here to see. You've gone mad, my girl.*

No. That wasn't it. That wasn't possible.

I wasn't mad.

There had to be another explanation.

Does there?

Shaking my head, I scanned the room again, searching for Camille and the Graces. We were going. We were leaving this awful, evil place and then—

I let out a shriek only I could hear.

Where the cake had once been rested a large platter. A sea turtle—the biggest one I'd ever seen—was showcased on a bed of dead eels. His great shell had been hacked, slashed, and sliced. He had not died an easy death. Tears welled in my eyes.

I dared to creep closer to the proud beast. He was enormous and obviously quite old. Barnacles dotted his back, and his flippers were scored with battle scars. I reached out to trace one of the long lines, but my hand stopped as the turtle's head shifted.

Was he alive? Surely nothing could have withstood the

wounds racked across his body, but there it was again, the slightest spasm of his head. I rubbed his flipper, letting him know he was not alone. Even though he was in pain and scared and probably about to die, I wanted him to know someone loved him and was sorry.

The head flopped toward my touch, and I dared to dream I might save him. My sisters and I could snatch up the platter and race it back to Highmoor. I'd fill the solarium's pond with salt water. He could live there until he recovered enough to return to the sea.

His head jerked again, and I leaned in. If he was about to open his eyes, I wanted to be the first thing he saw. The beak moved, and my heart jumped in anticipation.

The turtle's eyelids burst open as a string of fat white maggots fell from the hole. They poured out of the poor loggerhead's skull onto the platter. His body was full of them, ready to explode.

I turned away, certain I was about to be horribly sick, and ran into the leering dragon man. He caught hold of my elbows, keeping me from falling.

"Are you enjoying the refreshments?" he asked.

There was such a lightness in his voice, so completely at odds with what I'd just seen, it gave me hope the bloody mess was an illusion, just like the fountain. Turning back, I expected to see the cake and pretty punch bowls, but the gore was still there, spread across the tables in a sadistic buffet.

"I feel faint," I confessed, my head swooning with the smoke. "Can you find my sisters or Fisher? Can you find Camille?"

My knees gave way, and he lowered me to the floor, his hand at the back of my neck. The room faded in and out of darkness.

As the dragon man leaned over me, streaks of sweat ran down his face.

I wiped my fingers across his cheek. They came back black and oily.

The Weeping Woman.

"Dance with me," she whispered into my ear.

My stomach heaved, threatening to lose control, and I forced myself away from the wicked wraith. The floor felt sticky as I crawled forward. Sticky and moving.

Maggots spilled off the turtle's platter onto the dance floor, writhing in time to the orchestra's cheery tune. The floor was thick with their repugnant bodies. There were thousands of them. They crawled on me, into my shoes, under my skirts, and I finally opened my mouth and screamed.

31

"ANNALEIGH!"

From somewhere far away, in the depths of my swoon, I heard shouting. I just wanted to stay where I was, in the deep and silent dark, but the voice kept yelling my name, louder and louder. My shoulder jerked back as if shoved.

"Annaleigh, you have to wake up!" Another shove. "Now."

I came to with a gasp, fuzzy with confusion. My mouth was dry, and a sour, metallic funk coated my tongue. I squinted against the glare of my bedroom's sconces.

"What time is it?" I muttered to Hanna, sitting up, ready to push myself off the bed.

But I wasn't in bed.

And Hanna had not woken me.

"Cassius! What are you doing in my room? Papa will have your head if he finds you here." I blinked hard and used my hands to shield the light away. Why did the room feel so bright?

He knelt beside me, grabbing my shoulders, his fingers sinking in deep.

"Look at me," he demanded, pushing back my hands. He took

hold of my chin, forcing me to meet his eyes. His face was deathly pale; a sheen of sweat beaded his brow. He looked terrified.

"Let go of me. That hurts." I wrenched free from his death grip.

Instantly, he jerked his hands away from me. "You're awake?"

"Obviously. Why are you in here?"

I pushed myself up, wincing. Had I rolled out of bed while I slept? Or somehow fallen asleep on the floor after the ball? My body ached, and as I took a step toward my vanity, a stab of pain shot up my foot.

Lifting the hem of my dress—why hadn't I changed into a nightgown?—I winced. My feet were raw with bruises and blisters. We really did need to get new shoes before going dancing again.

I froze as the memories came slamming back, hitting me with the force of a storm-swept wave.

The ball.

The bloody massacre at the banquet tables.

The Weeping Woman.

I sank down on the chair as a cry escaped me. The Weeping Woman had been at the ball. Not in my dreams, but actually there, beside me, her long fingers clasped over my wrists. I closed my eyes, struggling to remember what had happened after I saw her.

I'd fainted. But then what?

"Did you help bring me back after I fainted—did you carry me back?" Cassius's blue eyes were dark with incomprehension. "Did you see me faint at the ball?"

He pressed his lips together, forming his words with care. "Annaleigh, there was no ball."

It suddenly felt as if the temperature had dropped several degrees, and I pushed back a flurry of shivers. "You didn't come? I could never find you there. Was the door closed once you caught up?"

Cassius knelt beside my chair, taking my hands in his. "There was no door to go through. You've been in your room all night long."

I pushed back the tickle of a laugh threatening to escape. "That's absurd. I was in Lambent. I can tell you anything you want to know about the castle. I was there, and so were Camille and the Graces, and—I was dancing. Look at my feet!"

He glanced at my tattered hemline and blistered heels and nodded slowly.

His silence was infuriating. "How do you explain that if there was no ball? If you didn't go—you fell asleep or forgot or whatever—just come out and say it, Cassius. I know I was there. We all were. Except you!"

He stood up, jaw tightening, and held out his hand. "I think you need to come with me."

"Why?"

"Annaleigh, please. You need to see this for yourself."

With wary hesitation, I followed him out into the hallway. The sconces were at their lowest setting, giving just enough glow to highlight the portraits hanging along the walls. I'd never noticed how my sisters' eyes seemed to flicker with life, as they did now, following our passage with knowing stares. With a shiver, I hurried after Cassius.

He stopped outside Camille's room. Her door was ajar.

"What am I meant to see?"

He nodded at the bedroom. "Go on."

The room was dark, and I was about to turn around, not wanting to disturb Camille's sleep, when I spotted her. My mouth fell open, as though icy water had been thrown over me, snapping me to my senses.

She was dancing.

In the middle of the room.

Not with anyone but also not entirely by herself.

Her arms were out, positioned as if resting on a phantom partner. The silk of her gown trailed after her like a ghost as she spun around the room. Her eyes were shut tight, a beatific smile on her lips. Was she sleeping?

"Camille! What are you doing? What are—"

I turned back to Cassius to see if he could make sense of the scene. His mouth was set in a grim line.

"What is she doing?" I whispered.

"Dancing."

"But with whom? Camille—"

He reached out, stopping me. "Don't. If she's in a fugue, jarring her awake could hurt both of you." He rubbed at a reddened patch across his cheek. Had I struck him? "Have you ever known her to sleepwalk before?"

I shook my head. "Never."

As we watched, Camille maneuvered through a series of intricate steps. This was not the make-believe dancing we'd played at in our youths, with our skirts twirling around us until we were breathless with laughter.

She flung herself backward, dipped by a partner who was not there. Her back arched far enough for her feathered hair clip to brush the floor. Impossibly, her right leg kicked up, and she was balanced in this painful contortion on the ball of her left foot. Had she been in the arms of a handsome consort, the pose would have been stunning. But with no one supporting her weight, she looked abnormal.

Unnatural.

Possessed.

Cassius tugged at my sleeve, pulling me down the hallway. I followed after him reluctantly, not wanting to leave Camille alone in such a state.

He raked his fingers through his hair. "Where are the little girls' rooms?"

I frowned. "Down the hall."

"Show me, please."

"That's Mercy's room," I said, indicating the closed door to our left. I kept a watchful eye over my shoulder, certain Camille would come gliding after us in her eerie solo pas de deux.

"Perhaps you ought to be the one to go in."

I palmed the doorknob, a painful knot of worry digging under my ribs. What was I about to find?

Mercy's curtains were drawn, and it was too dark to see anything at first. Then a white figure flashed through the shaft of light spilling in from the hall. I jumped back, bumping into Cassius.

Mercy was dancing in her sleep, just like Camille.

I watched her for a minute before racing across the hall to Honor's room. She was performing a pretty pirouette, eyes closed, mouth slack in sleep.

I crept to Verity's room, my eyes on fire with unshed tears. With trembling hands, I opened the door and waited for my eyes to adjust.

Verity was scared of the dark and always kept the curtains partially open, allowing moonlight to spill in. Her room was still, and I tiptoed in, praying I'd find her snug and secure in bed. Cassius remained at the doorway, his figure silhouetted against the hallway gaslights.

Pushing back the bed curtains, I wanted to cry. The bed was empty; the sheets were undisturbed.

"Annaleigh," Cassius murmured as a small figure glided by me.

Verity was waltzing, her steps graceful and far surer than I'd ever seen them in real life. I fell back on the bed to keep her from running into me. As she passed through a beam of moonlight, she turned and smiled at me.

Her eyes were open. Wide open and pitch-black, weeping dark, oily tears.

"Care to cut in?" she asked, but it wasn't Verity's voice. It was the thing from my nightmares, somehow inhabiting my sister.

"Verity?" Tears of my own streamed down my face. What had happened to my little sister?

Cassius turned the gas knob fully on. Just before the sconces flared to life, the Verity-thing whipped around, glaring at him, but as the room lit up, the Weeping Woman's face was gone, and it was just my little sister once more.

She collapsed to the floor like a marionette with slashed strings, up one moment and in a tangle of limbs and tulle the next.

"Verity!" I howled, racing to her. I cradled her small body against mine, choking on my tears as her eyes flickered open. They were green, not black, and I brought her up to me, embracing her as tightly as I dared with a sob of relief.

"What are you doing in here, Annaleigh?" she asked, her voice thick and raspy.

Just as mine had been when Cassius woke me. . . .

"Are you okay? Are you all right?" I asked, stroking her curls, needing to reassure myself it truly was her.

"I want to go back to sleep," she muttered drowsily, her eyelids fluttering shut.

"No!" I patted her cheeks, trying to keep her awake, but she nuzzled against my neck and drifted off once more.

"What is happening?" I asked, turning to Cassius. "What's wrong with my sisters?"

"I think it might be—" He paused, ducking back out into the hallway. "Do you hear that?"

I cocked my head toward the door, listening. I seemed to hear a series of knocks, but they were muffled, too far away to properly discern. "The front foyer?" I guessed.

"I'll be right back," he said, leaving us.

I sat in the middle of Verity's room, clutching her to my chest. I was terrified to let her go, certain she'd rise up and start dancing again. I wanted to keep her safe and snuggled next to me, but as the minutes passed by, she grew heavy, pressing uncomfortably into my hip bones and fidgeting in her sleep. I staggered up, hoisting her prostrate body to the bed.

I brought the quilt up to her chin and watched the rise and fall of her chest. Her eyes danced beneath her lids. She looked so content, it was difficult to imagine she'd been waltzing about the room, with that thing using her face, moments before.

The knocks turned into indistinct shouts, and I heard footsteps race up the stairs. Someone must have been going for Papa.

I drifted toward the doorway, wanting to keep an eye on Verity but also hating to miss what the commotion was. I heard

Papa's muttered curses mingled with the thud of his feet in the stairwell.

"Papa?" I called down the long hallway. "What's going on?"

"And you've woken everyone in the house!" he chided Roland. They were both still dressed in bedclothes. "Go back to sleep, child. It's only a messenger."

A messenger in the dead of night?

I threw a glance over my shoulder to Verity, still peacefully slumbering. Dimming the sconces—I didn't want her to wake in total darkness—I dashed out of the room, bolting past my sisters' doors. If they were still twisting and twirling with their phantom partners, I did not want to know.

By the time I arrived in the foyer, a crowd of cooks and footmen, maids and groomsmen, had gathered. They circled around a ragged-looking sailor. He was soaked to the bone, with a wool blanket thrown over his shoulders. Still, he shook, nearly frozen from the cold night. He frantically searched the room until he spotted my father.

"My lord!" the sailor cried. "I bring awful news. There's been a shipwreck just off the northern coast of Hesperus. Many have died. They're trying to salvage the cargo, but the clipper is taking on water fast. We need help."

Papa stepped forward as those gathered gasped at the news. "Why have you wasted all this time coming here? Silas needs to light the distress beacon. Men from Selkirk and Astrea will come to your aid."

"We tried Hesperus first, my lord, but something is wrong there. That's why the clipper ran aground. The light was out. Old Maude has gone dark!"

32

"OUR FIRST PRIORITY IS GETTING TO THE WRECK," PAPA said, pacing in front of the large fireplace in his study. Above the mantel hung our family crest. The eyes of the Thaumas octopus glittered in the candlelight, as if it were amused by our predicament.

Cassius, Roland, the sailor, and I perched on chairs scattered about the room. Large maps and ocean charts, held in place at the corners with anchor-shaped paperweights, covered Papa's desk.

"We need to save whatever lives—and cargo—we can." Papa nodded to Roland. "Wake every able-bodied man we have, and set sail for the *Rusalka* immediately." He peered out the window behind the desk, studying the weather vane attached to the lower gable. "The winds are in our favor, at least." He tapped the map where the sailor said the ship had struck rocks. "If they hold up, you should be able to reach it in two hours' time."

Roland was gone with a click of his heels, taking the sailor with him.

"Papa, what about Old Maude?" I asked. "Shouldn't we send someone to check on Silas? I can't remember the light ever going out before."

He sank into his chair, staring into the crackling flames as he rubbed at the circles under his eyes. "I just don't understand what is happening. First Eulalie, then the girls. Now this. It's almost as if . . ." He shook his head, clearing away his dark thoughts. He looked at me in confusion, as if truly seeing me for the first time that night. "What are you wearing, Annaleigh?"

"I . . ." I trailed off, unable to truly answer.

He waved it aside. "It doesn't matter. Old Maude needs to be relit. I'll wake Fisher. He needs to return and get the light back up and running."

My mind wandered upstairs to my sisters' rooms. Fisher had been at the ball with us. Would we find him dancing about his room as well?

"Papa—there's something else I need to tell you," I began, but Cassius shifted his head, warning me to stop.

"You have so much on your plate right now, sir," Cassius said. "Let me go and wake him."

"That would be very kind of you. I really ought to check on Morella. She was in such a tizzy when Roland woke us. Thank you both."

I watched him head toward the foyer, his shoulders hunched with too much weight.

"Where's Fisher's room?" Cassius asked, drawing me to the task at hand.

"On the second floor, just above the kitchens on the servants' side."

We hurried up the stairs, moving aside as Roland clattered down the steps past us, a group of sleepy-eyed footmen following after him.

"You said he was at the ball with you?"

I nodded, leading him down the dimly lit hall. The walls were stark white, the doors plain with brass handles. I'd been to Fisher's room once, when we were children. Hanna had boxed his ears when she found out. "Is he going to be like Camille and the others?"

"I don't know," Cassius answered. "I honestly don't know what to expect from this night."

"Was I like . . . that?" I asked, stopping outside Fisher's room. I did not want to imagine myself spinning about and contorting into the poses I'd seen my sisters perform. That the Weeping Woman might have somehow forced me to made me want to cry.

"You were," he confirmed quietly. "I thought it was some horrible prank, but you went through a beam of moonlight and I saw your face. . . ."

"Were my eyes all black?" I asked. My voice felt impossibly small and tight.

"It might have been a trick of the shadows . . . but it was awful, Annaleigh. It was like you were just . . . gone. I was so scared I'd lost you somehow."

I grasped his hand, bringing it to my lips. "I'm here. I'm still yours."

His mouth curved up in the shade of a smile. "Mine? Truly?"

"All yours," I promised, and kissed his fingers again.

He drew me in, pressing a kiss to the top of my head. I wanted to stay there, wrapped in the warmth and security of his embrace, but we couldn't linger. Old Maude needed to be lit again.

Blowing out a shaky breath, I stepped away from Cassius's side. "I'm so scared to open this door."

"I'll do it," he said, twisting the knob and pushing. After a second's hesitation, he went in.

"Cassius?" I called out when the silence grew loud enough to be deafening. I ducked my head in, squinting in the dark. I could make out a low, narrow bed with a quilt neatly tucked around it and a small desk and chair. Fisher's clothes hung on a series of pegs on the wall. But no Fisher.

"He's not in here."

"Maybe Roland woke him?"

"We would have seen him go down the stairs with the other men," Cassius said, poking out into the corridor.

"He could have heard the commotion and come down earlier," I tried, thinking out loud.

I pushed back strands of hair that had come loose from my twisted updo. It just didn't make any sense. When had I gone from being awake to dreaming such horrific nightmares?

"Do you think he's in the Grotto? Maybe he went down for the ball and—"

"There was no ball," Cassius repeated firmly. "He's not in the Grotto. I checked there when you never came down. It was empty. No people, no parties, no magic door." He let out a sigh. "There are a hundred places he could be right now, but we don't have the time to look. The beacon needs to be relit. As soon as possible."

"I might be able to light it."

Cassius looked surprised. "You?"

"Papa took me to visit Old Maude often when I was a little girl. I think I remember everything Silas showed me."

"Get dressed in warmer clothes and meet me in the garden, out from under all the trees. Hurry."

I raised my eyebrows. He'd said the same thing the night we traveled to the House of Seven Moons.

"We're going to Hesperus."

33

I HEARD THE CRASHING WAVES BEFORE I EVEN KNEW we'd left Salten.

Unused to the speed at which Cassius could travel, I clung to him for a moment, regaining my sense of equilibrium. Opening my eyes, I spotted Old Maude, her cheerful white-and-black spiral muted with a sheet of ice and jagged with hundreds of icicles hanging from her rails. In the dark starlight, they were like frozen teeth.

She looked so strange without her beacon to light up the night sky, a silent husk staring down over Salann with unseeing, dead eyes. I'd never seen the island so dark before. The moon hung low overhead, but dark wisps of clouds raced by. A storm was coming.

We'd landed at the east end of the island, far from Old Maude and Silas's little house. I took off down the narrow path, keeping a watchful eye out for Silas. He would never have let the light go out. Something was terribly wrong.

Far below us was the shoreline, black sand crusted with white swirls of snow. Having spent so many hours here as a child, I knew this island like the back of my hand. Despite the anxieties and exhaustion weighing upon my chest, my heart rose at seeing the familiar rocks and crags.

We rounded a bend, coming out near the lighthouse's cliff.

"Oh my," Cassius murmured, seeing the vast ocean before us.

I smiled, pleased it impressed him. Waves pounded the base of Maude's cliff, and the air was alive with crashes and a salty tang. Whitecaps dotted the water as far as we could see, and out at sea, a thick wall of clouds was building. Lightning danced through them—this promised to be a monster of a storm. We'd have more snow on Salten before the night was out.

Cassius spun in a slow circle, taking in the layout of the island and looking up at the enormous structure before us. "What's that?"

I followed his gaze to the top of the lighthouse. "It's a lightning rod. It draws bolts to it to protect the rest of the structure."

"I'm sure it'll get plenty of use tonight. It's strange to see so much lightning with a snowstorm, isn't it?" He squinted against the howling winds.

Down the hill from us stood Silas's house. All the windows, narrow and thickly paned to withstand the winds off the Kaleic, were dark.

"The key should be inside," I said, unable to tear my gaze away from the windows. It felt as if something stared back at us. I burrowed deeper into my scarf. "Silas keeps it on a hook in the kitchen."

We entered the cottage through the side door and stood in the mudroom. Tall waders hung upside down off long pegs above a drip mat, and a heavy ulster, once black but now stained with salt, rested on the top hook of a coatrack.

"He wouldn't have left the house without this," I murmured, fingering the heavy overcoat's worn wool. "Silas?" I called out, raising my voice. "It's Annaleigh Thaumas. Are you here?"

We paused but heard only the wind building outside. It raced past the house, growing into a low howl.

"You said the key is in the kitchen?" Cassius asked, prompting me to step deeper into the house.

On the table in the center of the small parlor was a hurricane lamp, and I fumbled to find a box of matches. I tried picturing Fisher and Silas in the threadbare armchairs, huddled around the fireplace as they took turns checking on the beacon's light. Did they play cards to pass the time? Sing songs or tell outlandish tales? The wick flickered to life, its warm glow casting off some of the night's eeriness.

Armed with the light, we quickly found the ring of iron keys hanging by the back door. As I picked it off the hook, there was a creak above us, as if someone had stepped on an uneven floorboard.

"Silas?" I called out. "Is that you?" I turned to Cassius. "We should go up and check. What if he's sick?"

"I'll go," he volunteered, his eyes finding the rickety stairs leading to the second floor. "You stay here."

I shook my head as another squeak sounded. "Silas knows me. I should go too."

Cassius handed me the lantern and picked up a poker from near the fireplace. He swung it low to the ground, testing its weight. "Stay behind me, at least. Just in case."

"In case of what?" I asked as we crept up the stairs.

"In case it's not Silas," he hissed under his breath.

I swallowed a surge of fear as we climbed the last steps.

There were three rooms on the top level. All the doors were closed. Cassius nudged open the one nearest to us. It was Fisher's empty bedroom.

The next was Silas's office, crammed full of books and ledgers. An old globe rested beneath a partially open window. As a gust of wind rushed by, the sphere spun around, creaking as it turned on its rusty axis. I prayed that was the noise we'd heard downstairs.

The final room was Silas's bedchamber. It was almost spartanly bare, except for the stacks of books lining the floor. The plain cotton curtains were pushed back, giving a spectacular view of Old Maude. Directly across from the window was a wide brass bed.

"Oh, Silas," I whispered, seeing the still form beneath the navy-and-white quilt.

He lay propped up on a pillow, a book open across his chest. His lined and weathered face looked so peaceful, he could have been dozing. But he didn't move, and there was a sour scent in the air, wrinkling our noses. He probably crawled into bed a day or so ago, after a long night tending the flame, and never woke up.

I looked out the window at Old Maude. She seemed to be anxiously peering in, unable to help her old friend. I hoped his beloved lighthouse had been the last thing he saw before shutting his eyes. Tears welled in my own as I remembered his crooked smile and gruff bark of laughter.

Cassius felt for Silas's pulse, a cursory gesture, before raising the quilt up over his face. We tiptoed out of the bedroom and carefully shut the door behind us, as though we might wake him.

"We'll have to send the High Mariner out at first light," I said once we were downstairs. My voice quavered, thick and sad. "And Fisher too, of course."

"I'm sorry he's gone, Annaleigh," Cassius said, squeezing my shoulder gently. "But it looked as though he lived a good, long life."

"You don't think he suffered, do you?"

He wiped the tears from my cheek, pulling me into a hug. "I'm sure he didn't."

"Old Maude must have run out of kerosene, and the beacon went out." I reached into my pocket, feeling for the keys.

"You know how to refill it?"

I nodded. "Silas always had me carry the bucket of oil up the steps. He said young knees could do it in half the time with half the exertion."

"We ought to hurry, then. Once the storm hits, I won't be able to get us back to Highmoor."

I drew my scarf up over my head once more, securing the ends so it wouldn't blow away. "You can't travel in storms?"

"Not in lightning. It's too unpredictable."

"Then let's not waste any time." I palmed the doorknob, poised to run to the supply shed. Silas kept large drums full of kerosene oil there. "Are you ready?"

We stepped out into the wind. The air was even colder now, whistling across the island and whipping snowflakes in our eyes. I unlocked the door, found an old tin bucket, and filled it three-quarters of the way up. The sharp aroma of kerosene burned my nostrils.

"Won't you need more? I'll carry it up. Don't worry about the weight," Cassius said.

"The tank won't hold more than this," I said, shutting off the kerosene spigot. "This will keep the flame going for a handful of days, at least until Fisher can return. Come on."

We made our way out toward Old Maude, careful to avoid patches of ice on the cliff's steps. I paused at the threshold, brushing a bit of flying grit from my eye. A gust of wind raced past the lighthouse and slammed the door shut with a loud crash. Startled, I dropped the lantern. The globe shattered, flames greedily flickering across the fuel. There was a burst of light, and we were left in utter darkness.

"I'm so sorry!" I exclaimed, reaching out to feel for Cassius. "The door hit me and—"

"It's all right," he said, finding my hand and giving it a reassuring squeeze. "I'm sure there's another one back at the cottage?"

"We don't have time. The storm is almost here. There's a lantern midway up the stairs. I'll go up and light it. Stay here so we don't spill any of the fuel."

Faint starlight filtered through the lighthouse from the gallery windows above. The spiral staircase's railing was barely visible. I grabbed it and felt around with my foot for the first step, then the next, and the next after that.

Keeping one hand on the railing to secure myself in the dark void and the other on the rough stone wall, I felt around for the lantern.

I was about twenty steps up when something grazed my hair, a phantom caress that jerked me to a stop.

"Dance with me," whispered a soft voice just behind my ear.

"Cassius?" I called out. Had he decided to come up too, rather than wait on the light?

"Yes?" His voice came from below me, in the center of the shaft.

Gripping the railing, I waved my other hand around in the dark, certain I would hit another person's—another thing's—body and scream. But there was nothing, only the cold, moist air.

"Dance with me," the voice repeated beseechingly.

"Do . . . do you hear that?" I asked, struggling to keep my voice level.

"I can't hear anything over that wind," he answered. "Should I come up?"

When my fingers brushed against the small globe of glass, I wanted to cry with relief. I fumbled open the lantern door and found the wick. Just before I struck a match against the wall, I had an awful premonition when I did, the Weeping Woman would be there in front of me. I pictured myself, startled, falling down the metal stairs and ending in a jagged pile of broken and bloody limbs.

But it was just me, and as the wick flared to life, a soft glow of light warmed the stairwell. Cassius was looking up at me, bucket in hand.

"Are you all right?" he asked, stepping around the glass shards from the broken lantern.

I nodded. "My imagination just got the better of me for a moment."

He headed up the spiral steps, hauling the kerosene. "I shouldn't wonder after everything that's happened tonight. Where are we taking this?"

I pointed up the shaft of the lighthouse, where the stairs curved around and around, narrowing in on themselves at the top like the tightly curled body of a seashell. "All the way up to the watch room. The beacon's base is in there."

He put the heavy bucket down for a moment and wiped his brow. "Lead the way."

I set my lantern on the watch room's table and checked the beacon's tank. It was empty.

"We have to crank the piston back up, then put the kerosene oil in," I explained, spinning the handle. Once the weight was raised, I had Cassius pour the oil in, then reset the weight. "The piston presses the oil up through the pipe here," I said, showing him the copper tube running up to the burner in the gallery room. "As the wick burns the oil, it's replenished by the tank."

"Until it runs out," Cassius said, setting down the bucket.

"Exactly. Now we just need to light the burner, and the beacon will be back."

Cassius peered out one of the windows, eyeing the storm. "We should have just enough time."

"Stay here in case I need the piston lowered again to get the kerosene flowing," I instructed, leaving the lantern with Cassius as I scurried up the stairs.

The gallery was a mess of dark shadows, but I found my way to the beacon and the lamp. Wrapping my skirt around my fingers—oils from my skin would cause the glass to heat unevenly and shatter—I slid the plate aside and lit the wick. It sputtered to a start, flickering as the kerosene pushed up from below. Once the flame was full and unwavering, I put the glass back in place and studied the rotating mirrors. They ran on a pendulum system, much like a grandfather clock.

"How does it look?" Cassius called. The beacon's flame offered me just enough light to see him through the opening in the floor.

I knelt down, pointing through the hole. "See those chains near you? Hoist the weights all the way up and then flip the catch. That will start up the mirrors, sending out the flash of light."

Squinting into the dark, I watched him work, checking the wick every few seconds to make sure it was still going strong. I tilted one of the glasses, instantly blinding myself as the room burst into light, amplified by the series of mirrors.

"It's working!" I exclaimed, rubbing my eyes. Dozens of brightly colored dots flashed across my vision, making it impossible to see. I heard Cassius on the stairs, coming up to see our work. "Watch out for the flash," I warned. If Silas were here, he would have fallen over laughing at so amateur a mistake.

"Annaleigh?"

I caught the note of concern in Cassius's voice. Squinting, I could just barely make out his form on the stairs. Stars danced around him.

"Annaleigh, come to me."

"What? Why?"

He was staring past me, looking at something huddled at my ankles. I turned, and a shriek ripped from my chest, splitting the world in two.

There, on the floor, twisted with rigor mortis and darkened with decay, was Fisher.

34

MY KNEES HIT THE WOODEN PLANKS AS I CRUMPLED to the floor. I tried to cover my mouth, but nothing would stop the guttural, choking screams from pouring forth. Fisher's neck was wrenched horrifically to the side, his joints splayed in unnatural angles. Milk-white eyes stared back at me from sunken sockets. I knew they couldn't actually see me, but they seemed to plead for release.

"Fisher?" I sobbed, crawling toward the corpse. My trembling hands reached out to somehow help before falling back. There was no helping him. He'd been dead for a long time. The fetid stench of rotting flesh was overpowering, coating my tongue and throat. A wave of sickness climbed up into my mouth, and I turned, spitting it out. "I don't understand," I moaned.

Cassius was at my side in an instant, arms around me, pulling me away from the decaying body of my childhood friend.

"I saw him not five hours ago. How is this possible?"

A low chuckle came from the shadows, seemingly from Fisher himself. It grew louder and louder, morphing into a cackle of triumph. Cassius pulled me to my feet and pushed me behind him as he stood guard, and drew a hidden dagger from his boot.

"Who's there?" he demanded, pointing the blade at the corpse. "Show yourself."

There was an impossible ripple across Fisher's chest, and his arm lolled off his body, thudding to the floor with a slap.

"Fisher?" I breathed, daring to hope that somehow he was still alive.

The arm flexed, contorting as his legs struggled to push the lower half of his body from the floor. They couldn't seem to find purchase and had to push again, testing their strength. His other arm jerked beneath him, so that he looked like a crab flipped on its back and scrambling to right itself. His torso twisted and writhed, muscles and sinews crunching, snapping, and popping into painful angles.

A low, keening wail rolled out of my chest as I cowered behind Cassius, my fingers tight around his sides, anchoring myself to him. He was real. He was here. Everything else seemed like something out of a dark nightmare I'd soon wake from.

Fisher righted himself, standing on legs too far decayed to hold weight. Knees bowed low, his back lurked over, hunched and hulking. He eyed us for a moment with a flat, stony glare, then began to cough.

Thick, viscous phlegm spewed from his mouth, landing on the floor like globs of tar. His body shook from the force, struggling to expel whatever was lodged deep in his throat. When his lips began to peel away, curling back like rolls of coiled tree bark, I pressed my face into Cassius, fighting the urge to throw up. I did not want to see whatever came next.

But I couldn't mask the gasps and groans as my very dead friend heaved and wrestled against the foreign object. With a wet burst, something awful gave way and fell to the ground. I peeked over Cassius's shoulder, unable to not look.

Fisher's body lay split open, pieces and parts flung out in a gruesome explosion. In the center of this absolute horror stood a figure, her back turned to us. Covered in viscera, she rolled her neck from side to side, stretching her muscles, delighting in her sudden freedom after such a tight confinement.

She turned slowly, gazing about her surroundings. When she saw us, her dark mouth flashed into a smile, even as oily tears ran down her face.

Her terrible black eyes met mine. "Dance with me?"

"Kosamaras?" Cassius gasped.

"Hello, nephew," replied the Weeping Woman, squinting at him.

My mouth fell open with alarm. "You know this . . . thing?"

"My aunt." Cassius lowered the dagger, putting things together that I was not privy to. "The balls, the dancing . . . that was all you?"

The Weeping Woman's eyes were wild in the pulsing light. "It was, it was. It may be my best work yet. Of course, it's not quite finished." She cocked her head to the side, staring around him at me. "I do hope you've not grown too attached to this one. She's next on my list."

"List?" I repeated. "Cassius, what's going on?"

Every fiber in my body was screaming at me to leave, to bolt down the stairs and out into the cold, away from this creature, away to safety. But where was safe? Not this island, and certainly not Highmoor. And with the storm's rapid approach, even the sea would be dangerous. There truly was nowhere for me to go.

"Kosamaras," I whispered, repeating the name he'd called her. I'd heard it before. Dredging up memories from childhood lessons on the canon of the gods, I sifted through them until it came to me. Kosamaras was Versia's half sister, not wholly a goddess but definitely an immortal. "Harbinger of Madness."

She ran her tongue over the pointed tips of her teeth. "And Nightmares," she added. "Everyone always forgets the Nightmares. It shouldn't bother me, I know, but it really is my favorite part." She spread her hands out, gesturing to the ruined bits of Fisher. "I'm just so good at them."

"What are you doing here?" Cassius demanded.

She laughed, a nasty little clicking tone deep in her throat, like a cicada seeking its mate. "I've been summoned, dear boy, why else?"

"By whom?"

"You know I won't tell you that, darling nephew of mine." She breezed past him, making a beeline for me, and I nearly tripped over my skirts to get away from her. Backing me into the glass window, she pressed her body into mine. It was surprisingly cold, sending a shudder of goose bumps down my arms. "We've had quite a few fun times, haven't we, little Thaumas girl? You always were my favorite partner." She cupped my cheek, running her fingers over my jawline.

"The dancing?" Every inch of me ached to squirm free of her grasp, but she was stronger than she looked, and her grip on my wrist was like a shackle. "The parties weren't real? Any of them?"

Kosamaras laughed in delight. "Now you're putting it

together!" She turned back to Cassius. "You know, I must give credit where it's due. Your little sweetheart was much harder to beguile than most of her sisters. The boy had to slip her something every time, just to knock her out enough to dream. Wine, tea, champagne, whatever." She shifted her attention to me again. "But I always got you dancing in the end."

"You had Fisher drug me?"

She slapped my cheek to the side and drifted over toward the beacon, like a moth to a flame. "Him?" she asked, turning back to the pile of Fisher. "It's never been him. Not truly. He's been a moldering sack of meat for weeks. *I*"—she drew out the word with preening importance—"controlled everything."

"That's not possible. I saw him alive just—"

"You saw what I wanted you to see!" she snapped, every trace of mirth gone from her voice. Around her eyes, dark webs of spider veins throbbed with rage, and a fresh wave of tears cascaded down her cheeks, dripping to the floor with abandon. "Everything you've seen, everything you've done, has been what I wanted you to." Her eyes flickered across Cassius. "Well, nearly everything."

A bolt of lightning danced by Old Maude, striking the cliffs far below us. I wanted to cry. The storm was here, and we were trapped on Hesperus until it let up.

"So you sent the girls dancing," Cassius said. If he'd noticed the lightning, his voice did not betray him.

I spotted the dagger still in his hand, limp at his side, and briefly entertained the thought of stealing it to plunge into her chest. But a little bit of steel wouldn't even scratch an immortal and I shuddered to think what she would do to me if angry.

"It's quite an impressive beguiling, very elaborate, I'm sure.

But I don't understand your endgame. Why send them off to dance in extravagant castles in pretty dresses? It hardly seems your style."

Kosamaras stepped over Fisher's ankle to stare out the window. She tapped on it once, leaving a bloody smudge across the glass. "I see what you're doing, nephew—cajoling me into telling you more than I should." She shrugged. "It's not as if anyone's going to believe either of you, though, is it? Not with me in their minds." She hummed a pretty waltz, dancing around pieces of Fisher. "I admit, the complexity was part of the appeal. Controlling the visions of eight girls at once, with none of them the wiser . . . it was a challenge I couldn't pass up. And they were all so moony and swoony. It seemed the perfect theme. I lured them in with baubles and brilliance, then let their own madness take over."

Another strobe of lightning briefly lit the sky, far brighter than Old Maude's beam.

"Two already danced themselves to death," she continued, her voice swelling with pride. "Straight out into the cold like lunatics, spinning around and around until they froze into blocks of ice." She whirled back to us. "And this one—she's close, so close, Cassius. I wouldn't be surprised if she takes her own life any day now. You can't have nightmares like mine every night and not break. You should have seen the way I made her squirm. Did you like the turtle, Thaumas girl? I made it especially for you."

"What turtle?" Cassius asked, turning back to look at me. His eyes were heavy with worry.

"You killed Rosalie and Ligeia," I murmured, ignoring him as I remembered that horrible day, running through the forest, so hopeful that we'd find them alive. "The third set of footprints in the snow was yours."

"His, technically," Kosamaras said, pointing down at Fisher. "I've been inside him for a very long time."

There were so many thoughts swirling in my mind, gaining speed as they flew in and out of focus, demanding attention. But they all snapped to silence at her words. "How long?" I demanded, my voice so much stronger than I felt. "How long have you been doing this to us?"

"Annaleigh," Cassius cautioned, reaching out to stop me.

"No, I have a right to know. You said you make us see things—was that what Elizabeth saw? We all thought she had a touch of madness in her—was it you all along? Did you use Fisher to push Eulalie from the cliff? Octavia from the ladder? When did he stop being my friend and become whatever *that* was?" I pointed to the festering pile of body parts. "How many of my sisters are dead because of you?"

"You mortals are all so ridiculous, trumped up and puffed out with your petty importance. Who are you to question me?"

"Tell me!"

Her eyes narrowed, still and contemplative, before bursting into a skittering, jittery blur. She was on me in an instant, mottled thighs straddling my chest. Her knees pressed into my collarbone, cutting off my air supply. Though she was smaller than me, her weight was crushing, pressing me into the wooden floor until I thought my bones might shatter. As she leaned in, two giant moths—just like the ones I'd seen that night in the gallery—crept out from her hairline. They crawled over her forehead before reaching out with hooked feet to latch on to my hair. Moldering wings brushed against me, and I felt one's spiral tongue uncoil, licking at my cheek.

"Just two," she hissed. "For now." She snorted in amusement. "Plus the little clockmaker."

Cassius drew up the dagger once again. "Let her go, Kosamaras."

She looked him over and laughed as more tears fell down her face. "Maybe I'll just finish this one off now. Especially as she knows so much." She tightened her grip, and I groaned as the room blinked in and out of darkness.

"Please!" His voice quavered, contorting with anguish. "This girl means the world to me. Name the price and it's yours."

Just before my ribs cracked, she rolled off me, striding to the other end of the room as if nothing had upset her. I struggled to sit up, gasping for breath. Cassius rushed over, stroking my hair, finding my heartbeat, whispering reassurances. I sensed the pressure of his lips on my forehead but didn't truly feel them. Everything inside me had gone numb.

"Spare me your offerings. You're never going to save her. This will not have a happy ending for you. Especially you," she said, winking at me.

"I'll tell my sisters everything. They'll know not to—"

"Not to what? Not to sleep? Not to dream? We're past that point, Thaumas girl. Now that I'm in here"—she pirouetted back to me and tapped my forehead—"I don't need you to sleep. I don't need you to dream. I'm with you everywhere."

I watched in horror as her skin peeled away, leaving bloody fingerprints on everything it touched. Including me.

Cassius swatted her hand away. "Who summoned you? Who started this?"

A roll of thunder shook the island, rattling the glass panes of the gallery with an angry ferocity. The beacon's flame flickered, pulled into an eerie dance by a draft. It caused the shadows in the room to loom around us with menace before retreating back to the edges. Almost like . . .

"The dragon man," I whispered. "I know who summoned you," I said, raising my voice. "The man with the three-headed dragon."

Cassius blanched, his eyes darting to Kosamaras. "Three-headed dragon? A Trickster? Is this true?"

I felt her black eyes roll over me, examining me with fresh interest. "Your sweetheart sees more than I thought. It was stupid of him to come dancing."

"Who?" Cassius demanded. "Say it out loud."

"Viscardi," Kosamaras rasped, drawing out the *s* and *r* into a long roll. A boom of thunder rumbled over us, echoing her tones.

"That's not possible. The Thaumases would never traffic with him."

Her face broke into an unnaturally wide grin. "Shows how little you know, nephew. You think everyone in that house is such a stalwart human, a pillar of the community? Viscardi was needed. Viscardi was called."

"Call it off, please, Kosamaras. I know you have sway with him. If anyone could do it, it's you."

She threw her head back, laughing. "This is the most exciting bargain I've ever been a part of, and you think I'll end it just because you asked politely? No." She paused, listening to something we could not hear. "I'll leave the girl alone—"

"Thank you, Kosamaras," Cassius started.

"—for this one night only," she continued. "But come the

dawn, all promises are off." She turned to me, fresh tears falling from her eyes, painting her mouth black. "We're going to have so much fun later, you and I. So. Much. Fun. Goodbye for now, dear Annaleigh. Dream of me, won't you?" She tapped my nose once before releasing her hold on me. "Have fun playing with your little poppet while you can, nephew."

"There must be something to persuade you to end all this, please, Kosamaras," Cassius said, approaching his aunt, hands up in supplication. "Something you want."

Her grin turned sharp and pointed. "You know, there is something I'd like right now. I fancy a dance with the littlest one, the little—what's her name? Patience? Prudence? Charity?" Her sharpened teeth winked, a wolf going in for the kill. "Verity. I've been visiting her for a very long time. Her little mind is just so open to everything I throw at it—dancing, balls, ghosts. . . ."

My heart thudded. "You're behind all her visions."

"Every last one." She beamed. "If you only knew the things I've shown her . . . You wouldn't believe how she screams." Her eyes sparkled, imagining fresh new horrors. "Hurry back to Highmoor. You won't want to miss it."

"No!" I screamed, throwing myself toward her, but with a crack of thunder, Kosamaras was gone.

35

I WAS HALFWAY ACROSS THE WATCH ROOM, READY TO race down the spiral staircase and out into the storm, before I realized I was alone. "Cassius?"

I heard his footsteps on the stairs, heavy and regular. When he finally appeared, his face was stricken gray. "I can't get us back there now." As if to prove his point, a white flash of lightning skittered across the sky. "It's too dangerous. Something could happen—"

"Something *is* happening! You heard what she said: she's going after Verity. I can't just stay here and let that happen!" A sob pushed up from my throat, begging to be released. I balled my hands into fists. I couldn't give in to tears now. I had to do something, had to act. "There's a boat! I'll go myself."

"In this storm? You'll never make it. Annaleigh—" He grabbed my shoulder.

"No!" I cried, whirling around. "I've lost too many people tonight. Silas, Fisher . . . I can't stay here, doing nothing, and have Verity added to that list. It will kill me."

"And she's counting on that," Cassius shouted over the storm.

"Kosamaras knows she riled you. She wants you to do something stupid."

The sob rose up again, this time bursting free. "Why? Why would she do any of this? We've never done anything to her!"

"She's not targeting you personally. Viscardi often uses her to collect his end of bargains. He's drawn toward the theatrical, and Kosamaras never disappoints." He sighed. "She's the Harbinger of Madness, creating so many false visions and skewed realities that the poor soul takes his life just to end the torment."

Laughter, bitter and hollow, barked out of my throat before I could block it. "She's going to try that with my sisters. I have to stop her."

"We'll figure out a way." Cassius pushed his hair back. "I know it's hard, but we need to forget about Kosamaras for a moment. She's just the puppet here. Viscardi is the one holding the strings. We need to figure out who agreed to his bargain."

"Then what? Politely ask them to end it?"

His eyes shifted away. "Not exactly . . . This could get very dangerous, Annaleigh."

I recalled Fisher's broken body, Lenore's silent stares, Verity pirouetting around her room with Kosamaras's black eyes. "It already has. . . ." I rubbed my temples, trying to think clearly. "I suppose we can't kill a Trickster?"

"No, they're immortal. But . . ." His eyebrows furrowed. "If the dealmaker died before the bargain was met . . . it would have to be over. Viscardi can't fulfill his end of a trade with a dead partner."

"And another person dies," I muttered, looking up to the ceiling. Above us, Old Maude's beacon flashed, again and again. Exactingly precise.

I'd loved that light ever since my first trip to Hesperus. Camille and Eulalie had been bored within minutes, wondering, rather loudly, why the lighthouse didn't do something more exciting. They'd wanted flares or fireworks, something big and bold. They couldn't see the simple beauty of something working with quiet efficiency, doing just what was needed.

But I saw it.

I breathed in deeply. "What if I make a bargain with Viscardi myself? I could stop this from happening, and no one else would have to die."

He looked horrified. "Absolutely not."

"Cassius, it might be the only way to stop this before someone else gets hurt. I can't lose another one of my sisters."

"And I can't lose you," he said, his eyes flashing over mine like burning stars.

Hot tears fell down my cheeks. "There must be something I could offer him, something that wouldn't hurt anyone."

He shook his head. "That's what everyone who summons him thinks. They all think they'll be the one to outsmart him. They'll be the one who can create a truly perfect deal. It's never happened. Viscardi always has an edge."

He sat down on the top step, leaving room for me to join him.

"I heard a lot about his bargains while growing up. Pontus likes inviting Viscardi into the Brine. No one amuses him like the Tricksters. They were all terrible. Viscardi always manages to sneak in some twist, create some mischief. He told Pontus about a pair of sisters who each had her heart set on the same man. When the man fell for the younger sister, the older one, heartbroken, summoned Viscardi."

I sank down beside him. "I can't imagine wanting something badly enough to summon a Trickster."

"When certain kinds of people get desperate enough, they're willing to do anything."

Thunder, booming and wild, echoed around his words. The storm was growing even stronger, and I too wanted to howl. I tried not to think about what was going on at Highmoor in our absence. I would only drive myself mad. Turning to Cassius, I fixed my eyes on him. "What happened with the sisters?"

"Viscardi appeared and listened to the older sister's request. He said he'd give her her heart's desire, happily, but he required one small thing. Just a memento, really. He wanted something of the younger sister's. Something she deemed precious."

It sounded so simple, such an inconsequential bargain. If I'd been in the younger sister's place, what would Viscardi take from me? One of Mama's necklaces? My favorite hair ribbon? What did I truly deem precious?

Verity flashed into my mind, safe and warm in sleep. Camille beside me at the piano, our fingers bumping into each other as we stumbled through a new song, laughing with every wrong note. The triplets, the Graces . . .

A cold snake of horror slithered deep inside me, coiling in the pit of my stomach. "She didn't agree, did she?"

Cassius nodded slowly, knowing I'd already guessed the outcome. "The older sister was betrothed to the man and did marry him, as the bargain promised. It was a beautiful wedding, and the villagers said she made a lovely bride. But at the altar, as the man finished saying his vows to unite them, Viscardi arrived, demanding payment. 'Payment?' the bride exclaimed, mortified at the interruption. 'My sister is over there.' She pointed. 'She's even wearing her prized hair combs. Take them from her and leave me be.'"

I grabbed his arm to stop the story. It was too terrible to imagine, and I sensed that the actual ending would somehow be even worse. Snow pelted the windows, tapping at the glass. I glanced up, suddenly worried I'd see the dragon man out on the gallery, peering in, begging to come inside.

I rubbed my arms, trying to stop the shudders that raced through me. "I can't believe someone I know would deal with him."

"Perhaps it's an act of revenge. A bargain for justice. Is there anyone you know who's had a disagreement with your father? Someone at court? Or maybe one of the staff?"

"Papa never mentioned any problems. Everyone has always been treated well, with kindness." The answer came easily enough.

Only it wasn't entirely true. I remembered the look of terror in the cobbler Gerver's eyes as he was cursed and berated in his own shop, Papa's rages over the slightest mishap in the shipyards, the fury with which he'd hurled the brandy bottle at a butler during Churning.

Churning . . .

"Are you all right?" he asked. "You've gone pale."

"Uncle Sterland." My mouth twisted around the treacherous words.

He drew a sharp breath, recognition dawning. "He was supposed to marry your aunt Evangeline. . . . You said she died . . . how?"

I nodded miserably. "She and Papa were twins. Evangeline was the firstborn—she would have become the Duchess, inheriting everything."

"What happened?" Cassius prodded gently.

"Sterland's father had been a respected admiral in the King's Navy and was one of my grandfather's closest allies. When the admiral died at sea, Sterland and his mother were invited to stay at Highmoor."

Outside, the wind howled, low and guttural, like a woman sobbing.

"As children, the three of them were inseparable. As they got older, Evangeline and Sterland became sweethearts. When the boys left to train at the naval academy, my aunt cried for months. She begged her father to bring them back. She refused to eat and grew pale and sick. The only way Grandpapa could appease her was to promise she could marry Sterland once he graduated and that he'd never leave Highmoor again."

Cassius sucked in his breath. "I don't suppose that went over well with your father?"

I paused. "There are . . . stories. Rumors, really. I've never believed them, but if Sterland does . . ." I pressed one hand to my clenched stomach, feeling sick. "But surely he couldn't."

"Tell me what happened, Annaleigh."

I looked out the windows at the dark sea surrounding us. A jagged bolt of lightning struck from above, splitting open a tree growing from the side of the cliffs.

"Grandpapa wasted no time preparing Sterland as Evangeline's future consort. He sent long letters and books detailing the family history, catching him up on politics and the Vasa shipping business. From what I understand, Sterland teased Papa unmercifully about all this, joking that all the Thaumas wealth and honor would soon be his."

A gust of wind blew by, kicking up a fine mist of snow. For a moment, I could see the past unfolding before me in the fog, as if I were watching an opera at the theatre.

"They boys returned home for Churning, and Evangeline was delighted to have the trio reunited once more. She wanted the ten days to be just like old times: picnics in the maze, trips to Astrea, playing hide-and-seek in the forest. . . . But a bad storm rose up without warning. Papa said he raced back to Highmoor. Sterland returned, hoping Evangeline was with Papa. . . . They didn't find her body for days."

"So Ortun became the heir and Sterland lost everything," Cassius filled in.

I nodded. "I know this doesn't paint him in a good light, but Papa would never have harmed Evangeline."

Cassius rubbed my arms. "It doesn't matter if he did or didn't, if Sterland believes it. . . ."

I felt sick with guilt, yearning to protest. This man was like an uncle to me. Even if he truly wanted to hurt Papa, how could he offer up my sisters and me? And to what end? What could he possibly hope to get from it?

But then I recalled the way his eyes had darkened in quiet rage at First Night. The bitterness that seeped off him like a bag of tea clouding clear water. I remembered the look of hatred boiling just below the surface as he'd joked about solving the mystery of the shoes and finally claiming what was due him.

"We have to tell Papa," I whispered. I grabbed his hands, beseeching him as tears fell from my face. "Cassius, I know it's dangerous, but please . . . take us back to Highmoor."

Lightning singed by Old Maude, taunting me, and we jumped as the following thunder smashed into our chests.

"We'd never make it in all this."

Rivers of tears ran down my face. I pushed them back, desperate to find a way out of this nightmare. I'd never felt so helpless. Cassius folded his arms around me, tenderly cradling me, letting me scream and cry. When I smashed my fist into the metal stairs, wanting to hurt something as badly as Kosamaras had hurt us, he let me. He held me until my frenzy passed and exhaustion settled over me.

Still, he smoothed my hair, running tender fingers through the tangled mess. I relaxed against him as my eyelids fluttered shut.

"Annaleigh?" Cassius's voice was warm and low against my ear.

I came to with a start. Had I dozed off?

"I think the worst of the storm has passed. We should try to get back to Highmoor before it reaches Salten."

With a weary nod, I followed him up the stairs. Shielding my eyes from the dark mess in the corner, I opened the glass door. We slipped through it before the cold breezes could blow out the beacon.

Cassius studied the sky for a long moment before holding out his hand. I wanted to join him but hesitated. "What are we going to do?"

"Your sisters need to know about the balls, first and foremost. Even if we can't stop them from sleeping, they need to know they can't trust anything they see. We have to tell your father everything as well."

"And Sterland?" I asked, hating the sharp bolt of fear spiking my voice.

His jaw clenched. "We'll let him speak, of course, but if it comes down to it . . . if the only way to end the bargain is to . . ."

He reached toward his dagger, squeezing the pommel. "I'll be the one to do it."

"Cassius, I can't ask you to—"

"And you haven't." Though he smiled, his eyes remained dark and unspeakably sad.

I stepped forward, wrapping my arms around him and holding him close. I wanted to thank him, wanted to say how much it meant that he was here, ready to fight with me when it wasn't his battle. I wanted to tell Cassius I'd fallen in love with him, deeply, truly, but before I could, we disappeared, leaving Old Maude in a swirl of snow and salt.

36

WHEN I OPENED MY EYES, HIGHMOOR LOOMED IN front of us, a dark, watchful monolith. But it didn't look like the home I knew and loved. It looked like a beast ready to devour me.

We arrived at the far side of the hedge maze just as the winds were picking up. It was disconcerting to be in the midst of a storm one minute and to see it approaching from far away the next. Clouds churned as the storm picked up strength over the Kaleic. When it finally hit Salten, it would be much, much worse.

A ball of worry gnawed deep within me. Would anyone believe us? The story sounded completely outlandish. If I hadn't seen it for myself, I would never have thought it possible. I leaned into Cassius's warmth, wishing it was enough to set everything right again.

"Did you really mean what you told Kosamaras? Up in the lighthouse? About me?"

"You are my world," Cassius said solemnly, without a moment's hesitation.

"And you are mine," I echoed.

He reached out to run his fingers through my locks, gathering a dark mass of them between his hands before kissing my forehead with gentle lips. Just once. It made me feel warm, protected, and cherished.

"We're going to get through this. You and I. Together."

I took a deep, steadying breath. "Then let's get inside."

In what now felt like another lifetime, my sisters and I had loved to watch approaching storms in the Blue Room. We'd curl up on the couches with tea or cocoa, wrapped in blankets and laughter. Those days were long gone, but perhaps everyone had still gathered out of habit.

My stomach churned with every step. My nerves were raw, sensitive to the slightest movement around us. When a maid opened the door to the linen closet, I nearly jumped out of my skin.

As we entered the drawing room, everyone looked up. For a moment, the room was full, crowded with even my long-dead sisters. Ava stood in concern, her hand clutched to her spotted bosom, and the triplets were reunited once more, though Lenore seemed not to notice her frozen sisters sharing the chaise. I blinked hard, clearing away Kosamaras's tricks.

"Thank Pontus!" Papa cried, crossing the room in three great strides to embrace me. Over his shoulder, Sterland perched on the end of a sofa and stiffened. "Where have you been? We've been so worried!" He looked past me, searching. "But where's Verity?"

I counted my remaining sisters. Camille in an armchair near the fire. Lenore on the chaise. Mercy and Honor on the floor with a picture book between them.

"What do you mean? Verity wasn't with us."

"She never came down for breakfast. When we went upstairs,

her room was empty, as was yours. We thought she was with you. Where have you been?"

A wave of nausea swept over me as I envisioned my sister's tiny body laid out in the snow, another victim of Viscardi's bargaining and Kosamaras's beguiling.

Camille made a small noise, a sound of horror lodged deep in her throat. "Oh, Annaleigh, what have you done?"

Gasps rose around the room, and Camille leaned forward, her eyes hot and accusing.

I felt as though the floor had dropped out from beneath my feet. "What do you mean?"

"Where is she? What did you do to Verity?"

"Do? Nothing! I was on Hesperus, relighting Old Maude's beacon. Silas died in his sleep. . . . And Fisher . . ."

Papa's face grew hard with confusion. "Fisher died weeks ago, Annaleigh."

"No . . . I mean, yes, he did, but we didn't know until—"

"Know?" Camille repeated. "There was an accident on Hesperus. One of the oil cans exploded. . . . We went to his funeral. Don't you remember? You cried the whole way there."

"And back," Mercy added.

"What?" I heard their words, understood each one's individual meaning, but when they were put together—when they were strung together in an accusation—it was like hearing an unfamiliar language.

And then I heard the laughter.

It started in the corner of the room, growing louder and deeper until the cackles rang across the arched ceiling, threatening to bring it crumbling down. But no one else looked up. I turned to Cassius, silently pleading for help, but he only shrugged. He didn't hear it either.

"Kosamaras is behind everything! She's making you misremember—all of you."

Papa and Camille exchanged uncomfortable glances. "That doesn't make any sense, Annaleigh. Why would a Harbinger be here?"

I balled my hands into fists, wanting to shriek. How could they not see this? "She's messing with your memories. That funeral never happened. Fisher has been here since the triplets' ball."

"Annaleigh, you know he hasn't." Camille stood up. "You've been acting strange for weeks. First with Eulalie, then that whole scene in the marketplace with Edgar. And I thought it must have been terrible for you, finding both their bodies. Then Rosalie and Ligeia went missing—only to be found, again, by you. And I tried to push away the thoughts, the wonderings. I tried to tell myself you'd never hurt one of us. You loved us too much. But now Verity? Annaleigh, how could you?"

My mouth dropped open. "You can't believe that. You're not seeing things clearly."

Camille crossed over to me, each step a fresh threat. "You've been blaming the curse, but it was you all along, wasn't it?"

I wanted to flee but was frozen in place, too shocked to react. Even though I knew Kosamaras was playing Camille, her words still stung, wounding deep. "What are you saying?"

"I think you've been wanting to be the heir all along. Inherit Highmoor, inherit everything."

"Camille!" I cried out. "You know that's not true! I'd never do anything to hurt any of you, least of all Verity! Killing her wouldn't put me any closer to inheriting Highmoor. Surely you see how mad that sounds."

"Mad," she agreed. "Seen any moths lately?"

My eyes darted to Papa. He was the only one who knew about that night in the gallery.

"Roland!" Camille shouted, calling for the valet.

"He's not here. He's at the shipwreck," I said. "All the footmen left for . . ."

I trailed off as Roland entered the room. He paused at the threshold, his eyebrows raised, waiting for instruction.

"You're not really here," I murmured. "You can't be."

I felt my family's eyes fall on me, their weighted stares ranging from pity to horror, all pressing in on me until I couldn't breathe.

The room spun around me sharply, and I sank to my knees. Colors leached away, leaving everything in shades of gray, then suddenly flashed back, vivid and more saturated than ever. I squeezed my eyes shut against the brightness, and somewhere in the back of my mind, I saw exactly what was about to happen.

Roland would haul me from the room and lock me away. Cassius wouldn't be able to stop them. They'd say I would be taken to Astrea to stand trial, but Camille wouldn't let her sisters' murderer leave Highmoor unscathed, especially with a Harbinger feeding her lies.

Would Camille poison one of my meals? Make it look as if I'd used the bedclothes to hang myself? Kosamaras would cross my name off her list, one step closer to her murderous goal.

Candlelight caught on oily tracks running down Camille's face. Though they were faint, it was enough to see Kosamaras was at work, altering her memories.

Without thinking, I grabbed Cassius's dagger and whirled around, brandishing it at Sterland.

"Annaleigh, no!" Cassius shouted behind me, but I did not waver.

"Annaleigh, put that down," Papa ordered, approaching me from the side.

I countered, keeping the blade trained on Sterland. "He did this. He made the pact. He's behind everything, Papa."

Sterland's face turned red. "What? What are you talking about?"

I tried to still the tremor in my hands as I stared down the dagger's blade at my father's lifelong friend. "Tell them! Tell everyone about Viscardi and the bargain. Tell them the dancing and the balls weren't real. Tell them all about the deal you made!"

"Deal? What deal? Annaleigh, you've gone mad!" He glanced around, presumably searching for a weapon.

"You're punishing Papa because he became the Duke, stealing everything from you."

His mouth opened in surprise. "What? I would never—"

"Sterland, is this true?" Papa asked, eyes widening. "You think I killed Evangeline? My own sister? Just for some title?"

"Of course not," Sterland said. He raised his hands as I took a step toward him, swishing the dagger back and forth. "I admit it's crossed my mind before, but I never truly . . . Ortun, I don't know what the girl is talking about. I never made a deal—certainly not with a Trickster."

"Papa, do something!" Honor or Mercy—I couldn't take my eyes off Sterland to be certain—let out a strangled sob.

A thought trickled down, running through my head like

rainfall on a stone wall. Though it seemed clear Kosamaras was using Camille's accusations to have me killed, maybe she was creating all this confusion to make me strike at Sterland first?

Which meant Sterland hadn't made the bargain . . .

Or had she known I would jump to that conclusion and wouldn't be able to kill him, thus protecting the dealmaker?

Or, worse, was she putting these ideas into my head now, overloading me until I snapped? My temples pounded, my mind cycling through too many possibilities. How was I ever to know which was right?

"Annaleigh, why don't you give me the knife?" Papa said, approaching slowly, hands raised in supplication. "You're upset, obviously. You've been through a lot these last few weeks. Let's talk, and I'm sure we'll come up with a solution."

"No. Sterland has to die before the bargain can be completed. This is the only way to fix it. Tell them, Cassius."

I glanced over my shoulder. I needed his reassurance. This was rapidly spinning out of my control. But when I looked to the doorway, he was gone.

A sound of confusion escaped me. I hurried out into the hallway, but he was nowhere to be found. "Cassius?" Crossing back into the room, I scanned it more thoroughly. "Where did he go?"

Camille frowned, confusion clouding her face. "Who?"

37

"CASSIUS." I TURNED BACK TO MY SISTERS. "HE'LL EXplain everything, Camille. I didn't do anything to Verity, I promise you—"

"Who are you talking about, Annaleigh?" Camille's voice was calm and measured, as if she were talking to a madwoman. The real glint of fear in her eyes gave me pause. She was looking at me as if I *was* a madwoman.

"Cassius . . . Cassius Corum. Captain Corum's son."

"Captain Corum is dead."

"I know that. His son took his place at Churning. Why don't you remember any of this?" Despite my best efforts, my voice rose in pitch as I spoke, verging dangerously on hysterics.

"It's like Elizabeth all over again," Papa murmured. His face was ashen. I'd never seen him look so old. He offered Sterland a look of spent resignation. "I'm so sorry, old friend. Would you allow us a moment with just Annaleigh?"

Sterland edged away from the chair, patting Papa on the back with remorseful condolence. "Of course, of course. Family affair and all that." His eyes lingered on me, deep with sorrow. "If there's any way I can be of assistance . . ."

Papa thanked him and waved him away.

"You're just going to let him go?" I asked, watching him leave the room a free man. "Papa, he—"

"Sterland isn't the issue here." The look on his face said everything his words did not.

"I am?" I asked, aghast. "Me?"

"No one else is seeing people who don't exist."

My dagger clattered to the floor as the room swam in and out of focus. This was a mistake. It had to be. Cassius was real. I'd been with him. All night. He was the one who told me everything about Viscardi and the bargain. Kosamaras and her games.

Her games . . .

She's the Harbinger of Madness, creating so many false visions and skewed realities that the poor soul takes his life just to end the torment.

With his words ringing in my ears, I sank to my knees, shivering uncontrollably. Had Kosamaras made me imagine Cassius? Was she powerful enough to create an entire person from thin air? We'd had so many conversations, shared so many kisses. I remembered the look in his eyes when he said he liked me best. I could still feel his hands on my body. That couldn't be manufactured, could it? He was real. He had to be.

I remembered talking about him with my sisters. They'd seen him—I wasn't the only one! But as quickly as my triumphant thought came, it was snatched away, like trying to hold on to the changing tides with your bare hands.

Rosalie and Ligeia had spoken with him. They were dead and couldn't vouch for him or me.

"Honor! Mercy! You were with him at the tavern in Astrea. He bought you cider." They stared blankly at me. "The day that Edgar . . . the day we got new slippers to replace the fairy shoes . . ."

Even as I said this, I spotted a twinkle of jade. Incomprehension flooded through me as I pushed aside my skirts, staring at my fairy shoes, whole and intact. They looked as new as the day we'd unwrapped them. I quickly covered them back up, wishing I'd never noticed them.

"Camille, you've seen him, I know you have. He sat right next to you at Churning! He was at the ball in Pelage. . . ." I shook my head, trying to dislodge that thought. The balls weren't real, and Cassius hadn't been there.

The truth crashed through me, falling from above like an anchor settling on the seafloor.

Cassius hadn't been at the ball in Pelage, even though I was so certain of his presence.

Kosamaras had made me see him there.

She'd made me see him everywhere.

Slowly, watching Papa for approval, Camille crossed the room and knelt beside me. She rubbed soothing circles across my back, the way you would comfort a frightened horse, crazed from a storm. "You mean the triplets' ball? Annaleigh, no one named Cassius was there."

"Not that ball. Stop saying my name like that."

"Like what?"

I shoved her arm away from me. "Like I've gone mad. Like you're trying to calm a mad person."

"No one thinks you're mad, Annaleigh," Papa said. "We're just worried about you."

"And Verity," Honor chimed in.

I whipped around to her, a snarl rising in my throat. "I told you, she wasn't with me!"

Camille bit her lower lip, eyes shiny with growing tears. "But maybe she was with . . . this . . . Cassius?"

A sharp blade of fear stabbed into my stomach. "How could you think I'd do something to Verity? It's absurd! You know I could never hurt her!"

"I'm sure there's an explanation for all of this," Papa said, snatching the dagger from the floor. Now in his hands, it was clearly nothing more than a butter knife, no doubt plucked from breakfast earlier that morning. The memory shimmered in my mind, bright and clear. I saw myself pick it up from the buffet and hide it in my skirt.

"No," I murmured, staring at the tiny bit of brass. "No, no, no, no." I curled into a ball, gripping my arms over my head, trying to make the pieces fit together. "What's happening to me?"

The dark cackle rose up again in the corner of the room. Camille stared at me, worry etched on her face. It was obvious she heard nothing. Just as suddenly as before, it sounded now from the right. I knew without looking Kosamaras would not be there. The laughter continued, creeping closer and closer to me until I realized it had been inside my mind all along, fusing itself into my brain until I broke.

I smacked my temple to dislodge this most unwelcome intruder, but the cackling only grew. I hit myself again. And again, using more force. Part of me was aware of Papa and Camille rushing in to wrestle my hands away, deterring the strikes, but I couldn't stop. When they pinned my arms back, I flailed forward, trying to smash my head on the floor. If I could just break it open, even a little, the voice could escape and leave me in peace.

The sound of porcelain shattering momentarily broke through my fit, causing me to pause. A vase from one of the bookshelves had exploded into hundreds of sharp pieces across the floor.

I was so relieved to see everyone's heads snap toward the noise, I sobbed.

A marble bust of Pontus slid along the edge of a higher shelf, pushed by unseen hands. It balanced precariously for a moment, as if waiting to make sure everyone was watching it, before plunging to the ground.

Honor and Mercy shrieked, racing away from the broken bits. Neither had on shoes—they'd staunchly refused to go about the house in the sailor boots Papa had issued—and they wailed as the wicked shards sank into their feet.

Echoing them, a prolonged scream sounded from upstairs. The hairs on the back of my neck stood at attention as the pitch grew higher, trailing off to a ragged end.

"What now?" Papa groaned.

Lenore straightened, sitting at the edge of the chaise. For the first time since the morning Rosalie and Ligeia went missing, her eyes looked sharp and present. She pointed to the ceiling.

Another cry tore the air apart.

"Morella," Mercy said, following Lenore's finger.

It punched through my stomach, clearing my thoughts—and that awful laughter—from my head. "The twins."

"Stay here. All of you," Papa ordered. Morella's howls swelled louder, ripping through the house like a tsunami, bathing everything in their pain and misery.

"With her?"

I turned back to what remained of the Graces. They were scared of me. Tears stung my eyes as I watched them cower from my gaze. "Mercy?"

"Papa, please don't leave us," she whimpered, holding her arms out, clearly wanting to be carried out of the room.

With a growl of impatience, he doubled back and knelt beside Mercy and Honor, folding them both into his arms.

I grasped my fingers, twisting them together in painful knots, ashamed to meet my sisters' faces. I'd frightened them. They truly believed I'd done something to Verity.

My breath hitched.

The night of the moths, Eulalie's ghost had accused me of murdering her. I'd passed it off as a bad dream, a case of sleepwalking gone horribly wrong.

What if it wasn't?

What if Kosamaras had used me to push Eulalie from the cliffs? And Edgar from the shop—I'd obviously not been with Cassius when it occurred.

But no. I would never have hurt my sisters, no matter what. This was just the beguiling.

Wasn't it?

If Kosamaras could bring a dead man back to life, create dozens of balls from thin air, and make me believe in a person who wasn't real, I shuddered to think what else she had in store for me.

What had I done to my little sister?

Papa broke their hug. "Morella needs me, and I need you to be brave right now." He kissed their foreheads, one after the other. "My brave little sailors. Camille . . . I'll likely need your assistance."

She blanched. "But I don't know anything about childbirth. Annaleigh takes care of her. She's the one who's been talking with the midwife. She helped with Mama's deliveries."

He looked me up and down, then sighed. "I'm not taking her up there in this state."

I hated the way he spoke over me, as if I wasn't fit to be included in the conversation. Studying the butter knife in his hand, I supposed he might be right.

I opened my mouth, forcing my voice to remain even. "The midwife left a book the last time she was here. There are pictures in it. You and Camille should be able to follow them. They're very detailed."

A wave of relief washed over Papa's face. "Thank you, Annaleigh. Can you get it for us?"

Feeling like a marionette being jerked and tugged by strings against my will, I crossed to the bookcase the statue had fallen from. I pulled the thick volume off the shelf and ran my hand over its worn cover.

On my way back to Papa, I skirted around the mess of porcelain and marble, then froze. Written in the dust, by an unseen fingertip, was a message.

I EXIST.

Mercy and Honor were the only two who'd been near the mess, but they'd run away as soon as the bust fell. They wouldn't have had time to write this. A faint flicker of hope warmed my heart. Had Cassius somehow written it? My head swam as I realized Kosamaras could have just as easily written it, wanting to drive me mad with uncertainty.

"Annaleigh?" Papa prompted.

I glanced back down at the floor before giving him the book, certain the words would be gone, that they were only in my mind, just as everything else had been. But they remained in place.

"Papa, there's something you should see—"

A fresh scream cut through the air.

"Not now," he said, rushing from the room with Camille.

A hot flash of lightning shot across the sky, followed seconds later by a rumble of thunder. It echoed in my chest, knocking my breath away. Even it could not drown out the sounds coming from the fourth floor.

"Someone ought to send for the midwife." Honor crossed to the window, watching another bolt of lightning. "Do you think they'd make it in such a storm?"

"I'll go," I volunteered. It was a fool's errand, but I was desperate to show my sisters I wasn't the monster they now believed me to be. "I can take the skip, or the dinghy if the winds are too strong."

Before anyone could talk me out of it, the gold clock sailed off the mantel, smashing to the floor in a pile of cogs and gears. Across the room, the piano came to life, clanging and clunking out an ugly series of notes as the keys pressed down on their own accord. It looked as though someone was walking down the length of ivory, stomping their feet. Our poltergeist had returned.

Mercy howled, bolting from the room, with Honor fast on her heels. Lenore silently looked to me, clearly uneasy.

"You should go after them. They're likely to run right up to Morella's room, and they don't need to see anything that's going on there."

She bit her lip, then nodded.

"Lenore?" I asked as she got to the doorway. "You really don't remember Cassius?" She shook her head. "What about the balls? The dancing? Did I make that up too? You were with me at nearly all of them."

She opened her mouth, looking as if she was about to deny the memories, but paused. She shook her head once, twice, as though clearing it from a fog. For the first time since the funeral, she spoke. "I do remember dancing, but—"

Another crash of thunder interrupted her train of thought, then a pair of shrill screeches.

"Go. I'll stay here, I promise."

She turned and raced down the hall after the girls.

Lightning danced dangerously close to the window, and the responding boom was so loud, I ducked, covering my ears. The glass panes rattled in their casings. Had that bolt struck the house?

An unearthly howl came from upstairs. Memories of Mama's labors sprang to mind, but it was far too early for Morella, wasn't it? Even if the twins were conceived before she'd married Papa, as Camille was so very certain, she was only six months along. Maybe. It was too soon. Far too soon.

I paced the room, feeling like a caged animal.

Morella's cries of anguish grew louder and louder, spilling into my mind as pervasively as Kosamaras's laughter. Were the twins part of the bargain? Was Morella? How many people were fated to die today?

One loud, long scream rang through the house before it fell into an eerie stillness. The storm raged on, with flashes of lightning and rumbles of thunder, but there was only silence from the fourth floor. I dared to cross into the hallway, straining my ears for the sound of a baby's cry.

Only silence.

Then Camille. "Annaleigh? Annaleigh, we need you *now*!"

38

RUSHING INTO THE BEDCHAMBER, I WAS STRUCK BY A wall of iron-tainted air. The sheets were a tangled horror of blood and viscera. The babies had come.

Morella sprawled back into a pile of pillows, dozing or unconscious, I couldn't say for certain. For a moment, I worried she was dead, but even from across the room, I could see her chest heaving. Papa knelt at the side of the bed, his hands enveloping hers as he whispered a silent prayer.

"The babies?" I asked stupidly, struck by how silent the room was.

Camille turned, holding out a blanket-covered bundle. I feared she'd cringe from me, as Honor and Mercy had. Tears streamed down her face, and I knew my math was right. It was too soon.

Wordlessly, she offered me the baby. Peeking inside the stained swaddling clothes, I spotted a beautiful tiny face, eyes closed. They would never open. He was a boy. Papa's only son. Stillborn.

"What happened?" I kept my voice low. There was no other

bundle in the room. This boy had been the first. Morella needed all the rest she could get if she was to deliver another child on this hellish day.

Camille glanced uneasily at the bed, then beckoned me into the hallway. I couldn't bear to leave my brother, however small, however dead, by himself, so I took him with us. I rubbed his back, wishing that could return him to us.

"She was already in labor when we got here. She said the contractions came on fast and horribly strong. She'd been fine at breakfast, but then . . . She was bleeding so much. I didn't know if that was normal. I can't imagine that it was." She nudged back a lock of hair with her wrist. I'd never seen her look so exhausted. "She started pushing, and he just came out in a rush of fluids and more blood. Papa caught him and . . . he never made a sound. He tried hitting him on the back, but he never woke up. I can't do that again, not by myself. I know you're not wholly well right now, Annaleigh, but I need you to be. I need my sister." She held back a sob.

"Oh, Camille." I threw my arms around her, not caring about her blood-soaked clothing, not caring about her accusations or the bargain. Relief raced through my body as she hugged me back.

"What is happening to our family?" I could barely hear the question with her face buried in my neck. "What were you talking about downstairs? A bargain?"

"Cassius . . ." She jerked away and I trailed off, seeing the nervous glint in her eyes. "I think someone in this house made a bargain with one of the Tricksters, Viscardi. I thought it was Papa, maybe. So he could have the twins. Then Sterland. But now I don't know what I believe anymore."

"Did Cassius tell you this?" Her voice was skeptical but not unkind.

My laugh was short and tasted like bitter coffee, brewed too strong. "He told me all kinds of things, but what is real and what isn't? Are we actually here, having this conversation? What about him?" I raised the baby higher up on my shoulder. "Is he really dead, or is it just an illusion?"

"An illusion?" she repeated. "I don't understand what you're talking about. Of course he's dead. Feel his chest. There's no heartbeat. Listen to his lungs. They never drew breath."

"But that could be what she wants us to see."

Camille stamped her foot, her patience drawn too thin. "What she? Who are you talking about?"

"Kosamaras." I rubbed circles across my brother's tiny back. "She can make us see whatever she wants us to. Even a captain's son no one else remembers."

"Oh, Annaleigh." She put her hand on my shoulder, her voice flush with understanding. "But why would she be here? What did we ever do to anger her?" I could see her wanting to listen, wanting to believe, but I didn't know if she truly trusted what I was saying or if it was simply easier to think that than to know your sister was a murderer.

"She's working for Viscardi. Tormenting us was part of his bargain."

She glanced up, meeting my eyes with exhausted resignation. "Verity is dead, isn't she?"

"I don't know." Tears came, swift and sudden. My throat felt clogged and thick. Kosamaras had gotten to her somehow, and I hadn't been there to stop it. I'd never see her lopsided grin or her happy green eyes looking up at me again. "I think so."

Camille let out a sob and bit into the back of her hand to stifle it. I hugged her again, holding our half brother between us.

Groans from Morella's room interrupted us.

"She must be waking up. Do you think the other twin will come today?"

There was too much death already. I could not lose either of them as well. "We should go in and see."

"Oh, Annaleigh, you're here!" Morella held out her hands, beckoning me to join her.

Papa glanced at Camille. "Are you certain this is a good idea?" After a considered beat, she nodded, and he grudgingly allowed me access.

"How are you feeling? Have there been more contractions?"

"Not as intense. Not like before." Her lips were pale—nearly the same shade the sheets had been—raw, chapped, and cracked from her screaming.

I spotted Hanna lingering in the corner. She looked as if she'd aged a decade since I last saw her, and I wondered again if everyone but me remembered Fisher's death. Were those tired circles under her eyes etched from grief or another illusion from Kosamaras?

"Hanna, can you bring water, please? And fresh linens. Several sets." I turned back to Papa. "Find a new nightgown for her?" I climbed into the bed, skirting the bloody mess as best I could. "We'll get you cleaned up, Morella, all right?"

She sank backward, her eyes rolling shut. "You don't need to bother. I think I'm dying."

"You're not," I said with more confidence than I truly felt. "Tell me what happened."

"You've seen your brother?" She broke into fresh tears. "I was resting after breakfast when there was a sudden sharp pain. Right here," she said, pointing to her side. "It was like being ripped apart from the inside. Then a great gush of water. Maybe it was blood. Just when I thought the pain couldn't get any worse, it did. Down . . . down there. I don't remember much after that. But Ortun . . ." Sobs racked her body.

"Sometimes these things happen. Papa knows that."

Thunder rumbled over Highmoor, shaking the breath from our chests. There was no way a midwife would make it to Salten in time.

Hanna returned with new sheets, and Papa tenderly scooped Morella up from the bed, heading to their bathroom. Camille offered to help clean and dress her while Hanna and I struggled with the bedding.

"Burn them," I instructed, looking at the bloodied sheets. Stringy black streaks of discharge stuck to them like pitch tar. There was no way they'd ever be cleaned. "And have someone bring up warm broth for her. She'll need to keep up her strength."

Hanna glanced at the chaise, where I'd carefully rested my baby brother between soft throw pillows. "What should we do with . . ." She couldn't finish.

In truth, I did not know. He'd eventually need a proper funeral, down in the crypt. When his little body finally returned to the Salt, would he know to look for his other sisters? Surely they'd be kind to him and show him love.

"Let me take care of him," Papa volunteered, reentering the

room. He tucked Morella beneath the clean sheets. "I will take care of my son."

Morella burst into a fresh set of tears once he and Hanna left the room. "He's going to hate me." Her lips trembled, and I took her hand. It was shaking.

"He loves you," I repeated. "You need to calm down. You've got the other baby to think about."

She shook her head with such violence, she managed to undo the careful braid Camille had just plaited. "No. No. I'm not going through that again. I can't deliver another dead child."

My hand settled on her belly, searching for any sign of movement from the other twin. My heart sank as I shifted positions, praying to Pontus for a sign of life. Just as I pulled away, her stomach jumped, the baby inside lashing out as if to say, "I'm still here. Don't forget me."

She grimaced.

"See? The other baby is alive and well. And feels very strong!" I tried to laugh, hoping she'd smile back, but she rolled to her side, away from me.

"I can't do it," she whimpered.

At the edge of the bed, Camille shifted, clearly uncomfortable waiting. She raised one eyebrow at me, silently asking what we should do. Remembering the tray of lotion and oil, I crossed to the bureau.

"Why don't Camille and I rub your feet?" I suggested, picking up the little vial of lavender oil. It would relax her and hopefully mask some of the foul odors lingering in the room. Breathing through my mouth helped only so much. I could taste the blood in the air, like copper coins weighing heavily on my tongue.

We knelt on either side of Morella's legs. Spilling out several drops of the silvery fluid into my palm, I showed Camille how to rub the arches of her feet with ever-increasing pressure.

Morella groaned as a mild contraction clenched her abdomen. When it passed, she continued to weep. Her hysteria built, growing ripe and foul like a great blister, ready to burst and soak us all with its poison. She'd drive herself crazy, lingering on the agony and pain of the first delivery. She needed a distraction.

"This smells nice, doesn't it?"

Her fingers clenched, balling up the sheet into a tight fist before smoothing it out, stretching the linen till threads snapped and unraveled.

"Does it remind you of the lavender fields near your home?"

She'd mentioned the fields of flowers before. Perhaps if I could get her talking about her childhood, she'd relax and stop putting so much stress on the remaining child.

Another contraction passed, and she frowned. "My home? No, we didn't have lavender in the mountains."

It was my turn to frown, though she didn't see. Her eyes were shut, anticipating the pain of the next wave. "I thought you lived in the flatlands."

She shook her head. "No. I grew up near one of the sharpest peaks in the range. But there were the most beautiful flowers just outside my village. Scarlet red, like shining rubies. They have a peculiarly sweet scent. It's hard to describe but impossible to forget. I miss them so." Her face scrunched as she tensed again. When the tightness passed, she opened her eyes. "There's one on my vanity, that little glass flower." Her bottom lip pushed out wistfully. "You can't smell it, though."

Camille slid off the bed to retrieve it for her. "It's beautiful," she said, handing it to Morella to focus on. "Like an exotic geranium."

A memory stirred inside me. I'd heard something about little red flowers before. Something Cassius had said . . .

The Cardanian Mountains. The Nyxmist flower and the People of the Bones . . .

Viscardi's people.

Another contraction, harder and longer than those before. Morella dropped the little bauble into the bedding as she doubled around the pain.

When her breathing returned to normal, I picked up the glass sphere, considering. "I'm sure once this is all over, Papa will get you a bouquet of these, the biggest you've ever seen. He'll probably fill the whole house with them!"

Her smile was weak, her energy drained. "They only grow outside that village. It's so far from Salten, they'd never make the journey."

All of this sounded exactly like the People of the Bones. Surely a follower of Viscardi would have no qualm brokering an agreement with him. I dug my fingers into her arch, rubbing her foot with a sharp focus. I'd jumped to the wrong conclusion with Sterland before. I didn't want to make that mistake again. "That's too bad. They're Nyxmist, aren't they?"

At the sound of the flower's name, she froze. "You've heard of Nyxmist?"

I dared to meet her eyes, going for the jugular. "I never realized you were from the Cardanian Mountains. You never talk about it."

Camille frowned, unaware of what Morella was about to give away. "You told me you grew up near Foresia, on the plains."

Eyes widened, she felt herself caught in the lie. "I moved there . . . later. Once I became a midwife."

"A governess," I reminded her. Her ruse was showing, unraveling like a spool of thread. "Papa said you were a governess."

She pushed a lock of hair back behind her ear. It was damp with sweat. Her nightgown was already drenched as she curled around another contraction. My instincts screamed to help her, to ease her pain, but I ignored them and slid out of the bed. When the contraction passed, she lay back into the pillows, feigning sleep.

"How could you?"

She kept her eyes closed.

Camille's mouth dropped open. "It was you? You made the bargain?" She'd put everything together.

Morella's eyes slowly fluttered open. "You really don't remember me, do you?"

Her voice was so weak and dry, rustling like leaves. She didn't look long for this world.

"I knew the little ones wouldn't, but I worried about you two."

"Remember you?" Camille asked, appraising her with fresh eyes. "Remember you from what?"

"I served as one of the midwives for your mother's confinement with Verity."

I frowned, scanning hazy memories of the women in white who had descended upon Highmoor during Mama's last pregnancy. Papa had spared no expense, saying he wanted the very best possible care for her. There'd been so many midwives and healers, I couldn't recall them all.

"I was much younger," she whispered. "Obviously. I never did live in the flatlands or work as a governess. Your father and I made all that up. I was born in the Cardanian Mountains and sent to the capital to study midwifery, like my mother and her mother before." She took a deep breath. "Could I have some water, please?"

Camille turned to the pitcher at the bedside table, but I reached out, stopping her. "When your story is done."

She sighed, rubbing her forehead. "Oh, what does it matter now? I'm going to die tonight anyway. Someone ought to know the truth." She turned toward the window, her eyes flickering back and forth as if watching her story unfold like a play onstage. "I'd never seen the sea before. Or a house as lovely as Highmoor. I spent most of my first afternoon here dreaming of someday being mistress of such an estate. . . . When I felt Ortun's eyes on me, I decided someday was too far away."

A bark of laughter burst from me. "You're lying. Papa was devoted to Mama. He never would have strayed from her."

"Don't be so naive. I knew he wanted me. I could see it in every one of his glances." She smiled so widely, her lower lip cracked open and began to weep blood as a stab of lightning danced outside the window.

Camille made a noise of disgust.

Morella's eyelids fluttered shut. "After Verity was born, your mother was so weak. So tired and worn out. Birthing twelve daughters . . . No one was truly surprised when she died. . . ."

Hearing the words Morella didn't speak made my blood run cold. Her forehead tightened as another contraction hit. When it passed, she dared to meet my stony gaze.

"It was an act of kindness, Annaleigh, truly, you must believe me. She was in pain, so much pain. I mixed a bit of hemlock into her nightly medicine, and she died in her sleep, none the wiser."

"You murdered Mama?" Camille's face twisted in rage. She grabbed an iron poker from the fireplace, wielding it at her. "You bitch!"

"It wasn't a bad death," she gasped. "She didn't suffer."

"Are we supposed to be thankful for that?" Camille brought the poker down over her legs—not hard enough to break bone, though it did leave a nasty welt. Morella shrieked and scooted away from the rod's reach.

I held out my hand toward Camille. "Let her finish. We need to hear everything. You killed Mama. Then what?"

"Annaleigh," she pleaded, "it wasn't murder. She was going to die anyway, probably. I just . . . helped."

I clenched my teeth, trying to hold in my fury. "What. Next?"

"After Cecilia's death, we were all sent away. My mother begged me to return home, but I stayed in the capital. One day I crossed paths with Ortun—he was there on business at court, and he . . . he was so lost without Cecilia, so in need of comfort and care . . . so I got him over his grief the only way I knew how to." She smiled, her face relaxing for a brief moment as memories washed over her. "Ortun sent for me every night that week. . . . When he returned here, he wrote, saying how he longed for me, yearned for me." She closed her eyes again. "And like a stupid calf, I believed him."

Another contraction. Another crash of thunder.

"It went on like this for months. Nights of bliss, followed by weeks of waiting for him. Publicly, he needed to mourn Cecilia. I only needed to wait a year. Just one little year." She swallowed. "Five years passed. Every time one of your sisters died, Ortun had to start the mourning process all over again. He said I needed to be patient and then we could be together, but I . . . I should have known better."

Morella paused, her face blood red and thick with sweat.

"One night, I was coming home from a delivery and I saw your father. I didn't know he was in town. He hadn't written, hadn't sent for me." Morella pushed back a damp lock of hair, wheezing. "And on his arm was a woman. Just a girl, really."

She rippled in pain, but I couldn't tell if it was from a contraction or memories of that night.

"I flew at him, cursing and shouting, making such a scene." She gasped, then let out a deep groan. "Water, please."

Camille pointed the poker toward her neck, and she tipped her head back, cringing. "Keep talking."

"He struck me. In front of his new little whore. He didn't even care that she saw. He called me names, screamed, berated me. Said I was a fool for ever believing a person like him would marry a nothing like me. I wasn't titled, I wasn't rich. I was just . . . me." Tears now openly streamed down her face.

Despite the horrors she'd confessed, in this one awful moment, with my own words ringing in her voice, I wanted to comfort her. She'd been hurt by my own father, a man who claimed to love her.

A sharp crack of thunder sounded directly above us, snapping me back to my senses. Impossibly, the afternoon grew darker still, the storm ready to slash the sky to bits.

"He left me there, lying in the street, as if I'd never mattered to him." She let out a broken sob. "But even after all that . . . I still wanted him."

A groan welled up from the very bowels of Morella's belly. Her legs flailed with such force, it gave the impression there were more than two under the sheets. My gaze strayed to the Thaumas octopus at the top of the bed's canopy. Its eyes seemed alive with condemnation, squinting down in judgment as it listened to her tale. Its arms spiraled down the posts, beaten metal against dark mahogany, reaching out in retribution. The silver reflected shots of lightning outside, and the wind picked up, howling past the windows in uneven pitches.

"So you summoned Viscardi," I filled in. "You summoned him to make Papa fall in love with you?"

Morella nodded. "And to become pregnant with a son. If I was with child, Ortun would have to marry me. After all I'd done for him . . . I deserved that much. Once I returned to Highmoor, I saw Eulalie watching closely. She was starting to remember. Then that awful night . . . she confronted me, saying she was going to tell everyone. I . . . I couldn't let her ruin everything."

Edgar's shadow on the cliff.

"You killed Eulalie?"

Her fevered eyes darted over mine, beseeching me to understand. "She wouldn't keep it a secret."

I recoiled, as if hit in the stomach. I'd befriended this woman, and all along she'd been killing off my family with no greater pain than crossing items off a list. A red mist clouded my vision, and my heart beat in double time. Fury raced through my body, pulsing from my core out to the very tips of my fingers. I grabbed the poker from Camille and pointed it at Morella's throat.

"You used us as payment for a son."

She cringed back toward the headboard, trying to escape the metal hook. "And it was all for naught. My son is dead, and I will be too before the night's end."

"Good," Camille spat out.

A crack of thunder exploded directly over us, and Morella began to laugh, clinging to her belly as the next contraction ripped through her. A commotion rose at the far end of the hall, shouts and screaming.

"Go see what it is." I kept the iron trained on Morella. "I'll stay with her."

Morella watched Camille go before meeting my gaze once more. "Annaleigh, you must believe me. I didn't want you to die. I . . . I did at first, before I knew you—I wanted to make Ortun pay for how he'd treated me—but then . . . You've been so kind to me. You took care of me, befriended me. I didn't know Viscardi would use the Harbinger to collect his payment, truly I didn't. That's why I gave you the book to read . . . so you wouldn't sleep at night. So you wouldn't dream of that *thing*."

I said nothing.

A feeble mewing squeezed out of her. "I can't do this, I can't," Morella groaned, shoulder blades popping. Her lower jaw jutted forward, sinking into her upper lip. "You could do it, you know. Just go ahead and do it."

"Do what?"

A crazed sheen glazed her eyes. "Hit me. I know you want to. You know you want to."

"I don't."

"Just raise it up and bring it down over my head. Then it'll all be over."

I backed away from the bed, looking out into the hall as the shouting grew. Servants ran by with buckets of water and towels. Smoke poured out of a room at the far end.

"Do it, Annaleigh," she called out. "Bash my head in. Bash my brains out. I killed your mother. I killed your sisters. Take your revenge and kill me." A bloodcurdling howl ripped from her mouth, and a spot of red appeared on her nightgown, growing larger and wet over her thighs. "Please!"

"I don't care what happens to you, but I'm not killing my brother."

Laughter erupted past bared teeth, cruel, sharp pieces of shrapnel ricocheting off the walls. "You idiot girl." She groaned and hunkered down as she began to push, pushing around the contractions, pushing past the pain, pushing the baby free. Her voice was low and grating, like metal skidding down a cliff. "This is not your father's son."

My stomach lurched. "What?"

She gasped for air. "Viscardi and I had to seal our bargain somehow. . . . Once it was set, Ortun fell at my feet, begging for forgiveness, begging for another chance, begging to come back to my bed. And I let him. I let them both in. And then . . . I let them ravish me."

Her groans turned to a shriek of anguish as a dark shape hurtled from her, spilling onto the bed in a mess of tangled limbs and dark, membraned wings. My eyes couldn't seem to focus on the details, couldn't make sense of the shapes flailing through the air. A mouth too wide, too full of teeth, opened and let out a lusty wail.

It wasn't a baby. It was a monster.

39

CAMILLE BURST BACK INTO THE BEDROOM, HER FACE flushed and smudged in soot. "Lightning struck the roof. The fourth floor is on fire! We have to get out!" She came to a screeching halt as she saw the writhing mass on the bed.

The thing flipped over, exposing its winged back, and grabbed at its umbilical cord. It tugged on the opposite end, and Morella cried out in pain, clutching her stomach. Raising the cord to its mouth, it bit through the muscle in one snap, freeing itself. I turned to the side, unable to stop myself from throwing up.

Camille grabbed my arm and pulled me toward the door. Servants ran by, shouting for us to hurry downstairs. The fire couldn't be controlled. We needed to escape now.

"Wait, don't go!" Morella called to us, her voice high and reedy. For a brief moment, her eyes lost their madness and she looked like our stepmother again. "I can't get downstairs by myself! You wouldn't leave me to burn to death, would you?"

Standing on the threshold, I dug my heels in, stopping Camille's race for the stairs. "We can't just leave her here."

She groaned in exasperation. "That's exactly what she'd do to us!"

Morella struggled to free her blood-soaked legs from the wet sheets. She tilted her head, listening to something beyond our hearing. From the adjoining sitting room came the sound of heavy footsteps. My mouth went dry as a black spider of fear sank its fangs deep into my stomach.

Viscardi had arrived.

Camille yanked on my arm again. "We can't stay here! The fire is already in the hallway!"

The door to the sitting room whipped open with a crack, stopping us in our tracks. A familiar dark figure appeared, silhouetted in smoke and flames. His silver curls sprang out, writhing like snakes.

As he strode past the fireplace, like a king traversing his throne room, he cast a shadow on the far wall. A great horned three-headed dragon was shown in stark relief, wings puffed out in ferocity and teeth bared.

Morella burst into a fresh set of tears before him. "My lord, I don't understand. My son was born dead. You betrayed me!"

He raised up one finger with fluid grace, swishing it back and forth. His voice dripped like honey, melodious and modulated. "Morella, my sweet. Is that any way to greet me?"

"You lied!"

In a shaky, jittering flash, he stood over her, looming, leering like a gargoyle from hell. On the wall, his dragon shadow glowered, flexing and snapping, while Morella's writhed beneath it.

"I. Never. Lie!" he snarled.

"My son is dead!"

He shook his head. "Our son lives."

"Ortun's is gone. You swore I would have a son! You swore—"

He held up his hand, silencing her. "I swore you'd have a son. And you did. Was the little body taken from this room by your husband not the perfect specimen of maleness?" His face turned stony, his eyes narrowed. "Next time you summon the god of bargains, remember to ask for exactly what you want."

"I did!" she howled.

Viscardi shook his head, his eyes hidden in the dark shadows. "You went into great amounts of detail with what you wanted—the husband, the house, the son you so foolishly thought would inherit the estate—but you failed to specify the child should be born alive." He reached out and cupped her cheek, running an elongated thumb across her lips. "But just think, my darling. Your boy provided ours with all the nourishment he'll need for the long trip home."

He scooped up the squalling monster from the bedclothes, peering down at the tiny, fanged face. Viscardi's visage softened with tenderness. He even gurgled coos as the creature bit at his finger.

"No!" Morella cried, struggling to stand on the uneven mattress. "No! I gave you your son. You've taken two of the Thaumas girls. Our deal is off. I want this bargain broken!"

He whirled back to her, cradling his son in the crook of his arm. "Broken? Who are you to take back an oath?"

"I don't want any part of this oath. You took my son; you don't get the other girls!"

With fire swirling in his eyes, he licked a forked tongue over his teeth, considering the small woman in front of him. Across the wall behind them, the dragons reared back, giddy with bloodlust. "You can't just say you want our bargain ended and expect it to be so. You know the price I demand. The only thing I'll accept in payment."

Morella blew out a shaky breath and nodded, resignation clouding her face. She glanced over his shoulder, meeting my eyes. "Don't tell your father any of this. Tell him . . . tell him I loved him. Always."

Viscardi looked back at us again, his lips—too thin to even call them that, really—raised into a painful smile, and he winked. Then, in that strange blur of movement, he descended on Morella, suddenly so much more than a man. Wings and scales and talons slashed in and out of the bedlam.

Cries rose from the chaos, and for one awful moment, they echoed the sounds I'd heard her make when I'd walked in on her with Papa. But the pleasure was short-lived, and her whimpers of ecstasy soon turned into shrieks. The shrieks turned to screams. And then the screams cut off into silence.

Camille covered her mouth, holding back cries of her own as we spotted the pale curve of a rib rising from the bedding. Morella had come from the People of the Bones and was now reduced to nothing but a pile of them.

A man once more, Viscardi turned to us, a lusty appreciation shining in his flaming eyes. "I always did like dancing with you two best," he said, his gaze burning over our bodies like scorched earth. "Pretty, pretty Annaleigh and my darling Camille . . . what fun we could have together . . . you need only ask."

Camille's jaw clenched as she stepped forward. "How powerful are you, Trickster? Are you able to change the course of things? To change the past?"

"Camille, no!" I shouted, sensing what she was about to do. I grabbed at her arms, pulling her away from the grinning god.

"He could bring back our sisters!" she hissed. "He could bring back Mama!"

"At what cost?"

"I could," Viscardi said, raising his voice to be heard over us. "I could do all that and more." A forked tongue slithered out from his blood-covered mouth, beckoning us. "And you might find you quite enjoy the trade."

I shook my head. "Never!"

He looked at me with his glittering, fiery eyes. "You're worried about what happened to Morella? I understand completely, Annaleigh. But you'd never be so foolish as to make the same mistakes she did. You're far more clever and so much more . . . dazzling."

My feet started to inch closer, seemingly under my control, but as I tried to force myself to stop, they continued forward. He drew me toward him like an anglerfish luring in prey with its hypnotic, flashing orb.

His fingers traced over my cheek, caressing the skin with a seductive tenderness I was unable to resist. It wasn't until I nuzzled back into his palm that I realized it was covered in Morella's blood.

"Annaleigh, stop!" Camille cried out, grabbing my hand and yanking me out of the trance and far from Viscardi's reach. She squeezed me tight, rooting us to where we stood.

Viscardi sighed, a cloud of sulfur wafting from his lip, but shrugged it off, offering a low bow to us both. "Suit yourself." Swooping up his wailing progeny, he disappeared in a crack of thunder.

Camille and I stared into each other's eyes, gasping in the smoky air, as we absorbed everything that had happened on this horrible day.

Was it truly over? I'd expected to feel different, to feel less marked. Surely there ought to be something to signal the bargain was broken—but there was nothing.

A cry from the corridor snapped us back to the present. The fire raged unchecked through Highmoor. If we didn't leave right now, we would not get another chance.

We raced into the hall as a ceiling timber, blazing as red as Viscardi's eyes, splintered to the floor, catching the runner on fire. Orange flames licked up the wallpaper, and in a sudden burst of fire, an oil painting of Eulalie and Elizabeth was gone.

"The back staircase!" I had to shout to be heard over the crackling flames.

"The third floor is already on fire," Camille said as we reached the landing. "Where are the Graces?"

"They were on the first floor with Lenore." I prayed they'd not ventured upstairs.

The fire traveled fast as we fled down the stairs, a monstrous orange fist trying to smash us. Bursting out into the garden, we choked back smoke. The storm raged across Salten, whipping sharp flakes into our eyes. It should have been cold, but the blaze threw off so much heat, we were in no danger of frostbite.

People gathered around the fountain, huddling together for warmth and comfort. I sobbed in relief as I spotted Lenore, Honor, and Mercy pressed together under a blanket.

"Camille? Annaleigh!" Hanna cried, seeing us. "Thank Pontus! The main staircase was already in flames when we tried to go up for you. I was so scared we'd lost you both." She pulled us into a painfully tight embrace. "Have you seen Fisher?"

I stared at her dumbly.

"Fisher!" she screamed again, as if I'd simply misheard her. "I couldn't find him when the fire broke out. Did he go with Roland and the others to the shipwreck? Did you see him then? I don't know where he is!" Hot tears ran down her face.

I ran my fingers over my own cheeks, smearing soot and pushing aside the last of Kosamaras's beguiling.

It had been a lie, earlier in the Blue Room, one of Kosamaras's tricks. There'd been no accident. No funeral. I was the only one who knew Fisher was already dead. Had died before ever arriving for the triplets' ball.

Lenore left the fountain, joining us. Her eyes were bright with tears, and the flames reflected across them, reminding me of Viscardi's burning irises. "Where's Papa? Why isn't he with you?"

Hanna let out another wail. "He helped the little ones out, then ran back in, saying he was going after Lady Thaumas. You were up with her . . ." She trailed off, taking in our silence. "Didn't you see him?"

I locked eyes with Camille. She shook her head, silent tears welling up.

"We didn't see him. Not since he took the baby . . . not since he went downstairs."

"We must go after him." Hanna let go of us, looking for other servants to rally. As I squinted through the snow, I could see there weren't many to call upon. Roland and many of the footmen were missing. Regnard and Sterland too.

I grabbed her sleeve. "The back stairs were already engulfed as we came down. He wasn't there."

As if confirming my words, there was a great rumbling crash from deep within Highmoor, a section of flooring giving way under the weight of charred wood and flames. Honor and Mercy let out shrieks, and Hanna started crying again.

I wrapped my arms around Camille, bracing myself against her sobs. No one ever needed to know what had actually taken place tonight. We held on to each other with a fierce protectiveness and watched Highmoor burn.

40

AS THE LATE AFTERNOON WORE INTO TWILIGHT, MORE servants escaped from the house, piling out the back doors and making their way to the garden. Camille joined the girls at the fountain, snuggling against them, comforting their tears. She beckoned me to come too, but I couldn't sit still. Wandering through the groups of people, I tallied how many had made it out, who was still missing.

Every male servant was gone. The *Rusalka* had truly run aground, and they'd all gone after it. Seeing Sterland and Roland in the Blue Room had just been another beguiling.

As the flames made their way down the wing, windows shattered in the heat, raining shards of glass like wicked snowflakes. Something inside exploded—stores of wine or kerosene oil, no doubt—and a ball of fire burst free. It flew down the steps, throwing itself into a snowbank.

It wasn't part of the explosion—it was a person!

Horrified, I raced over and threw handfuls of snow to stifle the flames.

With trembling fingers, I turned the body over and saw not one but two people.

Verity gazed up at me, flushed and smeared with soot but looking relatively unscathed.

"Annaleigh!" She hurtled into my arms, tears streaming down her blackened cheeks. "Annaleigh, you're alive!" She turned back to the other figure, lying motionless in the snow. "Is Cassius okay?"

I looked over at the pile of burnt clothing, trying to see the form beneath. "What did you say?"

"Is he okay?" She pulled away a piece of fabric, revealing his face.

My heart stopped. It was Cassius. He was real. Verity saw him, and I could feel his body beneath my fingertips. Kosamaras had beguiled us into forgetting him. "Cassius?"

Verity pawed at his legs, seeking a reaction. "It was so awful, Annaleigh. I woke up this morning and no one could see me or hear me. It was like I didn't exist. I followed Mercy and Honor everywhere today, but they didn't know I was there. I fell asleep in the Blue Room when the storm came. When I woke up, there were flames everywhere. But then Cassius came, and he could see me! He pulled me out of the fire. He saved me!"

I leaned over the blackened body. "Cassius?" I gently shook him, rousing him back to consciousness.

His eyes flashed open but couldn't focus. They were bloodshot from the heavy smoke. Had the fire blinded him?

"You see me?"

I pressed a kiss to his blistered palm. "I do, I do."

He coughed. "I wrote you that message in the dust. . . . I didn't want you to think you were alone. . . . Is she all right? Is Verity okay?" His voice cracked, his throat raw from breathing in the noxious fumes.

"She's safe. She's right here."

Verity ran her little hand over his ruined face, and he smiled. "You saved my life, Cassius."

His eyes closed for a moment. "Good. That's good." He fumbled for my hand, the flesh of his fingers bubbling with charred blisters. "It wasn't Sterland, was it?"

I shook my head. "Don't worry about that. You need to save your strength. The bargain was broken. Everyone is going to be safe. That's all that matters."

He tried to smile, though it clearly cost him. "Not everyone."

Tears streamed down my face, landing on his. "Don't you dare give up! You're out of the house, and the storm will end soon. We'll send for your mother! There's the wall of wishes at her abbey. . . . Everything will be all right."

He raised his hand, stopping me. "Will you take me out farther into the garden? Please? Out from under the branches? I want to see the stars."

Verity and I looked up into the storm. There was no way Cassius would be seeing any stars tonight.

"It's storming, my love. Stay here and rest."

For a moment, his eyes lit up and he looked like the Cassius I knew and loved. "Did you say *love*?"

I pressed the softest kiss I could to his cheek. "Of course I did."

"Then take me out from under the trees, Annaleigh."

With Verity's assistance, I picked him up as gently as possible and helped him walk farther from the house, out from under the oaks' obscuring branches.

A great cough racked his chest as we lowered him to the ground. Blood flecked across his lips, and I wanted to howl. This wasn't how things were supposed to play out. Eulalie's novels always had the villains defeated and the lovers safe and sound, ready to start their lives together.

"Cassius, isn't there a way to stop this? To summon your mother and—"

He clasped my hand, his head moving with a nearly imperceptible shake. "Oh, my darling Annaleigh, remember when you let the turtles go? Some things can't be kept." He cupped my cheek, and my tears trickled down his fingers. "Be brave. Be strong. You'll always have my whole heart."

He coughed again, his hand falling slack into the snow.

"No!" I screamed, and Verity sobbed, wrapping her arms around my neck. I rocked back and forth, holding her as tightly as I dared. The smoke on her clothes and hair singed my nostrils, grounding me into this horrible, awful moment. I wanted to punch the ground, kick and stomp and rip my shattered, useless heart from my chest.

He couldn't be gone.

I waited, praying to hear the wicked cackle of Kosamaras's laugh, but this wasn't part of her tricks. The beguiling was over, and Cassius was dead.

The snow swirled as the night wore on into morning, piling up on us, on Cassius, until he was tucked under a blanket of white. Hearing our cries, my sisters gathered around us, huddling together, warm and safe, the last of the Thaumases.

As the storm cleared and the sun rose over the smoking facade of Highmoor, Camille stood, inspecting her ruined estate. She held her body stiff and erect, trying to be strong, but her shoulders shook.

I pushed myself to my feet, knowing she needed comfort,

someone to hold her hand and meet this challenge with her. But I needed to see Cassius one last time. I wanted to say goodbye while he was still just mine. Not a half god. Not Versia's son. Just mine.

But when I looked back, the body wasn't there.

I pushed through the snow, brushing handfuls away, rooting through it, but he was gone, vanished as if he'd never existed.

But he had. Verity had seen him. She was pressed against me, alive and well, because of him.

I looked up into the sky. Had Versia somehow spirited him away, back to her moonstone palace? Back to the Sanctum? I wanted to race to the Grotto's door and travel to the House of Seven Moons, demanding answers, but stopped short. There was no door. There never had been. I had no way to reach her and would never know.

A great piece of the East Wing's wall toppled over, sending tremors through the garden and gasps through the crowd.

"What do we do now?" Lenore asked. "Where will we go?"

Camille's eyes, pink and watery, flickered over the crumbling edifice. "We're not going anywhere. We're the People of the Salt. We're tied to this land, to these seas. Fire cannot force us to retreat." She turned, her eyes looking over all of us, the final six Thaumas sisters. "We rebuild."

Seven Months Later

"HOLD ON TIGHT, DON'T LET THEM GO JUST YET!"

"But I have my wish already! I don't want to forget it!" Verity exclaimed, jumping impatiently from foot to foot.

"Me too!" Honor held on to the edge of her paper lantern with just her fingertips, dangerously close to releasing it.

"You have to wait for mine to be lit, and Annaleigh's," Mercy snapped. "You just want your wish to get there first!"

A summer breeze danced around us, light with the scent of seaweed and salt, and for a moment, Mercy's wick wouldn't catch. It sputtered out once, twice. When it finally lit, the paper lantern filled with warm air, and I handed it off to her. I hurried to light mine before the Graces' patience wore out.

"All right, do we all have our wishes?" My sisters nodded eagerly, their eyes reflecting the happy glow of the flames. "Then, on the count of three, we'll release them. One . . . two . . ."

"Three!" we cried together, and let go.

The little white lanterns slowly rose into the sky, twirling and twining around each other, caught in a dazzling ballet. They floated higher and higher to join with the stars.

Was Versia looking down on us right now, on this beautiful and clear summer solstice? From our perch on Old Maude, the sky seemed dizzyingly infinite, a sparkling forever. The stars twinkled with an extra amount of radiance, as if they too knew it.

A lump grew in my throat as I thought of my wish. I wanted Cassius here beside me on this exquisite perfection of a summer evening. Nights like this were meant to be shared, remembered, and talked about for years to come. Skies like this were made to be kissed under.

"What did you wish for?" Honor asked.

Verity shook her head. "You can't tell or it won't come true!"

Honor sighed and turned her face back up to the sky. "How long do you think it takes for the wishes to come back?"

I shrugged. "I don't know. That's part of the fun, isn't it? Every time you see a shooting star, you can be happy because someone's wish is being returned to them."

We watched until the lanterns could no longer be distinguished from the stars.

"I hope my wish comes true first," Honor said, rather uncharitably.

Mercy's mouth dropped. "No, mine!"

"Bedtime," I announced before a squabble could break out.

With minimal grumbling, the Graces headed back into the gallery, still sharp with the scent of fresh paint, and down the lighthouse's inner spiral staircase. We marched back home, to our little cottage on the cliff, and they readied for bed. After a story and a kiss on their foreheads, each fell asleep with childlike swiftness, leaving me to my work as Keeper of the Light.

After that horrible night at Highmoor—as threads of Kosamaras's false memories came back to my sisters—it became clear Old Maude would need a new Keeper, and quickly. Camille, as Duchess of Salann, gave me her blessing immediately, sending the Graces with me. With all the construction going on at Highmoor, they'd been hopelessly underfoot, and I think she was glad to have them out of her hair as she settled into her new position.

Now that the weather was warm again, Lenore visited often, bringing Hanna and baskets of treats from home. Each time she came, her eyes looked a little less haunted, a little more present. During her last stay, she'd mentioned she was thinking of leaving Highmoor once the renovation was complete. She wanted to stay and help Camille but felt trapped under the weight of memories. She didn't know where she wanted to go but was excited to discover more of Arcannia.

I understood how she felt. I'd always love my childhood home, but I was glad to be free of it. Though the work on Hesperus was often hard, I felt flush with purpose and woke each day with a happy heart. I often imagined Cassius working alongside me, hauling oil for the flame, tracking ships and the tides. His absence lingered, filling me with an ache deeper than anything I'd ever known. I knew I'd spend the rest of my life pining for him.

As I made my way back to Old Maude, a friendly breeze played with my braid, inviting me to go off course. It was too pretty a night to go back inside just yet. On our afternoon walk, we'd spotted several sea turtle nests on the beach, great mounds nearly as wide as Verity was tall. The sand on top of them shifted as we watched. The hatchlings would soon be ready to go out to sea.

Wandering down to the black sands, I kicked off my shoes. The warm waves washed over my bare feet, tugging at the thin linen of my dress, pulling me out to deeper water. Cicadas hummed in the trees farther inland, competing with the soft lapping of water against the shore. I closed my eyes and drank in the wonder of this night. The ocean's brine filled my nose, my lungs, my whole being, and I breathed it all in, completely at peace.

A disturbance in the water broke me from my reverie, and I opened my eyes in time to see a shooting star streak across the dark sky. I smiled as it raced toward the horizon. Some lucky person was about to have their wish returned to them. Hearing another splash, I turned, hoping to see a little army of hatchlings making their way down the beach and into the waves.

I froze, spotting a tall figure standing ankle-deep in the water, silver starlight caught in his wayward curls.

Cassius.

Every fiber of my being longed for it to truly be him, not a fantasy haunting my eyes as he did my heart. It wasn't him. It couldn't be.

But he looked so very real.

A seagull cried out overhead, and for one intoxicating moment, the stars seemed to glow brighter, dazzling the sky with an unnatural luster. A small sliver of hope sparked inside me, burning brightly. Had Versia received my wish? Was that shooting star for me?

"Cassius?" I dared to whisper, half certain this was a dream.

Don't wake up....

When he moved, wading into deeper water, my breath caught in the hollow of my throat. He wasn't going to reach me. He'd open his mouth, but I'd never hear his words. I would wake up in the watch room of Old Maude, all alone, all over again. My heart panged in anticipation of the painful disappointment to come.

Don't wake up. . . .

With a smile that began deep in his sparkling eyes, Cassius pulled me into a close embrace. I ran my hands over his arms in wonder. They were impossibly covered in smooth skin, without a trace of burns.

It was a dream. It had to be.

Then he ran his thumb across my cheek. His eyes were bright with a heated joy, and his lips parted, about to speak.

Don't wake up!

When I didn't, I reached up, my fingertips tracing the back of his neck, feeling his curls against them. Cassius released a murmur of pleasure before sweeping me into a kiss. His mouth was soft against mine before his arms tightened around me, pulling me into a more intimate kiss, a sweeter ache.

"You still taste like the Salt," he whispered.

"Is this actually happening?" I breathed. "Are you really here?"

Cassius nodded. "I'm really here."

"For how long?"

His grin deepened. "For as long as you'll have me."

My fingers trembled as I cupped his face, looking up to meet his eyes. I wanted to memorize everything about this miracle in front of me. "Truly?" He nodded. "How?"

"Of all the wishes tonight, yours was almost the loudest, nearly the most hopeful." He smiled. "The second easiest to grant."

A chorus of splashes sounded from the shoreline. We turned and saw a dozen small sea turtles paddling into the sea, swimming out into open water. One brushed my leg, giving my ankle a friendly tap with his flippers before heading off into the blue unknown.

"Almost?" I asked, looking up at the night sky. Starlight rained down around us, and I couldn't imagine a more achingly perfect moment than the one I was in now, nestled between the stars and the salt with the man I loved, who was equal parts both.

"There was only one louder," he murmured before his lips descended once more. "Mine."

ACKNOWLEDGMENTS

Shortly after my daughter was born, I set out to write *House of Salt and Sorrows*. Juggling a notebook and pen with a snuggly, sprawled-out baby might not seem like the best way to create a story, but my heart spills over with love whenever I remember those peaceful afternoons in her nursery. Grace, thank you for your patience and for being with me every step of this journey, from jotting down the first words to helping me drop my contract into the mailbox and pronouncing it "Good, good!" Watching your love of books, typewriters, and pink Post-its grow is truly one of my favorite things in life. I'm so proud to be your mama.

Sarah Landis, thank you for seeing something special in me and my words and knowing what on earth to do with them. You are amazing, and I'm so lucky to have you as my agent.

A huge wave of gratitude to Wendy Loggia, Audrey Ingerson, Alison Impey, Noreen Herits, Candy Gianetti, and everyone at Delacorte Press for your time and care with this book. Wendy, I'm still squealing with glee and am so darn grateful my book is in your capable hands. Fairy shoes for everyone!

I'd like to thank Jason Huebinger and #PitDark for such a wild

ACKNOWLEDGMENTS

whirlwind. I never thought one little tweet could change the world, but it certainly did mine.

To all of my dear family and friends, beta readers, and agency sibs—Jonathan Ealy, Sarah Squire, Sona Amroyan, Charlene Honeycutt, Maxine Gurr, Susan Booker, Scott Kennedy, Kaylan Brakora, Jenni Bagwell, Jeannie Hilderbrand, Kate Costello, Peter Diseth, Jeni Chappelle, Jennie K. Brown, Jessica Rubinkowski, Shelby Mahurin, Ron Walters, Meredith Tate, and Julie Abe: I couldn't ask for a cooler group of people to go on this journey with! Your support and laughter mean everything to me. Thank you!

So much love and gratitude to Jessica Hahn, who taught me everything I know about the history of dress and design. I owe you so many sparkling ball gowns.

Hannah Whitten, you magnificent creature. I think you've read this book almost as many times as I have! I can't imagine doing any of this without you—and furthermore, I wouldn't want to. You are incredible, and I'm lucky to have you for a critique partner and friend!

To my sister, Tara Whipkey: you've been reading my stories for as long as I've been writing them. Thank you for afternoons racing around the log cabin, imagining we were mermaids or the Boxcar Children, for talking about my characters like they are real people, and for being the best sister a girl could ever ask for. You are a true joy, and I love you like crazy!

Paul, you are my always. Thank you for believing in me, for making me a tasty breakfast every morning, and for never believing me when I say we can go to a bookstore "just to look around." I'm so blessed to have you for my husband and best friend.

This book would not exist without my parents, Cyndi and

ACKNOWLEDGMENTS

Bob Whipkey, who filled my childhood with Margie the Monkey, Anne of Green Gables, and all the girls from the Baby-Sitters Club. Thank you for every trip to the library, for endless batteries and flashlights to read under the covers with, and for never telling me my dreams were too big or wild. I love you so much.

If you were swept away by *House of Salt and Sorrows*, get pulled back in with *House of Roots and Ruin*.

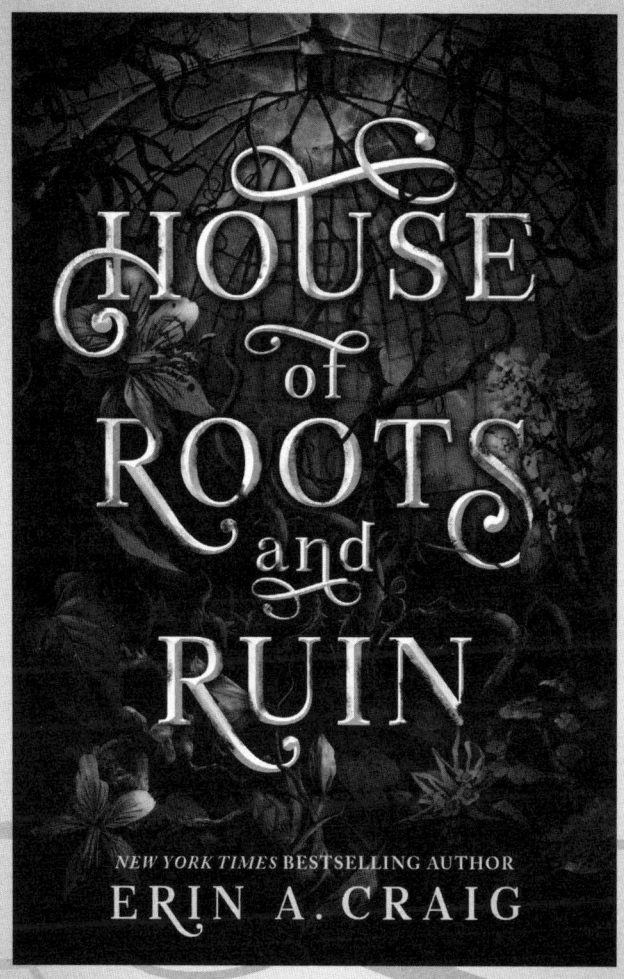

Turn the page for a sneak peek!

House of Roots and Ruin excerpt text copyright © Erin A. Craig, 2023
Cover art copyright © Marcela Bolivar, 2023
First published in Great Britain, Republic of Ireland and Australia by
Rock the Boat, an imprint of Oneworld Publications Ltd, 2026

THE PAINTBRUSH WAS TOO WET.

Pigment concentrated through the boar-hair bristles, sluicing out in irregular blots and smudging the line I'd wanted crisp.

"Hold still," I murmured, barely moving my lips as I dabbed the brush on a rag, lest I somehow jar the moment before me and lose its magic forever. "Just one minute more."

The corner of Artie's lips trembled as if fighting the urge to break into a grin.

"I'm almost finished," I promised. "Just . . ." I flicked the brush across the canvas, capturing the gleam of impish merriment brightening my nephew's eyes. "There. It's perfect."

"I want to see! I want to see!" Artie exclaimed, falling out of his carefully arranged pose and tumbling over himself as he dashed behind the easel. His eyebrows fell. "That's not what I look like. Is it?"

I studied the rendering with a critical eye before glancing back to the little boy before me. Thick waves of dark hair like mine, like most Thaumases, but with his father's button nose. "I think it's a fine likeness."

"Very fine," a voice affirmed from the doorway behind us.

"Mama!" he cried, racing off to give his mother a hug. "Am I done now?"

Camille raised an eyebrow at me, seeking confirmation. I set down my palette and nodded.

"All done." Camille pressed a swift kiss to the top of his head before he was off, racing down the hall, breathless with pent-up energy.

"How was he?" she asked, entering the Blue Room to study the portrait more closely. Her amber eyes missed nothing. "This arrived for you this morning," she said, handing me a thick envelope. It was marked with several palace seals.

Mercy.

"A little squirmy but that's to be expected." I ran my thumb under the flap, ready to rip open the envelope and dig out my sister's letter, but I paused, watching Camille take in the painting.

"It's a lovely painting," she complimented. "I can't believe he's five now. Where have the years gone?" My sister brushed a strand of burnished auburn hair from her face and her fingers fluttered over the corner of one eye, feeling at the nonexistent lines she worried were beginning to creep in.

"*My* birthday is coming up, you know," I mentioned, keeping my voice as light and casual as I could.

She frowned as though I'd accused her of something. "I wouldn't forget that, Verity."

"I didn't mean— Only . . . maybe we could talk about what we should do this year?" I turned on my stool, looking up. "I thought perhaps we could go to the mainland? To the capital? Mercy said—"

"It's not Mercy's place to say anything," Camille said, glancing at the envelope in my lap. I could see she wanted to snatch it up and read the missive for herself but instead she stepped forward, squinting at a brushstroke.

"She said that I *could* still be presented at court, if we wanted to. Eighteen is a little older than most girls, but—"

Her sigh stopped me short. "I would have loved to take you at sixteen. You know that."

"Only I was at Hesperus, helping Annaleigh with the baby," I supplied, knowing her excuses by heart. "But last year—"

"Last year we were in the middle of the east wing renovations. It was hardly the time for a long, extravagant trip."

"I know," I said, tucking a bit of hair behind my ear. She was bristling for a fight, and if she started snapping, I knew it would be impossible to sway her. "I know, I know, I know. But now . . . the house is all done. The children are old enough to travel. I'm sure they'd all love to see Arcannus."

Camille shook her head, backing away from the canvas, her eyes drifting around the room as if looking for something to improve. She approached a chaise and plumped a down pillow until it stood on its own like a tuft of meringue. "Oh no. The children would never come with us to court. They'd stay behind with their governess, of course."

I took a quick breath, hope reaching high into my chest like a man drowning at sea and grasping for a life raft. "But we . . . we could go? Oh, Camille, think of how fun it will be! We haven't been to the mainland since Mercy moved to court. Annaleigh could come, too, and I'm sure Honor would join us. Foresia isn't that far from the capital, and perhaps even Lenore . . ." I stumbled to a halt as I always did whenever Lenore came up.

My third oldest sister was a complete mystery to me.

"Lenore is Lenore. I doubt she'd . . ." Camille ran a quick hand over her hair again, as if assuring herself that everything was still in place. "All of that does sound . . . It could be quite agreeable," she allowed. "But your birthday is next week. There's no possible way we could have everything ready by then. The travel alone is a full day by our fastest clipper. Perhaps we could arrange something this fall? Before Churning."

My face fell.

We wouldn't.

The weather would grow bad.

The twins would get sick.

Camille would have half a dozen excuses by then, none of which I could argue against because she was older and wiser and a duchess and you might be able to lead a spirited debate if it were simply the first two but her title was as formidable as a citadel high atop a hill. Bordered by a barbed stone wall. And a moat.

Camille crossed to the giant windows overlooking the Salten cliffs. She made a beautiful silhouette in front of the dramatic landscape, and my fingers itched to sketch her. I could envision the first long lines, gently curved to indicate the flow of her mauve skirts. It would be the perfect juxtaposition for the thick, short spikes I'd use for the cliffs.

"We *should* do something festive, though," she mused. "What about a party?"

I was too surprised to respond. Once Camille fixed her mind on something, trying to budge her from it was like prying a barnacle off the seawall.

"What do you think?" she asked, turning back to me, the weight of her stare cool and steady.

Erin A. Craig is the *New York Times* bestselling author of *House of Salt and Sorrows*, *House of Roots and Ruin* and *The Thirteenth Child*. She has always loved telling stories. An avid reader, decent quilter, rabid basketball fan, and collector of typewriters, brass figurines, and sparkly shoes, Erin makes her home in West Michigan with her husband and daughter.